Praise for *After the War is Over*

"I loved this book! Jennifer Robson is a gifted, compelling storyteller who creates memorable characters. In this novel she perfectly captures the hopes and fears of a generation in the turbulent times of post-war Britain. I look forward to her next!" —Hazel Gaynor, *New York Times* bestselling author of *The Girl Who Came Home*

"Jennifer Robson returns with mastery once more to the World War I era. . . . She evokes true beauty by showing the hope and courage in rebuilding lives and the promise of a world born anew. This is a moving and memorable book." —Pam Jenoff, author of *The Winter Guest*

"A beautifully old-fashioned novel of the very best sort." —Deanna Raybourn, *New York Times* bestselling author of *The Dark Enquiry* and *A Curious Beginning*

Praise for *Somewhere in France*

"Utterly engaging and richly satisfying, Somewhere in France depicts the very best in love and war. Fans of Downton Abbey will devour this novel!" —Erika Robuck, bestselling author of *Hawthorne House*

"Set in the turbulent years of the first world war, *Somewhere in France* is a heartfelt portrait of love, courage, and self-discovery. Robson deftly weaves a tale richly steeped in the atmosphere, drama and heroism of an evolving and war-torn world. A compelling and memorable read." —Lynn Sheene, author of *The Last Time I Saw Paris*

". . . the fiercely independent Lady Elizabeth Neville-Ashford (Lily) will be sure to inspire readers." —Huffington Post

Moonlight Over Paris

Also By Jennifer Robson

AFTER THE WAR IS OVER
SOMEWHERE IN FRANCE

Moonlight Over Paris

A Novel

JENNIFER ROBSON

wm
WILLIAM MORROW
An Imprint of HarperCollins*Publishers*

P.S.™ is a trademark of HarperCollins Publishers.

MOONLIGHT OVER PARIS. Copyright © 2016 by Jennifer Robson. All rights reserved. Printed in the United States of America. No part of this book may be used or reproduced in any manner whatsoever without written permission except in the case of brief quotations embodied in critical articles and reviews. For information address HarperCollins Publishers, 195 Broadway, New York, NY 10007.

HarperCollins books may be purchased for educational, business, or sales promotional use. For information please e-mail the Special Markets Department at SPsales@harpercollins.com.

FIRST EDITION

Designed by Diahann Sturge

Library of Congress Cataloging-in-Publication Data has been applied for.

ISBN 978-0-06-238982-4

17 18 19 20   OV/RRD   10 9 8 7

To my editor, Amanda Bergeron, and my literary agent, Kevan Lyon. I am so grateful to you both, and so lucky to count you among my friends.

PART ONE

The best way to make your dreams come true is to wake up.

—Paul Valéry

Prologue

Helena had heard, or perhaps she had read somewhere, that people on the point of death were insensible to pain. Enveloped in a gentle cloud of perfect tranquility, all earthly cares at an end, they simply floated into oblivion.

It was rubbish, of course, for she was in agony. Pain seized at her throat and ears, so fierce and corrosive that she could sleep only when they drugged her, and even then it chased her from one nightmare to the next. She hurt from her scalp to her fingernails to the soles of her feet, and despite that very real reminder of her state among the living, she knew the truth, too—she was dying.

She had heard the doctor say so not a half hour earlier. He had told her parents there was no hope, she had heard her mother weeping, and she had wished, then, that she had lived when she'd had the chance. There were so many things she ought to have done, and would never have the chance to do, not now. Not with the doctor so certain and her parents so broken.

She slept, waking only when day had faded to night and her room was empty of everyone apart from one woman, a stranger, dozing in the corner. A nurse, she supposed.

She felt a little cooler, and the ache in her throat was a trifle less pronounced. A drink of water would be nice, but if she called out the nurse would insist on painting her throat with that bitter substance again. Something-something of silver. It ought to have been cool, for silver put her in mind of moonlit nights and alpine lakes, but instead it burned horribly and made her choke.

So she lay still through the slow, beckoning hours before dawn, and presently it occurred to her that doctors were sometimes wrong. People did rise from their sickbeds and astonish their families from time to time, and there was a small chance—admittedly a vanishingly small one—that she might be among the few to do so. She had always been a healthy girl, never much given to illness, and had recovered from the Spanish flu in record time only a few years earlier. Perhaps she would survive after all.

And if she did? What next? Another twenty years of trailing dutifully after her mother, all the while knowing what people were whispering behind their hands?

Cast aside at the eleventh hour, all so he might marry the governess. *Such a tragedy for her. And her poor parents—the shame of it all. The shame. . .*

For five years she'd been engaged to a man who scarcely noticed her existence, treating her as an afterthought in his life. And then, after their engagement had been called off, nearly everyone she'd known in London had erased her from their lives, choosing to believe she had been at fault. No one, apart from her parents and sisters, had defended her.

Invitations had ceased. Callers had stopped coming by.

Doors had been shut in her face. Lord Cumberland had been a war hero, awarded a chestful of medals for his valor, and she had, it was assumed, heartlessly cast him aside. No matter that she had released him from their engagement only after he begged her to do so. After he confessed that he had never loved her, and had agreed to marry her only because of pressure from his family.

Looking back, it seemed almost impossible that she had stood meekly by and allowed people to treat her so shamefully. Why hadn't she defended herself with greater vigor? Why hadn't she simply gone abroad? It seemed obvious now, but it hadn't once occurred to her then.

It was high time she moved past all of that. She would go somewhere . . . she wasn't sure where, but it would be somewhere *else*, somewhere new where no one cared about her disappointments and failures. And she would . . . she wasn't sure what she would do, not yet.

But she was certain of one thing. If she survived, she would *live*.

Chapter 1

Helena tapped her forefinger into the pot of rouge and rubbed a dot of color into the apple of one cheek and then the other, just as her sister Amalia had instructed. She was to start with the slightest wash of color, and build from there. Rather as she would do when painting, though this was the first time she'd ever applied pigment to her face.

She pulled back from her dressing table mirror and surveyed her reflection with an unflinching eye. The rouge had helped to reduce the pallor of her complexion, a little, though nothing could be done about the thinness of her face, nor the dark circles that ringed her eyes. Worst of all was her hair, which the doctor had ordered be shorn when her fever refused to break. After four months it had scarcely grown at all, and was only just beginning to curl around her ears and nape. It was rather pleasant to be free of the bother of arranging it, at least until it grew back, but she could have done without the sympathetic sighs and half-hidden stares. On the other hand, women everywhere were shingling their hair these days; this was simply a more radical version.

It wouldn't do to remind her parents of her illness too forcefully, however, so she wrapped a long scarf around her head, tied it at her nape, and let the ends trail down her back. The effect was rather bohemian, but fetching all the same, and the bright blue of the patterned silk, a gift from her aunt Agnes, helped to brighten her eyes.

The letter from Agnes had arrived a month before, dropping into her lap like a firecracker.

> *51, quai de Bourbon*
> *Paris, France*
> *12 February 1924*
>
> *My dearest Helena,*
>
> *Words cannot express my joy when I received your letter of Tuesday last and was able to read, in your very own words, that you have recovered from your illness and are nearly restored to health. Your account was so terribly moving—I have read it through a dozen times already and it never fails to bring tears to my eyes.*
>
> *I must commend you for your resolution to effect a wholesale change in your life. The past five years have been so very difficult for you, and you have borne your sorrows admirably—but it is long past time that you thought of your future, and I think any course of action that takes you away from London is a sound one.*
>
> *I have two suggestions that I hope you will consider. First, I would be very happy if you would come to stay with me in France. You said in your letter that you wished to LIVE—I so love your use of capital letters here—and where better than France for such an endeavor?*
>
> *Second—and let me emphasize that this is a suggestion and not an edict—if you do come to stay I think it best if you find some way to*

occupy your days. I live quietly, and I worry that you would quickly find my company boring—but if you have something to do you will be much happier for it. Given your interest in art, and your undeniable talent in that regard, I think you ought to consider a term of study at one of the private academies in Paris. To that end I have enclosed the brochures for three such schools, and it is my fervent hope that you consider enrolling in one of them for the autumn term.

I leave for Antibes at the end of this week—write to me there, no matter what you decide.

With affectionate good wishes
Auntie A

Folding the letter away, Helena looked in the mirror one last time. It was time.

Her parents weren't expecting her for luncheon; had she mentioned it, during her mother's visit that morning, she'd have been subjected to a visit from Dr. Banks, whom she had grown to detest, and then guided down the stairs by two maids at the least. Before she could set her plans in motion, she had to show Mama and Papa that she was fit to rejoin the world, and that began with dressing herself and walking down the stairs without anyone hovering at her elbow.

It was only the third or fourth time she'd ventured beyond her bedroom door since the fever had broken and her recovery had begun, and despite herself she felt rather cowed by the number of stairs she had to descend in order to reach the dining room on the floor below. But she had done it before and would manage it again. One step, and another, and finally she was crossing the hall and smiling at Farrow the footman, who looked as if he might faint when he realized she was alone.

"Don't worry," she whispered as he opened the door to the dining room. "If they fuss I'll tell them you helped me."

The vast expanse of the dining table was empty, apart from a trio of silver epergnes that marked its central leaves, for her parents had chosen to sit at a small table in front of the French doors overlooking the garden. Helena cleared her throat, not wishing to startle them, and braced herself as their expressions of delight turned to concern.

"Helena, my dear—what are you doing out of bed? When I saw you this morning—"

"I told you I felt quite well, Mama, and I feel perfectly well now. May I join you for luncheon?"

"Of course, of course," her father chimed in. "Take my place," he offered, pushing back in his chair, but Helena stopped him with a hand on his shoulder.

"No need, Papa; look—here is Jamieson with another chair, and Farrow has everything else I need."

In moments she was seated, a hot brick under her feet, a rug on her lap, and a shawl about her shoulders, her parents deaf to her insistence that she was perfectly warm. Too warm, in fact, and though it was heavenly to feel the sun on her face she began to hope that a passing cloud might offer some respite.

"Are you quite comfortable? Shall I ring for some broth? And some blancmange to follow?"

"Oh, goodness no—I'll have the same as you. Dr. Banks did say I might resume a normal diet."

"I know he did, but you must be cautious," her mother fussed. "Any sudden change—"

"I hardly think a few mouthfuls of trout and watercress will do me in."

"Let the girl eat in peace, Louisa. She's been cooped up in

this house for far too long," her father insisted. "Past time she returned to the land of the living."

They ate in silence, companionably so, and in no time at all Helena had finished everything on her plate. She cleared her throat and waited until she was sure she had her parents' full attention.

"I have something to tell you. The both of you."

Her mother set down her fork and knife, her face suddenly pale, and folded her hands in her lap. "What is it, my dear?"

"I've been thinking about what I ought to do. I'm feeling ever so much better, you see, and I should like so much to go somewhere warm, perhaps—"

"Splendid notion," said her father. "I've always been partial to Biarritz at this time of year."

"It is lovely, I agree, but I've decided to go to the Côte d'Azur. To stay with . . . well, to stay with Aunt Agnes."

"Ah. *Agnes.*"

"She is your sister, Papa, and she is very fond of me. And the weather in the south of France will do me good."

"Of course it will," her mother agreed, "and you know how we adore dear Agnes. But she lives a . . . well, a rather unconventional life. You really ought to stay with a steadier sort of person. Maudie Anstruther-MacPhail, perhaps? She's wintering in Nice this year."

"I scarcely know the woman, and Aunt Agnes would be awfully hurt if she found out."

"You're still so fragile. Remember Dr. Banks's warning—any sudden upset or disturbance—"

"I'm a woman, not a piece of spun sugar, and I am perfectly capable of making sensible decisions. You know I am. Even if Aunt Agnes got it into her head to go off on one of her adventures, I would simply stay put. She has plenty of servants. I wouldn't be left on my own."

"And would you promise to be perfectly careful of your health?"

"Yes, Mama."

"John? What do you think of this?"

"Agnes is a good sort. Always has been. Shame about that husband of hers, of course, but she rallied. She always does."

"A summer in the sun will do you good, I suppose," her mother mused.

"Yes. Well, the thing is . . . I'm staying for longer than that. For a year, in fact."

"For a *year*? Why so terribly long?"

"I have enrolled in art school, and the term runs from September to April."

Silence descended upon the table, as cold and numbing as November rain.

Her mother was the first to recover from her shock. "Art school? I don't know about *that*. Filled to the brim with foreigners, and the sort of art that is fashionable these days—"

"Degenerate rot," her father finished. "Makes no sense. Why bother with a painting that doesn't look like anything? If I buy a portrait of my wife, I want it to look like my wife. Not a hodgepodge of shapes. Who has a head shaped like a box, I ask you? No one!"

"Cubism is merely one approach among many, and the school I have in mind is far more traditional," Helena insisted, mentally crossing her fingers. "Maître Czerny isn't interested in what is fashionable. His focus is on technique."

Her mother wrinkled her nose. " 'Chair-knee'? What sort of name is that?"

"I believe it's Czech, originally. But he is a Frenchman. And he would be willing to take me on—"

"What? You've been corresponding with this man?"

"Only regarding his school, Mama."

"What of the other students? Foreigners as well?"

"I don't know. Most likely most of them will be French. Possibly there will be some Americans, too."

"Good heavens," her mother said. She had begun to worry at the lace on her cuff, which was never a good sign. "I really don't know if we can agree to this."

It was time to dig in her heels. "Mama, I am twenty-eight years old, and I have money of my own. I have the greatest respect for you both, but you must remember that I have the legal right to go and do as I please."

"But Helena, darling—"

Her heart began to pound, for she'd never stood up to her parents in such a way before, and it went against her nature to do so now. But she had to hold her ground. Before her resolve crumbled, she needed to step away.

"If you'll excuse me, I think it's time I return to my room. If you wish to speak with me about my plans I will be very happy to do so."

BACK IN HER bedchamber, Helena took up her notebook and pencils, and looked around for something she might draw. Settling on the window seat, she began to sketch the wrens that came to perch on the sill each afternoon. They were sweet little creatures, tame enough to alight on her outstretched fingers, and cheery despite the threatening rain. It was spring, after all; they had survived the winter, and seemed to know that blue skies lay ahead. If only she could be as certain.

She had no education to speak of, nor was she beautiful or witty or elegant. But something came alive in her when she picked up a pencil or brush. She had the makings of an artist in her, she was certain of it, and she was determined to keep the promise she'd made to herself last December, in those bleak, lonely hours when death had crept so close. Her parents wouldn't stop her, she knew, but it would be so much easier, and pleasanter, if they were to support her decision.

She meant to close her eyes for just a moment, but when she woke the sun had sunk beneath the garden wall and her mother was at her side, a cool hand smoothing her brow.

"You shouldn't have fallen asleep there," Lady Halifax fretted. "You might have caught a chill."

Helena crossed the room and settled in one of the easy chairs drawn close to the fire. "I'm fine. Not cold at all."

Her mother perched at the edge of the other chair, her stays creaking a little, and smiled rather wanly at Helena. "Papa and I have been talking. As you said earlier, you have always been such a good girl, and we *do* trust you. While we have our reservations about this, ah, this *academy* you wish to attend, we have decided to support your decision to go to France for a year."

"Thank you, Mama. I really am very grateful."

"I know you think I worry too much, but I can't help myself. I know how you have suffered, how people have treated you since your break with Lord Cumberland. I know how lonely you've been—"

"I've always had you and my sisters, Mama. It hasn't been that bad."

"It has. And it's so unfair. Just look at Lord Cumberland. He's been happily married all this time, has children of his own, and no one says a thing to *him*."

"It's in the past, Mama. You mustn't dwell on it."

"How can I not? You're almost thirty. Before long it will be too late for children, and then what decent man will have you? Please be sensible."

"I have always been sensible, and that is why I have no interest in marriage with some stranger who is indifferent to me. I was lucky to escape such a fate with Edward."

Her mother pulled a handkerchief from her sleeve and dabbed at her eyes. "How can you say you were lucky, when he all but ruined your life? If only you knew how it weighs upon me. What if something were to happen to your father? You know we cannot depend on your brother, for that wretched wife of his won't wait five minutes before tossing us all out of the house. I don't much care what happens to me, but you, my darling—what will become of you?"

Helena took her mother's hands and pressed them reassuringly between hers. "Listen to me: if the worst were to happen, and David's vile wife were to throw us out on our ears, we would take my bequest from Grandmama, buy a little house, and live quite comfortably together. But that is *not* going to happen, not least because Papa is as healthy as an ox, and likely to remain so for many years." She smiled at her mother, willing her to believe, and received a feeble nod in response.

"I am going to France to live with Auntie A for a year, and to try to become an artist, and when the year is done I will think seriously about what I must do next. But I need my year first. Agreed?"

"Agreed," her mother offered, her voice wobbly with tears, though she dried her eyes quickly enough. "Now, my dear: be honest with me. Are you well enough to travel?"

"Not quite yet," Helena answered truthfully. "Perhaps in a fortnight?"

"Very well. Shall we see how you are at the end of next week? If you feel improved, I'll have Papa's secretary book passage for you to Paris."

"Aunt Agnes is already at her house in Antibes, though. Wouldn't it be better if I took the Blue Train from Calais?"

"That does make sense. Shall I have a tray sent up with your supper?"

"Yes, please."

"Tomorrow we'll go for a nice walk together. And we must see about getting you some pretty things for the seaside."

"Thank you, Mama. For everything, I mean."

As soon as the door closed behind her mother, Helena erupted from her chair and jumped up and down, taking great skips around the room, though it made her breathless and so unsteady on her feet that she had to sit again almost right away.

She had done it.

She would have her year in France, a year away from the whispers, stares, and malicious half-heard gossip that had blighted nearly every moment of the past five years. She would . . . her mind reeled at the possibilities. She would eat pastries and drink wine and wear short skirts and rouge, and she would sit in the sun and burn her nose, and not care what anyone thought of her.

Best of all, she would go to school and meet people who knew nothing of her past, and to them she would simply be Helena Parr, an artist like themselves.

Helena Parr. Artist. Merely thinking the words filled her with delight—and it reminded her of one task that simply couldn't wait.

Returning to her desk, she took out a sheet of notepaper and began to write.

45, Wilton Crescent
London, SW1
England
16 March 1924

Dear Maître Czerny,

Further to my earlier inquiry, I should like to reserve a place at your school for the September 1924 session for intermediate students. I shall send a bank draft for the required deposit under separate cover.

Yours faithfully,
Miss Helena Parr

Chapter 2

$\mathscr{S}$trange to think she'd never been on a sleeper train before. She'd been to the south of France often enough, but her father detested rail journeys and invariably insisted they go by ship. As Helena was a poor sailor, she'd always dreaded the voyage to Marseille.

But *this*—this was heavenly. Her first-class compartment on the *train bleu*—she supposed the name came from the cars' midnight blue exteriors—was a tiny marvel of modern luxury, and rather than set down her valise and take off her coat she simply stood at its entrance and stared.

It was scarcely more than two yards wide, and perhaps a little longer from door to window. Every vertical plane was covered in gleaming mahogany panels, their lacquer polished to a mirror finish. To her right was a plush banquette, not yet transformed into her bed for the night. She reached out and unlatched the curving door to her left. It revealed a sink with hot and cold taps, chrome-framed mirrors, and an electric light that switched on automatically.

The train wouldn't be leaving Calais for another half hour, so she might as well unpack before they started to move. With only a single case for the overnight journey, her trunk having been stowed in the baggage car, she didn't have much to do. She shut and latched the door to her compartment, folded out the little table beside the window, and set out her valise. She'd brought a frock for dinner and another for her arrival in Antibes, neither of them much creased; these she hung on the back of the door. There was even a little rack for shoes at the bottom. Her nightgown and underclothes could remain in the case for now.

Mama had wanted her to bring one of the maids, fearing that Helena wouldn't be able to manage, but Helena had refused. Even before her illness, and the months of constant scrutiny by physicians and nursemaids, she'd rarely been left on her own. There had always been servants around, always, and though most of them were agreeable and friendly, and were usually quiet and unassuming, they were simply *there*.

Here, though, there was no one to mind her, watch her, hover over her. She had twenty-four hours to herself to do as she pleased, to act as she liked, and to be anyone she chose to be. For the first time in her life she was wonderfully and blissfully alone, and she would savor every single, intoxicating minute.

The train shuddered to life, lumbering out of the station with painful slowness, but before long they had left the coast behind and were rolling through the peaceful farmland of the Pas de Calais. Helena perched on the banquette and stared out the window, too excited to open her book, and watched as the countryside gave way to the outskirts of Amiens, their only stop before Paris. As they slowed to cross a low, rather rickety bridge, she glimpsed a faded sign that gave a name to the river flowing languidly below: *la Somme*.

The Somme. Simply reading the name made her shiver. She was pretty certain the battles had been fought farther away, farther to the north—she could still remember, if hazily, the maps of the front lines that the newspapers had included whenever there was a new advance to report. And the war had come very close indeed to this ancient town, for hadn't there been a Battle of Amiens toward the end?

At the time, she'd read the newspapers compulsively, trying to make sense of it all, but understanding had proved elusive. What sense could be made of something so futile? The broken men at the hospital where she'd volunteered, their faces still so vivid in her mind's eye, had been testament enough of the nature of war.

The banquette was giving her a backache, so she determined to go in search of the ladies' lounge car. She'd boarded at one end of the train, and had only passed through a single car of sleeping compartments, so any Pullman cars would be in the other direction.

"May I be of assistance, Lady Helena?" Waiting in the corridor was the same steward who had escorted her onto the train earlier.

"Yes, thank you. I was wondering if there might be a lounge—a Pullman car for ladies?"

"I am so sorry, but not on this service. If you wish, you may certainly take a table in the restaurant. Allow me to show you the way. I believe afternoon tea is being served."

Suddenly, tea seemed like a very good idea. Only moments after taking her seat at a table for two, a smiling waiter set a tiered tray of fancies before her: wafer-thin cucumber sandwiches, toast triangles with crème fraîche and caviar, currant-studded scones, and petits fours that were almost too pretty to eat. A pot of tea, perfectly brewed, joined the sweets and savories, along with a trio of cut-crystal bowls that held lemon curd, clotted cream, and a most unexpected delicacy: early strawberries at their peak of fragrant ripeness.

With a speed that would have appalled her mother, Helena inhaled all of it, every last crumb, and was contemplating how best to scrape the last smear of clotted cream from its bowl when the waiter returned.

"*Bien fait,* Lady Helena! I see that you enjoyed your afternoon tea very much."

"It was delicious, thank you. Would you mind very much if I sat here for a while?"

"Not at all. As you can see, most of our passengers have yet to embark. Not until we arrive at the Gare de Lyon will we have a full house, as you say it."

"How long will that be, do you expect?"

"Not long, not long. First we will stop at the Gare du Nord, and then we go to the Gare de Lyon. We will be there for about an hour. It will be a good time for you to—how do you say?—stretch your legs."

"I think I will, thank you."

She stayed at her table and watched the countryside give way to the growing suburbs of the great city, and then Paris was upon them, the train hemmed in by looming embankments and grim stone walls. They remained at the Gare du Nord for only a few minutes, just long enough to take on a few more passengers, before circling south to the Gare de Lyon.

Helena returned to her compartment to fetch her hat and coat, gloves and reticule; she wouldn't be leaving the train for long, but it was only sensible to have some ready cash on her person. According to her wristwatch, she had a little less than half an hour to walk up and down the platform before they departed for Lyon and points south.

She recognized the smell right away. No one who had ever been to Paris would forget that heady mélange of coal dust, drains, frying onions, fresh bread, Turkish tobacco, and here and there a whiff of some exotic, expensive perfume. Perhaps she would buy a bottle of scent when she returned in the fall, something rich with gardenia or lilies. Never mind that she quite liked the verbena-scented cologne she'd always worn. Now that she was in France, she would do as Frenchwomen did.

She walked from one end of the platform to the other, then, a little fearful of the train leaving without her, returned to her compartment and dressed for dinner. Her frock was new, in a streamlined style that was kind to her too-thin frame, and so short that Mama had been alarmed. But her mother had complete trust in Madame Rose, never mind that the seamstress hailed from Ripon and not the Rive Gauche, and Madame Rose had insisted that everyone, absolutely everyone, would be shortening their skirts for the season. The frock felt fashionable to Helena and was very pretty indeed, its turquoise silk chiffon adorned with a geometric pattern of gold and copper paillettes.

She surveyed her appearance in the mirror next to the sink. She was still far too thin, though a steady diet of French bread and pastries would surely take care of that problem, and her hair made her look more like a young boy than a woman in her late twenties. On a woman with more striking features, or coloring that was more dramatic, such short hair would be memorable. On her, with her plain oval face and plain brown eyes, it looked rather pathetic.

But there was nothing to be done; she hadn't thought to pack Amalia's pot of rouge in her overnight wash bag, and she hadn't so much as a scarf to cover her shorn head, not unless she wished to pair her chiffon frock with the green felt cloche she'd just removed. So be it.

The restaurant car was a little more than half full, most of the other diners unfamiliar. But then she recognized two women, sisters she'd known from the summer of her debut, and their failure to acknowledge her was as familiar as a cup of tea. They'd both been married for years, she recalled, with husbands who'd waited out the war in reserve battalions that never crossed the Channel. They had children and homes of their own and everything she'd once thought she, too, would have.

Although there were two empty places at their table, the sisters didn't beckon her over, didn't wave in her direction, didn't so much as raise an eyebrow to indicate they'd seen her. Women like that never did. It wasn't because they disliked her, for they barely knew her. But they feared being seen with her, or anywhere near her, and so it was easier to pretend she was invisible.

The waiter, the same friendly man as earlier, greeted her with a wide smile and showed her to a table for two. She would have a cocktail, something terribly strong, and it would go straight to her head and she wouldn't care what anyone thought of her. "Do you serve American cocktails?" she asked.

"But of course. Do you prefer a beverage prepared with gin, with rum, or with Scotch whisky?"

"I've no idea," she admitted. "I've never had one before."

"In that event, I advise a moderate approach. May I suggest a sidecar? It is made of Cointreau, brandy, and lemon juice."

"It sounds delicious."

She would drink it down, every last drop, no matter if it tasted like kerosene straight from a lamp. The waiter returned several minutes later, a single glass on his silver tray, and set the drink before her with a flourish.

"*À votre santé*," she said, and took a large sip of the cocktail. It tasted bright and citrusy, but that first impression was quickly overlaid by a sensation of searing heat as the brandy made its presence known. Stifling the urge to cough, she took another sip, and another, and decided she liked it.

"Shall I allow you a few moments to look at the bill of fare?" the waiter asked.

"I'm not terribly hungry," she confessed. "Perhaps some soup to begin, and then some fish—what do you have tonight?"

"We have sole meunière with new potatoes and white asparagus."

"Perfect. No pudding; just that. And I should very much like another one of those cocktails."

Chapter 3

"Good morning, Lady Helena, and welcome to the south of France. May I bring in your *petit déjeuner*?"

She'd slept well, lulled by the soporific effects of the two sidecars she'd imbibed and the cradling rhythm of the train, only vaguely aware of the stops it had made during the night. Apart from a mild headache, she felt quite well, and more than ready for a spot of breakfast.

"One moment," she called out, reaching for her robe. She unlatched the door and stood aside to let the steward into her compartment. Moving as gracefully as Nijinsky himself, he set out her breakfast tray and prepared a bowl of café au lait.

"We will be leaving Marseille shortly, my lady. You are disembarking at Antibes, yes?"

"I am, thank you. How long do I have?"

"It is two hours to St.-Raphäel, and then another hour to Juan-les-Pins. The station for Antibes comes one quarter of an hour later."

The train's modern conveniences did not extend to WCs in each compartment, alas, so Helena dressed quickly and hurried to the toilet cubicle at the end of the car. It, too, was decorated in sumptuous style, with mosaic floors that might have been plundered from a Roman villa. Back in her compartment, she perched at the edge of her bunk and made short work of her breakfast: two croissants, which she spread with butter and raspberry jam, and washed down with the still-scalding café au lait.

The steward had brought two newspapers with her breakfast. The first, a day-old copy of the *Times,* she had read at her hotel in Calais. The other was a European edition of the *Chicago Tribune.* It stretched to only eight pages in total, and was a curious mix of news about American politicians and criminals, descriptions of lunches and gala dinners at dull-sounding places like the Board of Trade, and mystifying tables of statistics that appeared to relate to the sport of baseball.

Soon they were on the move again, heading east under a radiant turquoise sky. Thinking to freshen the air, Helena cranked down her window a scant inch, but the breeze was so warm and fragrant that she quickly lowered the pane to its full extent and let the wind rush into the compartment. It smelled of pine trees and sunshine and salt air, without so much as a wisp of locomotive exhaust, and felt like heaven on her face.

The steward came by once more, to take her tray and fold away her bunk, and as soon as he was done she returned to her perch by the window. They had turned south, or so it seemed from the angle of the midmorning sun, and presently he called out for St.-Raphäel.

She packed the last of her things, even rolling up her coat and stuffing it into her valise. It would look ridiculous with her linen frock and straw cloche hat, she reasoned, and Aunt Agnes wouldn't fuss over her catching cold as Mama would have done.

They halted in Juan-les-Pins, its modest station dwarfed by gargantuan palm trees, and then, only minutes later, the steward called for Antibes. As soon as the train had shuddered to a halt he took Helena's valise, helped her down the steps, and thanked her profusely when she tipped him with some paper francs from her handbag. She really ought to check the exchange rate; for all she knew, she had just handed over most of her monthly allowance.

"Helena! Oh, Helena darling!"

"Auntie A!"

The last time she'd seen her aunt, a little more than two years ago, had been at the memorial service for Agnes's husband, a Russian grand duke who had died under tragic circumstances. They had all been dressed in deepest black, though no one apart from Agnes had ever met the man—she'd married him only a few months before his airplane had crashed en route to Tangiers. Family was family, however, so they had observed the proprieties and attended a terribly baroque service at a Russian Orthodox church near Victoria Station, and afterward Agnes had drunk an astonishing amount of vodka with Dimitri's Russian friends and declared that her life was over.

Evidently she had overcome the worst of her grief since then, for she was the picture of happiness as she swept her niece into a feathery embrace. It was an odd sensation, one that made sense once Helena realized that the neckline and cuffs of Agnes's chartreuse chiffon frock were trimmed with dyed-to-match marabou.

"You look wonderful," she said truthfully. "I can't tell you how glad I am to see you."

"And I you, my darling girl. When I received the telegram

from your father—the first one, I mean, the one that said you were *dying*—I swooned. I absolutely did—didn't I, Vincent?"

"You did, madame."

Vincent was her aunt's chauffeur, butler, bodyguard, and confidant, and had been with her as long as Helena could remember. Nearly everything about him was mysterious, from his nationality to his life before Agnes, but his loyalty to her aunt was unquestionable.

"Hello, Vincent, it's lovely to—"

"You see, Helena? *Swooned*. And then, when the second telegram came—"

"In which I lived?"

"Yes, dear, in which you *survived*—well, I simply collapsed. I was in bed for *days*, and Hamish was ever so worried for me, wasn't he?"

"Hamish is still . . . ?"

"Oh yes—Vincent, hand over Hamish to Helena. I'm sure she'll want a cuddle."

Hamish was Aunt Agnes's stout, elderly, and very smelly cairn terrier, who had been at death's door at least a dozen times over his long lifetime but somehow always rallied with the help of expensive veterinary care. He was a dear old thing, though, and seemed to recognize her, so Helena set down her valise and tucked him under her arm. He thanked her with a soft huff, then a gentle belch.

"The poor dear—his tummy has been giving him *such* trouble. Vincent, take Helena's bag—you don't have anything else, darling?"

"I've a trunk in the baggage car."

"Go see to it, Vincent, while we get settled in the car. Hurry, now!"

Agnes took Helena's other arm and guided them to the station exit. The car was idling at the curb, a huge, gleaming beast of an open-topped coupe, its interior upholstered from stem to stern in leather that was softer than velvet. Aunt Agnes had never been one for scrimping on luxuries.

Vincent returned with the news that the trunk would be delivered that afternoon, so with nothing to keep them in town they set off for Agnes's villa. Helena couldn't recall its exact location relative to the shore, only that its garden had a marvelous view.

"Do you remember the villa? You won't have been here for years, of course. We must throw you a party, something simply *wild,* and we'll invite all my friends. We'll have such fun together!"

"That sounds lovely, Auntie A, but perhaps not quite yet—"

"Of course, of course. You need to build up your strength, and what better place than here? A little sun will do you such good. Of course you're terribly pale, but that's true of everyone when they arrive. I mean, poor Peggy Guggenheim looked like a *ghoul* back in March, and now she's as brown as a walnut."

"Do you think we can send a telegram to Mama and Papa, to let them know I've arrived? I ought to have said something before we left the station."

"Never you mind—you can write it out as soon as we get home and Vincent will drive it down to the post office. He won't mind—will you, Vincent?"

"Not at all, madame."

"Oh, look—we're here. Welcome to Villa Vesna!"

Away from the seafront, with its grand hotels and more modest pensions, the residences of Cap d'Antibes were hidden behind whitewashed walls or tall hedges, so Helena had little sense of how her aunt's neighbors lived. The car slowed, turning carefully into a short drive, and drew up by the front door of a square, squat, flat-roofed house that charmed her with its pale pink walls and turquoise shutters.

Far more striking, though, was the garden, which spilled down the hillside in three lushly planted terraces. Framing the magnificent view were trees that would never survive an English winter—date palms and olives, figs and mimosa. There was even a little grove of lemon and orange trees. Whitewashed trellises supported tangled vines of clematis, heliotrope, Chinese roses, and bougainvillea, while spreading beds of thyme, chamomile, and lavender tumbled over their low stone walls onto undulating pathways of crushed limestone. Birdsong was everywhere, melodic and joyful; later, she knew, it would be eclipsed by the rising drone of cicadas.

"Helena? Shall we see you settled? We'll do that, then we'll have a late breakfast out on the terrace, and after that we'll go down to the water and have a sunbath. Do you have a bathing costume with you?"

"There's one in my trunk."

"Oh, good. Leave your valise—Vincent will bring it in. And you can put Hamish down. He knows the way."

Inside, all was dark and cool, the villa's windows still shuttered to keep out the heat of the day. Aunt Agnes led them to a flight of stairs, its banister a sinuous curve of weathered wrought iron, and the three of them climbed the steps, Hamish's claws clicking softly against the terra-cotta floor tiles.

"I've given you the best of the guest rooms, darling—my room is at the other end of the corridor. I think you'll *adore* it. Do come in and tell me what you think."

Agnes hurried to fling open the shutters on two large

windows, revealing an expansive view of the terraced garden and, beyond, the infinite azure arc of the Mediterranean. "Will the room suit? I mean, apart from the view? You've the bed, and a desk and chair, and a little fauteuil if you feel like lounging. Is anything missing? I do want it to be perfect."

"It is," Helena promised.

"Oh—I almost forgot! Come with me—I've been dying to show you. Perhaps you could carry dear Hamish? He's a little out of breath."

Helena scooped up the dog and followed her aunt back downstairs and outside again, this time via a side door. They stood on a round, elevated patio that was shaded by a pergola blanketed in the scarlet blooms of a trumpet vine. Just beyond was a low, stuccoed outbuilding, its façade dominated by a set of rough-hewn doors. Her aunt opened both doors wide and beckoned impatiently to Helena. "Come in. Come and see."

The interior was dim, especially compared to the glare of the midday sun. She lingered at the threshold, intrigued by her aunt's enthusiasm for the shabby old shed, and blinked as her eyes struggled to discern what lay beyond.

She saw the easel first. She blinked, and a table came into focus. A long table, pushed against the back wall, its surface covered with everything to tempt an artist's heart: stacks of stretched canvases, reams of paper, boxes of pastels, tins of watercolors, a clutch of sharpened pencils in a tin. There were empty palettes, too, and an open case of brushes, every size and shape, all waiting for her.

And there were tubes of oil paint, scores of them, set in rows on the tabletop, their neatly lettered labels the only clue to the colors hidden within. All new, all untouched.

"I wasn't sure what to buy, so I ordered one of everything

You don't mind, do you? I thought it would be nice to surprise—"

"Oh, Auntie A. It's . . . I don't know what to say. It's perfect. I never dreamed—"

"Don't cry, dear. It's just some paints and paper, and the shed wasn't being used."

Helena blinked away her tears, not wishing to spoil the moment with theatrics, and pulled her aunt into a heartfelt embrace.

"Is there enough light? I know you artists need to have plenty of light," Agnes persisted.

"It's perfect, I promise. Like a dream come true."

"Oh, good. Let's go back inside. I'll remind you where everything is, and of course you won't have met Jeanne and Micheline. My cook and housemaid. Such dears, though they don't speak a word of English, and I've barely any French. Still, we get on well together, and Vincent can translate in a crisis."

Her heart full, her mind's eye awhirl, Helena cast one last glance over her studio—*her* studio—and followed Agnes inside.

Chapter 4

Villa Vesna
Antibes, France
5 July 1924

Dearest Amalia,

I'm afraid I don't have much in the way of news for you this week,
for life on the Côte d'Azur continues in much the same vein as it has
done since my arrival. I quite enjoy the routine—up at dawn, a solitary walk down to the water, some sketching there if I feel inspired,
then back home for breakfast on the terrace with Auntie A. After that
I move to my studio and work up sketches from the day before, with
a break for lunch around one o'clock. I did try asking the cook if I
might simply have a sandwich on a tray, but I only managed to hor-
rify the poor woman. So lunch at table it is, with the addition once
or twice a week of Auntie A's friends.

You won't be surprised to hear that our aunt knows everyone
here: the great, the good, the notorious, and the merely interesting,
too. At first, when people visited, I was a little concerned they might
have heard of my social difficulties back in London, but no one has

said a thing. Not yet, at any rate! Agnes introduces me as her niece, says I am visiting from England, and that is that.

In the afternoons, I go down to the seaside for a swim, for the water is much warmer now. Auntie A comes with me from time to time, but she insists on being driven down the hill, and tends to fuss about everything—the heat, the wind, even the sand that clings to Hamish's paws.

Most evenings we go out to dine, most often with Sara and Gerald Murphy. I'm sure I mentioned their arrival in my last letter, and since then I've seen them at least three or four times. At present they are staying at the Hôtel du Cap with their children, for their villa is being renovated and won't be ready until the end of the summer.

Helena sipped at her tea, though it had already gone cold, and smiled at the memory of her first meeting with Sara. It had been the spring of 1914, not long after her own debut, and she had been feeling rather adrift at a particularly dreary tea party. She'd joined a conversation, drawn by the talk of modern art, as well as the American voice she overheard, and had been introduced to Miss Sara Wiborg, lately of East Hampton, New York.

Sara had been defending the work of Marcel Duchamp to a clutch of disbelieving and pinch-faced matrons. Though normally shy when meeting new people, Helena hadn't hesitated before chiming in, avowing her admiration for Duchamp and his fellow Cubists. She and Sara had talked non-stop for the rest of the afternoon.

The Wiborg family had departed for Italy not long after, but Sara and Helena had maintained a faithful, if irregular, correspondence throughout the intervening years. In 1915 she had married Gerald, and not so long ago they had moved to France, it would seem for good.

As far as Helena had known, they'd been living in Paris; she had meant to call on them once she was settled there in September. So it had been a lovely surprise to discover the entire family at the little beach at La Garoupe one afternoon a few weeks earlier, and then to learn they were staying for the rest of the summer.

> *Tonight Auntie A and I are dining with the Murphys, along with an American friend of Gerald's. As I write this it's nearly eleven in the morning, so if I'm to get in any plein air work today I must be off. Although people don't really dress for dinner here in Antibes our aunt does expect me to be presentable—and that means I need to set aside a solid hour at the end of the day to scrub the paint from under my fingernails and render the rest of my person fit for company!*
>
> *I promise to write again soon—Auntie A sends her best wishes—*
>
> *With much love,*
> *Helena*

Having packed her satchel after breakfast, it remained only to fetch a sandwich and a flask of water from the kitchen, leave the letter to Amalia on the hall table for Vincent to post later, and haul her bicycle out of the garage. She'd found it a few weeks earlier, tucked away in the back of the old stables, and although it was old and rather heavy it worked well once Vincent had cleaned off the cobwebs and set it to rights.

The ride into the hills north of Antibes was ever so pleasant, and in the hours that followed she made some very satisfactory sketches of lavender growing wild in an ancient grove of olive trees. She worked happily for ages, only noticing the time when she paused for a drink of water, and realized the afternoon was nearly gone.

She packed up her things and began the journey home, but her bicycle dropped its chain before she'd gone even a mile, and despite her best efforts the chain stubbornly refused to stay put. Helena was so intent on trying to fix her bicycle that she didn't hear the approaching vehicle until it pulled to a growling halt only a few yards away.

Turning around, she expected to see one of the goods lorries or delivery vans that comprised most of the limited traffic on the narrow, unpaved roads. Instead, she was surprised to discover a small and low-slung coupe, its exterior painted with red and blue racing stripes. The driver, a man only a few years older than she, switched off the engine.

"Do you need a hand there?" he asked in a faintly amused American baritone.

He seemed friendly enough, but he was looking at her far too boldly, and she felt certain he was holding back a smile. No, not a smile—a smirk. He hadn't even bothered to say hello, or to introduce himself properly.

"Thank you, but no. I'm quite all right." She stared back, unblinking, her posture so perfect even her mother would have approved. Only then did she realize he hadn't spoken to her in French. "How did you know . . . ?"

"That you're English? You don't often see Frenchwomen on bicycles."

"You aren't French, either."

"Nope. My accent give me away?" He grinned at her.

"Well, yes. That and . . . I suppose you just look like an American."

"Huh. I guess I'd better take that as a compliment."

He clambered out of his motorcar and walked over to look at her bicycle. It was a wonder he'd even fit in the coupe, for he was well over six feet tall, and broad-shouldered besides. He wore a linen suit, rather crumpled and dusty, and his shirt was open at the neck. On his head he sported a long-billed American cap, but he pulled it off and tossed it in the car, revealing short-cropped auburn hair.

"Why don't I see what the problem is, Duchess?"

"I'm not—" Helena began, but stopped short when she realized he was only teasing her. In vain she tried to think of something amusing to say, but her mind remained stubbornly blank.

Crouching by her bicycle, he pulled at its chain, muttering a little under his breath. He sat back on his haunches and began to rummage about in the grass. "I need a stick, nothing too big . . . here we go." Using the stick as a guide, he looped one end of the chain over the rear cog, and then eased it around to fit over the front chain ring. He then grasped the nearside pedal and turned it slowly round until the chain clicked into place.

"There. Fixed."

"Really? I tried that half a dozen times but I couldn't get it to stay on."

"You'd have probably got it on eventually. Using the stick helps."

"Of course. That's, ah, that's terribly helpful. Thank you so much, Mister—"

"Howard. Sam Howard."

"Well, thank you, Mr. Howard. I'm Helena Parr." She wondered if she ought to offer her hand for him to shake, but remembered, just in time, that it was dirty. Of course his hands were dirty, too, so it really ought not to matter.

"Do you need any more help, d'you think?"

"No. You've done more than enough. I mustn't keep you." She winced at the sound of her voice, so prim and starchy compared to his unaffected friendliness.

"So long, then. Perhaps I'll see you around town." He smiled then, really smiled, and she saw that he had a dimple in one cheek and a sprinkling of freckles across his nose and cheekbones. She'd never known a grown man with freckles, or perhaps she simply had never noticed before.

"That would be very nice." What was wrong with her? *Very nice?* Even as a green debutante of eighteen she'd been capable of conversation that was ten times as sparkling.

"It was good to meet you, Miss Parr. You're sure you don't need me to stay? Just to make sure you're fine?"

"I'm sure. I mean, I'm sure that I'm fine. Really, there's no need to stay. Thanks ever so much."

"As long as you're sure, then," he said, and smiled at her once more. It made his eyes crinkle at the corners in an awfully endearing fashion, and it also made her notice, rather unwillingly, just how handsome he was. "Good-bye."

He returned to his car, somehow managed to fit his long legs into its cockpit, or whatever one called the driving compartment of a motorcar, and drove off in a cloud of dust and exhaust.

By the time she got home, a half hour later, Helena was grimy, terribly thirsty, and suffering from a tremendous headache. Leaving her satchel in the studio, she hurried upstairs to the bathroom, praying there would be enough hot water left in the cistern for her to have a modest bath. She opened the hot water tap all the way, and went to look at herself in the cheval mirror while the tub filled.

It was even worse than she'd imagined. Her frock, fortunately an old one, was streaked with bicycle grease and dust from the road. Her face was nearly as dirty, and her hair, which now reached to her earlobes, was standing on end. She might have been one of the urchins from Fagin's den of thieves. Her laugh echoed in the tiled room—no wonder Mr. Howard had been grinning at her. Between her disheveled appearance and her tongue-tied responses, she must have come across as decidedly strange.

The tap began to clamor and clank; that was the end of the hot water. She added a splash of cold, so she wouldn't scald herself, and poured in some lemon bath essence. She would wash her hair, wash every inch of her person, and then she would swallow two tablets of aspirin and take a short nap. When she awoke, she would be perfectly rested and ready for a pleasant evening with her aunt and the Murphys—and then, maybe tomorrow, she would locate her wits and what little dignity she still possessed, go into town, and find Mr. Howard to thank him properly for his help.

Chapter 5

Helena was, indeed, much restored by the time they left. She wore the nicest of her dinner frocks, a simple shift in heavy, midnight blue silk charmeuse, its inky darkness brightened by scrolling silver embroidery at its neck and hem. Her hair was now long enough to look fashionably bobbed and not simply shorn, and apart from setting a slim diamanté clip in the locks by her left temple, she left it alone.

Agnes was wearing one of her glorious velvet *devoré* caftans, this one in a burnt orange color that ought to have looked dreadful but instead suited her admirably. In her hair, which had been hennaed to a shade that very nearly matched her frock, her aunt wore a peacock feather aigrette, its clip adorned by a diamond the size of a quail's egg.

The Hôtel du Cap, which occupied an enviable swath of seafront at the southeastern tip of the cape, was all but deserted in high summer, its wealthy and titled clientele preferring to holiday in milder climes. Monsieur Sella, the hotel's proprietor, had been planning to shut the hotel for the summer, Sara had confided, but Gerald had persuaded him to keep it open.

Gerald and Sara were sitting with a single man, his back to

them, when she and Agnes arrived. The table, which had been set for five, was at the edge of the dining room, its linen napery fluttering in the soft evening breeze.

Gerald was the first to notice them. "Sara, darling, they're here!"

Just then, the man turned to face Helena and Agnes, and she was astonished to see that it was Sam Howard. It was such a surprise that she simply stood and gawped while Gerald made their introduction.

"Sam Howard, may I introduce you to the Princess Dimitri Pavlovich, and to her niece, the Lady Helena Montagu-Douglas-Parr. Ladies, may I introduce you to Mr. Sam Howard, a correspondent with the European edition of the *Chicago Tribune*."

"Good evening," they chimed.

He was somehow even taller than she remembered, though not as young as she'd first thought, for there were deep-set laugh lines around his dark blue eyes when he smiled. His hair, in the lamplight, looked more brown than auburn, but his freckles were just as noticeable.

"Good to meet you, Princess Dimitri, Lady Helena."

"Please do call me Agnes, or Mrs. Paulson if you're obsessed with minding your elders. Our royals anglicized their names, so why shouldn't I? Besides, all that grand duchess folderol seems so terribly old-fashioned to me. I know dear Dimitri expected it, but he was the great-grandson of a czar, after all."

"Well, then, Mrs. Paulson it is. Glad to make your acquaintance."

It seemed as if Mr. Howard was about to say more, but the arrival of their waiter forestalled any further conversation until everyone had been furnished with their first course of sliced tomatoes with olives and a basil dressing.

"The chef is short-staffed, so I ordered for the table ahead of time," Gerald explained. "After this we'll have grilled leg of lamb, and then some figs and cheese to finish." Instead of wine, they had one of Gerald's cocktails with their first course. "I call it 'Juice of a Few Flowers.' My own recipe. Orange, lemon, grapefruit, and lime juices, with just a splash of gin. What do you think?"

Helena took a careful sip, for she had learned to be wary of Gerald's concoctions, and promptly choked on it when Mr. Howard spoke again.

"Lady Helena and I actually met earlier today. On the road into town. She was having some trouble with her bike, so I stopped to see if I might help." He smiled, revealing the boyish dimple in his cheek again.

"Helena! You didn't say a thing," Agnes chided. "You know how I feel about your riding miles and miles on that contraption. You might have become ill with sunstroke."

She directed a frostbitten glare at her aunt. "I was fine. I *am* fine."

Mr. Howard drained his cocktail, grimacing a little, and shook his head. "It wasn't anything worth worrying about, Mrs. Paulson. Just a slipped chain. We fixed it in no time."

Helena couldn't help but smile at his generous use of the collective pronoun. "There was no 'we,' I'm afraid. I'd still be there if Mr. Howard hadn't come along."

"You *divine* man," Agnes all but cooed. "You must come for lunch—tell me you will. Tomorrow? I insist absolutely."

"Oh, Auntie A," Helena pleaded. "I'm sure Mr. Howard has better things to do than—"

"I'd love to, but I'm only here a few days," he explained. "One of my colleagues is in Nice for the summer with his family. They took the train down, but he wanted his Peugeot, too. So we drew straws, all of us on the rewrite desk at the paper, and I won. Wish I could stay longer, though," he added, and he looked directly at Helena.

"You're staying here at the hotel?" Agnes asked.

"Yes, ma'am."

"Lovely. How long have you known Gerald and Sara?"

"Oh, three or four years—does that sound right, Gerald?"

"We have mutual friends in Paris," Gerald said. "Archie and Ada MacLeish."

"Archie and I were friends at Harvard, and then we served together during the war," Mr. Howard added. "He and Ada have been nice enough to introduce me to people of taste and refinement, unlike the crowd I run with most of the time."

"Your colleagues at the newspaper?" Helena asked, belatedly realizing how insulting that sounded. "I beg your pardon. I didn't mean—"

"Don't worry about it," he said with a grin. "They're Philistines, almost to a man. And we deskmen are the worst of the lot."

"What's a deskman?"

"I work on the rewrite desk most evenings. Though I'll sub in on days if they need an extra body."

She nodded, though she still had no real notion of what he was talking about. "I've seen your paper. There was a copy on the train when I came here. It was very interesting."

"Thanks. I'm glad you liked it. What do you do, anyway?" he asked.

It was such a surprising thing to be asked that she yet again found herself lost for words. Most people, after hearing her title, and learning a little about her upbringing, simply assumed she did nothing. That she had no identity beyond being the youngest daughter of the Earl of Halifax.

Sara answered him first. "Helena is an artist, and we all think she is terribly talented. She's starting classes in September at the Académie Czerny."

"I can vouch for Helena's talent," Gerald said. "She has a fine eye, particularly for color. Far better than my own."

This was a grand compliment indeed, for Gerald, though largely self-taught, was an artist of some renown, with work that the great Picasso himself had praised. Only that spring, one of his paintings had caused a sensation at the Salon des Indépendants.

"Gerald and Sara are too kind. I still have so much to learn."

"No better place than Paris. Not that I'd know—I can hold a pencil well enough to scribble down notes, but that's about it. Is that the connection between you and my friends here? Art?"

"You know, I suppose it is," Sara answered. "I was in London just before the war, and met Helena when I was there. Of course I was quite a bit older, but we soon discovered we had a lot in common. She came to my rescue one day, when I was trying to champion Cubism to some grandes dames—"

"You were doing perfectly well on your own," Helena insisted. "I merely contributed some moral support."

"All the same, I was very grateful to find a friend with similar interests and enthusiasms."

"I was heartbroken when you and your sisters left for Italy," Helena added.

"We'd hoped Helena might visit me in America, but the war got in the way, and then . . . well, you know what they say about one's best intentions. We're making up for lost time this summer."

Sara and Helena reminisced throughout the rest of the meal, while Mr. Howard divided his attention between Gerald and Agnes. As they were eating the last of the figs that had been serving in lieu of pudding, the Murphys' children were brought in to say good night. A little surprised by the lateness of their bedtime, Helena glanced at her watch and saw it was only a quarter to nine. Hardly more than an hour had passed since her and Agnes's arrival at the hotel.

"Honoria, Baoth, Patrick. Please say good night to Mrs. Paulson and Lady Helena, and to Mr. Howard."

"Good night, Mr. Howard," they chimed, coming round to shake his hand. "Good night, Mrs. Paulson. Good night, Ellie."

"Good night, my dears," Helena replied, not minding their use of her childhood nickname at all. "Shall I see you on the beach tomorrow afternoon?"

"Yes, oh yes! Yes, pleeeeease!" shouted Patrick, who was only four years old. "We're going on a treasure hunt!"

Gerald smiled indulgently. "You won't be going anywhere if you don't listen to Nanny and hop straight into bed. It's already an hour past your bedtime."

The Murphys were such wonderful parents, and their children really were delightful in every way. It did pain Helena at times, the knowledge that she was unlikely to ever have her own children, but moments like these went a long way in making up for such disappointment. And it was something, besides, to be everyone's favorite aunt.

With the children settled and their meal at an end, Gerald suggested they go out to the terrace and watch the sunset. So they trooped after him and stood before the modern, chromed railing as the sun descended ever closer to the wine-dark, slumbering sea.

Gerald passed around his cigarette case, but Helena's parents had forbidden her to smoke when she was younger, and consequently she had never taken up the habit. In any case, she quite disliked the smell. Rather to her surprise, Mr. Howard declined as well, and moved a little distance away from the others.

"Gassed in the war," he explained. "Smoking just makes it worse."

"I see," she said. "I'm sorry to—"

"So . . . Ellie," he said, turning to face her, his hip against the railing. "You don't seem like an Ellie."

"It's my pet name. From childhood. Didn't you have one?"

"Well, I was christened Samuel, so I guess that Sam is it. Never felt like a Samuel. That's my uncle's name."

"I don't feel like an Ellie, not really. But I don't mind when the children use it. Or my aunt."

"Earlier, when I was fixing your bike, you introduced yourself as Helena Parr."

"I'm only the daughter of an earl," she protested. "The 'lady' is a courtesy title; no more. I'm nothing in my own right."

"Aren't you?" he asked, suddenly serious.

"You know what I mean. It's something that belongs to my father, not me. That's why I don't like to use it. And it does seem rather, well, pretentious. Especially when speaking with an American. Please call me Miss Parr."

"Would you mind if I called you Ellie instead?"

Oddly enough, she wouldn't. "No," she said, and found herself smiling up at him.

"And would you mind if I join you at the beach tomorrow?"

"Not at all. Do you know how to dig for buried treasure? Build a sand castle? The children will expect us all to join in."

"Does an American know how to play baseball? Of course I do."

"Then I'll—"

"Helena, dear, do you mind awfully if we trundle back home?" Aunt Agnes called.

"No, I don't mind." She took a step back from Mr. Howard and offered her hand. He shook it firmly, just as he'd shake hands with a man. "Good night, then," she said.

"Good night, Ellie. See you tomorrow."

Agnes, normally so chatty at the end of an evening out, complained of a headache as they got into the coupe for the short trip home, and the resulting silence gave Helena a chance to reflect on their dinner with the Murphys and Mr. Howard. She decided that she rather liked him, and not only because he was handsome and interesting and really quite amusing. He was, she reflected, simply unlike any man she'd ever met in her circle of acquaintance at home. He was honest and straightforward, and she hadn't discerned even a hint of artifice or pretense in his manner.

With the exception of Gerald, whom she knew by virtue of her friendship with Sara, she'd never had a male friend before. There had been her fiancé, and before him a handful of suitors, but she couldn't honestly say they'd known anything about her. Certainly she'd never felt she could speak to them with candor, or share her thoughts and feelings in any meaningful way. Yet Mr. Howard, on the strength of a few hours' acquaintance, had asked her questions and, even more surprising, had actually listened to her answers.

Most surprising of all, she'd managed to speak with him as Helena Parr, a confident and articulate adult. The shy and awkward debutante of ten years past? Gone. The rejected fiancée, so cringing and apologetic, of five years ago? Absent.

Just the thought of it made her smile. And it made her wonder: here, in France, might she finally be free of the past?

Chapter 6

Helena rose at dawn the next day, and spent a happy and solitary morning in her studio, fortifying herself with cups of tea from her aunt's silver samovar. She fueled it with lumps of the ersatz coal the French called *boulots*, which threw off about as much heat as a firefly's dying breath, but the samovar didn't seem to mind. It did look rather ridiculous amid such rustic surroundings, but it boiled water quickly without heating the already-warm studio and meant she didn't have to invade Jeanne's kitchen whenever she wanted a cup of tea.

Having decided to work up one or two of her sketches from the day before in pastels, she looked them over and chose one that was little more than a few penciled lines. A swath of lavender had colonized a ruined drystone wall, rooting wherever pockets of soil had collected, and she'd been entranced at the way the plants spilled in a leggy jumble over the scattered blocks, as if there were no place on earth they'd rather be growing.

She began with blocks of color, which she pressed onto the paper with broken pieces of hard chalk pastels: a pale gray, almost white, for the mass of the wall, a bluish gray for the undulating mass of the foliage, and airy smudges of cornflower blue and violet for the blossoms. Dipping a flat brush in water, she used its damp bristles to sharpen the pigments here and there, adding intensity to the blossoms and depth to the ruined wall. She worked quickly, never lingering in any one spot for fear of overworking the pigments.

At this stage, the painting needed some time to dry, so she made herself a cup of tea, washed and dried the brush she'd used, and walked down to the edge of the top garden terrace. The sky was a dazzling blue already, without a shred of morning cloud. It would be another fine day, and very hot. Perfect weather for an afternoon on the beach.

She stood at the edge of the terrace and sipped at her tea, and tried to recall what life had been like before she had discovered she could draw.

She could still remember, if vaguely, how she had loved to make sketches of her toys and pets when she was very little, and how her parents had been pleased when presented with examples of her artwork by her nanny and governesses. No one had ever encouraged her to do anything more, however, and after a while she had become frustrated by her inability to capture what her eyes saw.

And then, the year she'd turned twelve, Miss Renfrew had been engaged as governess to her and Amalia. The woman hadn't been especially friendly or kind, and most of her lessons had been extremely boring, but she had known a little about art. Miss Renfrew had taught Helena the basic rules of composition and perspective, had shown her how to use pastels and watercolors, and had encouraged her to always carry a sketchbook and pencils, just in case inspiration struck when she was far from home. When Miss Renfrew had been replaced by another, less artistically inclined governess the following year, Helena had been disconsolate, but she hadn't given up. She had, instead, saved for months to buy an illustrated guide to figure drawing, and once she had memorized its precepts she had bought and devoured similar volumes devoted to watercolors and pastels.

And there she might have stayed, a self-taught but woefully inexperienced artist, if not for the war.

In the early years of the conflict, she hadn't done much in the way of volunteer work, apart from the same sort of Red Cross meetings and bandage-rolling parties that every other girl her age seemed to do. She had been bored and restless, and before long had started to pester her mother for permission to do more.

It had taken months and months, but eventually she had worn Mama down. By the middle of 1917 she had begun to volunteer at a small auxiliary hospital in Grosvenor Square. At first her work had been confined to letter-writing for men too weak to do so themselves, but one day she had found herself at loose ends, and without anything else to do had pulled out her ever-present sketchbook and pencil and had sketched one of the wounded men. He had been turned away from her, his face in profile, and it had been surprisingly easy to capture his likeness. One of the nurses had noticed, and complimented her, and soon every patient on the ward was asking for a portrait to send home.

Art had sustained her that year and the next, all those long, bleak months at the rag end of the war after Edward had gone missing and her happy, naïve dreams for the future had melted away like so much sand before the tide. In the years that followed, art had become her salvation. No matter how horrid people had been to her, no matter how lonely she had become, she'd always been able to escape to her room, to her easel by the window where the light was best, and forget everything.

Helena returned to her easel, again working with fragments of hard pastels, breaking them as needed to find a sharp edge for the details she sought. A mossy green traced the length of individual stalks of lavender, a shard of dark indigo further shadowed the crevices between the wall's ancient stones, and tiny pools of warm white, softened with her fingertip, caught the fractal path of sunbeams through a parasol of olive leaves.

She took a step back and surveyed her work. It was a simple scene, nothing that would ever turn the world on end, but it nonetheless filled her with a deep sense of satisfaction. Out of nothing more than a sheet of paper and a handful of broken pastels, she had created something beautiful.

And a year from now? What would she be capable of creating then? The possibilities alone were enough to make her feel nearly dizzy with excitement.

Just then, a bell rang inside. Micheline was reduced to almost comical levels of anxiety at the thought of interrupting Helena while she was painting, so they had come up with the bell as a tolerable means of summoning her to meals. She tidied away her things and headed back to the house.

The villa was cool and dark, its shutters still drawn against the sun, and its tiled floors felt pleasantly cool against Helena's bare feet as she went upstairs to wash her face and hands.

Agnes had a love of cold soups, the more exotically flavored the better, and as Helena joined her aunt in the dining room she braced herself for that day's offering. The soup from yesterday, which had contained ground almonds, of all things, had reminded her unpleasantly of melted ice cream.

Today's first course, however, was a concoction of tomato, cucumbers, and onions, as well as a headily fragrant amount of garlic; when they'd first had it the week before she had thought it delicious.

"I've forgotten the name for this," she said.

"It's gazpacho. The Princesse de Polignac has a Spanish chef and I persuaded him to explain how it's made. So wonderfully refreshing."

It was, and Helena had a second helping before devouring a plate of cold, grilled vegetables and several slices of day-old bread, also grilled, that had been rubbed with olive oil and yet more garlic.

"What are you doing this afternoon?" her aunt asked.

"I'm going down to the beach, as usual. Why don't you come with me? The Murphys have half a dozen parasols all set up, so you'll be in the shade, and—"

"Not today, my dear. I didn't sleep at all well last night. Bad memories, you know."

"Then you should stay here and rest. May I bring Hamish, though? He loves playing with the Murphys' dogs."

"Those wild things?"

"They're no bigger than Hamish, and very friendly animals."

"Oh, I suppose," her aunt said, sighing gustily. "You will carry him home, won't you? He'll be far too tired to manage."

"Of course I will, and I'll have a spot in the shade where he can rest, and a bowl of water, too."

"Don't forget the lemon. He loves a squeeze of lemon juice in his water."

"I won't forget."

It didn't take long to prepare for the afternoon, for Helena kept a bag ready packed with almost everything she needed, her swimming costume included. All she had to do was rub some sun cream on her nose, put on her espadrilles, and clip Hamish's lead to his collar.

"Ready?" she asked.

"Rrruff," he answered, and together they set off for their afternoon in the sun.

THE MURPHYS WERE already at the beach, with Gerald hard at work, as he had been every day since their arrival, on the task of clearing away the mountains of seaweed that had been allowed to accumulate. Only the hardiest winter holidaymakers ever went swimming, and the locals appeared immune to the charms of sand and sea. The section of beach he and his friends had cleared, while modest, was more than sufficient for the purposes of their small group, though the smell of the remaining seaweed could be a trifle overpowering at times.

"Hello, Helena," called Sara from the water, where she and Honoria were paddling. "Agnes didn't come with you?"

"Not today. But I did bring Hamish." She bent to unclip his lead, watching fondly as he waddled off to join the other dogs.

"Do help yourself to a glass of sherry or lemonade. And there are sandwiches in the basket."

"I think I'll change first."

Never inclined to do anything by half measures, the Murphys had set up a small pavilion-style tent for use as a changing room. Helena slipped inside, taking care to tie shut its flaps—she didn't wish to see her modesty in tatters thanks to a sudden breeze—shrugged out of her frock, cami-knickers, and espadrilles, and wriggled into her bathing costume. It was new, bought in Nice at the beginning of the summer, and while not immodest, at least not compared to others she had seen, its skimpy décolletage and abbreviated skirt would certainly have alarmed her mother. What her father might think of it she didn't care to imagine.

Only then did she remember that Mr. Howard would be at the beach, and she very nearly balked before urging herself forward. Of course he wasn't likely to notice what she was wearing, or even care. It had been years since anyone had noticed her in that way, and that state of affairs was unlikely to change as a result of one passably chic swimming costume. Besides, she really did want to go for a swim.

She spotted Mr. Howard as she was leaving the tent, and rather than walk down to the water right away she stood and watched him for a moment, admiring the way he played so unaffectedly with the Murphy children. He had rolled up his trouser legs, shed his shoes, and, at the boys' direction, was patiently excavating a moat around a sand castle they were building.

"Helena! Are you coming?" called Sara. "If you are, could you bring me my hat? It's on the table."

"Coming!" she called back. She collected Sara's hat and, holding it well above her head, crossed the hot sand to the water's edge. A few more steps and the water was past her knees, then her waist, and then she was standing on tiptoes an arm's length away from Sara and her daughter.

"Here you are," she said, passing the hat to her friend. "I'm going to swim for a bit. Honoria—you will shout out if you see any pirates? Promise me you will."

"I will," the child said, giggling.

"Good. Don't start the treasure hunt without me."

The beach at La Garoupe was on the western side of Cap d'Antibes and oriented rather more to the north; as she paddled away from the shore, the view before her was of the smaller Baie des Anges, and not the great expanse of the Mediterranean. She wasn't a strong swimmer, but here, in the sheltered bay, the water was shallow and nearly still, and it was easy to touch bottom and walk back to shore when she did grow tired.

It really was such a joy to swim in water such as this. The seasides she'd known at home, in Cornwall and Devon, had been beautiful places, but their water had rarely been so warm, and certainly never as calm. Swimming there—and she'd never gone very far, for fear of the tumbling waves—had been bracing rather than pleasurable, and she'd never been tempted to linger.

In her first weeks in Antibes, Helena had been able to swim for ten minutes at most before stumbling, utterly exhausted, back to the beach. Now she swam for half an hour, sometimes more, taking pleasure in the feeling of strength in her limbs as she carved through the water, letting her thoughts wheel and wander as freely as the gulls overhead. It was glorious to feel like herself again, to feel young and alive, and so hungry for every experience life could offer her. For so long she'd been starving, in body and in spirit, but a banquet awaited her now.

Honoria was waiting with a towel and robe, all but jumping up and down with excitement, when Helena emerged from the water. "Come, Ellie, do come! Mother says that as soon as we've eaten we may start the treasure hunt. But we can't begin until you've had something, too."

She followed Honoria back to the little encampment the Murphys had established, accepted a glass of lemonade, and sat down on an empty mat near the children.

"Mind if I join you?" Mr. Howard asked.

"Not at all. There's room on the mat, or we could find you a chair . . ."

"The mat will do just fine. How was your swim?"

"Lovely. Very refreshing. You should go in. I'm sure Gerald has a swimming costume he can lend you."

"I'm all right here on the beach," he answered affably, and he did seem perfectly content, his long legs stretched out in front of him. His feet were bare, she noticed, and the cuffs of his khaki trousers were still rolled up. She flushed at the strangeness of sitting next to a man she hardly knew while looking at his bare feet and calves, so near to him that she could see the bright coppery gold of the hair on his legs.

Such a missish response to something entirely normal in this day and age. If she didn't pull herself together, she'd be laughed out of art school come the autumn. Good heavens—what if she were asked to draw a nude? Only the worst sort of small-minded country bumpkin would balk at that.

Lost in her thoughts, she didn't immediately notice that Mr. Howard was talking to her. "I beg your pardon," she said. "I wasn't attending just now."

"I was only saying that I'd give almost anything for a cold beer," he answered, then looked ruefully at his glass of lemonade.

"You don't care for sherry?" she teased, her sense of equilibrium beginning to return.

He shook his head. "On a day like this? No. What I want, right now, is a beer that's cold enough to make my teeth hurt. That's one of the things I miss most about home."

"Isn't it against the law to drink beer in America?"

"Ah, yes. Our delightful Eighteenth Amendment. A triumph of antediluvian legislation. Any American over the age of ten can walk into a corner drugstore and buy a bottle of patent medicine with enough laudanum in it to knock out a platoon of GIs, but it's against the law for a grown man—or woman—to have a cold beer on a hot day."

"Were you still living in America when it was enacted?"

"I was, but not for long. I've lived in France for a little more than four years."

"Do you miss it? Home?"

"Apart from the beer I can't legally buy? Sure I do. I miss my family, and my friends there. I miss being able to watch a baseball game, and I miss having a real winter—not months of rain and damp like they have in Paris. But I'm not sure I'll go back, not for a while. What about you?"

"What do you mean?"

"Have you always lived here? Or is England still home?"

"I only have the one year here," she admitted. "That is, my parents have been kind enough to let me come here for a year and study with Maître Czerny. But it's not a forever sort of thing. I can't just stay here."

"Can't you?"

Flustered by his question, she took a sip of lemonade and considered how best to answer. "I could stay, I suppose. My aunt wouldn't mind. But I said I would come home after a year. They . . . well, they worry, you see. As parents do."

"Yes, but most parents let their children grow up. How old are you, anyway?"

"I beg your pardon!"

"I don't mean to be rude. I just mean that you're not a child like Honoria. Why can't you decide where you'll live and what you'll do?" There was an edge to his voice as he spoke, as if her words had irritated or even offended him.

"I do. I mean, I have decided, and I'm happy to have just the year."

He shrugged and looked away, and she was struck even more strongly by the notion that she'd somehow disappointed him. Which was a ridiculous thought, for it wasn't as if he knew anything about her, or what had happened after the war, or indeed only a few months earlier.

"Have you ever been to the south of France before?" she asked brightly, hoping to find a neutral topic of conversation.

"No, this is my first time seeing the Med. I've gone to the Atlantic coast, though. I went to Brittany last summer with some friends. Reminded me of home."

"You grew up at the seaside?"

"In New York City. But we went to Connecticut most summers. My parents have a house there, right on the shore. I loved it."

"Do your parents—" she started to ask, but was interrupted by whoops and cheers from the children. Gerald had just presented them with a map for the treasure hunt, and they spread it out on the mat next to Helena and Mr. Howard, Honoria reading aloud so her brothers could follow along.

"We have to draw lines between each of these places, I think, and at the bit in the middle where they go crisscross, we dig for treasure. Is that right, Dow-Dow?" she asked her father, using the name she'd given him when she was just a toddler.

"It is. Where shall we begin?"

"With the mermaid's perch!"

The children ran off to a chalk-white boulder at the shoreline, in their excitement forgetting to bring along the map. Helena stood, brushing sand from her posterior, and admired the beautifully detailed work of art that Gerald had created for his children, which resembled in every respect a child's expectation of what a pirate map should be, down to its charred edges and weather-beaten appearance. He must have labored on it for hours.

Once the four markers had been located, the children decided that Mr. Howard, having the longest legs of anyone else on the beach that day, would pace out the intersecting lines. He readily agreed, though he complained piteously that the hot sand was hurting his feet. This just made the children laugh all the louder.

Once the X had been found, it remained only to dig down to find the pirates' "bunty," as Patrick called it. Mr. Howard was again pressed into service, though he began to protest when the hole had reached a depth of two feet with no sign of the promised treasure.

"What if we got it wrong?" he asked. "What if we're digging in the wrong spot?"

"Noooo!" they cheered. "Keep digging!"

At a yard deep, Mr. Howard's little spade—he was using Patrick's sand toys to dig—scraped against something hard. A wooden box, tightly wrapped in oilcloth, emerged from the hole. As the youngest, Patrick was accorded the honor of opening the box, and he nearly swooned with delight when the lid fell back. Inside were heaps of golden coins, so many he gave up on counting them right away, and a letter from a long-dead pirate that, by some miracle, was addressed directly to the children.

Once the excitement had subsided and the treasure had been tidied away for later play—the coins were checker pieces that Gerald had gilded—the children insisted on going for swim, and ignored Helena's protests that she'd already been in the water. Mr. Howard excused himself, explaining that he hadn't brought his swimming costume, but he promised t stand at the edge of the water and keep watch for sea serpents or enemy submersibles.

When they had finished their swim, which was really just an excuse for the children and dogs to frolic in the shallows, he brought her a fresh towel, which fortunately was large enough to act as a makeshift cloak. He didn't wink or smirk or even smile at her—was perfectly well-mannered in every respect—but she did feel uncomfortable. If only he'd thought to bring a swimming costume. That would have made things easier, since they'd have been on equal footing, sartorially speaking.

"When do you start your classes?" he asked, his gaze focused on the sea.

"In September. At the Académie Czerny."

"The name is familiar. Do you know the address of the school?"

"It's on the rue du Montparnasse, just off the boulevard."

"Then it's not far from where I live." He turned his head, one hand shading his eyes. "Will you look me up when you're back in Paris? You can send me a *petit bleu* at the paper."

"A little blue . . . ?"

"A pneumatic message. I doubt your aunt has a telephone—hardly anyone does—and the post isn't very efficient. You can buy the forms at the post office or stationers."

"When do you leave?"

"Tomorrow. I could only wrangle a few days off from my editor. Blochman fell down the stairs last week, and he and I are the only ones that can make much sense of the cables from New York. So back I go."

"Is he all right? Your colleague?"

"He'll be fine. Will teach him to avoid stairs when he's had a snootful."

It was the first time she'd ever heard that term, but for once it didn't have to be explained to her. American words were so terribly expressive.

"I had better go home," she said presently. "My aunt will be expecting me."

"Looks as if Gerald and Sara are marshaling the troops, too."

It really was a shame he wouldn't be staying longer. She wondered if she'd have the courage to find him in Paris. "Thank you again for your help yesterday."

"You're welcome, Ellie. Or should I say 'duchess'?" He smiled again, for the first time since she'd admitted her decision to stay only a year in France. "Look me up, will you? It's always nice to have an old friend in a new city."

"I will, though it may be a while. I'll need to get settled at my aunt's house, and I don't know how much time I'll—"

"I don't mind. I'll wait."

"Good-bye, Mr. Howard."

"Call me Sam. Please."

"Good-bye, Sam."

He walked away, holding little Patrick's hand as they followed the path up to the seawall, his head bent to listen to the child's happy chatter. She watched them until they were hidden by a stand of palm trees, and then she clipped Hamish's lead to his collar and set off for home.

PART TWO

Don't you ever get the feeling that all your life is going by and you're not taking advantage of it? Do you realize you've lived nearly half the time you have to live already?

—Ernest Hemingway, *The Sun Also Rises*

Chapter 7

The last weeks of the summer slipped by in a languid, sun-drenched blur. Agnes departed for St.-Malo in the middle of August, taking Vincent and Hamish with her, and without her animating presence the villa felt cold and silent, even on the hottest of days. Jeanne and Micheline stayed on, for they remained in Antibes year-round; and though they were friendly enough, their work kept them too busy to offer much in the way of company for Helena.

It would have been unutterably lonely if not for the Murphys. If ever she felt at loose ends, or in need of conversation, she had only to wander over and they made her welcome. Sara even invited her to stay with them at the hotel, but Helena hadn't wanted to intrude, or to be seen as presuming on their friendship. She still saw them at the beach most afternoons, and often went with them, too, when they paid visits to their villa, where renovations were nearly finished and the garden was in full, riotous bloom.

"It was here when we bought the place," Gerald explained. "The fellow who owned the villa before us was a diplomat, and every time he traveled he brought back something exotic.

We'll have to do some pruning and weeding, but not much of either."

Gerald had set up a studio at the hotel, too, for art was as vital to him as the air he breathed. He had begun a painting he hoped to exhibit at the Salon des Indépendants the following spring, a huge canvas that portrayed a disassembled watch, or perhaps clockworks; it was hard to tell at such an early stage.

At the end of August she packed up her things and bid a fond farewell to the Murphys, who wouldn't be returning to Paris until later that autumn, and even then would be living in St.-Cloud, a suburb on the outskirts of the city.

"It's too far for visits during the week," Sara advised, "but you can always visit on the weekend. Besides, we'll be at our apartment on the quai des Grands Augustins often enough—at least once a month, if not more."

VINCENT WAS WAITING at the Gare de Lyon when her overnight train arrived, not far past dawn, on the first of September.

"Good morning, Vincent. How are you?"

"I am well, Lady Helena. This way, please."

It was more than he'd ever said to her before; perhaps the man was warming up to her. Or perhaps she had worn him down. Either way, she was almost certain she caught him smiling, though only a little, as he bent to collect her valise.

It was only a short drive to her aunt's home, a grand old town house at the western end of the Île St.-Louis. She hadn't visited since before the war, but the exterior hadn't changed at all, nor had the neighborhood.

Vincent went to park the car in the old stables, and rather than walk back through the gates to the front, Helena went in through the side door. "Hello!" she called out. "Auntie A? Are you up?"

She walked the length of the main floor, popping her head into its various reception rooms—all empty. They'd been redecorated in an elegant but rather clinical contemporary style since she'd seen them last, in startling contrast to the faded and faintly shabby grandeur of the house itself. She walked upstairs, to the first floor with its bedrooms, calling out for her aunt as she went.

"Auntie A? Hello?"

"Helena? But you're early! Do come in—I'm at the end of the hall."

Agnes was sitting up in bed, the morning's newspapers scattered around her, wearing a silk and lace bedgown that was more confectionery than garment. Her breakfast of buttered toast and *chocolat chaud* sat on a japanned tray at her side, and Hamish, snoring loudly, was sprawled across the bed's embroidered silk coverlet.

"Helena, my dear! I wasn't expecting you for another half hour at the least."

Helena sat on the edge of the bed, rather a feat as it was impossibly high, and deposited a kiss on her aunt's cheek.

"How was your journey? How are you?" Agnes asked.

"Very well. How was St.-Malo?"

"Exceedingly tiresome, I'm afraid. Crammed with sad old bores, and the weather was frightful. I really ought to have stayed with you in Antibes. Are you hungry? Do you want any breakfast?"

"No, thank you. They fed me on the train."

"I thought I'd let you choose your room. Not the blue room, though—it smells of damp."

"I suppose it can't be helped when one lives so close to the river."

Agnes sighed dramatically. "My dear, if you only knew how many tears I have shed over this *ruin* of a house. It costs the earth to maintain, and every time it rains there is water in the *sous-sol*. I would leave, but dear Dimitri and I were so happy here. I couldn't bear it."

"But I thought . . . I thought you were only married for a few months before he died."

"Yes, my dear, but we lived here together for nearly ten years before that. Such a happy time."

Helena had always known her aunt was unconventional, but this was astonishing news. "You did? I had no idea . . . I mean, Mama never said a thing."

"Of course she didn't. She and your father were horrified. But love is love, and we weren't about to be parted simply because his wife wouldn't divorce him. Horrid woman."

Helena's head was reeling. "Is that why you never visited? Never introduced him?"

"Yes, but let's not talk of all that. So disheartening to think about. And I made my peace with your parents ages ago. Now you go along and choose a bedroom while I finish my *petit déjeuner*. Once I'm dressed we can go for a walk and talk about everything I missed when I was away."

The bedroom next to her aunt's was grandly furnished, all burnished walnut and quilted satin coverlets, and was clearly the best of the guest rooms; she would never sleep well there. The next room along was nearly as bad, but the last—perhaps it had been reserved, once, for a maiden aunt or some other overlooked relation—was perfect.

It was furnished with the simple neoclassical pieces of a hundred years before, now sadly out of fashion but much more to her taste than modern furniture. Two tall windows offered a pretty view of the central courtyard, with its arching plane trees and manicured flower beds. She opened the window nearest to the door and, leaning on the wrought-iron balustrade, let the beauty of the city seep into her bones.

She stood at the window and thought of her aunt and Dimitri, and understood, at last, the reason she'd seen so little of her aunt when she was younger. The reason that Agnes had never come to visit her family in England, and had never introduced Dimitri until after their marriage.

Their lives, if they'd lived in England, would have been unendurable. Would have been *made* unendurable, she corrected herself. They would have been outcasts, the object of pity, scorn, and contempt. No one would have received them, their own families included. But they had been happy together in France.

THE FOLLOWING WEEK, on the Friday before term began, Agnes greeted Helena with an announcement at breakfast.

"I think it is time for you to experience your first Paris salon. I've just had a note from Natalie Barney, and she's back from Normandy a little early this year. Such a fascinating woman, and friends with *everyone* in Paris."

"What happens at her salon?"

"Not much of anything, to be perfectly honest, but that's why I like it. One goes for the company, and of course the delicious food, and she keeps any attendant folderol to a minimum. Some obscure poet might recite a few lines from his or her newest work, but that will be the sum of it."

"What time does it begin?"

"Around four o'clock. You'll want to wear something chic—

your frock with the *broderie anglaise* will do. Oh, we shall have such fun!"

Vincent drove them to Miss Barney's house on the rue Jacob, although it was scarcely a mile away, and after parking the car on the street he escorted them to a set of green doors, wide and high enough for a carriage to pass through. Beyond was a cobbled courtyard, rather overgrown with moss, a small and very pretty pavilion, and, astonishingly, a grove of chestnut trees. Here in the heart of Paris, where trees were ruthlessly pollarded, and where they were expected to grow in straight lines flanking straight boulevards, a remnant of wild and ancient forest had somehow survived.

"Such a surprise," she murmured.

"The trees?" Agnes asked. "Or the temple?"

And there it was, a perfect, tiny, classical temple, its pediment supported by four Doric columns. "Natalie calls it her 'temple of friendship,'" Agnes explained. "It can't be any older than the pavilion itself, but it does look impressive, doesn't it?"

It had begun to rain, so they hurried to enter the pavilion. At the door, greeting Miss Barney's guests, was an elderly Chinese butler, who smiled and ushered them along. They walked to the end of a narrow, dark hall and moved into a large room, already so crowded with guests that Helena could discern little of its décor beyond the closely hung prints and portraits on the faded red walls. The light in the room was faintly green, tinted by the overarching boughs of the chestnut trees outside, and what few lights there were did little to dispel the late afternoon gloom.

"Agnes, my friend. You're here!" A woman approached them, her smile ready and genuine; it could only be Miss Barney. She might have been any age between thirty and fifty, for she had a beautiful, unlined complexion, and her chin-length hair was either blond or silver; in the dim light of the sitting room it was difficult to tell.

"Of course," Agnes replied gaily. "When have I ever refused one of your summons?"

"And is this your niece?" Miss Barney asked.

"Yes, indeed. Helena, allow me to introduce you to Miss Natalie Barney. Natalie, this is my niece, Lady Helena Montagu-Douglas-Parr."

Helena suppressed a sudden urge to curtsey, for there was something terribly regal about their hostess, and instead shook her outstretched hand. "I'm very pleased to make your acquaintance, Miss Barney. Thank you for including me in your invitation."

"It is entirely my pleasure, I assure you. Agnes tells me you are an artist."

"Yes, ma'am. I've come to Paris to attend classes at the Académie Czerny."

"I see, I see. Excellent school. Fabritius does have an eye for talent. You'll do well with him. We must talk some more—I can think of any number of people you ought to meet. Do excuse me; I must say hello to some people."

And with that she was gone, her attention drawn by the arrival of another group of guests.

"There. You have met the grande dame herself. Now, shall we have something to eat? We just need to squeeze past these people here."

Agnes looped her arm through Helena's and steered them toward the dining room, and as they made their way through the crush of people, nearly all of them women, she put names to faces for her niece's benefit.

"That's Djuna Barnes, I think; haven't seen her here before. Can't remember where I first met her. And there, with the Valentino look-alike, is Colette—yes, *the* Colette. Hasn't written anything worth reading in years, but she does add a certain spark to these affairs. That's Lily Gramont, the duchesse de Clermont-Tonnerre; she's one of Natalie's dearest friends. No sign of Romaine Brooks today, but that's no surprise. Let me see . . . the women over there, the ones in the awful suits? They're Sylvia Beach and Adrienne Monnier. Miss Beach owns Shakespeare and Company, the English-language bookshop. She published Joyce's *Ulysses* when no one else would touch it. Ah—here we are. No one feeds her guests as handsomely as Natalie."

The table before them was tiled with tray after tray of cucumber sandwiches, éclairs, meringues, almond *tuiles,* and *palmier* biscuits. Helena filled a plate, accepted a cup of tea, and followed Agnes to a relatively uncrowded corner of the dining room.

"As soon as we've eaten I'll take you round and introduce you properly," her aunt promised, and once they'd emptied their plates Agnes took her arm and led Helena on a tour of the salon and its sophisticated guests.

Nearly all the conversation was in English, for almost everyone was American or English, and though she could have taken part Helena simply stood and listened to the discussions of poetry and fiction and art and dance that swirled around her.

They left after an hour, in concordance with her aunt's theory that one must always leave a party when everyone is at their most amusing, and after thanking Miss Barney and promising to come again, they left the hidden courtyard behind and found Vincent waiting with the car.

"What did you think of Natalie and her friends?" Agnes asked immediately.

"I liked them, very much. They were all so interesting, and their conversations were interesting, too. None of the usual drivel about husbands and quarterly allowances and problems with the help."

"That's because none of them have husbands, or if they do the men are just window dressing."

"I don't understand."

"Natalie and her circle are nearly all of them lesbians." Agnes let her words sink in, and then, a frown creasing her brow, turned to look Helena in the eye. "You aren't one of those tiresome people who rail against such relationships?"

"Of . . . of course not," Helena stammered, more than a little embarrassed by her naïveté. She knew that women might be drawn to other women, just as men might desire other men, but until that afternoon it had been an abstraction, no more real to her than Sappho on her island.

"I didn't know it was possible to live so openly," she added after a moment. "Aren't Miss Barney and her friends bothered by the police?"

"Not usually. From time to time the authorities become obsessed with homosexual activity in Pigalle, at places like Chez Graff and the like, but prosecution is rare here. I'm not sure if lesbianism is even considered a criminal offense in France."

"I'm glad . . . I mean, I should hate to think of Miss Barney being harassed in any way. She and her friends . . ."

"Yes?"

"I envy them, that's all. They were so confident. So assured. I do hope I'll make friends of my own at school."

"Of course you will. Simply keep an open mind and a smile on your face and you'll be awash in friends in no time."

Chapter 8

Helena arrived at the academy early, that first morning, and dutifully queued for her *carte d'étudiant*, an *horaire*, and a shapeless artist's smock that was far too large for her slight frame.

"Excuse me," she called out, trying to catch the clerk's attention. It was no easy task, given the general din in the room and crush of students, all just as eager to be done with their paperwork. "May I exchange this for another size?"

"One size, Mademoiselle. Next!"

Rather than make a fuss, and possibly incur the enmity of everyone else in the queue, she retreated to the hallway, and then, finding it full to bursting with yet more students, ventured upstairs. Presumably the timetable she'd received, now rather crumpled, would include details of her classes' locations as well as their times.

She walked to the end of the corridor, where it was somewhat less congested, and unfolded the *horaire*.

Mlle H. Parr—septembre 1924
lundi, 10 h à 12 h, dessin, grand salon

mardi, 10 h à 12 h, dessin, grand salon

mercredi, 10 h à 12 h, dessin, grand salon

jeudi, 10 h à 12 h, dessin, grand salon

vendredi, 10 h à 12 h, dessin, grand salon

They'd made a mistake. In the school's prospectus, the curriculum for intermediate students had included classes in watercolors, pastels, and oils. No sculpture, which had been a shame, but everything else had definitely been mentioned in the brochure. On her timetable, however, she was only enrolled in one two-hour drawing class each day.

"Oh, bother," she muttered. Now she would have to go downstairs and brave the masses again.

"Is anything the matter?" asked a young man standing nearby. He was dressed in the shabby, informal way that amounted to a uniform among the artists of Montparnasse: a worn and none-too-clean coat, a wrinkled shirt with an open collar, and no hat whatsoever. He was also astonishingly good-looking, with beautiful green eyes and straight brown hair so long that it brushed his shoulders.

"I think there's a mistake. I've only been signed up for the drawing classes, but I'm sure there—"

"Turn it over," he said, smiling. "Voilà. There are the classes for October."

Feeling terribly silly, she looked on the reverse of the page, and there it was:

Mlle H. Parr—octobre 1924

lundi, 10 h à 12 h, dessin, grand salon; 13 h à 15 h, pastels, salon B

mardi, 10 h à 12 h, dessin, grand salon; 13 h à 15 h, aquarelles, salon C

mercredi, 10 h à 12 h, dessin, grand salon; 13 h à 15 h, pastels, salon B

jeudi, 10 h à 12 h, dessin, grand salon; 13 h à 15 h, aquarelles, salon C
vendredi, 10 h à 12 h, dessin à modèle vivant, grand salon

"Thank you. I was worried I'd have to go downstairs and join the queue again."

"And that is a fate worse than death, hmm?"

"Nearly. How do you do?" she asked, remembering her manners. "I'm Helena Parr."

"And I am Étienne Moreau, and very pleased to make your acquaintance." He had a lovely voice, his accent just noticeable enough to make everything he said sound charming. Smiling again, he shook her outstretched hand. "Shall we go in?"

Behind them, halfway down the corridor, students were streaming through a set of open doors. Her first class was beginning.

The *grand salon* was a large but not enormous room, and most of its space was taken up by sets of easels and stools, around forty in total. At its front was a low platform about five feet square and half as high. Light streamed in from a huge bank of windows; even on a dull day, she saw, the salon would be bright enough for work without artificial light.

Mr. Moreau took a spot on the left side of the salon, near the back, and she sat next to him, her heart pounding. She had never been given to attacks of nerves before, so why was she so anxious now?

"*Courage*," her new friend whispered, using the French pronunciation. "And put on your smock. We're using charcoal today, and you don't want to ruin your clothes. Shall I help you roll back the sleeves?"

"I think I can manage, but thank you."

"Excuse me, but is this seat taken?" A young woman,

American by her accent, now stood by the last stool and easel in their row.

"It isn't—please do take it."

"Thank you so much. I galloped nearly all the way here," she said, rummaging through her handbag, "and I was late all the same." Finding a handkerchief, she patted invisible drops of perspiration from her brow. "Thank heavens I got here in time. Oh—you're wearing your smock. I'd better put mine on, too. I wish it wasn't so big."

Helena smiled at her, and was about to say something re-assuring when she realized that a man had entered the salon and was standing at the front. Rather than ascend the stage, however, he stood next to it, his expression impossible to read.

He was middle-aged, perhaps in his early fifties, and was dressed more like a banker than an artist, with a collar and tie and rather old-fashioned coat. His hair, which he wore swept back off his brow, was less conventional, for it was dark and wavy and fell almost to his shoulders, and he had a carefully trimmed Vandyke mustache and beard. She wasn't sure if he was handsome, or merely striking. Either way, he wasn't the sort of man one ignored.

He waited, his demeanor unchanging, until the room was entirely silent, and only then did he speak.

"I am Fabritius Czerny. I expect one-quarter of you, per-haps as many as a third, to flee by the end of this week. I make no apologies. This is a difficult course of study, and far beyond the talents of many here today. If you find the work I give you too challenging, you are free to withdraw from the course, or you may wish to join our class for beginners."

His voice was soft and low, and only lightly accented. Under dif-ferent circumstances, Helena might even have thought it beautiful.

"I will be blunt: I am not a pleasant person. I am not, as the Americans among you might say, 'a nice guy.' I am not here to be your friend or your mentor, and I have no interest in your thoughts or opinions.

"We shall begin from the beginning. You may think you know how to paint, but you do not. You know *nothing*. And so you must unlearn all the rubbish you have been fed, like so much pap, by your other teachers. You must forget all so you may learn all."

He surveyed the room, a dark-maned lion assessing a herd of terrified gazelle, but rather than hide behind her easel, as others were attempting to do, Helena straightened her back and didn't look away when his gaze swept across her. She was made of sterner stuff, and she'd faced disapproving stares before. Compared to the first ball she'd attended after Edward had ended their engagement? This was nothing.

"Most of you are American or English, so I shall teach this course in English. If you have difficulty understanding, ask a neighbor, and don't even think of bothering me. You shall now embark on a series of sketches. Before you is paper sufficient for the exercise, as well as a selection of charcoal."

Maître Czerny set a tall stool upon the center of the stage and then strode to the side of the room, to a set of shelves that was crowded with objects of every color, shape, size, and substance. He selected a bowl of apples and, returning to the stage, placed it on the stool.

"You may begin. You have ten minutes. Do not bother to prepare the paper; simply draw. Draw what you see before you."

Never in all her life had Helena been as apprehensive of a task as she was now. Withdrawing a stick of charcoal at random from the cup on her easel, she sketched a light outline—but she had chosen a piece of soft charcoal by mistake, and it left a thick, almost jet-black line on the paper. She scrubbed at it with a lump of putty eraser, and succeeded only in smearing the paper. Praying Maître Czerny wouldn't notice, she flipped the paper over, found a thin stalk of vine charcoal, and began again. Outline. Shadows. Shadows softened.

She needed to remove some of what she had added, and so add highlights, but the light in the salon was coming from two sources, the bank of windows and the electric lights that dangled overhead, and was reflected in quite different ways by the apples, which she was certain were papier-mâché or wax, and by the bowl, which was made of a dark, almost opaque glass. She needed to—

"Enough!" Maître Czerny carried the bowl and apples back to the shelf and returned with an ornate and heavily tarnished silver candelabrum. "Take up a fresh sheet of paper. This time you have five minutes. Begin!"

Her hand flew over the paper, trying in vain to capture what her eye saw, but she got the proportions all wrong, and she hadn't the time to erase what she'd done, and the finer details of the silver were vanishing into a misshapen blur that bore more resemblance to a dead tree than a piece of antique silver, and—

"Enough!" He removed the candelabrum and replaced it with a wreck of a violin, its strings broken and tangled. "Two minutes!"

The shape of the instrument was easy to capture, but she'd barely sketched its outline when the dreaded order came— "Enough! One minute!"—and the violin was replaced with an enormous conch shell, pale ivory with a delicate pink interior, its curving lines so—

"Enough! That is all for the moment."

Helena set down her charcoal, her hands shaking so badly that she had to fold them into her lap. Her sketches were crude, unfocused, and amateurish, while Mr. Moreau's—she couldn't help but glance at them—were elegant and effortlessly graceful.

"Choose the best of your efforts, and set it on your easel," their teacher commanded.

Maître Czerny walked along the rows, muttering to himself in French and what Helena took to be Czech. Periodically he would groan loudly, or run a hand through his hair. Two or three times he examined a sketch for a few seconds longer, and then, before moving on, nodded curtly.

At last he was at their row. He paused by Mr. Moreau's sketch, a marvel of simplicity that captured the conch shell in four or five sweeping lines, and nodded approvingly. For Helena's sketch, he offered no response, instead moving past as if he hadn't even seen it. A moment later, she knew she'd been lucky to escape so easily, for his groan of disdain upon seeing the American girl's work was accompanied by yet more hair-pulling and grumbling.

When he had finished his inspection he returned to the front, scrubbed his hands over his face, and raised his eyes to the heavens. "Terrible. Simply terrible. Try again," he commanded the entire class.

Ten minutes to sketch a vase filled with ostrich plumes, five minutes for a heap of red and gold brocade, two minutes for a forlorn and moth-eaten stuffed pheasant, and finally one minute for a green glass fisherman's float.

"A few—a *very* few—of these sketches show promise," he said upon his return to the front of the salon. "The rest belong in the bottom of a chicken coop. There is only one thing to be done: you will start at the very beginning.

"Cone. Cylinder. Sphere. Cube. Torus."

Someone at the front must have grumbled, or made a face, because Maître Czerny was across the room in a flash, looming over the poor fellow, all but shouting in his face. "Did I not say I care nothing for your opinions?"

He paced the width of the salon, back and forth, pulling his hair back from his brow so forcefully that Helena's eyes fairly watered at the sight.

"You long to be successful, do you not? You long to be the young new painter everyone is talking about. But you do not wish to do the work. And you cannot become great without learning how to *draw*.

"It does not matter if you wish to paint like an Old Master or a Cubist—the education is the same. If you cannot draw, you are nothing. And your art? It is *nothing*."

He went once again to the shelves, and this time took down a plain wooden cylinder. This he placed on the stool. "I will give you one half hour to draw this cylinder. Begin."

Calm yourself, Helena thought. Calm. She could draw a cylinder in half an hour. This, she could do.

Helena decided to prepare the paper before she began—not as painstakingly as she would ordinarily do, but enough to provide some depth to the sketch's background. She dug a flat piece of compressed charcoal from the cup on her easel and, holding it flat against the paper, spread an even layer of light gray across its entire surface. No rag had been provided, so she used the cuff of her smock to blend the charcoal to a pale, even wash of silver. Turning the stick on end, she sketched the cylinder's outline in quick, confident strokes. Shadows came next, and then highlights, which she created with swift, sure touches of her putty eraser. She worked carefully, pausing now and again to survey her progress, blocking out all thoughts of Maître Czerny and the other students.

"Enough!" he called. "We have only enough time for one more shape. Shall we see what ruin you can make of a sphere? Begin."

Moments later, it seemed, the bells at Notre-Dame Cathedral began to chime the hour. It was noon.

Maître Czerny went to the door, issuing a final directive before departing. "Take your work with you. I have no use for it. For tomorrow, I expect you to prepare one example of each shape, executed to the best of your sadly limited abilities. *À demain*."

Chapter 9

As soon as the door had closed behind Maître Czerny, air began to fill the salon again. Helena took a deep breath and tried to collect her thoughts.

"You seem a little *bouleversée*," Mr. Moreau said. "I am not sure of the word in English. Overturned?"

"Bowled over, perhaps?"

"Yes, exactly. I was thinking we should—"

"Étienne!"

They were interrupted by the arrival of another student, a woman who had been sitting on the other side of the salon, and whose work had elicited several rare nods from Maître Czerny. She and Mr. Moreau kissed cheeks and began a conversation in French that was far too animated for Helena to follow.

"Miss Parr, allow me to introduce you to Mathilde Renault. I was about to ask if you'd like to share a coffee with me."

"Yes, please. But you must both call me Helena. I insist."

"We shall. We should all be on a first-name basis, should we not? As comrades in arms? Yes?"

"I have the time for one coffee," said Mathilde. "But what of your other friend?" she asked, looking over Helena's shoulder at the American girl, who was slowly gathering her sketches into a bundle.

"Of course," Étienne agreed. "Excuse me, Mademoiselle—would you like to join us?"

"I'd love to," she said, her expression brightening.

"I am Étienne Moreau, and these are my friends Mathilde Renault and Helena Parr."

"I'm pleased to make everyone's acquaintance. I'm Daisy Fields."

No one spoke for a moment. The American girl simply had to be teasing them.

"Truthfully—that is your name?" Étienne said, his eyes wide with amazement.

"Well, my real name is Dorothy, but my parents called me Daisy when I was little and I guess it just stuck. It's pretty silly, I know."

"Not at all," Étienne insisted gallantly. "I think it suits you very well. Now—where shall we go? Mathilde?"

"The Falstaff is not so very far."

"The Falstaff it is. *Allons-y!*"

As they filed out of the *grand salon* and down the stairs, they were joined by a middle-aged woman who had been sitting on a stool in the corridor.

"Do you know her?" Helena whispered to Daisy, for the woman's eyes were focused to a disconcerting degree on her new friend.

"That's just Louisette. Daddy insists she accompany me everywhere. We hate one another."

"Oh . . . I see."

"I shouldn't use the word 'hate,' I know. But she does get

on my nerves. When Daddy first hired her, I tried to be nice. I'd invite her to sit with me, to have what I was having, but she always said no. So now I try to pretend she doesn't exist."

When they got to Falstaff's, which was just down the street from the academy, Daisy politely but firmly banished Louisette to a table at the far side of the café and asked the waiter to bring the woman a glass of water. But she didn't touch the water, or ask for anything else. All she did was sit and stare at Daisy and, by extension, the rest of them. It really was quite unnerving.

Soon, though, Helena was caught up in their conversation and having a grand time, though she barely touched the *café noisette* she had ordered. Étienne was on his third *café express* before he noticed.

"Is there something not right with your coffee?"

"Nothing at all. It's simply . . . well, it's a bit strong for me. I would normally have a café au lait, but—"

"But the garçon would faint if you asked for such a thing after nine in the morning," Étienne agreed. "The milk in the *noisette*—it isn't sufficient?"

"I think the trouble is that it still tastes like coffee to me, and I'm used to tea," she admitted. "Don't mind me. I'm in Paris now, and this is how Parisians take their coffee. I'll learn to like it."

The Falstaff was a curious place—a café-bar in the heart of Paris that was decorated to resemble a British public house, with forest green banquettes, framed prints of hunting hounds and Scottish stags, and enough oak paneling to satisfy a Tudor. At least Helena assumed that had been the decorator's intent, for she'd never actually been inside a public house.

Their conversation so far had centered on Maître Czerny and their morning class. Daisy and Helena were still feeling bowled over, while Mathilde and Étienne were more phlegmatic. It seemed that tyrannical behavior was not uncommon among the city's art teachers.

"I was in a class once where the maître ripped our drawings to pieces when they displeased him," Mathilde recalled. "And there was another teacher—remember Maître Homard, Étienne?"

"God, yes. That wasn't his real name, but we called him that because his face would become as red as *un homard*—how do you say it in English?"

"A lobster?" Daisy offered.

"Yes, that's it. Once, I remember, he was so enraged by one student's efforts—I think the poor fellow had overworked his paint—that he came leaping across the studio, waving a palette knife, and slashed the canvas in two. Right down the middle!"

"Goodness me," Daisy said. "That does put things in perspective."

"Do not be disheartened," Mathilde advised. "Czerny will not always be so fierce."

"How do you and Étienne know one another?" Helena asked. He seemed to be in his early twenties, while Mathilde was nearer to thirty, she judged; as their accents when they spoke French were quite different, she doubted they had grown up together.

"We were students at the École des Beaux-Arts together, last year," Mathilde answered. "But we both found it . . . I'm not sure how to say . . . *désagréable*?"

"Disagreeable."

"Ah. Nearly the same. Yes, it was disagreeable. I thought the teachers too rigid. Too attached to old traditions."

"I was asked to leave," said Étienne with mischief in his eyes. "I consider it a great honor."

Thinking it impolitic to question him on the reason for his expulsion from the prestigious school, Helena turned to Daisy.

"Did you come over from America specially for the course?" she asked.

"Oh, no. I've been here for years. My father's a doctor, and during the war he came over to oversee the American hospitals here. My mother had died a few years before, and he needed someone to run the house and act as his hostess when he entertained. That kind of thing."

"I see," said Helena, thinking that Daisy would have been awfully young for such responsibilities, at least when they first came to France.

"Daddy's retiring at the end of the year—they asked him to stay on after the war, which is why we're still here—so I suppose we'll be going home then."

"Why are you taking the course?" Mathilde asked. "Have you studied art before?"

"No, not really. After the war, I worked in a studio for a while, helping with the supplies and some preparatory work. I learned a little while I was there, and then, after the studio closed, I bought some instruction books and tried to learn that way. Daddy wasn't very keen on my going out to school, you see. But I convinced him, finally, that I should have some lessons. So here I am, although it may not be for long . . ."

"For someone who's never had an art class in her life, you are very good, you know," Helena reassured her. And it was true. Maître Czerny had been wrong to dismiss Daisy's work so cruelly, for several of her sketches had been competently executed.

Étienne reached across the table to pat Daisy's arm. "Here we say *le chien qui aboie ne mord pas.* The barking dog does not bite,

I think? He is a loud man, and a rude man, but you must not be afraid of him."

"And you, Hélène?" Mathilde asked. "Why are you here?"

"Just after Christmas last year, I came down with scarlet fever, and I nearly died. Even after the worst was over, I was bedridden for ages. Once I was a little better, I told my parents that I wished to come to Paris and learn how to paint properly."

"They let you come to Paris all on your own?" asked Daisy, her mouth agape in wonder.

"Heavens, no. My aunt lives here, otherwise I'm sure they'd have made a huge fuss. And I think the only reason they did agree is because they felt so badly for me."

"Shall you return home when the course ends?" Étienne asked.

"I think so. Although if Maître Czerny keeps making faces when he looks at my work I may be home before Christmas!"

"No, no," Étienne said, shaking his head. "You will be fine, and so will you, Daisy. Now—it is time for lunch. Shall we order something?"

"*Désolée*, Étienne, but I cannot stay," Mathilde said. Something passed between them—a look of understanding, something that hinted of shared hardships? It made her very curious to learn more about her new friends.

"I'm sorry, too, but I must go as well," Helena said, gathering her things. "It was lovely meeting all of you. *À demain?*"

"*À demain.*"

She had done it. She had made it through the first day of classes, her dignity more or less intact, and she had made three new friends who knew her as Helena Parr, an art student like themselves. Just the thought of it made her so happy she could hug herself, for with friends at her side, she knew, she could weather any storm—even the unpredictable gale of the maître's ire.

Chapter 10

10 October 1924

Dearest Amalia,

I hope this letter finds you well and happy, and that Peter and the children are also in fine form.

Today marked the end of my first month of classes—four weeks of dessin, dessin, dessin, and yet more dessin, all with Maître Czerny. There are days when I feel as worn-down as the stub of charcoal I use for sketching, but there are good days, too, when everything suddenly makes sense and the drawing I produce comes close to matching the one in my head.

Although the maître is a difficult man, I can't say I regret my decision to attend his academy and not another school. Our focus here is limited—there are no classes in sculpture, for instance, as the maître says it bores him. He doesn't much care for watercolors or pastels, either, and so those classes, which began last week, are being taught by others. But he is a very good drawing master, and I know I have made progress, even if he has yet to tell me so.

I am rather nervous about his class in oil painting techniques.

Each year he chooses only twelve students for the class, and I have a terrible feeling I won't be one of them. It's not that the maître dislikes me or my work—the problem is that he doesn't seem to notice that I exist.

But that, I must admit, is a small problem set against the joys of my life here. Auntie A is a delight, as ever, and I've made some wonderful friends, all of them students at the academy. My health is even better than it was before my illness—all that swimming in the Med, and now the long walks I take each day from home to school and back again.

In response to your question—no, I haven't yet written to Mr. Howard, and now I rather regret having told you about meeting him. He is a perfectly nice man but he is not, no matter what you may be thinking, a potential beau. While I'm not opposed to furthering my acquaintance with the man, I have no intention of embarking on any sort of romantic entanglement, so please do put that idea out of your head!

I've enclosed a little portrait of Hamish that I thought the boys might like to see when they're next home from school—isn't he a dear old thing?

With much love,
Your devoted sister,
Helena

She did have every intention of writing to Mr. Howard. Once or twice, she had very nearly asked her aunt for a *petit bleu* postcard, for she had seen Agnes using them when arranging visits or appointments. But something had stilled her tongue. What if the man she remembered from that day on the beach was a concoction of her memory? What if he had only been making conversation, and was himself uninterested in furthering their acquaintance?

She had warned him that she would be busy; a few weeks here or there wouldn't make much of a difference. Besides, she was busy enough with her friends from school. Unsurprisingly, Étienne had become the star of their class, and while he clashed with Maître Czerny nearly every day their teacher seemed to like him all the more for it. Mathilde was another favorite, and his criticism of her work was mild at best.

It was poor Daisy who most frequently attracted the maître's ire, which Helena thought horribly unfair. Her friend had made terrific progress in the last month, but Czerny didn't seem to notice or care. Daisy's problem, he told the class on more than one occasion, was her lack of passion.

"Miss Fields has no fire in her belly. I see nothing in her work that engages my imagination, nothing that seizes me by the throat and shouts in my face. She might as well be creating wallpaper."

As for what he thought of Helena's work? As she had said to Amalia in her letter, he had yet to notice her. The terror she had first felt, when he roamed the aisles of the salon searching for prey, had faded once she realized he simply wasn't aware of her presence in his class. She had improved, she knew she had, but her drawings attracted neither his praise nor his anger. She, and they, were invisible to him.

She knew she ought to say or do something—anything to make him see, but fear stopped her throat time and time again. It was silly, and childish, to let one man's indifference push her from the path she had chosen, but she simply couldn't bring herself to address him directly or, even more terrifying, challenge him openly as Étienne often did.

She simply needed more time; that was all. She would learn, and improve, and when she was feeling more confident she would make sure that he noticed her. For good or for ill, by the end of the year he would know her name.

In the meantime, there was the problem of her studio, or, more precisely, her lack of one. Agnes's house was large, but every room was crammed full of artworks and antiques, and the only space suitable for a studio and its attendant mess was an unheated garret.

Agnes had arranged for the contents of the studio in Antibes to be set up in the garret, and in September, when the days had been long and mild, she'd been happy working there. In recent weeks, however, her makeshift studio's failings had become all too apparent. It was cold, and would only get more so as winter approached; and the light that had seemed so abundant in the late summer was waning by the day.

Her friends were also desperate for studio space. Étienne's landlady had taken to complaining about the smell of turpentine and linseed oil, going so far to as warn him that he would be out in the street if he didn't find another place to work. Daisy's father, from what little she had said, disapproved of her "hobby" and discouraged her from practicing at all when she was at home. And Mathilde simply agreed that she, too, needed some room in order to work without distraction. What those distractions might be, Helena had no idea, and the French-woman's reserved, dignified manner discouraged curious questions.

Their mutual need for a studio soon became an obsession, although they never got very far with their discussions. The difficulty, as ever, was money. Studios, even grubby, rat-infested and terminally damp ones, were expensive; and landlords according to Étienne, were disinclined to rent them to students who had no visible means of support beyond their art.

If she'd had enough money to rent a studio for them all, she'd have done so; but the allowance she received from her parents, though perfectly generous, didn't stretch to such an expense. And there was no question of asking them for more, as they would never agree to such a proposal. "But we don't *know* these people," her mother would be sure to say. "We don't know anything *about* them." True enough, for Helena knew almost nothing about her new friends. She hadn't met their families, hadn't been to their homes, and couldn't honestly say that anything they had told her was, in point of fact, true.

She considered dipping into the money her grandmother had left her, but to do so she would have to consult with her father's solicitor, and he would be certain to tell Papa. Never mind that she was a grown woman and perfectly capable of deciding what to do with her own money. Papa would object, Mama would fuss, and she would be forced to admit the truth.

Agnes would have offered up the money for a studio without hesitation, but her aunt had already been far too generous. So she said nothing of her dilemma, and after dinner most evenings, sitting in the *petit salon* at home with her aunt, she avoided the subject of her classes at the academy, and instead talked about her new friends and their talents and interests. Before long Agnes was insisting that she invite them for dinner.

"I won't take no for an answer, Helena. I simply won't. In every one of her letters, your mother persists in asking me if I approve of your friends—but how can I answer if I haven't met any of them? What if she should take it into her head that I'm hiding something? You know how she can be. No one is better than her at sniffing out a lie or half-truth."

"Fine, Auntie A. I'll ask them tomorrow."

Agnes would charm them, she knew, but it still gave her pause. While she knew little of her friends' lives, they knew even less about her. Would meeting her aunt, and seeing where she lived, change how they thought of her? It was all rather antediluvian, but she'd never been friends with ordinary people before. Her childhood friends had all hailed from the top-loftiest branches of the aristocracy, just like herself.

None of those friends had proved faithful or true, however, and she had no reason to believe that Étienne, Mathilde, or Daisy would be envious or jealous, or even disconcerted by her background. They would surely discover the truth one day, so better to be honest with them now.

She didn't say anything until Friday, when they had gathered for lunch at a cheap and nameless café on the rue Delambre that was marginally less expensive than its grander cousins on the boulevard du Montparnasse. Rain was pelting down outside, as it had all morning, and after their one-franc meal of soup, bread, *saucisson*, and cheese they lingered over their coffees.

Helena had nearly finished her *café crème*, which she had almost learned to like, Daisy was lost in her thoughts, and Étienne and Mathilde were smoking like chimneys, as usual. She hated the smell, which clung to her clothes for hours afterward, but since nearly everyone else in the café was smoking it didn't seem right to ask them to refrain.

"You know I live with my aunt," she said, after waiting for a pause in the conversation. "She is, ah . . . she's keen to have all of you to dinner. Or to lunch on a Friday, if that's better."

"I'd love to meet her," said Daisy, glancing at Louisette, who perched as grim as a gargoyle on a nearby chair, "but Daddy likes me to be home in the evenings."

"I can't manage dinner," said Mathilde. "Lunch is better."

"Étienne?" Helena asked.

"I am at your disposal, my dear Hélène."

"Shall we say next Friday? We can walk there after school."

"Where does your aunt live?" asked Étienne.

There was no way around it. "Her house is on the Île St.-Louis."

"A house, you say? Not a flat?"

The man was relentless. "Yes, Étienne. An entire house."

"Who *is* this aunt of yours?" Mathilde asked, her curiosity piqued.

"Her name is Agnes Paulson, although that's . . . well, it's a translation. Her husband was Russian."

"Go on," said Étienne, his eyes sparking with interest. "I can tell there's more."

"He was a grand duke. There. Happy now? But he was killed in an airplane crash several years ago."

"Interesting. What was your aunt before she married him? A cancan dancer?"

The mental image this provoked was decidedly bizarre, and enough to bring a smile to her face. "No, silly. She was just an English lady."

Mathilde leaned across the table. "Does 'lady' mean a woman, or does it mean the relative of a lord?"

"The latter," Helena admitted.

"And are you . . . ?" Mathilde pressed, not unkindly.

"My full name is Helena Montagu-Douglas-Parr, but I prefer to use only the last part of my surname. My father and Agnes are brother and sister."

"Who is your father?" Mathilde persisted.

"The Earl of Halifax."

"So that makes you *Lady* Helena Montagu-Douglas-Parr, does it not?" Étienne asked.

"Yes, but I don't use it. The title, I mean. To my friends I'm Helena. Even Ellie, if you feel like teasing me." She held her breath, waiting and worrying. Wondering if this would change things. America and France were republics, after all. They'd had revolutions to rid themselves of such pretensions.

"Ellie," Étienne said at last. "I like it."

"That's all? You're not going to tease me?"

"Why? Paris is filthy with aristocrats. Do you know how many people I've met with a 'de la' in their surname? And none of them have two sous to rub together. So—lunch with the grand duchess this time next week?"

"Oh, please don't call her that. She honestly prefers Agnes."

"Then I shall call her Agnes, but in the French fashion. 'Ahnyess.' Far more elegant that way."

"Mathilde? Daisy? Will you come, too?"

"Yes," said Mathilde, meeting Helena's gaze squarely. "We will be there."

Chapter 11

A week later, they set off together for the walk to the Île St.-Louis. Helena had spent the entire morning in a welter of nerves, her hands so clammy she had difficulty holding her pencils, and the drawings she'd produced in their only class of the day—a two-hour life drawing session with Maître Czerny—had been fit only for the bin.

Her friends hadn't seemed affected at all by her admission regarding her background, and no one had mentioned it since. Even Étienne hadn't teased her about it. But Agnes's house was so very grand, and it was hard not to worry that they might find it intimidating, or be moved to think of her differently as a result.

She was worried about Étienne, too, for he'd shown up with a black eye and a deep cut across the bridge of his nose. She'd been horrified, of course, but he had insisted he was fine, and had only slipped on some wet leaves. And yet . . . would a simple fall explain the injuries to his right hand, which was so bruised and swollen he could scarcely hold a brush?

Agnes must have been watching out for them from one of the upstairs windows, for she was at the front door, waving gaily, as they came over the Pont St.-Louis and walked the short distance north to her town house.

"Hello, hello! Welcome to my home!"

Introductions were made, cheeks were kissed, and Agnes announced her intention to give everyone the grand tour before sitting down to luncheon. "I have a few bits and pieces you might like to see—nothing particularly fashionable, but they were considered quite avant-garde at the time they were painted."

With Hamish trotting at her heels, she led them first to the *grand salon*, which had been expensively decorated in a style Helena privately thought of as "steamship nouveau" and did little for the magnificent seventeenth-century architecture of the space. Above the hearth hung a full-length portrait by John Singer Sargent, painted when Agnes was in her late twenties and at the height of her beauty. On the opposite wall, between two lacquered cabinets, was a smaller portrait, also of her aunt, by Augustus John. Agnes's gaze was so bold, so sensually inviting, that the painting had caused a minor scandal when exhibited at the Royal Academy in 1907.

"Come with me into the dining room—I want to show you my favorite. It's the only portrait I have of dear Dimitri."

She led them to the hearth at the far end of the room, above which hung a modestly sized painting that depicted Dimitri and Agnes, dressed in the fashions of a decade earlier, their heads framed by a bower of roses in full bloom.

"Is that a Bonnard?" Étienne asked reverently.

"It is. He painted it in the garden here. Wasn't my Dimitri handsome? He was a great patron of the arts, I'll have you know, and Monsieur Bonnard was a particular favorite. We used to have any number of his paintings, but after Dimitri died his dreadful relations stole nearly everything from me. Ghastly people."

They were saved from a longer discourse on the greed and duplicity of Dimitri's family by the arrival of Vincent, who advised them that luncheon was ready and they might take their seats. It was a simple meal by Agnes's standards: lobster bisque to begin, followed by roast capon, braised celery, and souffléd potatoes, with poached pears in Riesling to finish.

The conversation was animated, dominated in the main by her aunt's stories of adventures abroad with Dimitri. Only when they retired to the *petit salon* for coffee and petits fours did the discussion turn to their classes at the academy.

"I'm sure Hélène is too modest to tell you," Étienne said in a confiding tone, "but she has done some marvelous work so far. We are all of us in awe at her abilities."

"I knew it. I simply *knew* it," Agnes trilled, clapping her hands in delight. "All she needed was a bit of encouragement and practice."

"Precisely," said Étienne, and there was something in the intent look he directed at her aunt, or perhaps the way he leaned forward, capturing Agnes's gaze, that convinced Helena he was up to something.

"Although," he continued, "it would be so much easier for her if she had a studio in which to work."

Agnes turned to Helena, her brow wrinkling with concern. "Isn't the space you're using upstairs agreeable? I was worried there might not be enough light, but you said—"

"I think the difficulty, Madame Paulson, is that her little garret, or rather her studio, is rather cold. And I'm sure you don't want her to catch a chill . . ."

"Of course not," Agnes agreed. "Could I have the furniture

cleared out of a spare bedroom? Would that do?" she asked, turning to Helena.

"I suppose . . ."

"I think perhaps Hélène has been too shy to say anything, but the four of us, we have been talking of trying to find a studio to rent."

Agnes's face brightened immediately, her relief palpable, and if Helena had been close enough to kick Étienne under the table she'd have done so. What was he playing at?

"That's a marvelous idea. Why didn't you say anything before, Helena?"

"Well, I . . . I wasn't sure if you'd approve. It would keep me away from home, and I thought . . ."

"Of course I approve. Why wouldn't I? Now, Étienne, have you begun your search?"

"Not yet, I'm afraid," and at this he stared wistfully into his empty coffee cup. "We need to save up. Studio space is expensive, alas."

"Forgive me if I seem impertinent, but how much is the monthly rental for a studio?" Agnes asked.

"Oh, around two hundred francs? Three hundred at the most."

"But that's nothing—I can pay it. I *will* pay it," Agnes insisted.

Mathilde, only now realizing what was afoot, shook her head, her mouth twisting into a frown. "I am very sorry, and I do not wish to appear rude, but I cannot accept such charity. I do beg your pardon."

"I quite understand. Shall we say this instead? I will pay for a studio for Helena, and she, in turn, is free to ask her friends to share it. I don't believe that could be constituted as charity. I am only seeing to the immediate needs of my niece, you see."

"I don't know," said Daisy. "My father is sure to refuse. He's so very protective, and—"

"My dear girl," said Agnes, and she reached out and patted Daisy's hand. "I have every respect for a parent's finer feelings. Truly I do. But sometimes it is best that we not share every part of our lives with them. Hmm?"

"He'll know. Louisette will tell him."

"Who is this Louisette person?" Agnes asked. "Is she that sour-faced woman who was trailing along behind you?"

"Yes," Helena answered. "She's Daisy's maid, and goes everywhere with her. The problem is that she is rather unpleasant. Certainly she won't keep a secret for Daisy."

"I see. Perhaps I could write your father a letter? Charm him along?"

Daisy remained unconvinced. "I don't know . . . I'm not sure it will work."

"We won't know until we try, and I can be very persuasive. I'll use my stationery with the imperial crest. Have the letter delivered by Vincent himself, in his best livery. *That* will make an impression. Forgive me for saying so, but you Americans are terribly susceptible to such things."

"I guess there's no harm in trying."

"There you have it. You are all in agreement? Helena?"

"Oh, Auntie A—you've already been so generous. It doesn't feel right to ask anything more of you."

"Nonsense. It will give me great pleasure to support you in this fashion. Tell me, Étienne, where shall you look? I sense you are the engine driving this scheme."

"I'll start in the *sixième*. We don't want anything too far from school; otherwise we'll spend half our lives walking back and forth."

"Very well. Once you find a suitable space, advise me at once and I'll have dear Vincent sort out the paperwork. There isn't a landlord in Paris who can get the best of *him*."

ÉTIENNE'S REPORT, DELIVERED on Monday at lunch, was dispiriting. He'd visited half a dozen studios on Saturday, and all of them had been unsuitable.

"I'm certain the first place I saw was being used as a brothel at night. The one on boulevard Raspail looked pleasant enough, but it had an *odeur*—a stench? is that the word?—of cat urine that was most disagreeable."

"And the others?" asked Mathilde.

"Too far away, too small, too expensive. But I shall keep looking. There is one place, on the avenue du Maine; my friend Léon told me about it this morning. But it's expensive—two hundred and fifty francs a month. Would your aunt balk at that, Hélène?"

"I've seen her spend that much on a hat without blinking, so I don't think she'll mind."

Agnes may have been happy with the arrangement, but Helena still felt uncomfortable. She couldn't properly say she was taking advantage of her aunt, for Agnes was wealthy enough that 250 francs a month meant nothing to her; but all the same she wished she had money of her own to pay for the studio. If, one day, she managed to sell any of her work, she would repay her aunt right away, no matter how she protested. At the very least she would buy Agnes a trunkful of stylish hats.

"Shall we go this afternoon?" Étienne suggested. "Otherwise we risk losing it to someone else."

As soon as their afternoon class had finished they set off, with Louisette trailing five paces behind; as Étienne had promised, the studio was an easy ten-minute walk from the academy. They almost walked past the alley in which it was located, for the entrance off the street was narrow, its archway shadowed by a mantle of ivy, and the cobbles underfoot were thick with moss. The buildings themselves had a faintly ramshackle appearance, as if they'd been constructed from scavenged materials—a hod of bricks, a weathered greenhouse window, an ancient stone lintel—and one or two of the structures seemed alarmingly close to collapse.

Étienne led them to the end of the alley, about seventy yards back, where a red-painted door had been left open.

"*Allô?*" he called, stepping inside.

"*Entrez, entrez!*" came an answering voice.

Étienne led them upstairs and introduced everyone except Louisette to the concierge, Madame Benoît, who had been sweeping out the empty studio.

It was a large, open room, perhaps ten yards along its longest wall, its chief appeal a great bank of windows that began at knee height and soared up to the twelve-foot ceiling. Some of the window panes were cracked, and ivy had crept inside a number of the casements, but the light would be wonderful once the glass had been cleaned. Here and there were bits of furniture—a paint-splattered table, a threadbare settee, several wobbly chairs—and Helena was relieved to see a small pot-bellied stove and a deep porcelain sink.

The negotiations that followed, in which Étienne and Mathilde both participated vociferously, were nearly impossible for Helena to follow, and there was one moment when she feared they might come to blows with the concierge, who was a large lady and perfectly capable of knocking any of them flat with her sturdy broom.

And then, quite suddenly, all was resolved, and Madame Benoît was smiling and shaking her hand, and Daisy's, too, and with a round of final good-byes they retreated to the alley and the avenue beyond.

"What just happened?" she asked, more than a little bemused.

"We discussed the terms of the lease," Mathilde explained. "I told her the studio was in a shocking condition and we would certainly not pay two hundred and fifty francs a month for it. She disagreed, but offered to clean it and repair the windows. I said we would do the work ourselves and pay two hundred a month for the first three months."

"Wait—*we* have to clean the studio?" Daisy asked.

"Yes. There's nothing wrong with it that soap and hot water can't fix."

"And some whitewash," Étienne added. "She agreed to pay for that, too."

"But I . . . I don't know how to do any of that. I've never had to do anything like that," Daisy protested.

"Then you will learn."

Chapter 12

The next day, Helena confessed the truth to Mathilde: she, too, had never held a broom, mop, or duster in her life. Servants had always done such things for her, and apart from her paintbrushes and her own person she'd never cleaned anything.

Mathilde bore this news with good grace, and if she was irritated at having to show the other women how to grate soap into hot water so it would dissolve properly, or how to sweep without raising clouds of dust, or how to scrub and wax wooden floors, she never betrayed it.

True to her promise, Agnes had written to Dr. Fields, and whatever she had said in her letter had worked, for he had agreed to Daisy spending a few hours in the studio most days. He had not, however, relented on the matter of Louisette, who continued to shadow Daisy's every step. She even came into the studio with them, where she perched on a stool in the corner, never saying a word, her gaze as bright and baleful as a raven's.

While Mathilde, Daisy, and Helena swept and polished, Étienne cut away the ivy that had grown over the windows and replaced a score of cracked and broken panes, fitting the glass as expertly as a glazier. When that was done, he repaired the chairs and settee and steadied the table, and even constructed a set of shelves from some scrap lumber that Madame Benoît had been about to burn.

It took almost a fortnight of work, a few hours at a time, until Mathilde was satisfied. All that remained was an application of whitewash to brighten the space.

It was Friday afternoon, and they'd just finished applying a second, and final, coat of whitewash. At Étienne's suggestion, they abandoned their usual haunt for the marginally more luxe surroundings of Le Dôme, where the wine was served in bottles, the menu was printed on paper and not scrawled on a chalkboard, and the tables were covered with clean white cloths.

She was poring over the menu, trying to decide between the baked endive with ham or a mushroom omelet, when a group of Americans entered the restaurant. She looked up—even in Montparnasse, where there were so many foreigners, she always noticed when she heard people speaking English—and there he was. Sam Howard.

She blinked, and he was still there, as appealingly tall and handsome as she remembered.

"Sam!" she called out unthinkingly.

He turned, his expression softening into a smile, and came over to her table. "Ellie Parr. I'd given you up for dead."

"I'm sorry. I've been so busy since I arrived. I hadn't forgotten my promise, though."

"Sure you did. But I don't mind."

"Hélène, why don't you introduce us to your friend?" Étienne interjected.

"Of course. Sam Howard, these are my friends from school:

Étienne Moreau, Mathilde Renault, and Daisy Fields." Sam's eyes widened a fraction when he heard Daisy's name, but to Helena's relief he only shook their hands and returned their greeting.

"Sam and I met in Antibes last summer. He works at the Paris office of the *Chicago Tribune*."

"We're old friends," Sam added, and gave her a pointed look. "Listen, Ellie, I'm here with some colleagues. I should probably go—"

"Why don't you join us?" Étienne asked. "This table here is empty."

"Please do," Helena added.

"Well, then. I'll ask—they could stand to lap up a bit of culture." He returned to his friends, said something that set them to laughing, and in a moment they had pushed the tables together and Mr. Howard was seated next to her on the banquette, so close that his shoulders brushed hers as he unwound his scarf.

"Geoff Fraser and Larry Blochman, let me introduce you to Helena and her friends from school—Étienne, Mathilde, and Daisy. Fraser and Blochman are deskmen at the paper with me," he explained.

"Deskmen?" asked Mathilde.

"We work the rewrite desk at the paper. Wires come in from New York, but they're short. A few words per story. We fill in the blanks, I guess you could say."

"Is today your day off?" Helena asked.

"No. Only day off is Saturday. We start in an hour and work till one in the morning."

"Tell her where they sent you today," said Mr. Fraser, or perhaps it was Mr. Blochman.

Sam aimed a sharp look at his colleague, but complied. "Gloria Swanson landed in town. I went to a press conference at her hotel, me and a couple of dozen other hacks, to ask her the usual bunkum. How she likes Paris, what her new film is about, are the rumors about her and Valentino true—that sort of thing."

"What was she like?" asked Daisy excitedly.

"I've no idea. I was at the back of the scrum. Couldn't hear a word she said."

"How are you going to write your story?" Helena asked.

"I'll use my imagination, I guess. How's this sound?

"'Miss Gloria Swanson, fresh from her recent triumph in Manhandled, was a vision in white at the Hôtel Crillon today. She has come to Paris to begin work on her new film, a romantic romp set at the court of Napoleon Bonaparte. When asked what she thinks of the City of Light, Miss Swanson said that she's in love with Paris already and can't wait to see the sights. Judging from the crowds that greeted her earlier in the day at the Gare St.-Lazare, Paris is equally smitten with Hollywood's most dazzling star.'

"That about right, Fraser?"

"Spot-on, Howard."

"Earns me a few extra francs, and a byline for my troubles. Not bad for an hour's work."

Their waiter had arrived, and Helena was unaccountably pleased when Sam ordered cassoulet for himself and his friends in fluent French. She would have to ask Mathilde or Étienne if his accent was acceptable to their ears, but to hers it seemed just fine. It was silly to care about such a thing, but so few foreigners made the effort to learn French—even she and Daisy had got into the habit of speaking English with their French friends.

Mr. Fraser and Mr. Blochman had begun to talk about horse racing, a topic that Sam apparently found uninteresting, for he turned to her, ignoring his friends entirely, and bent his head so his words rumbled against her ear.

"I lied just now. I did mind."

"Mind what?"

"That you didn't look me up."

"I didn't forget," she said, and looked him in the eye. "I was going to send you a *petit bleu*. Once I was settled."

"Are you happy? With your classes?"

She almost told him the truth. That she was afraid she'd made a mistake, that she was failing, that she would never get the maître's attention. That she would not be chosen for the oil painting class. Le Dôme wasn't a confessional, however, and she didn't wish her friends to know of her fears, so she couched her answer in the same platitudes she used to calm her aunt.

"I'm enjoying it very much," she said, loudly enough that Étienne, sitting to her left, would be able to hear. "Last month we were only allowed to draw, but we have classes in pastels and watercolors now. In November a dozen of us will be chosen to work in oils with the maître himself."

"Not all of you?" he asked. "Don't all of you pay the same fees? Shouldn't everyone be entitled to learn?"

"I hadn't thought of that before," she admitted.

"You make an excellent point, Monsieur Howard," Étienne said. "It is most unfair. I shall ask the maître about it on Monday."

"Oh, don't," Helena pleaded. "What if he should take offense? He might expel you from class."

"I doubt it—you know how he adores me. Even today, when he was in such a temper, he still had praise for me."

"We have our life drawing class on Friday mornings," she explained for Sam's benefit. "Today the model was an *ancien combattant,* and he had trouble maintaining his pose. Maître Czerny was frightfully rude to him. But Étienne calmed everyone down."

"Yes, well . . . I'm a peace-loving man. And I could see that Daisy was creating something quite remarkable with her drawing. I didn't want her work cut short."

They all looked to Daisy, who was blushing furiously.

"It was lovely. I ought to have said so earlier," said Helena.

"Thank you. I, ah . . . I spent some time among the wounded," Daisy stammered. "Years ago, that is. During the war." Her eyes darted to Louisette, who was sitting at a table near the door, her sharp gaze ever watchful. They were too far away for the woman to overhear their conversation, so why was Daisy so apprehensive?

The conversation over lunch was unremarkable, turning on the falling franc, the League of Nations, and the rising cost of bread. Sam listened, asked questions when the discussion faltered, and ate every scrap of his enormous serving of cassoulet. When his friends progressed from beer to brandy, he instead ordered a *café allongé.* "Keeps me awake," he explained. "Was up early this morning."

Daisy left as soon as she'd finished her soup, fearful that her father would worry, and though Helena was sorry to see her leave it was also a relief to be rid of Louisette. In Daisy's absence Étienne and Mathilde switched to French, which they spoke so rapidly that Helena could only make out one word in ten. Sam's friends had moved on from horse racing to baseball, but he ignored this new conversation and simply sipped his coffee.

"Hold still," he said. "I just noticed something."

Reaching across the table, to a glass of ice water Daisy had left untouched, he dampened the corner of his napkin and touched it to her temple. "There's a smudge of paint here," he explained. "I only saw it now, when you tucked your hair behind your ear."

"You don't have to . . ."

"All done. I have to go to work now, but I'm off tomorrow. Will you come to dinner with me?"

His manner was so appealingly open and straightforward, and it really did seem that he wished to be friends. Nothing more; simply her friend.

"I . . . yes. Yes, I will."

"Do you want me to come to your aunt's house?"

"You don't . . . I mean, there's no need. It's out of your way, I'm sure. I'll take a taxi."

"Fine. Let's go to Chez Rosalie. Rue Campagne Première. Seven o'clock?"

"Yes, seven is good."

"Until tomorrow, Ellie. I hope you don't change your mind—but if you do, send me a *petit bleu*."

Chapter 13

Helena's taxi turned off the boulevard du Montparnasse onto the dark and narrow rue Campagne Première. Peering through the window, she could just make out CHEZ ROSALIE in faded lettering on an old-fashioned storefront near the corner. A man stood outside, his shoulders hunched against the rain, and though his face was in shadow she knew it was Sam.

"*Ici, s'il vous plaît,*" she told the driver. She paid her fare and went to open the door, but Sam was there already, taking her arm as she stepped down onto the cobbled street.

"You didn't have to wait outside," she chided. "You must be soaked through."

"I'm fine. The sign's hard to read at night. Didn't want you to miss it." He held up an umbrella, still tightly furled, and made a show of tucking it under his arm. "And this isn't rain, besides. More like one of your London fogs. Didn't even bother to put up my umbrella."

"How very stoic of you. Shall we go in? I can smell something delicious."

"Everything here's good. It doesn't look like much, but I think you'll like it. Rosalie is a real character, that's for sure."

He guided her through the door and several steps down, into an establishment that might charitably be described as modest. Four long marble-topped tables, with room at each for eight stools, took up nearly all the space; at the back, through a single door, came the sounds and smells of a busy kitchen.

A large man, his apron none too clean, was wiping glasses at a bar to their right. Recognizing Sam, he threw down his cloth and came rushing over. He greeted Sam in Italian, which Helena understood only imperfectly, and in short order had seated them at a table, which they shared with six other diners, and brought them a basket of bread and a carafe of red wine.

"That's Rosalie's son, Luigi. He'll tell her we're—oh, here she comes. *Signora! Come estai?*"

Rosalie was a short and stout lady, somewhere north of fifty years old, her person enveloped in a grease- and tomato-spattered apron. It was nearly impossible for Helena to follow her and Sam's conversation, but she was fairly certain that the signora was pleased that he had brought a young lady to dinner, and that Rosalie would bring them the best of everything from her kitchen. Sam said something more, gesturing at Helena as he did so, and this seemed to please Rosalie immensely.

"What did you say to her?" Helena asked as soon as the signora had retreated to her kitchen.

"I told her you're an artist. She approves."

"How did she come to be so far from home?"

"I've no idea. I know she was an artist's model for a while. When that came to an end, she opened this place. She does all the cooking, the tables are always full, and if you can't pay she'll ask you to sweep the floor or wash a few dishes. You've heard of the sculptor Modigliani, who died a few years ago? When he was flat broke and halfway to starving one winter, she took him in and let him sleep in the back. Never asked for anything in return."

Luigi brought their first course, huge servings of vegetable, bean, and pasta soup, and as they ate they talked of home and food and the things they missed. Helena confessed to missing currant scones and properly made tea, and spent some time trying to explain the appeal of bread sauce to a mystified Sam.

"If I'm ever in England, I promise to try it," he said, but she could tell he wasn't convinced.

"What do you miss about America?" she countered.

"Lots of things. And d'you know what? At this time of year, when it's getting close to November, I really miss Thanksgiving."

"That's an American holiday, isn't it?"

"*The* holiday. Here it's just another Thursday in November, but at home it's a big deal. You try to be with your family, if you can, and the table is piled with food. Roast turkey with all the trimmings, and American things like corn pudding and baked squash and pumpkin pie."

"Pumpkin?" she asked, wrinkling her nose at the thought.

"Don't make that face. It's really good."

Their main course had arrived, a pork stew with dark, garlicky greens, and for a few minutes they ate in silence, lost in their appreciation of Rosalie's cooking.

"This is delicious," Helena said. "I've never eaten anything like it before. My parents aren't overfond of foreign food."

"Their loss," he said, wiping his plate clean with a chunk of bread.

"It is. Where did you learn Italian?"

"Here and there. At college I took a course in Italian Renaissance literature. Dante and the like. Thought it would be easy but I barely scraped through."

"So Dante isn't your favorite poet?" she asked, thinking to tease him a little.

"I don't know if I have a favorite. School put me off a lot of poetry—hard to love something when you're forced to read it."

"I loathe Coleridge for exactly that reason."

"See? I don't mind some of the more modern stuff, though. Have you ever heard of Rainer Maria Rilke? Not much of his work has been translated, and I don't read German, but I've one book of his poems."

"What are they about?" she asked.

"Same thing as most poetry. Love. I remember one bit—

> " 'In the deep nights I dig for you, O Treasure
> To seek you over the wide world I roam,
> For all abundance is but meager measure
> Of your bright beauty which is yet to come.' "

Their eyes met, and something passed between them, an acknowledgment of some sort, and she was certain he was about to speak when Rosalie bustled up and pinched Sam's cheek and the moment was lost. The signora said something in Italian, he laughed, and Luigi came over with a scrap of paper, which Sam examined and returned to him with a five-franc note.

"She wants us to finish up and move along," Sam explained. "She loves me, she said, but I am costing her money. I should have asked before I paid—do you want a coffee? Something sweet?"

"No, thank you."

"Then let's be on our way. Where's your aunt's house? Is it far?"

"It's on the Île St.-Louis, just across from the cathedral. A little less than two miles."

"Do you want me to find a taxi, or shall we walk? The rain is pretty light. And we've got my umbrella if it really starts to pour."

"Let's walk, please." She didn't want the evening to end, not yet, and if that meant a damp coat and hat she didn't mind at all.

Inches apart, never quite touching, they walked north along the boulevard St.-Michel, its eastern side packed with smoky cafés made raucous by wine-fueled laughter and impassioned arguments.

"Where do you live?" she dared to ask.

"I've a room in a hotel on the rue de Vaugirard. Most of my colleagues from the paper live there, too. It's nothing much to look at, but it's cheap and clean."

In the distance, a rumble of thunder sounded. Lightning split the sky and a hard, cold rain began to fall. They stopped short, looking at one another disbelievingly, and then Sam pulled his umbrella from under his arm.

"Here—take this," he said, and thrust it at her. She reached out, but a sudden gust of wind snatched it from her cold-numbed hands and sent it cartwheeling across the street and under the wheels of a passing taxi.

"I'm so sorry," she gasped.

"I don't mind," he assured her, grinning. "It was Blochman's umbrella. He lost mine a few months back. Now we're even."

Helena tried to look up at him, but the brim of her hat was so sodden that it had flopped down over her eyes. She pushed it out of the way, shielding her face from the downpour as she did so, and saw that Sam had removed his hat for the same reason. Their eyes met, and they both dissolved into helpless laughter.

"Let's go to my place," Sam suggested. "At least until the rain stops. I don't want you to catch a chill."

"Are you sure? I can take a taxi home," she offered.

"Haven't seen one pass since we left the restaurant. Trams are packed, too."

"I'll be f-f-fine," she protested, but her chattering teeth betrayed her.

He ignored her, and instead took off his mackintosh and draped it around her shoulders. "Here. This will help a bit. At least until we're inside again."

"Y-your c-c-coat . . ."

"Come on." He took her hand in his, and she shivered at the sudden contact between them. "Should we run for it? It's not far now—only a few hundred yards to my street."

By the time they reached the lobby of the Hôtel de Lisbonne, Helena was soaked through, with even her shoes squeaking under her toes, and Sam was even more bedraggled. They dashed up the stairs, leaving puddles in their wake, and made it to his room without encountering any of his colleagues from the paper. Heaven only knew what they'd say if they saw her going into Sam's lodgings in such a state.

His room was on the top floor, tucked under the eaves, and seemed ridiculously small for a big man like Sam. It was dominated by a wide bed, hastily made, that had been shoved against one wall. A small coal stove had been installed in the hearth, and beside it sat a bucket of coal *boulots*. A desk and bookcase took up the opposite wall, and at the end of the room, which was longer than it was wide, a tall window looked onto the street below. To her left, inches away from the door, were a washbasin and bidet.

"Charming, isn't it?"

"I, ah . . ."

"Like I said, it's cheap and clean, and they keep it warm in winter. That's enough for me."

He went straight to the chest of drawers and, after rummaging through it, handed her a set of well-worn pajamas. "You can wear these. There's a robe on the back of the door and a towel on the washstand. I'll wait in the hall."

As soon as he'd closed the door, Helena stripped out of her sodden clothes and dried herself off with the towel. Moving as quickly as her shaking limbs allowed, she changed into his pajamas, which were so large that she had to roll up the legs and sleeves several times, and wrapped herself in his robe. Her clothes she gathered up in a bundle; perhaps Sam could suggest a way of drying them.

"All done," she called out.

"Good. You sit on the bed—there's a blanket you can put around your shoulders. I'll get the stove going and your things laid out to dry."

Adding several *boulots* to the fire, he built it up until she could feel its warmth on the far side of the room, and only then did he pull a rickety old clotheshorse from beneath the bed and set it out in front of the stove. Soon her clothes were draped across it, steaming gently, and that included *all* her garments, even her careworn old cami-knickers and stockings with darned heels.

Back he went to the chest of drawers, and this time extracted a fresh singlet and shirt. He shrugged out of his braces, and then, as if she weren't there, pulled his soaked singlet and shirt over his head and tossed them on the floor. She knew she should look away, but his shoulders and arms were heavy with muscle, and though he stood in profile to her she could see a dusting of red-gold hair on his chest. She swallowed, her mouth having gone quite dry, and then had to smother a gasp when he turned away from her and she saw his back.

For a moment she thought it might be a trick of the light, but as he moved, drying himself carefully, she knew her eyes hadn't deceived her. His back was covered with scars, the skin there mottled red and white, like a half-healed sunburn, and the marks extended down the back of his arms and beneath the waistband of his trousers as well.

"I wish I could make you a cup of tea," he said as he buttoned his shirt, "but I don't have a teapot, and I don't have any tea."

She smiled, glad to have a distraction from the questions racing through her head. "You Americans really are Philistines."

"How about some bourbon instead? It's a kind of American whiskey."

Heaven only knew what a glass of strong spirits might do to her precarious sense of equilibrium. "I'd better not," she said. "Thank you all the same."

It wasn't a safe or wise subject for them to discuss, but she needed to know what had happened to him during the war. "Back in Antibes, at our dinner with the Murphys, you said you'd served with one of their friends during the war. I can't recall his name now."

"It was Archie MacLeish. But that was only at the end of the war. I started out as a volunteer with the American Field Service. Was an ambulance driver for almost three years, mainly around Verdun."

"And this was before America joined the war?"

"Long before. I was young and stupid. Propelled by visions of glory. That wore off in no time, of course."

"If you didn't have to stay, if you were a volunteer, what kept you there?"

He shrugged. "I was needed. There were never enough of us, not in those early years. We did what we could."

"Don't make light of it. You did more than most."

"I suppose. Did you . . . I mean, did your parents allow you to do anything? You must have been pretty young."

"I was eighteen that summer, when the war started. I didn't do much, not at first, but I didn't like the thought of just sitting at home. So I talked my mother into letting me volunteer at a hospital near our house. It wasn't much, just visiting the wounded and writing letters for them. That sort of thing."

"I'm certain it meant a lot to the men you visited."

"When America joined the war, did you remain a driver?"

"For a while. And then . . ."

She waited for him to continue, holding her breath all the while.

"My brother was killed that summer. Six weeks to the day after he landed in France."

Whatever she had expected him to say, it hadn't been that. "I am so very sorry. What was his name?"

"Andrew. He used to tell me, in his letters, that he was proud of me. That's why he joined up. And when he was killed, I don't know . . . I guess I felt I needed to take his place. So I signed up. Was assigned to his old unit. That's when I met Archie."

"Your back . . ." she began, but let her voice trail away. She simply wasn't brave enough to ask outright.

"My scars? Sorry about that. I forgot. Should have changed in the hall."

"Don't apologize. Never apologize for something like that."

He leaned forward, his elbows on his knees, his eyes fixed on the floor, and when he began to speak his voice hardly rose above a whisper.

"I was a corporal in the 130th. It was the day before the Armistice. They wanted us to retake the ruins of a village called

Marchéville. It was crazy. There was nothing left of it, and we all knew the Germans were about to surrender, but out we went all the same.

"Someone—I've no idea if it was us or them—had used mustard gas a day or two earlier, and the ground was muddy. We were on our way back when I slipped. I fell on my back, in a low crater, and it was filled with the gas. The stuff is heavier than air, so it can sit there for days."

"So that's why your lungs are sensitive?"

"No," he said, and he laughed hoarsely. "I was gassed earlier in the war, but that was just chlorine. If I'd got any of the mustard gas in my lungs I'd have been dead inside a week."

"What happened after you fell?"

"I don't really remember. I woke up in a clearing station the next day. That's when they told me the war was over."

"Were you in hospital for long?"

"Two months or so. Burns weren't that deep."

"And now?" she asked, her voice trembling a little. "Does it still hurt?"

"Not really. I didn't need skin grafts or anything like that. My face and hands weren't burned, so people don't stare. It could have been a lot worse."

"You said you were a corporal. Why not an officer?"

"I could have been, I guess. They did ask me a few times. But I couldn't stand the thought of it. Left the States to get away from all those buttoned-up idiots I'd known at university. From . . . from all of that."

He sprang to his feet, walked over to the bookcase, and picked up a bottle of dark-colored liquor. "Sure you don't want that bourbon?"

"I'm sure, thank you. Where did you go to university?"

He poured himself a measure of spirits and returned to his chair. "Listen to you today. Asking questions like a newspaperman. I went to Princeton."

"What did you study there?"

"Classics. Then I went to Harvard, to law school."

"With the view to doing what? Becoming a barrister?"

He tilted the glass in his hand, letting the amber liquid swirl around. "No, not exactly," he said at last. "I was planning to work for my family business."

"Why are you here?" she asked softly.

He stared at the spirits in his glass, not once looking up at her. "It's hard to explain. I guess I could say that I love my family, but they want me to be someone I'm not. I felt terrible about it. I still do, but I just couldn't become that man. Not even for them. That's why I left."

"I'm sorry. I didn't mean to pry."

"You don't have to apologize, but would you mind if we talked about something else?" he asked, his smile wry. "I could ask you uncomfortable questions about your family."

"I've no secrets there."

At this he looked up, his expression doubting. "Really? What brought you here? You hardly ever speak of your family, apart from your aunt and one of your sisters. Did they cast you out?"

"Nothing so Gothic as that. I had scarlet fever last year. It was a normal enough case at first, but then I contracted some sort of secondary infection. The doctors told my parents there was no hope. I heard them talking. And I promised myself that if I survived I would change. I would make something of my life."

"Oh, Ellie," he said, his voice gruff. "You're so brave. You have to know how brave you are."

"I don't think so. Not really."

"You are. Most of us spend our whole lives with our heads down, walking in circles. It never occurs to us to want anything more, so we cling to what's safe. What we know."

Sam went to the clotheshorse and turned her clothes over so the backs of everything would dry. Then he sat down again, and this time he looked her in the eye.

"Will you stay on in France?"

"I don't know. There's nothing much for me back in England. That's the problem. I'm too old to dream of a home and family of my own, but my parents won't give up hope. I'm not sure they ever will."

"Is that what you want?" he asked. "A home and family?"

"I did, once. Before the war."

"You were engaged, weren't you?" he asked carefully, with no more affect than a stranger inquiring after the time of day.

"How do you know?"

"Sara," he answered simply.

"Edward and I were engaged just before the war—weeks before, in fact. I waited for him, of course. When he finally came home, he was changed, and not because he'd lost a leg and had been taken prisoner, although people later said . . .

"At any rate," she went on, "he realized he no longer wanted me, so we broke things off. It was for the best, really. Especially since he was in love with someone else."

"Did he break your heart?"

"He didn't. He honestly didn't. If we'd stayed with one another he'd have broken it eventually. But he never had the chance."

They regarded one another, the silence building and building until she could bear it no longer. Glancing at her wristwatch, she saw it was well past nine o'clock. "I ought to be on my way."

"I'll walk you home."

"No," she said firmly. "No, there's no need. It's late, and it's still raining. I'll take a taxi."

"I'll come down with you—oh, wait. I almost forgot."

He went to the bookcase and, crouching, rummaged through its contents until he found a slim paperbound volume. "Here—found it." Returning to where she stood, he put the book in her hand.

"Your Rilke poems," she said, touched that he should trust her with a favorite book.

"Yes. Doubt you can get them here, not even at Sylvia Beach's shop. Promise to take good care of them?"

"I will."

"I had better get dressed," she said.

"Of course. I'll wait in the hall."

When she had changed into her clothes, which were still damp but not unbearably so, he followed her downstairs and outside, and then he flagged down a taxi for her. He told the driver where to go, and then, stooping low, surprised her with a kiss on her cheek. "Good night, Ellie."

"Thank you," she said. "I had a lovely time."

"In spite of getting caught in a downpour."

"In spite of that, yes. And I did enjoy dinner at Chez Rosalie."

"Will you come out with me again?"

"Yes," she answered unhesitatingly. "I should like that very much."

Smiling up at him, she got in the taxi and let it bear her away. As they approached the corner, something made her look back. Sam was still standing there, watching, his kind eyes so serious and sad, and she nearly told the driver to stop the car so she could run back and say something, anything, to erase or ease the loneliness she saw on his face.

But she kept her silence, and the taxi turned the corner, and the moment was lost.

Chapter 14

The list was pinned to the corkboard in the Académie's front foyer, but try as she might, Helena couldn't get close enough to read the names. A bell rang, heralding the start of the morning sessions, and the crowd began to thin. She pushed forward, heedless of the crush, until her nose was all but pressed against the notice.

31 octobre 1924

Étudiants admis—peinture à l'huile

M. Dupont

M. Esquivel

M. Goodwin

M. Herrera

M. Kolosov

M. Martens

M. Moreau

Mlle Parr

Mlle Renault

M. Swales

M. Williams
M. Zielinski

She blinked, rubbed at her eyes, and read the list again. Her name was on it. Her name, and Mathilde's, and Étienne's. Daisy's was not.

How was it possible that her name was on the list? Maître Czerny didn't know she existed; and if he did, if by some means she had made an impression on him, it certainly hadn't been a positive one. In eight weeks—nearly a hundred hours of class—he hadn't directed a single comment at her, good or bad, and he had never, not once, spared a glance for any of her work. How could she have been chosen for the oil painting class when far more capable students had been left off the list? It simply made no sense.

Étienne had been brave enough, a week or so earlier, to challenge the maître's habit of only selecting twelve students from a class of two dozen or more. Silence had followed his question, a silence so profound she'd heard the thump of her own heartbeat, and Helena had feared that her friend would be expelled. At the very least, the maître would find a way to cut Étienne down to size.

"You remind me of myself at your age, Monsieur Moreau. I, too, questioned my teachers, especially when their decisions appeared unfair. So I have a certain tolerance, even fondness, for a young man who dares to speak his mind.

"Why do I choose only twelve among you? I do so because I am not a patient man. I am not a charitable man. And I do not have the patience or charity to waste my time on incompetent students. Understood? *Bien.*"

After class, when they began their walk to the studio, she

made a point of hanging back with Daisy, just so they might have a chance to talk. She'd wanted to say something earlier, but Étienne had been seated between them all day.

As soon as she fell into step beside Daisy, her friend smiled and linked her arm with Helena's. "Congratulations. I'm so happy for you."

"Thank you, but I—"

"I'm fine. I've worked in oils before and they're not my favorite medium. Besides, I'm not sure I could stand any more time in one of the maître's classes." She rolled her eyes, and Helena tried to smile.

"He's a brute, and we both know it," Helena said.

"Perhaps. But he was right not to pick me for the class. And I truly, honestly, am not upset. So don't worry about me. Promise?"

"I promise."

Mathilde and Étienne were walking just ahead, and Louis-ette trailed several yards behind. Helena was fairly certain the woman didn't understand English, but pitched her voice low just in case.

"Forgive me for intruding," she ventured, "and don't feel you need to reply, but I can't help noticing that your father is really very, ah, vigilant."

"He is," Daisy acknowledged, her expression resigned. "I know."

"How do you bear it? Having her follow you around day after day?"

"It was hard at first, but I got used to it after a while. What else could I do?"

"How long has it been?"

Daisy's sigh was almost inaudible. "Almost six years. Do you recall my talking about some work I did near the end of the war?"

"With wounded men? Yes, you did mention it. I did something similar. Writing letters for the men, and drawing portraits of them to send home. Was it like that?"

"Not really. It was . . . have you ever heard of the Studio for Portrait Masks? No? The wife of one of my father's colleagues founded it. Mrs. Ladd was an artist, a sculptor, actually, and she'd heard about a studio in England that provided masks to men who had been disfigured by their injuries. It made her think she might be able to do something similar in France. She went to England, to learn how to make the masks from the experts there, and then she set up a studio here at the end of 1917."

Helena nodded, trying to take it all in. "How did you come to work there?"

"I was bored, plain and simple. I got to talking with Mrs. Ladd at a dinner party one evening, and she told me about the studio, and then we met again so she could make sure I was serious about it. I mean, the last thing she needed was someone who'd take one look at a man who was missing his jaw, or his nose, and faint on the spot."

"Presumably you passed inspection."

"I did. It was upsetting at first—how could it not be?—but the only thing that really bothered me was how depressed most of the men were. Some of them had been rejected by their families because of how they looked, you see, and they'd pretty much given up hope of ever being able to walk down the street without people screaming or turning away."

"Did you make the masks?"

"Goodness, no. At first I just swept the floors and tidied up, and after a bit I graduated to sitting with the men and holding their hands while the plaster impressions were made of their faces. It's a very uncomfortable process, and I think it helped them to know someone was nearby.

"After a while, I began to experiment with some paints at home. I'd look in the mirror and then copy what I saw as exactly, and finely, as possible. Once I was certain I could do it, I showed Mrs. Ladd, and she let me help with the painting after that. I was especially good at eyes."

"What were the masks made of?" Helena asked, fascinated by her friend's story.

"Copper, hammered very thin, with a layer of enamel paint on top. They were held on with spectacles, even if the wearer didn't normally need them, because that helped to make the entire mask look more lifelike. At a distance, you wouldn't realize they were masks—that's how good they were."

"But how did working at the studio lead to Louisette?" Helena pressed, still not understanding.

"There was one patient, an American officer, and he and I became friends. He was so nice, you know. Just the nicest man. He'd lost an eye, and the occipital bones around it had been crushed, but he was still very handsome. At least, I thought he was handsome. We . . . well, we danced together, the day the war ended, and I so hoped . . ."

"What happened?"

"Nothing, in the end. I came down with Spanish flu, and spent nearly a month in bed. By the time I'd recovered, Mrs. Ladd had decided to return to Boston and the studio wasn't taking on any new commissions. And Captain Mancuso had gone back to America."

"I still don't understand why your father felt the need for Louisette."

Daisy's voice, already faint, faded to a whisper. "Daniel—Captain Mancuso—went home, or I suppose he was sent home, while I was sick with the flu, and I had no way of finding him. I asked my father for help, but he got very upset. He said it was wrong of me to ask, and that I should just forget about Daniel."

"Oh, Daisy," Helena said, and gave her friend a handkerchief so she might wipe her eyes.

"And then, almost right away, Daddy hired Louisette. For his 'peace of mind,' he said."

"It is rather odd," Helena ventured. "Does he know that you dislike her? Won't he consider someone else?"

"No. He says I'm meant to dislike her. That she's there to protect me, and not to be my friend."

"I thought my parents were strict, but this is terrible. Perhaps we can find a way . . ."

But Daisy was shaking her head. "I'm used to her now, and she can't stop me from spending time with you and Étienne and Mathilde. Only Daddy can do that, and ever since your aunt sent him that letter he hasn't complained once about the studio or my going out from time to time. So, you see, I can't really complain."

HELENA CERTAINLY DIDN'T have cause to complain about anything, for her life in Paris was perfect in nearly every respect. The exception, the single stone in her shoe, was oil painting, for her initial elation at having been chosen for Maître Czerny's elite class was slowly dissolving into despair.

The difficulty lay in the gulf between her expectations and reality. Back in Antibes, happy in her little studio overlooking the sea, she had imagined that learning to paint in oils would be a straightforward affair, though naturally demanding. It would simply require patient application on her part, and practice would eventually make perfect.

She had assumed that she would have a natural flair for painting in oils. She could not have been more wrong.

Squeezed from the tube, gleaming and fresh on her palette, the oils were gorgeous, like little puddles of melted jewels. Every time, admiring them, she believed. This time the paint would behave. This time the colors would remain true. This time she would create something worth saving.

She failed. Again and again, she failed. The paints, so bright and perfect and new, turned dull at the touch of her brush, and the more she worked at them the worse they looked. Around her, the other students worked so confidently; some, like Étienne, had been painting in oils for years. She was the only one who struggled. She alone was left to flounder with the desperation of an upended tortoise.

And always, always, the voice of the maître, strident, methodical, and unrelenting.

"Fat on lean. Thick on thin. Warm on cold. Engrave these words on your heart—have them tattooed into the skin over your hearts—and forget everything else. These are your commandments. These are the laws I compel you to follow."

She tried, harder than she'd ever tried at anything, but they were commandments, not habits, and they left her head so crammed full of technique there was no space left for inspiration. There were moments, rare ones, when she figured out the *how,* but the canvases she then produced were mannered, stiff, and lifeless.

Worst of all? It was impossible to hide from the maître in a class of twelve. He took notice of her now, but only to lavish upon her the disdain he'd once reserved for Daisy.

"Again, Mademoiselle Parr. Again you make of your paint *une pagaille* upon your palette. I must conclude that you wish to paint with mud, or perhaps you wish to depict mud? *En tout cas* you are hopeless."

At lunch and after class each day, Étienne and Mathilde were endlessly patient, never complaining when she needed help working up her paints. From them she learned when to make the paint lean by thinning it with white spirits, and when to fatten it with linseed oil. At Mathilde's suggestion she altered her brushwork, for the delicate manner she'd used with her watercolors led only to a bumpy mess of impasto on the canvas. At Étienne's direction she used fewer colors, combining them as needed on her palette.

"Monet often used only five or six," he explained. "Here—I've given you yellow ochre, golden ochre, viridian, vermilion, cobalt blue, and chalk white. These are all you need."

In the peace of the studio, helped by her friends, and freed from the simmering contempt of the maître, she worked up several small canvases that showed some promise. Back in the *grand salon*, however, with the maître pacing back and forth, muttering and tearing at his hair, her newfound knowledge and competence drained away like so much dirty bathwater.

"I need a rest," she told Étienne and Mathilde as they left class one afternoon; Daisy had gone home after the morning session. "It's only been a week and my head is spinning."

"It's the fumes from the paint," Étienne said teasingly. "We'll open a few more windows."

"Ha. I need more than fresh air."

"I wonder if perhaps you might like some company?" Mathilde asked. "I, too, feel in need of a short vacation from the studio."

"I should like that very much. I was thinking of taking a walk through the Luxembourg Gardens, but if you—"

"No, that would be most pleasant."

They bid adieu to Étienne, who was going directly to the studio, and set out for the gardens. Walking side by side, they shared a comfortable silence, rather as if they were old friends who had already disclosed every possible thought, opinion, and secret to one another, and were simply content to be together.

The Luxembourg Gardens were dormant and rather sad at this time of year, but they were quiet, a rarity in a modern city like Paris, and their cool beauty was exactly the tonic that Helena needed after the combustible atmosphere of Maître Czerny's class.

They walked north to the Musée du Luxembourg, and then, wordlessly agreeing that its paintings could wait for another day, made their way over to the Grand Bassin, and then to the playground. Finding a bench, they sat and watched as beautifully behaved children, their faces gravely dignified, waited their turn for a ride on the garden's carousel.

"My daughter loves to ride the carousel," Mathilde said quietly. "Although we have not come here in a while."

"You have a daughter? I mean . . . I feel as if I ought to have known."

"Her name is Marie-France. She is almost ten years old."

"Do you have a photograph of her?"

"Not here. But I may have . . . let me see . . ."

Rummaging through her bag, Mathilde extracted a sketchbook and handed it to Helena. "There—that drawing. That is my daughter."

"She's very pretty. Is her hair as dark as yours?"

"Yes. And it is just as straight. It will not hold a curl, no matter what I do."

"What color are her eyes?"

"Green, like my husband's."

Helena didn't say a thing, just held her breath and waited for Mathilde to continue.

"His name is Antoine. We have been married for twelve years. He was gassed during the war, and he lost his right arm, too. He cannot work, not any more. He does what he can, but . . ."

"It must be very hard for you both," Helena said, taking care to keep any trace of pity from her voice.

"We live with my parents. They own a café in the eighteenth arrondissement. I work there in the evenings."

"That is why you aren't able to come out with us . . . ?"

"That, and Marie-France. I like to be there for her supper, and to put her to bed."

Helena thought of the tuition she had paid for her own year at the academy, a not inconsiderable sum, and the money she had spent on paints and canvas and other art supplies over the past months. "How is it that you're able to attend the academy? I don't mean to pry, but it's—"

"I had an uncle. He never married, was fond of me . . . he saw how I loved to draw when I was in school. He encouraged me always. When he died last year, he left me a small legacy. He asked that I use it for art school. I had a term at the École des Beaux-Arts, but I hated it there. So I tried again."

"How do you manage it all?" Helena asked. "I can scarcely keep my head above water, and I only have to take care of myself."

"I don't really have a choice, do I? It's not so very hard. Of course there are days when I am very tired, but then I remember how fortunate I am. My husband returned from the war, though many did not. I have a roof over my head, enough to eat, family to share my work. I have a child who is happy and healthy. I am a very fortunate woman, am I not?"

Mathilde stood, the same soft smile upon her face, and turned to look down at Helena. "Shall we be on our way?"

Helena returned her smile gratefully. Given what she had just learned, she wouldn't have been surprised if Mathilde had hated her and Daisy on sight. Her friend carried so many burdens, and unlike Helena she never complained about them—she didn't even whine about Maître Czerny.

"Where would you like to go now?"

"Would you mind if we visited the cathedral? It's on the way home for both of us, is it not?"

"It is. *Allons-y*, then."

Walking north, Helena and Mathilde continued until the Seine was before them and they were facing the grassy prow of the Île de la Cité. They bore east for half a mile, to the narrow Pont au Double, which led them across to the busy forecourt of Notre-Dame Cathedral.

Long ago, she knew, the church's great west façade had been brightly painted, though she couldn't recall if the colors had been stripped away or had simply faded over the centuries. She tried to imagine what the cathedral would have looked like six or seven hundred years earlier, when its stonework had mimicked the stained glass of its windows. Modern eyes would find it jarring, no doubt, but it must have suited medieval tastes.

Helena hadn't returned to Notre-Dame since her first exploration of Paris in early September, but it promised peace, and sanctuary of a sort, as well. With Mathilde leading the way, they slipped inside, dodging the tourists and their guides.

They paused to make certain that Mass was not being said, then walked down the nave toward the high altar.

As they neared the transept, Helena bent her head, keeping her eyes fixed on the worn marble floor. She passed the first row of chairs and walked a yard or two farther, until she was at the center of the crossing. Only then did she turn to the right and raise her face to the jeweled radiance of the south rose window.

She had first visited Notre-Dame as a child, and she had overheard someone, possibly a guide, advising a fellow visitor to do the same. The beauty of the cathedral had moved her beyond words, and the light from the window sustained and nourished her even now. She would likely never achieve perfection in her own work, but someone else had, and the simple thought of this, of its possibility, comforted her beyond words or sense.

"Do you wish to stay here, or come with me to the chapel of St. Geneviève? I won't be long," Mathilde whispered.

"You go. I'll sit here for a while."

The choir had gathered, it seemed for a practice, and rather than linger before the altar Helena found a seat on the southern aisle of the nave. Sitting in the shadow of a looming pillar so high she could scarcely discern its terminus, she listened to the gathered voices, rising and falling, singing the same words in exquisite counterpoint: *Dona Nobis Pacem.* Give us peace.

She sat and listened, and presently she noticed a large plaque that had been affixed to a nearby pillar.

TO THE GLORY OF GOD
AND TO THE MEMORY OF
ONE MILLION DEAD

OF THE BRITISH EMPIRE
WHO FELL
IN THE GREAT WAR
1914–1918
AND OF WHOM THE
GREATER PART REST
IN FRANCE

A million dead across the empire, and millions more in Europe and beyond. How was she, or anyone else, to make sense of such numbers? Of such suffering?

Of those dead, how many had been artists? It wasn't the sort of thing that was summarized in war diaries and official histories, but many hundreds, even thousands, must have been artists like herself. They, too, had struggled and doubted themselves and wondered if they might be better suited to some other occupation. And now they were gone.

A year or so after the Armistice, she'd bought a book of poems by Wilfred Owen, who, she later learned, had been killed just before the end of the war. The poems had been difficult and troubling, raw in their beauty, and she'd read them over and over, using them to make sense of her own, pathetically insignificant sorrows.

"Foreheads of men have bled where no wounds were," he had written. Millions were dead, though they ought to have lived—ought to be working and loving and standing in the nave of Notre-Dame as the spangled light of the south rose window fell across their faces. Millions more, men like Mathilde's husband, had been left disfigured, maimed, and tormented.

What were her troubles, compared to that?

She would not despair. She would make the most of this

chance to study, to learn, and she would remember to look up and see the beauty that surrounded her.

Presently she felt a hand on her arm. It was Mathilde, her eyes aglow with sympathy and understanding.

"Shall we go?" Helena whispered, and her friend nodded in reply.

Outside again, they stood blinking in the afternoon sun.

"I didn't—" Helena began.

"I'm sorry," Mathilde said.

"I didn't lose anyone. I don't want you to . . . that is, I was engaged, and he was wounded, but we broke things off. He did, that is. He was in love with someone else."

At this, Mathilde shrugged ruefully. "So you are sad for him, but not because of him."

"I suppose so. Him, and other men I knew. I wanted to say . . ."

"Yes?"

"I am very glad to have you as my friend. Thank you for coming along with me today."

"It is nothing. I was glad of a chance to talk with you. All the same, I must be on my way. My family will be waiting."

"Shall I see you at the studio tomorrow?"

"Yes, of course." Mathilde kissed Helena on both cheeks, her face a little flushed, and disappeared into the crowds milling about the cathedral forecourt.

And then, for it was late in the day, and Hamish would be wanting his walk, Helena, too, went home.

Chapter 15

Helena's life had settled into a comfortable, and comforting, rhythm. On Monday mornings she woke at seven, had a hasty breakfast of café au lait and toasted *tartine* with marmalade, took Hamish on a walk around the perimeter of the island, turning up her collar against the late November chill, and set off for school.

Lunch was shared with her friends in their studio. Mathilde had brought in an old percolator, which produced murky but sustaining cups of coffee, and Madame Benoît had kindly lent them a mismatched set of cups, plates, and cutlery. Daisy and Helena contributed cheese, dried sausage, and ham from their kitchens at home—Agnes's cook was invariably generous—and they all took turns paying for a fresh baguette at the boulangerie at the corner.

Daisy always offered Louisette something, but the woman refused to accept even a glass of water. It must have been incredibly boring for the woman, sitting there hour after hour as she did, but Helena found it hard to muster even a scrap of sympathy for someone so uncongenial in spirit.

After lunch, it was back to the studio for another hour or

so, then home. Helena preferred to walk, but on cold or rainy days she would take the tram up the boulevard St.-Michel. As soon as she was home, she took Hamish out for a second time, since the extra exercise was good for both of them, and then dined with her aunt.

The exception to her routine was Sam, for she could never be sure when she might see him. Not only did he work odd hours, but he also was prone to disappearing for days on end, she assumed because of some story or another he was writing. Despite this, she'd managed to meet up with him half a dozen times, though they hadn't again bared their souls as they'd done that rainy evening in his garret room.

His first *petit bleu* had arrived the morning after their dinner at Rosalie's.

> *Dear Ellie—Woke up sneezing. Hope you're all right after our run through the rain. Menzies down the hall lent me his kettle and gave me a packet of tea. Said it will cure whatever ails me. Is he a liar? If not, how do I make a decent cup of tea? I know you have strong feelings on the subject. Sam*

> *Dear Sam—A proper cup of tea can cure even the worst case of the sniffles. As I don't recall seeing a teapot in your room, you may brew your tea one cup at a time. Measure one teaspoonful of tea leaves into the bottom of your mug, fill the mug with freshly boiled water, let the tea steep for five minutes (a few minutes more if you like it very dark), and add a drop or two of milk and some sugar if you must have it sweet, though honey is better if you have a cold. The tea leaves should settle to the bottom of the mug, but if they are bothersome you can decant the tea into a fresh mug. I do hope you feel better soon. Regards, Helena*

Dear Ellie—The tea experiment was successful. I added honey and a slug of bourbon. Slept like a baby afterwards. Thanks for the instructions. Sam

Dear Sam—You added spirits to tea? Where I come from that is very nearly sacrilege. I've heard that some Americans drink their tea cold—in my opinion a perversion of an otherwise perfect beverage— but your approach is nearly as bad. Shame on you! (Though I am very glad to know you are feeling better.) Regards, Helena

This coming Saturday they were planning to meet for dinner at Chez Rosalie with Étienne, and possibly Mathilde, too, if she could be spared from work at her family's bar.

Sam's *petit bleu* arrived on Friday morning, not long after dawn.

Ellie—Have been called away on assignment. Not back until Sunday P.M. Promise me you'll take a taxi home on Saturday, or have Étienne walk you. Sorry for short notice. Sam.

It was kind of him to worry, but she wasn't so silly as to walk home alone, especially since it was getting dark by seven o'clock. She scribbled out a reply and posted it on the way to school.

Dear Sam—Not to worry. Will be prudent. I forgot that it was your Thanksgiving yesterday. Do I wish you Happy or Merry? We shall dine on roast chicken when I next see you and pretend it is turkey. Regards, Helena

She and her friends spent Saturday morning and afternoon in the studio, though Daisy had to leave before lunchtime. Her father was feeling poorly again, and though Helena admired her friend's devotion to her parent she now suspected that Dr. Fields was in the habit of exaggerating his ailments as yet another way of keeping Daisy under his thumb.

Mathilde, who was needed at the bar after all, departed at five, leaving Helena and Étienne to continue on to the restaurant alone. Dinner at Chez Rosalie was never a drawn-out affair, for no money was to be made from diners who had eaten their fill, no matter how much the signora adored them. In less than an hour they had finished, paid, and were strolling north on the boulevard St.-Michel. Helena would have been content to simply walk and wander, but Étienne wanted wine and coffee, in that order, and of a better quality than Rosalie served.

"Her food is delightful, but the wine . . ." He shuddered in his oh-so-French way.

They found a table in one of the nameless cafés of the boul' Mich', as Étienne called the street, and settled in with a five-franc bottle of Burgundy and a *café express* for Étienne. A single coffee in the morning kept Helena feeling energized for most of the day; how her friend was able to consume the stuff at such a late hour, and in such a strong form, never ceased to amaze her.

"You'll never sleep, you know."

"I will. And the wine is a soporific. I'll sleep like the dead."

"It's very bad for you."

"I am fine. There is no need to fuss over me."

"That's what friends do. And you never talk of your family— who takes care of you?"

A flash of pain twisted across his face, and she wished she could snatch back her words. "You do, and Mathilde," he said, pouring himself another glass of wine. "You are all I need."

"Is your family in Paris?"

"No."

"But you—"

"You, Hélène—you never talk of *your* family. Only your aunt Agnes, and from time to time your sister. You never speak of your life in England, or your family there. Are you estranged from them?"

"Not at all. I'm very fond of my parents and siblings. I've three sisters and one brother, and nearly a dozen nephews and nieces between them. I write to Amalia every week, and my mother nearly as often."

"So why am I convinced the scarlet fever is not all that brought you here? There is something in your manner, you know, when you speak of home. And you are very adept at changing the subject when it comes to speaking of the war." He swallowed a gulp of wine, his eyes never leaving her face. "I wonder . . . did you lose someone, perhaps?"

She could have lied, told him he had an overactive imagination, but what would that serve? She knew she could trust him.

"In a manner of speaking . . ."

"I *knew* it." He really did have the look of a cat that had learned how to open a birdcage.

"It's hard to hide anything from you."

"I am very observant. That is why I am a great artist."

"And such a humble man," she teased. He made a face, refilled both their glasses, and waited for her to tell him everything.

"I don't like to talk of it. It happened so long ago. I was . . . I was engaged. I cared for Edward, but I wasn't in love with him. I didn't know him well enough."

"What happened to him?" Étienne asked softly, carefully.

"He was taken prisoner. For months, we thought he was dead. And then he came home, and he'd lost a leg, and he was different. We all knew it, but no one said anything, not at first."

"Did you break it off?"

"No, of course not. I'd never have done that to him. He was struggling, and so unhappy, but I didn't know how to help. I don't think he wanted me to help him. It went on for months, and then he came to see me one day and broke the engagement, just like that. He told me that I was too good for him and that we would make one another unhappy."

"Was he right? Would you have been unhappy with him?"

"I think so. He married someone else not long after. I think he was in love with her all along."

"Ma pauvre Hélène."

"It didn't hurt me. It didn't. They are happy together, from what I've heard. And she was nice to me, the one time we met. I don't blame either of them."

"But . . . ?"

"But the gossip was *awful*. No one would believe that our parting was amicable. They assumed it was my fault. That I'd broken things off because of his missing leg. That I had done something to *deserve* being set aside."

She took a sip of her wine, embarrassed at how her hand trembled. It had been so long since she'd allowed herself to think of that dark time, and still it upset her. "It has been so lovely to make friends here and not have to worry about any of it. I so dreaded it, that look in a person's eye—"

"I know what you mean. You are introduced to someone, and before you have even opened your mouth they have weighed you on some invisible scale, and found you wanting."

"That's happened to you?" she asked incredulously. "How

could anyone not like you? You're kind, and generous, and you are very handsome, though I shouldn't say so."

"Darling girl."

"And you've always been so nice to me. Since the moment we met, just before our first class, you've been so kind."

"Why wouldn't I be nice to you?" he asked, and though he smiled his eyes were sad. "You smiled at me, you were civil to me. Why would I not do the same in return?"

"Of course I was civil to you. Anyone would have been."

He smiled again, his eyes even sadder, and kissed her cheek. "Do you remember last month, when I had a black eye?"

"You'd slipped on some wet leaves."

He shook his head. "No, *ma belle*. I was set upon. I was walking with a friend; we'd been at Chez Graff, in Pigalle—"

Understanding dawned. "I've heard of it. My aunt said that's where the . . . well, where the homosexuals go . . ."

"Yes. And sometimes thugs who hate men like me. They call us *pédés* and they consider it a kind of sport to attack us."

Tears sprang to her eyes, but she blinked them away, not wishing to embarrass him. How could anyone wish to hurt this gentle, kind man? It defied all understanding. She reached across the table and clutched at his hand.

"So you, ah . . . you prefer men to women?" she said, lowering her voice, fearful that someone might hear and say something unkind to him.

"Yes."

"And your family?"

"Lost to me."

"Oh, Étienne. I am so, so sorry."

"It was a long time ago. It is in the past." He poured more wine into his glass.

"The man you were with, when you were attacked . . . is he your lover?"

"Not anymore," he said, and there was a world of regret in his voice.

"What if you'd been badly hurt? I can't bear it."

"And that is why I love you, my friend."

The bottle of wine was empty. Étienne called for another *café express* and drank it down straightaway, though it was surely hot enough to burn his mouth.

"Let's be off," he said. "Shall we walk on? I don't feel disposed to take the tram."

"Yes, let's walk."

They continued along the boulevard, the route so familiar to her, now, that she might easily have navigated her way home with her eyes closed. They walked arm in arm, and she was comforted by his closeness and steady warmth.

"I feel so silly. I ought to have understood," she confessed.

"I don't have a sign attached to my lapel. Don't apologize."

It then occurred to her that if she had failed to realize Étienne preferred men, she might have . . .

"Oh, Helena—your thoughts are written on your face. No, he is not homosexual."

"I, ah, I wasn't thinking—"

"Your Sam. He is assuredly *not* homosexual."

"Oh. Well. That's good to know," she said, and though she didn't have any romantic designs on Sam she was unaccountably relieved.

"You know," Étienne said, "your reaction surprises me. You do not appear to be disgusted or angry."

"Why should I? It would be terribly hypocritical. I know

what it's like to be shunned, and I wouldn't wish it on my worst enemy."

"You were very sheltered, were you not? When you were growing up."

"I was, I suppose. Perhaps it was a good thing. No one was able to teach me how to hate."

He hugged her close and kissed her cheek. "My heart is full to bursting. I am very glad you are my friend."

"I feel the same way," she said, and they walked on through the night, until they were crossing the Seine and she was almost home.

"I have decided that I must paint you," Étienne announced, just as they stepped off the Pont St.-Louis. She was so surprised that she stumbled, and would have fallen if not for his arm around hers.

"*Me?*"

"Yes. You are a beautiful woman. I must paint you."

"I'm flattered, but I . . ."

"Why do you hesitate?"

"I'm not sure. I've had my portrait painted, but it was something I did for my parents. And I didn't like it. I didn't like the way the artist looked at me. As if he were cataloging all my flaws, and trying to think of how best to conceal them."

"Then he was an idiot, for I look at you and I see only perfection," Étienne said. "It would be a pleasant experience for you. I am certain of it."

They were at her aunt's door. "May I think on it a little more?" she asked, still certain she would say no, but not wishing to upset or offend him, not after all they had shared.

"Of course. I shall kiss you good night now." He deposited a chaste salute on her cheek. "*Fais des beaux rêves, ma belle.* And thank you."

Chapter 16

With the beginning of December came winter, and rain, and afternoons so overhung with gloom that Helena could scarcely recall the feeling of sunshine on her face. Even in the studio, with its great bank of windows, the light was dull and gray, and most afternoons began with Étienne standing on a stool to hang lanterns from hooks in the ceiling beams. The lamp oil smelled awful, and the light from the lanterns was pretty feeble, but it was enough to keep them working until five o'clock most days.

Since natural light was so precious, Helena and her friends set to work as soon as they arrived after class, only breaking for coffee once the sun had set for good. They would sit around the stove, warming their hands with their cups, and talk of the work they'd done or the difficulties they were encountering with one piece or another, and in those few minutes she was as content as she'd ever been.

They ought not to have become friends, for they were as different as four people could be, and at another time, or in another place, they might instead have got on like chalk and cheese. Yet she looked forward to seeing them, enjoyed their company, and trusted their opinions. In only three months, she'd forged a deeper bond with these three friends than she had with any of her acquaintances from London.

One Monday afternoon, Mathilde had just poured their coffees when Étienne held high his cup and shushed them all to silence. "I propose a toast. It is the first of December, which means we have survived three months at the Académie, and—"

"A record for you, is it not?" asked Mathilde, a rare smile animating her face.

"It is indeed. I only lasted at the École des Beaux-Arts for ten weeks. All the more reason to toast our three months of friendship and hard work."

They tapped their cups together carefully, so as not to spill any of the scalding coffee.

"In five months we'll be done," Helena mused. "What do we receive at the end of the course? I never thought to ask."

"I've no idea," said Étienne. "Likely a certificate of some sort. Useful for lining birdcages, but not much else."

They laughed at this, which made him suggest other, even more vulgar uses for their Académie Czerny diplomas, and only when everyone had lapsed into a happy silence did Helena unburden herself.

"I have something to tell you," she said.

"It isn't bad news, is it?" asked Daisy worriedly.

"Not at all. It's only . . . my aunt has issued another invitation. To all of you."

"But that's marvelous," said Étienne.

"I'm not so sure. She's holding a dinner party, and I think she's invited half of Paris. It will be a terrible crush."

This didn't seem to faze him one bit. "All the better. When is it?"

"A little less than a fortnight, Saturday the thirteenth. Daisy—do you think your father will object?"

"I hope not. I'll see if I can ask someone to stay with him that evening. Just so he isn't lonely."

"I suppose he'll make you bring Louisette."

"He will, but she can sit in the kitchen with the chauffeurs. I won't let her spoil the party for me, or for any of you."

Mathilde hadn't responded, not verbally at least, but her expression was strained. "Will it be difficult for you to get away?" Helena asked.

"No. It is only that I don't have anything to wear, not for a formal dinner party," Mathilde said uncertainly. "Your aunt and her friends are sure to be, ah . . . I don't know the idiom in English. *Elles vont se mettre sur leur trente et un.* Étienne . . . ?"

"Dressed to the nines, I think."

"Yes, I suppose they will," Helena admitted. "But you're French. You could wear a burlap sack and still look chic." She hesitated, not wishing to offend her in any way. "Would you allow me to lend you one of my frocks? As one friend to another? As sisters do?"

After an everlasting pause Mathilde nodded, a little awkwardly, and smiled shyly at Helena. "If you truly do not mind, I would be most grateful."

They said their good-byes soon after, and as the evening was cold Helena took the tram most of the way home. Hamish wasn't at the door when she arrived, however, which was unusual enough to warrant an immediate search. She found him with her aunt, who was once again abed with a headache.

"You ought to see a doctor, Auntie A. This is your third headache in less than a week."

"I'm fine, I'm fine," Agnes insisted. "I only needed to rest my eyes. Now, tell me, what did your friends say?"

"They're all coming." The answering smile on her aunt's face made Helena regret her earlier irritation over the party. Agnes could be overwhelming at times, but she was very easy to please.

"And Sam?"

"I don't know. I'm hoping to see him on Saturday, so I thought I'd ask then."

"Heavens, no. What if he's asked to go away and write some story for his paper? No, you must ask him tonight. Send him a *petit bleu*."

"If you insist. But I—"

"Ooh—I almost forgot to tell you. I've made an appointment for us at Maison Vionnet tomorrow afternoon. It's at four o'clock, so I'll have Vincent collect you directly from the Académie."

"Vionnet? But that's one of the couture houses. Their clothes cost a *fortune*. I can't, Auntie A. Mama would have a fit."

"Forget about your mother. She is ridiculously frugal when it comes to important things like clothes."

"But I have a perfectly lovely frock—my blue and silver, from last year."

"That old thing? Do you wish to embarrass me in front of all my friends? No, I insist—you shall have a new frock, and only a Vionnet will do. Off you go, now. I need to rest, and Hamish needs a little walk. Don't forget to send that *petit bleu* to Mr. Howard."

Dear Sam—A formal invitation is forthcoming but want to let you know that my aunt is holding a dinner party on Sat. 13th. We

*both hope you can come. Dinner jacket as it's a formal shindig.
Sorry! Regards, Helena*

*Ellie—Thanks for advance notice. My tux smells of mothballs but
will air it out. Have a good week. Sam*

THE MAISON VIONNET, located in a monumental Second
Empire building on the avenue Montaigne, was every bit as
impressive as Helena had expected. The instant their car drew
up to the entrance, footmen were at hand to lead her and Agnes
inside. There they were greeted by Madame Charpentier, her
aunt's longtime vendeuse, who escorted them to the viewing
salon on the floor above.

Helena had grown up in beautiful houses filled with lovely
and valuable things, but the salon at Maison Vionnet was truly
jaw-dropping in its magnificence. Its neoclassical décor was
perfectly restrained; even her own mother, who had a horror
of anything even faintly arriviste, would have approved. Low-
backed armchairs, each with a matching table, were arranged
along the length of the room, while the walls were hung with
Lalique plaques, subtly backlit, of women in Vionnet gowns.

As soon as she and Agnes were settled, and had been served
cups of perfectly brewed English tea, Madame Charpentier
nodded to an assistant and the parade of frocks began. One
young woman after another appeared at the far end of the
salon, walked toward Helena and Agnes, paused, and moved
to wait a few yards away.

Twenty frocks were displayed to them in this manner, each of
them more beautiful than the last. How would she ever decide?

"Have you seen anything to your liking, Lady Helena?"
asked the vendeuse in impeccable English.

"They're all so pretty. I'm not sure . . ."

"May I take the liberty of suggesting three gowns that I think especially suitable?" At Helena's nod, Madame Charpentier called to three of the mannequins, who came forward while their fellows moved silently and impassively toward the door. "These are, I think, particularly suitable for your lovely English coloring."

All three frocks were sleeveless tunics with irregular hems, but that was the extent of their similarities. The first was of ivory crêpe embroidered with intersecting Japanese fans, the second of pale peach chiffon with bands of delicate apricot beading, and the third, rather more fitted than the others, was a pale gold silk charmeuse, with an overlay of darker golden net. Leaning forward, she realized the net had been decorated with hundreds of intricately appliquéd flowers.

How to decide? With her luck, she'd end up choosing the most expensive of the three. "The last one, perhaps? Aunt Agnes, what do you think?"

"The third. It is perfection. Though you may have all three if—"

"Only the one, Auntie A. That is what we agreed."

A further parade of mannequins was presented, this time with frocks for her aunt. It took Agnes an age to choose, but she eventually settled on a severe black tunic, its only embellishment a central embroidered motif that reminded Helena of the artwork from Tutankhamen's tomb.

Their selections made, she and Agnes were escorted to two smaller fitting rooms, where their measurements were taken and Helena's serviceable undergarments were tutted over. They were directed to return at the end of the week so their toiles might be fitted, and would then have to return again for a final fitting a few days before the party.

Madame Vionnet herself came to see them once they had dressed and were preparing to leave. She kissed cheeks with Agnes and shook hands with Helena, and inquired with grave politeness if they were pleased with the frocks they had chosen. The *couturière's* appearance came as a pleasant surprise to Helena, who had been expecting a chic and faintly terrifying figure cut from the same cloth as Gabrielle Chanel or Jeanne Lanvin. But Madame Vionnet was dressed in a shapeless white smock, had a motherly figure that would never have fit into any of her designs, and wore her silver hair in an old-fashioned chignon. If she reminded Helena of anyone, it was of her childhood nanny.

They were waiting in the grand entrance hall, for Vincent had parked around the corner and required summoning, when the great doors opened to admit Agnes's friend Madame Balsan. She was accompanied by a young man, who Helena was certain had not been present at Natalie Barney's afternoon tea in September, and who waited patiently while Agnes and her friend kissed cheeks and embraced and admired each other's hats.

To Helena's eyes, he seemed the very archetype of a Frenchman: slim, not overly tall, and beautifully dressed, with short, dark hair and a pencil-thin mustache. It wasn't the sort of appearance that made her heart sing, but she couldn't honestly say he was unattractive, either.

"I forget myself, dear Agnes—this is my husband's nephew, Jean-François d'Albret. Jean-François, allow me to introduce you to the Princess Dimitri Pavlovich and her niece, the Lady Helena Montagu-Douglas-Parr."

He bowed formally and then shook their hands. "Your Imperial Highness. Lady Helena. *Je suis enchanté de faire votre connaissance.*"

The handshake he shared with Helena was perfectly proper, although it lasted a trifle longer than her comfort allowed. She was more than happy when, only a minute or two later, Agnes cut their conversation short, citing an incipient headache and the momentary arrival of her car.

"Dear, sweet, *dull* Consuelo," Agnes groaned as soon as they were safely away. "I suppose I must invite her to the party. Shall I include that nephew of hers, do you think? He seemed rather charming."

"I suppose."

"Oh—I forgot to mention earlier, but I had a letter from your mother today. There's one for you, as well."

"Am I in trouble?"

"Not in the least. David's daughter, Rose, is engaged."

Her niece was only just eighteen, the same age that Helena had been when she'd become engaged. "Poor girl. Who's the groom?"

"That's the sticky part. It's George Neville-Ashford."

"Edward's brother? Heavens, no. I mean, from what I can recall he's a decent sort, but that mother of his . . ."

"I know. As you can imagine, Sophia Cumberland and I have *never* seen eye to eye."

"When is the wedding? If it's during term, I doubt—"

"It's at the end of April, so you've no reason not to go. Besides, the talk will be far worse if you don't. This way, you can be seen in the company of Edward and his wife, who by all accounts is a perfectly nice woman, and everyone will see you are in perfect accord, and that will be an end of it."

"It will be ghastly," Helena moaned.

"Of course it will. These things always are. Now, tell me. Did you enjoy your first taste of haute couture?"

"I did," said Helena, feeling more than ready to think of something else. "Mama always took us to a dressmaker for our clothes. She was very capable, and she made me some very pretty frocks, but . . ."

"They weren't anything out of the ordinary."

"I think Madame Vionnet must think like an artist. As if the frocks she makes are art."

"Her frocks are works of art, my dear, just as much as the paintings you create. You could turn anything she makes inside out and wear it without shame. Try to turn a painting to the wall and see what people say."

"I suppose that's why they're so expensive."

"Hush! No talk of money. You know how that upsets me."

"Yes, Auntie A."

"You will need another frock for the wedding, you know, since it's likely to be a morning affair."

"Are you sure? I have any number of lovely things already."

"Yes, but you'll want to look your very best. Like it or not, you'll attract attention. We both will."

"I suppose you're right."

"Would a knight of old ride into battle without his armor? Of course not, and neither shall we."

Chapter 17

Later that same week, at the end of a busy and satisfying Saturday in the studio, Helena and her friends had an early dinner at Chez Rosalie. At eight o'clock they went their separate ways: Mathilde and Étienne made for the Raspail Métro station, while Sam and Helena set out on foot for her aunt's house. After only a few hundred yards, however, he steered them across the boul' Mich' and onto a quieter street.

"Where are we going?" she asked, not particularly concerned.

"To Gertrude Stein's."

"Why didn't you tell me? If I'd known, I'd have worn something nicer. I've got paint on my shoes."

"Trust me—she won't care or even notice what you're wearing. And I only just thought of it now. I ran into her on the street earlier in the week, and she asked me where I'd been."

"How do you know her?"

"A few writer friends we have in common."

"Will I know anyone else?"

"You might. We won't stay for long. Half an hour at most. Make sure you get an eyeful of the paintings in the salon while you can, because Miss Toklas will drag you into the kitchen with the other women right off the bat."

"But why would Miss Stein . . . ?"

"She likes to be the center of attention, and you're both beautiful and interesting. That's why."

They walked on for another five minutes or so, and presently they turned left onto an even narrower and quieter street. "Here we are," Sam said, and he led them through a set of wide metal gates, across a darkened garden courtyard, and to a door at its far end. His knock was answered by a maid, who took their coats and hats and led them into a very large room.

The salon was long and high, with a large table, piled with books and papers, at its center; at the far end was a fireplace around which a number of people were seated. There were no electric lights, only candles and oil lamps, and at first it was hard to discern much more than the rectangular shapes of the paintings crowding the walls. But then Helena's eyes grew used to the gloom, and shapes and colors leapt from the frames, and she *saw*.

There was a Cézanne portrait of his wife, and what looked to be some of his watercolors, too; a half-dozen paintings by Matisse, among them his *Blue Nude*; and a few more by Juan Gris, she guessed, as well as other artists unfamiliar to her. Most thrilling were the Picasso paintings and drawings and collages, so many she couldn't keep count.

To the right of the fireplace hung a portrait by Picasso of a dark-haired woman, her expression grave and inscrutable. Beneath it, perched on an old wooden chair that rather resembled a throne, was the painting's subject, Gertrude Stein herself. She was dressed in a shapeless skirt and coat of brown corduroy, and her graying hair was piled rather messily on top of her head. Her smile, as they walked forward and she recognized Sam, was warm, and reached her dark, expressive eyes.

"I told you I'd come for a visit," he said.

"You did, and I'm happy to see you," she answered, shaking his hand as regally as Queen Mary herself.

"Miss Stein, this is my friend, Miss Helena Parr. She's attending classes at the Académie Czerny this year."

"Good for her."

Of the group of men seated around Miss Stein, only one bothered to get up and say hello. He was young, with a heavy mustache that couldn't quite hide his ready smile, dark hair swept back off his brow, and bright, inquisitive eyes. He and Sam seemed to know each other, and he shook Helena's hand with a grasp that left her knuckles aching.

A firm hand took hold of her elbow. "Why don't you come with me, Miss Parr? I'm Miss Toklas."

And that was that. Miss Stein resumed her conversation with the clutch of young men who surrounded her, and Helena was escorted to a gray and rather damp kitchen, where several other women were already gathered around a table.

Miss Toklas introduced Helena to everyone so quickly that she failed to catch a single name, and then directed her to sit in the only vacant chair. After fetching her a cup of dishwater tea and some delicious little pastries, Miss Toklas returned to her seat at the end of the table, took up some embroidery, and led the other women in a desultory conversation that revolved, in the main, around the scarcity of fresh fruit in December and the poor health of several relations back in America.

"Hello," said the woman at Helena's left. "I'm Hadley Hemingway." She had an American accent and was very pretty, with hair the color of a new penny and a wide, ready smile.

"How do you do? I'm Helena Parr."

"Are you here with your husband?"

"Oh, no. He's a friend. I mean, I'm here with my friend. Sam Howard. Do you know him?"

"I do," she said, her expression brightening. "He and my husband are friends."

"Is your husband at the *Tribune* as well?"

"No. He was with a Canadian newspaper, but he's given that up so he can work on his novel."

"Do you write, too?" Helena asked.

The question seemed to take Mrs. Hemingway by surprise. "Me? Oh, no. I'm not a writer. I—we—have a little boy. John, but we call him Bumby. He's just over a year old. Taking care of him and Ernest fills my days nicely."

"I'm sure it does," said Helena.

"Are you visiting France, or do you live here?"

"I'm living with my aunt while I go to art school, so a bit of both, I suppose?"

"And how do you know Sam?" Mrs. Hemingway asked.

"Through mutual friends. Sara and Gerald Murphy."

The mere mention of Sara's name prompted a broad smile from Mrs. Hemingway. "We're friends with them, too. I'm surprised you and I haven't met before now. Isn't Sara the nicest person?"

"She is," Helena agreed. "She has, well, I suppose I'd call it a knack for friendship. She and Gerald both. And I—"

"Are you enjoying your tisane, Miss Parr?" It was Miss Toklas, her raised voice instantly stifling the surrounding conversations.

"I am, Miss Toklas. And the pastries, too. They are delicious."

Her hostess smiled thinly at the compliment but made no attempt to continue their conversation; in any event the table was a long one, and a sustained discussion would have been impractical. It was rather a relief to be seated so far away from Miss Toklas, for her downturned mouth, pinched expression, and sharp, knowing eyes were unsettling, though not precisely malign. Perhaps she was shy, or unhappy at having to entertain strangers. Perhaps she would have preferred to sit in the salon with Miss Stein and the men.

Helena was about to resume her conversation with Mrs. Hemingway when a knock sounded at the kitchen door. It was Sam.

"Sorry to interrupt, Miss Toklas, but I'm taking Miss Parr away now."

"Leaving so soon?" she replied, as unblinking as an owl.

"Sorry. I have to head over to the paper. I didn't want to interrupt Miss Stein—will you pass on my regards?"

Helena whispered her thanks, said good-bye to Mrs. Hemingway, and made her exit with alacrity, although she did draw out the process of putting on her coat and hat so as to have a few more moments to admire Miss Stein's paintings.

"Was it worth it?" Sam asked as soon as they were back on the street.

"It was, if only to see all those paintings."

"I wasn't lying. I do need to stop by the paper. Do you want me to drop you off at home, or would you like to come along?"

"I'd love to see where you work, but I don't want to get in the way. Not if you have work to do."

"I don't. I'm waiting for a cable from the States, that's all. And it'll be a far sight less exciting than Miss Stein's. Just a roomful of sad-faced hacks and their typewriters."

They found a taxi on the rue de Vaugirard, and only after Sam had given the driver the address did Helena realize she'd no notion of where they were going. "Where is your office?"

"In the ninth, not far from the Opéra."

"I don't know why, but I'd assumed it was on the Left Bank. I hadn't realized it was so far from where you live."

"It's only a couple of miles. Takes no time at all to walk. Better than being cooped up on the Métro or a tram."

"I suppose. Before I forget—who was that young man who shook my hand? Tall, quite young, with a mustache?"

"That's Hemingway. He used to write for a Canadian paper, but I think he's working on a novel now. At least he says he is. Just had some short stories published."

"I sat next to his wife in the kitchen. She was very friendly."

"Everyone loves Hadley."

"Have you read any of his stories?"

"Only the one so far. I liked his writing but not the story—does that make sense? Miss Stein likes him, though."

"What about your writing?" she asked. "Are you still sure you don't have a novel in you? I remember our conversation, you know. On the beach that day."

"Sure I'm sure. I know because of men like Hemingway. I look at him and I can tell he has a fire inside—I can see it, and so can everyone else. I'm a better journalist than he'll ever be, but I'll never write like he does. It's the truth, plain and simple."

"Don't you wish you could?"

"Not really. We can't all be Shakespeare. Although . . ." His words trailed away, as if he were hesitant to hear them aloud. "I've thought about trying for a dayside job. Working as a correspondent for one of the big American or British papers."

"Is that what interests you?" she asked, truly curious. "Foreign affairs and politics and peace treaties?"

"Of course it does. It should interest all of us. Fascism is on the rise across Europe—just look at what's happening in Italy with that clown Mussolini. Germany has been beggared by war reparations, and if history has taught us anything it's that desperate times breed desperate men. Where do you honestly think Europe will be in twenty years?"

"I hadn't, ah—"

"Sorry. I didn't mean to lecture you."

"You didn't, and if I've learned anything in the past few months it's because of your articles. Have you inquired after any positions?"

He shook his head. "I want to, but it isn't that simple. I—"

The taxi pulled to a stop just then, and by the time he'd paid and helped her out of the car the moment was lost. She would have to ask him again, and perhaps even press him on the subject if he proved reticent.

Sam led them to a modest entrance at the corner. "Most of the building is taken up by *Le Petit Journal*," he explained. "They get the grand entrance on La Fayette and we use the tradesmen's stairs out back. Watch your step—there's hardly any light in the foyer."

The newsroom was on the third floor, behind a door marked "Archives," and was surprisingly quiet. She'd expected to see people rushing about and perhaps shouting at one another, but only four men sat at the central bank of desks, and the arrhythmic click-clack of their typewriters was the loudest noise in the room. The air was blue with smoke, with most desks anchored by an overflowing ashtray at one corner, and one of the men had an open bottle of Scotch whisky at his elbow.

"Look lively," Sam said to the men at the desks. "I've brought a lady in for a visit."

They smiled at her, every last man looking as if he'd just rolled out of bed and onto his desk chair, and one by one they came forward or reached across their desks to shake her hand.

"Gentlemen, this is Miss Helena Parr. Helena, these are my fellow deskmen. Fraser, Blochman—you've met them before—and here's Small and Calmer. Where's Paul?" he asked of no one in particular.

Blochman answered with a roll of his eyes. "He was howling at the moon earlier. Last I saw he was sleeping it off in a booth at Gillotte's. It's a quiet night, though. We'll be all right."

"Planning on joining us there later?" asked Fraser.

"Not tonight. I'll see you tomorrow. Just came in to fetch that cable. You remember the one I was talking about?"

"It's probably on Darragh's desk. Nice meeting you, Miss Parr."

Helena followed Sam to a fantastically messy desk at the far end of the room and stood by as he rifled through a towering stack of paper. Not far from the desk was a round table heaped with newspapers, all much fatter than the slim, eight-page European edition. She wandered over, curious, and saw they were day- and week-old copies of Paris and London papers.

"Keeping an eye on the competition?" she asked.

"Borrowing from them, more like it. Only our front page is written in-house. The rest is rewrite and filler. Mainly from the Paris papers, but we plug the gaps with whatever comes in from London and New York. Here—let me show you something."

He pulled a cable form from a wire basket and handed it to her. She read it, her incomprehension growing with each puzzling word.

GENLPLUTARCO ELIAS CALLES OATHTOOK
OFFICE PRESIDENT SMORNING ADNATL STADIUM
MEXCITY STOP PRES CHEERED PAROMNI
GLADSOME CROWDS COLORFUL CEREMONY
ATTENDED AILINGGOMPERS ETAMERICAN
REPSLABOR STOP ELN PRESCALLES SECURED
CUMSUPPORT LATAMUNIONS FUT DTF
UNRATIFIED YESTERYEAR BUCARELI TRTY STOP

"What on *earth* is this?"

"A cable from New York. They cost a bomb to send, so we've developed a sort of language to shorten them. 'Cablese,' we call it. Do you want me to translate?"

"Yes, please. It can't be in English."

"It is, after a fashion. Let's see . . .

"'*General Plutarco Elias Calles took the oath of office and was sworn in as president this morning at the National Stadium in Mexico City. Thousands of onlookers cheered the president in a colorful ceremony that was also attended by an ailing Samuel Gompers and American labor representatives. The election of President Calles, which was secured with the support of Latin American trade unions, has put the future of the as-yet unratified year-old Bucareli Treaty in doubt.*'

"That's the gist of it. Could use a bit more color—some background on Calles, Gompers, the treaty. But it's mainly there."

"So you take cables like these and translate them, and then you turn them into a story?"

"There's an art to it. This cable is pretty informative, but sometimes they're only five or six words long. Try spinning *that* into five hundred words."

"I see you what you mean. I—"

"Found it." He pulled a page from the pile and pocketed it

swiftly. "A cable from home. From my parents. Nothing serious, though."

"Thank goodness for that."

"We're done here. How about I see you home?"

They said good night to the deskmen and, after a few minutes' wait in the cold, found a taxi on La Fayette. When Sam got in as well, she realized he meant to accompany her and also pay for the taxi, the third they'd taken that night.

"Sam, don't. It's too expensive. I can pay."

"Don't worry about me. I'm flush tonight. Got paid yesterday."

The taxi was an old one, its backseat terribly cramped, and rather than fight to maintain her distance she let her head fall against his shoulder, softly, easily, as if she had a right to be so near to him. He was her friend, just as Mathilde and Daisy and Étienne were her friends, and it would be utterly foolish to think of him as anything else. As anything more. So why had her heart begun to flutter in her chest, and why were her palms faintly damp beneath her gloves?

"Seeing your office was terribly interesting," she said after a while. "It was nothing like what I'd imagined."

"That boring, huh?"

"Not at all. I'd had it in my head that it would be loud, and rather disorganized, and people would be running around shouting at one another."

"At some of the big papers it's like that, but we're small potatoes. No point shouting when it's only the half dozen of us sitting around."

"I think you ought to write as many pieces as they'll let you," she said. "I think you're a fine writer."

"I am? How can you say that?"

"I buy the paper every day. I've seen your, ah . . . your byline? Is that the word? I've seen it nearly every week. You may not wish to admit it, but you and I both know there's a lot more to you than rewrites and translations of cablese."

The taxi stopped; they'd arrived at her aunt's.

"Thank you for today, and for dinner, and for Miss Stein's. And most of all for showing me the newsroom."

"You're welcome, Ellie. I—"

"Sweet dreams. I'll see you next Saturday."

Chapter 18

"*Dépêche-toi, Hélène!* We were meant to be downstairs ten minutes ago."

Helena stepped back from the pier glass in her dressing room and cast a final, critical eye over her appearance. Her Vionnet frock was enchanting, like so much golden spun sugar, and it fit her so perfectly that it was all but weightless.

When it had been delivered, the afternoon before, its box had also contained a gift: someone, likely one of the seamstresses, had fashioned a bandeau for her hair from the same gold charmeuse fabric as the frock, and finished it with a posy of lace flowers that echoed the gown's metallic trim. It looked wonderful, far better than the simple diamanté clip she'd been planning to wear, and was so decorative that she decided against wearing any jewelry.

In deference to the occasion she'd applied, with advice and assistance from Mathilde, some rouge on her cheeks and lips, a sweep of cake mascara to darken her pale lashes, and just enough powder to blot the shine from her nose. Her mother would have swooned at the sight but Helena liked the way she looked—modern, confident, and striking.

Preparations for the party had begun before dawn, but when Helena had offered to help—it was a vague offer, as she hadn't the practical skills to help with anything important—Agnes had laughed and sent her off to the studio for the day. At the end of the afternoon Mathilde and Étienne had come home with her and, banished from the lower floors, the three of them had sought sanctuary in Helena's bedchamber.

Daisy had arrived at half-past seven, a good hour before the party was set to begin, and although her frock was not to Helena's own taste—it was an elaborate confection of pink chiffon that rather overwhelmed her friend's delicate prettiness—her excitement was so infectious that she soon had the four of them seized with giddy anticipation.

"You've no idea how long it's been since I had an evening out like this," she'd said with a happy sigh. "Daddy insists on living so quietly, and we hardly ever entertain. So this is just *wonderful.*"

When it was time to change into their evening clothes, Helena had sent Étienne and Mathilde off to two of the spare bedrooms, but both had returned at lightning speed while she was still buttoning the straps on her shoes.

It wasn't fair to keep them and Daisy waiting, though, so with a last look at her transformed self, she gathered up her gloves and joined them in the corridor.

"What do you think?" she asked, suddenly nervous. "Will I do?"

"I have only one word," said Étienne. "*Ravissante.* All three of you are perfection."

Mathilde had borrowed Helena's turquoise and gold frock, which suited her very well; Étienne, who didn't own a dinner jacket, wore his usual dark suit, albeit with a freshly laundered shirt. His necktie was a startling shade of purple, however, which might not have passed inspection at the Élysée Palace but wouldn't be out of place among the rather bohemian crowd already gathered downstairs.

"Shall we go?" Helena suggested. "From the sounds of it most of the guests have landed already."

It was a relief to enter the *grand salon* and have her friends—her allies—at her side. In the five years since the end of her engagement, she'd spent far too many evenings standing alone in corners, or trailing after her mother or siblings. This was a very different gathering, of course; although she didn't know her aunt's friends especially well, she was confident no one would deliberately shun her or whisper gleeful insults behind her back. And if they did? She would laugh in their face, and toast her newfound courage with her friends at her side.

The house's reception rooms had been transformed, their furniture rearranged against the walls so guests might stand and circulate freely. On every table and mantel there were huge arrangements of orchids, lilies, and tuberose, and though the flowers were very pretty their scent, in the rising warmth of the rooms, was quite overpowering.

All told, there were thirty invited guests at dinner that evening. As Helena led her friends from room to room, she made introductions and, if guests were already engaged in conversation, supplied their names sotto voce to her friends.

She introduced them to Natalie Barney and Lily Gramont, then to Djuna Barnes and Thelma Wood; others received a smile and wave as they passed by. "That's Mina Loy, just there, and Nancy Cunard . . . and Peggy Guggenheim is standing at the doorway. And there's Romaine Brooks, the painter; you'll have heard of her, I think. She's the one wearing a man's frock coat."

"Who is that very handsome young man by the window?" Étienne asked. "Fair, not too tall, standing with the dark-haired girl."

Helena stood on tiptoe; it was difficult to see, as there was rather a crush of people in the library now. "Oh, that's George Antheil and his—I suppose she's his girlfriend. He's a composer, and quite a radical one, from what I've heard. They live above Shakespeare and Company, the English bookstore on the rue de l'Odéon."

"Where is Sam?" Daisy asked. "I thought you said he would be here."

"He will. He was working earlier and thought he might be a bit late. But he'll be here."

Sara and Gerald were there, too, and though they had been at their house in St.-Cloud for some weeks it was the first time she'd seen them since the summer.

"When are you going to visit us?" Sara asked. "You must all come out and have lunch one day. The children are forever asking when their Ellie is going to visit."

"We will, I promise. Let me finish showing my friends around, and then we'll talk some more."

"We must. You look beautiful tonight. Is that a Vionnet gown?"

"It is. Does it suit me?"

"Admirably."

Helena had led her friends through the *petit salon*, the library, and the breakfast room, and she'd just finished her first glass of champagne, when she caught sight of Sam.

His dinner jacket was so perfectly tailored that it must have been made for him, and he was so very handsome and unfamiliar that her heart skipped a beat. He advanced across the room, his eyes never leaving hers, his gaze keen and appreciative. Normally his appearance was rather disheveled, to put it mildly, but tonight he was the very epitome of aristocratic elegance. If she didn't know better, she'd have assumed he was to the manor born.

He stopped when he was an arm's length away, not seeming to notice their friends. And then he smiled, a slow and easy smile that made her knees feel like jelly and her heart race in her chest.

"Good evening, everyone," he said, and he shook hands with Étienne and kissed cheeks with her and Mathilde and Daisy, and the moment between them, when it seemed as if they'd been the only two people in the room, evaporated.

"Where is your aunt?" he asked. "I didn't see her when I came in."

"I've no idea—making the rounds, I expect. We're seated near her at dinner."

A footman came forward with glasses of champagne on a silver tray, and they all accepted one, even Sam. She sipped at hers slowly, savoring the way it fizzed against her tongue, and was startled when he bent his head to whisper against her ear.

"Do you think I should ask for a beer? How would that go down in this crowd, d'you think?"

"Not well," she said, and giggled helplessly. It was the champagne, of course; giggling was for schoolgirls. "They probably drink champagne with their *petit déjeuner* every morning."

"*Attention, s'il vous plaît!*" Vincent, looking very distinguished in a corded silk tailcoat, had appeared at the threshold to the dining room, and was clapping his hands to gain the guests' attention. "*Mesdames, messieurs, le dîner est prêt.*"

THE DINING TABLE, which normally accommodated ten or twelve diners, had been fitted with enough leaves to bring it to a good thirty feet, and it now stretched the entire length of the chamber. Elaborate flower arrangements, ornate Georgian candelabra, and epergnes brimming with out-of-season fruit ran down the center of the table, which had been set with her aunt's sterling silver flatware, *bleu celeste* Sèvres porcelain, and Baccarat crystal.

Agnes was seated at the head of the table and had honored Helena and her friends by placing them nearby: Sam was at her right, with Mathilde and Daisy occupying the next two spaces. On the opposite side of the table, Étienne sat next to Agnes, with Helena at his left.

The identity of the person who was to sit at Helena's left remained a mystery until nearly everyone had found their seat; only then did a vaguely familiar figure take his place at her side. It was the man she'd met at Vionnet the other week, the nephew by marriage of Madame Balsan. She racked her brain for his name . . . Monsieur d'Albert. No, d'Albret. That was it.

All was well during the first course, which consisted of lobster bisque with a remove of *truite à la Véronique*. The table was too wide for her to easily join in the conversation between Sam, Mathilde, and Daisy, and Étienne was engaged in charming her aunt. That left Mr. d'Albret. Fortunately his manners were impeccable, and he had some interesting things to say about aviation and his time with France's Aéronautique Militaire during the war.

"While I cannot account myself an ace, I did have my share of kills," he said, dabbing at his mustache with the corner of his napkin.

"I suppose it was terribly dangerous."

"But of course. Only the best and bravest ever dared to become aviators."

Helena happened to look across the table, where Sam was engaged in conversation with Daisy. She couldn't be certain, but something told her that he had overheard.

"What are you doing now?" she asked her dinner partner.

"I have decided to pursue the Orteig Prize," he announced with gusto.

"Oh, yes," she said. "I've heard of it. A challenge—"

"It is the greatest challenge of our age. Monsieur Orteig is a hotelier in America, and he has promised twenty-five thousand dollars to the first man who completes a nonstop flight across the Atlantic between New York and Paris."

That was enough to induce Sam to join the discussion. "Orteig issued the challenge five years ago, and not a single attempt has yet been made. Most people think it's impossible."

Helena stared at him, taken aback by his skeptical attitude. He'd been the one to tell her about the prize, and to her best recollection he'd been enthusiastic when speaking of the challenge. Why he should now dismiss it out of hand was puzzling indeed.

"Only those who know nothing of modern aviation say it is impossible, Monsieur, ah—"

"Howard."

"Monsieur Howard. But I know better. I say it is entirely possible."

"It's got to be an expensive proposition," Sam persisted. "The outlay will far exceed the prize money. What is the going rate for a Fokker C-IV, anyway? I doubt you can buy one ready-made from your friendly neighborhood aircraft salesman."

"You speak of matters of which you are clearly ignorant—"

"The plane would need to be built to order," Sam mused, "with the extra weight stripped away, bigger fuel tanks, better instruments . . . that can't be cheap."

Mr. d'Albret's face had reddened, but rather than address Sam directly he turned to Helena and unleashed a dazzling smile. "I believe that questions of commerce should not enter into such a noble endeavor. I have decided to pursue the prize for the glory of France. I anticipate no difficulty in securing the support I require."

Although he was clearly expecting some kind of response, Helena only smiled and nodded, and then dealt with the awkward moment that ensued by taking a sip of wine. After that, Mr. d'Albret turned to the woman at his left, and Helena was left to listen to Étienne as he became ever more charming and loquacious, though she tried, with little success, to follow Sam's conversation with her friends.

A second course, of grouse in a morel mushroom sauce, was served; and then, though she could scarcely eat another bite, another course arrived, this time roast filet of beef with braised carrots and duchess potatoes.

"Your niece will not believe me, but I believe she is truly gifted." Étienne was singing her praises to Agnes and once again was exaggerating wildly. "Hélène has been experimenting with new mediums, you know, and is absolutely fearless in her pursuit of inspiration. Why, only the other day she was telling me of her plans to visit Les Halles at night to draw the workers there."

For a moment, no one spoke. Agnes had been stunned into silence, perhaps for the first time in living memory, and Helena herself could only stare, horror-stricken, at her friend. She had mentioned her notion that such a visit would be interesting, and possibly very useful, and they had talked of Étienne accompanying her on such an outing, but she would never have been so foolhardy as to venture out at night by herself.

Agnes recovered first. "Helena, how *could* you? Think of the danger—and what it would do to me if anything were to happen to you. I'm terribly disappointed, you know."

"I wasn't planning to go by myself. Tell her, Étienne. We were—"

"You're a grown woman, and I trust you to behave in a sensible fashion. Or at least I *did*."

"Auntie A, I would never have gone on my own. I'm not that foolish."

"I'll take her," Sam said. "I'm a night owl anyway," he added, "so it's not a problem."

"I don't need your help," Helena said, bristling at his description of her as *a problem*. "Étienne has already agreed to go with me."

"I don't mind if you prefer to go with Sam," said Étienne.

"See? All sorted."

"Fine," she muttered, though she felt anything but fine at their high-handed manner toward her.

Resolving to ignore all further discussion on the subject, she turned pointedly to Mr. d'Albret, set her hand lightly on his forearm, and offered up her most winning smile. "I do hope you'll tell me about your time in the Aéronautique Militaire. You must have been terribly brave . . ."

In this fashion she survived the final course, apricot tarts with vanilla ice cream, and followed her aunt dutifully to the *grand salon* when it was time for after-dinner digestifs.

Helena didn't partake, having drunk rather more wine at dinner than was her habit, and instead stood quietly and listened to Mr. d'Albret describe his wartime exploits, some of which were very impressive indeed. Sam remained nearby, and every time she looked in his direction he was watching her, his eyes merry with suppressed laughter, and she couldn't tell if he was laughing at her, or the Frenchman, or both of them.

At long last Mr. d'Albret took his leave, and when he bent to kiss her hand she very nearly snatched it away. Sam noticed, of course, and his apparent relish of her discomfort was so intensely irritating that she felt like shouting at him.

Mr. d'Albret was speaking to her again; she had to force herself to concentrate. "I wonder, Lady Helena, if I might have the honor of escorting you to dinner one evening? And perhaps we might go dancing afterward?"

She was about to refuse, but she made the mistake of looking to Sam yet again, and it seemed, from the expression in his eyes, that he was daring her to say yes.

"I would love to go to dinner with you, Monsieur d'Albret," she answered, and to her great satisfaction Sam looked every bit as annoyed as she had hoped.

She said good night to her friends; Étienne, rather the worse for wear, refused her offer of a guest room for the night, but Mathilde promised she would see him home safely.

"I shall also take good care of your frock," her friend whispered. "Thank you so much."

"It was my pleasure," Helena replied honestly. "I would offer to give it to you, but I think you would refuse. All the same, I hope you know you may borrow it, or anything else I have, anytime you wish. I do mean that."

And then it was time to say good night to Sam. If he was angry at her having accepted Mr. d'Albret's invitation, he betrayed no sign of it.

"When do you want to go?" he asked.

"Where? To Les Halles? But you don't have to take me. I can—"

"I want to take you. How about Wednesday?"

"You truly don't mind? You'll be so tired the next day."

"I'll be fine. I'll come by at three in the morning. And make sure you go to bed as soon as you get home from school. It'll be easier to get up when your alarm goes off."

"Won't you be bored?" she asked, still uncertain.

"I doubt it. I'll watch you work, which is always interesting, and I might even get enough local color for a piece on the market."

"I suppose. Well, good night, then."

"Good night, Ellie," he said, stooping to kiss her cheek. "You were beautiful tonight."

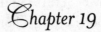

Chapter 19

On Tuesday afternoon, Helena went straight home after class, packed her satchel with a new sketchpad and box of sharpened pencils, ate an early dinner, wound and set her alarm clock, and put herself to bed. She woke on her own, not far past one o'clock, but rather than get up straightaway and face the cold and dark of her room she lay abed, her mind too busy for sleep.

She didn't know much about the market, only that Les Halles was a group of buildings where produce, meat, fish, and other fresh foodstuffs were brought into Paris overnight to be sold in the morning. That much of the fresh food to feed a city of millions might be seen, gathered together in one place, was difficult to imagine, and as she'd never been to any of the big markets in London, or indeed to any market at all, she'd no idea of what she would discover that morning.

It wouldn't do to keep Sam waiting at the door, however, so she forced herself out of bed and into the chill of her room. Before retiring, she'd set out the warmest and sturdiest of her clothes: thick stockings and flannel combinations, a woolen frock with an unfashionably long skirt, lace-up boots, her winter coat, a felt cloche hat, and a scarf that, once wrapped around her neck, was as high and enveloping as a monk's cowl.

Tiptoeing through the house, so as not to wake her aunt or any of the servants, she crept downstairs at a quarter to three and installed herself in the front foyer. Sam's knock on the door came a few minutes after the hour.

"Yes?" she called out softly.

"It's Sam. I've a taxi waiting."

She let herself out, locked the door behind her, and turned to her friend. He was wearing a proper coat for once, and a scarf, but his flat cap didn't look very warm.

"Won't you catch cold?" she asked.

"It's forty degrees out. Where I grew up, that barely warrants an overcoat. Don't worry about me."

The taxi took them north to the rue de Rivoli, then steadily westward along rain-slicked pavements. The moon hung low and full, its light a gleaming silver net flung wide over the empty streets and shuttered façades of a still-slumbering city.

As they drew closer to Les Halles, the streets grew busier and brighter, with long lines of heavy-laden carts stretching along the rue St.-Denis and the rue du Pont Neuf. They turned north again, and Sam leaned forward to speak with the driver. A few minutes later, the taxi pulled to a stop in the shadow of an imposing Gothic church.

"We're just north of the market," Sam said, helping her out of the car. "But I think we should have something to eat before you get started. Hungry?"

She was about to say she wasn't, but then she smelled some freshly baked bread and her stomach grumbled loudly in response. She nodded, hoping he hadn't heard.

"Let's go. Just up this street." He slung her satchel over his shoulder, and then, as if it were something he'd done a thousand times before, he took her hand in his. They'd walked arm in arm before, usually when returning home after dinner, but this felt far more intimate, the touch of a sweetheart, not merely a friend. His hand was so much larger than hers, and the warmth of his touch, though she could feel it but dimly through their gloves, was both comforting and exciting. If only they had farther to go.

She stole a sidelong glance, not wanting him to catch her staring. He was so different from other men. It wasn't just his coloring, though his auburn hair and fair, freckled skin were uncommon enough. And it wasn't his height, for her brother and former fiancé were tall men, too.

It had to be his manner, his wonderful American directness. He was honest, but not to such a degree that he ever injured her feelings, or those of anyone else. He was plainspoken, with none of the verbal affectations so common among the men of her social circle back home. And he was kind, the sort of man given to practical good deeds that meant so much more than bouquets of hothouse flowers or festoons of sickly-sweet compliments.

They walked north on the rue Montorgueil, past a bakery, shuttered but lit within, and the source of the fresh bread that had awoken her hunger; past slumbering draft horses, still harnessed to their carts, awaiting the long walk home; and past a dozen or more narrow-fronted restaurants, all full to bursting with blue-smocked farmers, weary porters, and stall holders just beginning their day.

The restaurant Sam chose had no sign and was even smaller and humbler than Chez Rosalie, but it, too, was full of men and women bent over steaming bowls of soup.

"They only serve one thing here, onion soup, but it's really good," Sam explained. "Go sit down—there are two places at the end of that table—and I'll get the soup."

He was back in no time, carrying two large bowls and spoons and nothing else.

"Aren't you going to have something to drink?" she asked. "The men at the next table have mugs of beer."

"No. Would only make me sleepy. I'll have a coffee later. Do you want anything? A glass of wine?"

She shook her head. "This is all I need."

The soup was simple, nothing but onions and broth and at the bottom of the bowl, she soon discovered, a piece of dark country bread. It was the single most delicious meal she'd ever had. In no time at all, she was staring into her empty bowl and wishing she had an extra piece of bread to soak up the last drops of remaining broth.

When she set down her spoon at last, Sam was watching her fondly. "Good?"

"Wonderful."

"Are you ready to go? We can walk around for a while, give you an idea of what there is to see. Have you been here before?"

"No. Étienne told me about the market, and a flower seller posed for us at school one day. I thought I might find interesting subjects here, that's all."

"You will," he promised, "though I doubt you'll find much in the way of flowers at this time of year."

They walked south, past the church where the taxi had left them, stopping just across the street from the market buildings, which were far bigger and taller than she had expected, the delicate tracery of their iron and glass walls reminding her of the greenhouses at her father's country estate.

"The halls on the right are for meat and tripe," Sam said. "To the left are the halls for produce, cheese, and fish. It's early still, so they're just setting up. Why don't we wander around outside?"

If she'd been amazed by the scale of the halls, she was even more surprised by the crowds milling between and around the market buildings. There was scarcely any room to move, for the lanes and streets were a surging mass of people, carts, horses, lorries, piles of boxes, and empty crates. In the space that remained, there were the vegetables.

She'd assumed the produce for sale would be inside, arranged on barrows in the market buildings, but for some reason many of the carts were unloading their contents directly onto the street. She saw ruffled heads of green-bronze Savoy cabbages, stacked in neat pyramids, and beside them baskets of leeks, onions, turnips, and swede, and the furled spears of winter chicory. There were carrots and parsnips by the hundredweight, fat bunches of radishes, knobbly fists of celery root, and huge burlap sacks of potatoes.

It was all rather overwhelming. She looked to Sam, not certain of what to do or where to begin, and once again he understood. "Let's find you a quiet place to stand," he said, his voice raised so she might hear him above the din. "It's hard to find your bearings in the middle of this."

He still held her hand, but now he drew her close and guided her through the crowds, until they were standing in front of a wine shop on the south side of the rue Berger. Several empty crates stood by its door, and, after testing them to ensure their sturdiness, he made a sort of stage for her to stand upon, just high enough that she might see over the heads of passersby.

There, protected from the bustle of the market, she worked

for more than an hour, making sketch after sketch of anything and anyone that caught her fancy. First there was a farmer's wife, presiding proudly over a heap of celadon-green cabbages; though the set of the woman's shoulders told Helena she was weary to the bone, she was good-humored in spite of it, laughing and joking as if she liked nothing better than standing out in the cold for hours on end. Farther along, a porter crouched low as the deep wicker basket strapped to his back was filled with sack after sack of potatoes. As he straightened, he staggered a little under its weight, but then, balance regained, he set off as though the load he carried were no heavier than a pair of down pillows.

She sketched a pair of nuns in pristine habits and starched white veils who haggled over every sou they spent but smiled beatifically at passersby; a ginger tabby cat, perched on a stack of empty fruit crates, delicately washing its face as it ignored the hubbub around it; and the arching tracery, only faintly visible in the gloom, of the iron roof supports of the nearest market hall.

She nearly sketched a *mutilé de guerre*, hobbling by on too-short crutches, his face drawn into a rictus of suffering, but compassion stilled her hand. It was one thing to draw people who were busy at their work, and quite another to capture the pain and desperation of a fellow human being brought low. She was about to dig in her satchel for some francs when Sam approached the man, who had halted only a few yards away. After engaging him in conversation, they walked together to a nearby soup vendor, at which point Sam paid for a serving of cabbage soup, handed it to the veteran, shook his hand, and returned to Helena's side.

"I offered him some money, but he said he didn't feel right

in taking it. So I asked if I might buy him something to eat instead."

"That was very kind of you," she said.

"No more than any decent person would have done."

Apart from his conversation with the veteran, Sam stayed close by her side, never commenting on her sketches, though he was tall enough to look over her shoulder. From time to time he scribbled in a small notebook, but that was all. He didn't stamp his feet or blow on his hands to keep warm, though she was nearly frozen to the marrow after more than an hour of standing still.

"I'm worried you're cold. Shall we find you a *café express*?" she asked.

"No, I'm fine. Are you ready to move on?"

"May we walk through the market halls? I won't take long."

"Take as much time as you like," he said, and helped her down from her perch.

They began at one of the halls given over to fish. Here she concentrated on quick, almost impressionistic sketches of the wares on display, adding notes in the margins to remind her of the colors she saw. There was an iridescent amethyst glimmer to the mussels, she noted, in beautiful contrast to the beds of moistened moss on which they were piled; nearby, delicate pink langoustines were arranged side by side, as neatly as soldiers on parade. There were barrels overflowing with the shimmering silver of herring and sardines, deep buckets full of squirming, ink-dark eels, heaps of carp and pike, fierce-looking swordfish, and even, at one stall, a bluefin tuna as big as a man.

The smell in the cheese and dairy hall was far less agreeable than the briny scents of the fish market, though the displays there were very pretty, with stacked towers of Brie, Camembert, and ash-covered chèvre; blue-veined rounds of Roquefort; gargantuan wedges of Gruyère and Cantal; and pail after pail of cream and milk and primrose-yellow butter. Helena adored cheese, the smellier the better, but a city's worth of cheese in one enclosed space made for an eye-watering experience.

Last of all they visited the flower sellers where, despite the lateness of the year, there were masses of violets, chrysanthemums, pinks, Michelmas daisies, winter camellias and hellebores, their mingled scents conquering even the stench of the now-filthy streets and an adjacent pissoir.

Dawn was breaking, the moonlight was fading from the sky, her hand was beginning to cramp, and her teeth wanted to chatter. "I suppose we ought to be going home," she said reluctantly.

"I'm happy to stay as long as you like, but you should try to get some sleep before class begins."

"What time is it?" she asked, too tired to look at her wristwatch.

"Coming up on six o'clock." He took her pencil and sketchbook and stowed them in her satchel, and then, before she could object, he bought a small bunch of violets. Wrapped in a corona of newspaper, their petals still streaked with soil, they made the prettiest posy Helena had ever seen.

"You don't have to—"

"I want to," he said, and he led her away, his hand once again in hers, to the relative quiet of the boulevard de Sébastopol, where they found a taxi for the short journey home.

She was too tired to say anything when they were in the car, but remembered her manners when they were once again standing at her aunt's side door. "Thank you."

He didn't answer, only smiled and bent his head, she

assumed to deposit a kiss on her cheek. But then his hand was touching her chin, encouraging her to look up, and before she had quite realized what was happening his mouth was on hers and he was kissing her, really kissing her, as no one had ever done before.

She knew she was meant to reach up and embrace him, twine her arms around his neck, but she would have to drop her satchel and posy. So she stood and let him kiss her, his big hands framing her face so gently, and all she could do was strain forward on tiptoe and press her lips ever more firmly against his.

If only it could have lasted forever, not only the kiss, but also his hand in hers, his presence at her side, his gift of violets fresh from the countryside. But the sun was rising, they were tired and cold, and she had to be at school in a few hours.

"I'm not sorry for that," he whispered, his words soft against her cheek.

"Neither am I," she managed weakly.

He dropped a lesser kiss on her brow. "Good night, Ellie."

"Sam, I—"

"Lock the door behind me. I'll see you soon."

Back in her bedroom, she undressed, changed into her nightgown, washed her face, and brushed her teeth, and all the while her mind was whirring and turning and trying to make sense of what had just happened. Sam had kissed her, she had kissed him back, and nothing was simple or straightforward or uncomplicated anymore.

She got into bed, arranged her pillows, sheets, and eiderdown so they were perfectly comfortable, and still she couldn' stop thinking about that kiss, and how, in the space between two heartbeats, everything had changed.

Chapter 20

20 December 1924

Dearest Mama and Papa,

I do promise to send you a proper letter very soon, full of every last detail of my birthday and Christmas, but I have to run off to class in a few minutes, and would you believe I've yet to buy any gifts for Aunt Agnes or my friends here? (I sent off a parcel to you last week—has it arrived yet? I do hope you receive it in time.)

Thank you very much for the beautiful bracelet. It fits my wrist perfectly and as you know I have always adored amethysts. I opened it the moment I awoke this morning, having forced myself (with great difficulty!) to leave the parcel alone when it arrived last week.

Thank you as well for your cheque, which I had no trouble in depositing at Auntie A's bank. Yesterday I went to Galeries Lafayette and spent nearly all of it on a new winter coat in a gorgeous raspberry color, and with the remainder I bought a matching hat.

Once again I am sorry to not be with you for Christmas, but Maître Czerny only closes the school between the 24th and 26th and I dare not miss any classes. I know you will be very busy, what with everyone

*coming to stay with you in Yorkshire, and I do hope that you will be
so occupied you won't even notice my absence. Please know that I am
thinking of you, and of course missing the both of you very much.*

With much love from your devoted daughter,
Helena

It was the Saturday before Christmas, and it was Helena's birthday. Not wishing for anyone to make a fuss, she'd said nothing to her friends and happily passed the day at the studio, hard at work on a portrait of the jolly farmer's wife she'd seen at Les Halles.

At five o'clock sharp Daisy packed up her things and left for home, mindful as always of her father's wish for company. That left the rest of them to continue on to dinner at Rosalie's at seven o'clock. Sam was waiting outside when they came around the corner, and he seemed exactly his normal self, if rather quieter than usual. If he had spent the last few days obsessing over their kiss he betrayed no sign of it, and in his manner she could discern no trace of tension or awkwardness. It was almost as if she had imagined the entire thing, and Helena couldn't decide if she ought to be relieved or disappointed.

"How did you spend the day?" she asked as soon as they were settled and Luigi had brought them bread and wine.

"I had to work. Was filling in for Geoff Fraser."

"Wasn't it your day off?"

"It was, but I lost a bet to him back in October, when New York lost the World Series to Washington, and he waited until today to make me pay up."

"The World Series?" Helena asked.

"Of baseball."

"How can it be a 'world' series if both teams are American?"

He rolled his eyes at this. "Fine. The baseball championships. So what does he make me do? Spend half my day standing around at the Rotary Club, waiting for some jackass assistant to an undersecretary of trade to show up and give a speech."

"Was it interesting?" Mathilde asked.

"God, no. It was so boring I can't even remember the man's name. Should be fun spinning a story out of *that*."

Helena wanted to enjoy dinner, and her time with her friends, but she couldn't manage to loosen the coil of apprehension that was tightening around her chest whenever she thought of what would happen once dinner was finished, and she and Sam were left alone for the walk home. Would he pretend the kiss hadn't happened? Would he wish to talk about it? She'd rather be paraded through the streets on a tumbrel.

Her anxiety was allayed, if only temporarily, when Étienne insisted they all go to Le Dôme for a round of drinks. "I need at least two glasses of *fine à l'eau* to wash away the taste of the vinegar we just drank. I am certain I felt my teeth dissolving."

"Like Cleopatra's pearls?" Helena teased.

"Just so."

They were able to find a tiny table at Le Dôme, crowding into a space that was better suited for two, and Étienne hailed the waiter with a snap of his fingers and, oddly enough, a wink.

Rather than come to them straightaway, the man did an about-face and vanished into the kitchens, appearing several minutes later with a plate that held a single chocolate-topped creampuff. He set it before Helena with a wonderfully Gallic flourish, extracted a tall and very thin candle from his apron pocket, lighted it with a match, and inserted it in the top of the cream puff.

Sam spoke first. "Happy birthday, Ellie."

"How did you know?"

"How do you think? Your aunt."

"She took me aside at the party," Étienne explained, "and told me then. She knew you wouldn't say anything, and she thought it was silly. So now—"

"Enough explaining," Sam interrupted. "It's time to sing. Do you know 'For He's a Jolly Good Fellow'?" Étienne shook his head and Mathilde simply shrugged. "No? I guess you'll have to keep up. Here goes."

He stood, his chair scraping against the tiled floor, cleared his throat, and began to sing in a lovely, deep voice.

"For she's a jolly good fellow, for she's a jolly good fellow, for she's a jolly good fellow, and so say all of us."

Within seconds, people at neighboring tables joined in, and then everyone at the bar, and soon everyone at Le Dôme, was singing Helena's praises.

"And so say all of us, and so say all of us, for she's a jolly good fellow, and so say all of us!"

After that, the barman stood them a round of drinks, and against her better judgment Helena had a *fine à l'eau*. The watered-down brandy burned her throat, but it helped to steady her increasingly ragged nerves.

"I must be off," Mathilde said, setting down her glass and buttoning up her coat. "Étienne, *toi aussi*." She leaned across the table and kissed Helena's cheek. "Happy birthday, my friend."

"I suppose we ought to go, too. I haven't seen my aunt since breakfast."

Helena and Sam walked home in silence, which was just as well since her heart was pounding so loudly she couldn't hear anything above the roar in her ears. Sam had offered his arm, as he always did, and she accepted it without protest.

It was cold enough that she was very glad of her new coat,

and grateful that she had also worn the plush fur stole Agnes had insisted on lending her. Sam, as usual, was bareheaded and immune to the weather. Even if it had been snowing he likely wouldn't have noticed.

Vincent was at the side door when they arrived, which was rather a surprise as normally she and Sam were left to say their good-byes in relative privacy.

"Good evening. Lady Helena, your aunt wishes for you and Mr. Howard to join her in the *petit salon*."

"Oh," said Helena, disappointed yet also, somehow, relieved. "That's lovely. I mean . . . do you mind coming in? Do you have time?"

"Of course I do," Sam said easily, following her inside.

A table in the *petit salon* had been set for dessert, with champagne on ice and Helena's favorite cake, a Victoria sponge, ready to be served.

"Happy birthday, my darling girl! Did you have a nice evening with your friends?"

"I did, Auntie A, but you didn't need to tell everyone."

"Of course I did. Come here, now, and have some champagne and cake, and then you must open your present."

Agnes's gift was a bottle of French perfume, Mitsouko, which Helena had never heard of before. "It's from Guerlain," her aunt explained. "Do try it on." So she opened the bottle and dabbed the stopper to her wrists, and at once was enveloped in roses and jasmine and another scent that she couldn't name, but which reminded her of Earl Grey tea.

"It smells just like the gardens at Villa Vesna," she said, and Agnes clapped her hands in delight.

"I thought so, too. You must wear it this winter and think of warmer days to come."

"I've something for Helena," Sam said quietly, and set a neatly wrapped parcel on the table.

She had a little trouble opening it, for the colored string that fastened shut its paper refused to be undone, and she had to wait for Sam to pull out his penknife and cut it free. It was a book, she was certain. The paper fell away and revealed a familiar binding. It was his rare, precious translation of Rilke's poems, which she had returned to him only last week.

She opened it to the flyleaf and saw that he had inscribed it, his messy, looping scrawl so distinctive she'd have known it anywhere.

> *To Ellie—*
> *an artist with a poet's heart*
> *—Sam*

"Oh, Sam," was all she could say, and suddenly she had to blink back tears.

"I thought you might like it," he said, and when she dared to look up she saw that his cheekbones were flushed, as if he were embarrassed by the generosity of his gesture.

"Well, I ought to be on my way," he said. "I've a story to finish up for tomorrow. Thanks for your hospitality, Mrs. Paulson."

"You're very welcome. Helena, walk Sam to the door."

Agnes didn't follow them, and so once again they were left to stand at the door, alone, as he shrugged on his coat and checked his pocket for the key to his room.

She stood by awkwardly, not knowing what to say, but he didn't seem to mind. "When will I see you again?" she blurted out.

"I have to work on Christmas Eve, but what about Christmas Day? We could go for a walk."

"Would you like to come for lunch? I was thinking of asking Étienne," she added. "I don't think he has anywhere else to go."

He smiled ruefully at this. "I guess I don't, either. What time?"

"I'm not sure. Perhaps one o'clock? I could send you a *petit bleu* once I know for certain."

He nodded slowly, and then reached out to tuck a strand of hair behind her ear, his touch wonderfully gentle. "I wish . . ." he whispered, his voice oddly strained.

"What is it? Do tell me."

"Never mind. Happy birthday. I'll see you soon."

IT WAS MONDAY afternoon, only three days before Christmas, before she was able to do any Christmas shopping. She began on the Right Bank, at Fauchon, where she bought a tin of Scottish shortbread and a canister of Lapsang souchong tea for Agnes. The weather promised to remain fine, so she walked to Magasin Sennelier in St.-Germain, where she found a set of squirrel-hair brushes for Étienne, a sheaf of fine watercolor paper for Daisy, and a box of intensely pigmented soft pastels for Mathilde.

Her final errand of the day was to a shop she'd heard about but not yet visited, Sylvia Beach's Shakespeare and Company. According to Sam, Miss Beach had the best collection of English-language books in France. There, Helena reasoned, she'd be able to find him the perfect gift.

The moment she entered the shop she was transfixed by the stupendous amount of books on display. They were jammed into bookcases that went all the way to the ceiling, they were heaped on the floor, they were stacked in precarious piles on the windowsills and the staircase at the back, and they tiled the surface of the long oak tables that ran down the middle of the front room.

The décor was eccentric, for much of the woodwork had been painted in bright colors, and in lieu of artwork there were scores of framed photos of writers, many of them signed, and a tattered poster proclaiming "The Scandal of Ulysses."

Miss Beach was sitting at a desk near the front, her attention on some papers she was collating. As Helena's approach she looked up and smiled warmly.

"Good afternoon. May I help you?"

"Hello, Miss Beach. I'm Helena Parr. We met a few months ago at one of Miss Barney's Friday salons."

"Of course, of course. Welcome to my shop, Miss Parr. May I help you in any way?"

"Yes, please. I'd like to buy something for a friend. Sam Howard. I know he comes in here often."

Another smile. "Oh, yes. I'm very fond of Mr. Howard."

"I'm not sure where to begin. I was thinking he might like a novel, something new, but he also likes poetry. I wish I had a better notion of his taste in books."

"Why don't I have a look in my files? I keep a record of everything I sell, and he's a member of the lending library here, too, so that should help to narrow things down."

"You don't mind?"

"Not at all. Why don't you have a look around, and I'll see what I can dig up."

Straightaway she knew she would be coming back after Christmas to find something for herself. The shop was a treasure trove, with surprises waiting on every shelf. In less than five minutes she'd come across a Kelmscott Press translation of *Beowulf,* an early edition of *Daniel Deronda,* and a bound volume of Japanese woodcuts; with enough time, heaven only knew what else she might discover.

The bell above the entrance rang, and when she looked over to see who had entered, for she was a little nervous of bumping into Sam, she recognized Hadley Hemingway's husband. She smiled at him and was gratified when he returned the gesture.

He went over to Miss Beach and spoke to her, the two of them laughing at some joke he made, and then he came over to Helena.

"Hello," he said. "You look familiar. Didn't I meet you at Miss Stein's the other week?"

"You did. I was there with Sam Howard."

"Of course," he said, and they shook hands. "I'm Ernest Hemingway."

"I'm Helena Parr. I came in to look for a present for Sam, though I'm not sure how I'll make up my mind. It's like Aladdin's cave in here."

"What were you thinking of getting him?"

"A novel, I thought. Or some short stories. You have a book of stories published, don't you? Sam told me about them. He said he thought you are a very fine writer. Perhaps I ought to buy him your book."

"That's a fine idea," Mr. Hemingway said, evidently delighted by the compliment. "I've two books out. Let me talk to Sylvia."

He was back a few minutes later, shaking his head. "She's sold all her copies of *Three Stories and Ten Poems,* and Howard already has the first two volumes of *in our time.* Sorry about that."

"Don't apologize. It's grand that you're such a success."

He looked back at Sylvia, who had prepared a parcel of books for him. "I'm sorry, but I must go. I'm taking my wife and son to Austria until the new year."

"Good-bye, then. Do wish Mrs. Hemingway a happy Christmas."

"I will, and the same to you."

She resumed her search, never quite finding the right thing, and then, standing slightly proud of its fellows, she spied a slim volume with the words *Al Que Quiere!* on its spine. Some instinct urged her to pull it from the shelf, though she didn't speak or read Spanish, and when she did the book fell open to a short poem titled "Danse Russe."

She read it through, and it was unlike any other poem she'd ever seen, and so she lingered over it, all but memorizing the lines where she stood. *"I was born to be lonely. I am best so!"*

She could buy it for herself, but it was the only copy in the shop, and she felt, somehow, that Sam would like it. She took the book over to Miss Beach, feeling apprehensive as she held it out. What did she know, after all, of poetry and fine literature?

"Ah—William Carlos Williams. I do love his work. He's been overshadowed by Eliot in recent years, but these earlier poems are striking."

"Do you think that Sam will like them?"

"There's no way to tell. He won't find them boring, though, and that's the most important thing."

On Christmas Day, Étienne and Sam arrived at one o'clock, each bearing gifts: Sam had a bouquet of hothouse lilies for Agnes and a sweet little posy of violets for Helena, while Étienne had brought a bottle of Russian vodka for them all to share. This latter offering pleased her aunt to no end, and she ordered it put on ice immediately so they might enjoy it with their first course.

In the dining room the table had been set for four, and though it had been reduced to manageable dimensions there was still a baronial gap between each of them when they sat down for lunch.

They began with oysters, which Helena secretly detested, though she managed to gulp down two with the help of some champagne; she had thought it prudent to refuse the vodka. Foie gras on toast, smoked salmon on tiny buckwheat pancakes, and grilled herring with mushrooms followed; the latter, according to Agnes, had been Dimitri's favorite dish.

For the main course, Agnes's cook had managed to find a turkey, which was served with chestnut dressing, haricots verts, and pommes de terres soufflés.

"Helena told me how you miss your American foods from home, so I thought it would be pleasant if we had one of your roast turkeys. Is it prepared properly?"

"It's delicious," Sam said. "Thanks for thinking of me."

For pudding they had a choice of Russian honey cake, English fruitcake, or *bûche de Noël*. The men ate heartily—Étienne in particular was able to consume vast amounts of food, to no ill effect—but Helena accepted only a wafer-thin slice of honey cake.

Most of the conversation over lunch revolved around Agnes's memories of grand Christmases past with Dimitri, for he had insisted on celebrating twice—once at the end of December, and again in early January, when the Orthodox feast was held. It all seemed terribly grand, a parade of caviar and royalty and Fabergé jewels, and Helena was still trying to wrap her head around the notion of Christmas breakfast in full court dress when her aunt turned to Sam.

"How did your family celebrate Christmas?" she asked. "Are there any odd American customs I need to know about?"

"Apart from eating turkey instead of goose? Not really. Most years we stayed in the city. It was just the four of us for Christmas Eve and Christmas morning, but the entire family would always come for dinner. Aunts and uncles and cousins, and any waifs and strays my mother had invited. Friends without family of their own, or people who were traveling and had nowhere else to go."

"Rather like our little group today," Agnes agreed. "Is it hard to be so far from home for Christmas?"

He swallowed, his gaze fixed on the table, and nodded slowly. "It is, I guess. But it's easier to stay away. My brother . . . he was killed in the war. My parents try, but it isn't the same."

"I quite understand, and I do beg your pardon if I've upset you at all."

"No," he said, and the smile he directed at Agnes was genuine. "This is the nicest Christmas I've had in years."

They repaired to the *petit salon* after lunch, and as Helena and Agnes had exchanged gifts the night before it remained only for her to give Étienne and Sam the presents she'd chosen so carefully. Étienne was very pleased with his brushes, and came over to embrace her heartily right away; Sam, however, reacted in an altogether different fashion, and simply stared at his book, his brow furrowed.

"Is anything the matter? I pulled it off the shelf, and one of the poems in it was so strange and lovely, and I had hoped . . ."

Sam cleared his throat, and then he looked up, his eyes bright. "I met Williams last January. He was at the shop, visiting Miss Beach, and we talked for a few minutes. He must have signed the book then." He held up the book, open to the title page, where a scrawling signature had been inscribed.

"I didn't know—I mean, I bought the book from Miss Beach, but I didn't look at the title page. You like it, then?"

"I do. I like it very much. Thank you."

She couldn't have said, afterward, what they talked of that afternoon. Étienne and Agnes worked their way through most of the vodka, and Helena and Sam polished off the rest of the champagne, and by the time her friends got up to leave her head was spinning.

She said good-bye to both men with a chaste kiss on the cheek, for she knew better than to expect a passionate farewell from Sam while Étienne stood nearby. As soon as the door closed behind them she returned to the *petit salon* to thank her aunt, and to ask if she might return to her room for a nap.

"Of course, but first come and sit with me awhile," said Agnes, who had the look of a cat sated with cream.

"Is anything the matter?"

"Not at all. You realize, of course, that he's halfway to falling in love with you."

For a moment Helena thought she might be ill. She pressed her fingers to her temples and took several deep, steadying breaths. "What? No, he can't be. I mean . . . we're only friends. I'm sure that's all we are."

"The man is smitten with you. It's as plain as the freckles on his nose."

"No, no . . . you're wrong. He can't be. It's impossible."

Sam was fond of her, and he certainly was attracted to her, but she felt certain that was all. If anything, he was feeling just as she did: confused about the path their friendship should take but reluctant to do anything that might threaten the bond between them.

No matter how he felt, he certainly wasn't smitten with her. That sort of thing happened in romantic novels, but not in real life.

Agnes patted Helena's hand, her shrewd gaze missing nothing. "Surely he's given you some notion of how he feels. Has he kissed you?"

Helena's hands flew up to cover her face. She wasn't having this conversation with Agnes. She wasn't. She'd had too much champagne and rich food; that was all. She would go upstairs and rest and the world would make sense again very soon.

"I'm not your mother, my dear. I won't have the vapors if you've shared a kiss with a man who cares for you."

"The night . . . the morning he took me to Les Halles," Helena mumbled, still hiding behind her hands. "He kissed me then. And then, the night of my birthday, I thought he might. But he didn't. Which was probably for the best, I suppose."

"Why would you say that? He's a terribly attractive man, and you're evidently fond of him."

"I am, and there have been, well, a few moments when I've wondered if there might be something between us, but I can't let myself hope for anything more. That life . . . it isn't for me."

"You mean marriage and babies and all of that?"

"Yes. Once I wanted it, or at least I told myself I did, but now . . . I'm not so sure."

"And what's to stop you from becoming his lover?"

Helena was so stunned she could only stare, openmouthed, at her aunt. Surely Agnes wasn't suggesting—

"Don't look at me like that. I'm not your mother. I won't condemn you for doing as I did at your age."

"I honestly don't know what to say."

"Would you consider it?" Agnes pressed.

"No! I don't know . . . perhaps? But what if he doesn't want me? He's only ever kissed me the one time, and that was weeks ago."

"Perhaps he is waiting for you, hmm? In any event, you don't have to decide anything today. Remain his friend, or become his lover—the only thing that truly matters is your own happiness. That, my dear, is the mark of a modern woman."

Chapter 21

January was a miserable month, cold and perpetually rainy, and Helena began to think she might never be warm again. It felt like months since she'd seen the sun, and with the dawn of each gray day she found her spirits wilting, inch by inch, their only prop the satisfaction she found in her work and the company of her friends.

Nearly every Saturday she, Étienne, and Mathilde went to dinner at Chez Rosalie. Helena always invited Sam, but his editor had been keeping him busy with writing assignments, and he'd only been able to join them once in the weeks following Christmas.

Her aunt was absent, having departed for a long stay in Antibes, and without her animating presence the great house on the quai de Bourbon felt awfully cold and lonely. Agnes had taken Hamish with her, and Helena was surprised by how much she missed her walks along the Seine with the little terrier. There really was nothing like a dog to make one feel as if one mattered to the world.

It was as well that she had precious few distractions, since her preparations for the Salon des Indépendants consumed her waking hours. Although there was no guarantee that the Salon organizers would accept her or any other student's work, Maître Czerny was a member of the placement committee, and this, Étienne assured her, was a virtual guarantee of their each having at least one piece admitted.

The maître had instructed them to prepare no more than three works of art, in any medium, for his inspection, and he would make the final decision on which to submit for consideration. This had kept Helena awake for more hours than was good for her: how to guess what would appeal most to her teacher, and thereby win a place in the Salon? Whether she cared for a given piece was immaterial; what Maître Czerny liked was key. And he was a difficult man to please, even on those rare days when he was in a tolerably amiable mood and didn't shout himself hoarse before lunchtime.

Since Christmas she'd been occupied with a series of paintings based on her drawings from Les Halles, and she'd begun to believe she might, one day, be capable of producing a grander piece—a painting that incorporated all the clamor, noise, filth, beauty, misery, and despair that she'd witnessed in her few hours at the market. But she was a slow painter, especially when working in oils, and she would never be able to finish such a painting in time for the Salon.

So instead she was focusing on a character study of the farmer's wife, but there was something missing, some animating spirit, from the preparatory drawings she had executed so painstakingly. In her mind's eye she could see the woman so clearly, see the way she'd brimmed over with life and joy despite her hardships, but time and again Helena wasn't able to capture her memories with charcoal and paper. The drawings were flat, hopelessly so, and she was running out of time. The opening reception, or vernissage, for the Salon des Indépendants was set for April 25, little more than three months away, and her other completed works were simply not good enough.

There was also the matter of Jean-François d'Albret, who had not forgotten her promise to dine with him. Just after Christmas he'd sent her a letter, which she had rather shamefully ignored; but it was followed by another, then another, and on two separate instances he had also sent her flowers. Each posed the same question: when will you be free for an evening of dinner and dancing?

Yesterday she'd received a *petit bleu* from Sam with the news that he was busy working on a story and once again couldn't come to dinner at Rosalie's on Saturday night. She had sat on the end of her bed for a good half hour, simply staring at his untidy handwriting that she now deciphered so easily. And then her gaze had fallen on her dressing table and the pile of messages from Mr. d'Albret, all unanswered, and she had decided she might as well give in and go to dinner with him.

She'd written out a response, posted it straightaway—and had immediately regretted it. The man, after all, had been a complete bore at her aunt's party the month before. What did she expect? That he would magically be transformed into an agreeable and interesting person?

His response arrived first thing the next morning, the expensive stationery smelling faintly of eau de cologne.

17 January 1925

My dear Lady Helena,

You cannot imagine the delight with which I opened your message. I had begun to fear that my pleas were falling on barren ground, so it is with the utmost pleasure that I accept your invitation to dinner this very evening. I will collect you at eight o'clock. Until then, please be assured of my sincere regard and heartfelt good wishes, for I remain,

Your devoted servant,
Jean-François d'Albret

It was a perfectly polite and proper response, although his choice of words was perhaps more flowery than she would have liked. She'd bristled at his suggestion that she had issued the invitation, but he was writing in a foreign language, after all, and it would be unfair to parse every word of the message.

All Saturday she worked alongside her friends and said nothing, not wishing to color her day with dread of the inevitable. It was also the case that she had a pretty good idea of how they would react.

Only when it was time to leave for dinner at Rosalie's, and they were putting on their coats and dousing the lanterns in the studio, did she admit the truth of her plans for the evening. Both Étienne and Mathilde were horrified; fortunately Daisy had already left, so she wasn't present to cast a third condemning vote.

"Are you mad?" Mathilde asked. "The man is *un cochon* . . . Étienne?"

"A swine."

"Yes. And I do not say this as a *critique*, for you are a lovely girl, I hope you know it, but this d'Albret person is in search of a fortune. Remember what your Sam said at dinner that night—"

"He's not 'my' Sam," she protested. It had been one month since he had kissed her, so long that even her carefully tended memories of the moment had begun to fade.

"Pfft," said Mathilde. "He said that these airplanes are very expensive, and d'Albret, he sees your aunt, he sees how she lives, and he thinks to use you to get some of it for himself."

"I only said I'd have dinner with him," Helena protested. "What harm can that do?"

"You know, Hélène, just because Sam is busy, that is no reason for you to look elsewhere," Étienne added.

"I'm not! I only thought it might be nice to go dancing. That's all. And I don't see what Sam has to do with any of this. Really I don't."

"*Eh bien.* I will be at the Dôme later, just in case. If you are bored, ask him to bring you there."

She'd taken the tram home, not feeling up to a walk through the cold, and had spent the absolute minimum of time and effort in preparing for the evening. Her Vionnet gown was too fine for the occasion, so she put on a simple frock of plum-colored wool, touched up her face with some rouge and powder, and declared herself ready.

Mr. d'Albret rang the doorbell at five minutes before the hour, and if he was surprised when she answered it herself—Vincent was in Antibes with her aunt, and the other servants were busy belowstairs—he didn't show it. He was beautifully dressed, and indeed looked very handsome. Nor could she fault his manners as he helped her in and out of his enormous black Daimler, then escorted her into one of the private dining rooms at Lapérouse on the quai des Grands Augustins.

It was rather alarming to be separated from the other diners and effectively left alone with a man who was little more than a stranger, but the restaurant's waiters were never far away, and the *chambre particulier* was very charming. It was small, less than half the size of her bedroom at home, and was extravagantly decorated with figured walnut paneling, very bad copies of Old Masters paintings, and mirrors in elaborate gilded frames.

The mirrors, she noticed, were covered in scratches, with scrawled initials here and there, which seemed rather odd given the luxury of their surroundings.

"I see you are wondering at the marks. They were left by courtesans. When their lovers gave them diamonds, they would test them on a mirror, for only a true diamond can cut the glass."

"Ah," she said, rather unnerved that he had brought her to an establishment known for assignations with courtesans. "Thank you for explaining, Monsieur d'Albret."

"Oh, please—you must call me Jean-François."

"Very well. I've, ah, never been here before," she said, hoping to steer the conversation in a more conventional direction.

"Where do you dine, if not in the finest establishments?"

"Well, I dine at home. With my aunt. And I do go to several restaurants in Montparnasse with—"

"*Pah.* That ghetto. With my apologies to your aunt's excellent cook, I fear this means you have not yet experienced the wonders of French haute cuisine." He snapped his fingers, and a waiter ran in from the corridor.

"I have decided that we shall both partake of the tasting

menu. To begin, I have ordered a bottle of their finest champagne."

"Oh, really, there's no need—"

"But I insist."

Dinner was endless, a parade of increasingly rich dishes that he devoured with great gusto, but which Helena barely touched. The tasting menu, disappointingly, included many of her least favorite foods, and she was simply unable to muster the appetite to eat more than a bite or two of each course. There were jellied langoustine, which looked disconcertingly insectlike, duckling in a viscous orange sauce, lamb's kidneys, and even frog's legs.

She had accepted only one glass of champagne at the beginning of dinner and had refused anything more; by the end of the meal, Jean-François had finished off the bottle, as well as an additional bottle of claret. He stumbled on the way out of the restaurant and had some difficulty in entering the car, but this in no way dampened his enthusiasm for the evening.

"Let us go to Le Grand Duc in Pigalle. It has the best American jazz music in Paris. After that, we shall go dancing at the Bal Bullier."

Although she would much rather have gone home, the prospect of hearing jazz music played live did appeal to her. She'd only ever heard it on gramophone records, and if she were lucky the music would be so loud that she wouldn't have to make conversation with the man, her store of conversational topics having petered out well before the second course at dinner. Of course, if he'd even once asked about her interests, or work, or friends, they'd have had plenty to talk about.

At the Grand Duc, they were ushered to a table near the front and provided with yet another bottle of champagne or ice. Helena ignored her glass, knowing it would only make her growing headache worse, and though she asked the waiter for a glass of water it never appeared.

None of that mattered once the music began. The musicians played without sheet music before them, often at dizzying speeds, and although she didn't know much about jazz it seemed that they were improvising some of the songs. It was the perfect music for dancing, though she'd no idea how one would dance to it. Perhaps Étienne might be able to show her.

Jean-François emptied the bottle of champagne at high speed, and thereafter he seemed to grow increasingly annoyed with the music, or perhaps the venue in general. Right in the middle of a song, and in front of the entire audience, he stood and beckoned for her to follow him out.

"We are going!" he shouted over his shoulder. "I've had enough of this degenerate Yankee music."

"I thought the musicians were very accomplished," she said as they got in the car.

"*Pah.* What would you know?"

"I beg your pardon?"

He giggled, a ridiculous sound coming from a grown man, and patted her arm in a way she did not appreciate, not one bit. "I do apologize. I meant only that a lady like yourself cannot possibly understand the vulgarity of such music."

"I think I should like to go home now," she said evenly.

"But the night is young! How can you even think of going to bed before midnight? And surely you do not wish to disappoint me, not after keeping me waiting for so long." His smile widened into a leer, and a wisp of panic took up residence behind her sternum. In this car she was trapped, for she couldn't depend on the driver to come to her aid, and d'Albret—she no

longer wished to think of him in a friendly fashion—seemed to
have abandoned his morals along with his sobriety.

An idea came to her then, for hadn't Étienne said he would
be at Le Dôme? If she could persuade d'Albret to go there instead of the Bal Bullier, she might enlist her friend's aid in
divesting herself of this disagreeable man. At the very least he
could distract d'Albret while she got into a taxi and went home.

"Very well. But could we go to Le Dôme first? The barman
makes the most divine cocktails."

"I suppose," he acceded. "But after that we must go dancing."

The café-bar was packed, but Étienne, disappointingly, was
nowhere to be seen. It was rather late; perhaps he had already
gone home. She would have to sort things out on her own.

D'Albret led her to a table in the back corner, but rather
than sit opposite he squeezed onto the banquette at her side.
He pressed against her, his breath hot against her ear, and she
had to remind herself that they were in public, in an establishment where she was known, and nothing bad could possibly
happen to her so long as she refused to get in his car.

He was talking again, this time about his plans for a passenger service via airplane between Paris and London. She longed
to tell him it was a ridiculous idea, for who on earth would risk
their life on an airplane when they could get from one city to
the other by ferry and train in less than a day, but she bit her
tongue and nodded approvingly.

Like Étienne, d'Albret was given to talking with his hands.
Unlike Étienne, he had a disconcerting way of allowing them
to settle on her shoulder or arm, or even, though she brushed
them away firmly more than once, on her knee.

It was unbearable, truly unbearable. She was going to stand
up and walk a pace or two away, thank him for a lovely evening

and go; she would hope, in that moment, that he wouldn't dare to make a scene. Before she could act, however, he whispered something in French that she couldn't quite make out, seized her chin, and turned her face toward his.

He was going to kiss her, she knew it, and she pushed against his chest to make him leave off, retreat, but he was surprisingly strong, and his other hand was around her waist, and oh, God, he really was going to press his mouth to hers—

And then he was gone. She heard, as if from a distance, the sound of chairs tipping over and glass breaking, and then her eyes cleared and it was Sam, right there, and he was the one who had pulled d'Albret away.

His cheeks flushed, his eyes glinting with murderous intent, Sam twisted d'Albret's arm behind his back and marched him outside, and she just sat and stared and told herself that she mustn't be sick, could *not* be sick, no matter how much her stomach was churning.

"Come on," came a voice, and there was Sam again, his arm outstretched, and he led her away and outside to the blessedly cool night. D'Albret had vanished.

"What did you do? Did you hit him?" she asked, her voice shaking so much she had to force the words past her teeth.

"No, Ellie, I didn't hit him. I shoveled him into his car and told him to sleep it off."

"Oh. I . . . I'm sorry. I didn't—"

"I may also have told him to keep his hands to himself, especially when he's around a lady. And it's possible that I also told him to never come near you again. Because if he did, I really *would* hit him."

She was shivering, although her coat was warm enough, and she badly needed to sit down. "How did you know we were here?"

"Larry Blochman was sitting at the bar. He recognized you, saw you were having trouble with that jackass, and called me at the paper. I got in a taxi and came down here as fast as I could."

"Ah. Well. I suppose I should go back to my aunt's."

"You should. Come on—the taxi's still waiting."

They didn't talk on the way home, and though she longed for him to comfort her, to tell her everything would be all right, he kept his silence. Not until they were standing at Agnes's side door did he speak again.

"Good night, Helena. Lock the door behind you."

"Please don't be angry," she implored. "I was about to get up and leave. I wouldn't . . . I wouldn't have let him kiss me."

"What were you thinking? What if he'd assaulted you? A man like that can't be trusted."

"I know. I shouldn't have gone. But he was so persistent, and I'd nothing else to do this evening . . ."

At last he looked at her, and his face was the picture of torment. Something was tearing him apart, something more than the shock they'd both just endured, but she'd no idea how to help, or what to say. So she stood on her tiptoes and pressed a quick, soft kiss to his mouth.

Before she could pull away, he backed her against the door, his mouth never leaving hers, and his hands went to frame her face, as he'd done the last time he kissed her. Only this kiss was different, it was wild and desperate, and though she wished to comfort him she also wanted more, so she pushed against him and opened her mouth and let his tongue press past her lips and clash against hers.

"No," he groaned, and he pulled his mouth away. He took a step back, and his expression was so anguished that her eyes filled with sympathetic tears.

"What is wrong? Did I do anything wrong? I'm sorry if I was forward. I only meant—"

"Ellie, you know I care about you. You must know."

"I do."

"And so what I'm about to say has nothing to do with you. *Nothing*. You must believe me."

"What is it? I told you I'm sorry about tonight."

"This isn't about tonight, and I'm sorry if I was mean to you just now. It wasn't your fault. I know that."

"Then what is the matter?" she asked, hating the piteous tone in her voice.

"I can't . . . the thing is, I can't offer you anything else. Anything more. Not now, at least."

"You don't want me? In that . . . in that way?"

"Of course I want you. You know I do. But it would be wrong of me to expect anything more, not when I . . . I wish I could explain."

"We could be lovers. I wouldn't ask for anything more."

Her words hung in the air between them, as vivid and unsettling as a neon sign. For long seconds Sam just stared at her, his eyes darkening, his face pale but for two flags of color high on his cheekbones. He took a step back, looked down, and scrubbed his hands roughly over his face.

"No," he said, and he shook his head vehemently. "No. I want to—if you only knew how much. But it wouldn't be right. It would be the farthest thing from right. I wish there was a way to make you understand."

"But I do," she said, and she did. He desired her, but not enough to act on it. He liked her, but couldn't conceive of a future with her.

"I hope you can forgive me," he said quietly. "I never meant to act like this. I never meant for you to be hurt."

"And I'm not," she insisted, wishing her voice didn't sound quite so wobbly. "We were friends before, and we're friends now. That's all that matters."

"Well, then. I guess I had better go. Good night, Ellie."

"Good night."

She couldn't bear to watch him walk away, so she went inside and crept into bed, her chest so bound by dread and disbelief that she could scarcely take a breath. Dawn came, and she was still awake, shivering under her eiderdown, her eyes hot with unshed tears, the words of that singular poem beating an endless refrain in her head. *I was born to be lonely. I am best so . . .*

They were true, the truest words ever written, for she was alone now, as she had always been, and perhaps, as the poet had said, it was best that she be so.

PART THREE

*Love consists in this:
that two solitudes protect and touch and greet each other.*

—Rainer Maria Rilke, *Letters to a Young Poet*

Chapter 22

Tuesday, 24 February

Dearest Ellie,

Wonderful news—I know that in my last letter I complained that there was no hope of my escaping the winter this year, but the Delamere-Strathallans have taken a villa in Biarritz for the season and Violet has invited me to stay! As you know I cannot bear the thought of a sea voyage that lasts one minute longer than necessary, so I shall be taking the train from Paris—and (if I have read the timetables correctly) that means I shall have nearly twenty-four hours in the city to visit with you! I arrive in the early afternoon Tuesday next and depart late the next morning.

I do realize it is terribly short notice but I am so looking forward to seeing you and meeting your new friends. Do you recall the day we spent together when we were girls, just before my debut? We had such fun—and though I'm rather long in the tooth for such antics it would be so lovely to wander around Paris together and see the sights.

*Do let me know if this is convenable, as the French say—I shall
cable you the exact details of my arrival as soon as I hear from you—*

With much love,
Your devoted sister,
Amalia

Helena did recall their long-ago day together. It had been
the spring of 1909, a bare month or so before Amalia's debut,
and they'd come to Paris so the final touches might be put on
her sister's gowns for the Season. Their elder sisters, Sophia
and Bertha, had made their debuts already and had been duly
married off to men who were so little known to Helena that she
always had trouble recalling their names. Although Amalia was
five years older, they had always been close, and the thought of
being left alone in the nursery until her own debut had been
weighing upon Helena for some months.

A day or two before their departure for home, Mama had can-
celed their engagements, for reasons Helena couldn't now recall—
likely she'd had a headache, or something of the sort. It had been a
beautiful day, so bright and warm that it was a shame to stay inside,
and Amalia had asked if they might go for a walk with Bessie, their
mother's maid. Rather to their surprise, Mama had agreed, insisting only that they return in time for tea at four o'clock.

They'd left their hotel on the Place de la Concorde and
walked through the Tuileries Gardens, which were pretty but
rather dull, and had crossed the Pont Royal and wandered
along the banks of the Seine, past the stalls of *les bouquinistes*
pausing now and then to admire a fine leather binding or
even rarer, a book printed in English.

She and Amalia had ventured into Notre-Dame, head

thrown back to wonder at the stained glass and ancient stone-work, and had even lighted candles at a saint's statue in a side chapel. She couldn't recall, now, if she had prayed for anything in particular. Had she known to ask for a reprieve from her sisters' fate? Probably not; although she'd been sad at Amalia's imminent departure from home, she'd also been excited at the prospect of her own debut, far-off as it had then been.

They had gone to a café, or a bistro of some kind, and had eaten *croque monsieur* sandwiches and crème caramel, and then, though Bessie had protested, saying it was time to be going back to the hotel, they'd walked along the boulevard St.-Michel until they'd encountered the fence that enclosed the Luxem-bourg Gardens. They'd followed it around, eventually arriv-ing at the entrance by the Musée du Luxembourg, and they'd paid their entrance fee for the museum, wandered through its galleries, and marveled at its astonishingly modern art.

After an hour, likely more, Amalia had insisted they see the rest of the gardens. There was a carousel, which they'd gone on twice in a row, and a Punch and Judy show, though the puppets were called Guignol and Madelon in French, and an ornamental pond where boys and girls alike played with elaborately rigged toy sailboats.

When they had returned to the hotel, well past teatime, Helena's shoes and stockings had been soaking wet, a casualty of her having rescued a toy boat in danger of capsize; Amalia, always so immaculate in her dress and manners, had torn the hem of her frock, which was very dirty besides, and lost her hat. They had been sent directly to bed, without any tea or supper, and Mama had grumbled for days.

Helena looked over her sister's letter again; she was arriving Tuesday next, so there wasn't much time to make plans. Not that they needed to work terribly hard to have fun in Paris, of course—all they required was a group of friends and enough francs to pay their way.

Amalia's visit would be just the distraction she needed. It had been more than a month since Sam had rejected her so comprehensively, and she hadn't seen or heard from him since. She'd wasted countless *petit bleu* forms on messages that went no farther than the wastepaper basket in her bedroom, her stilted invitations so cringingly worded that she very nearly felt sick when she read them over.

> *If you happen to be free and don't have anything else to do I should be so very happy if you could join me and my friends for dinner at Rosalie's.*

No; it was better to remain silent. If he wished to see her—if, as he said, he truly wished to remain friends—he would seek her out. She extracted a telegram form from a pigeonhole in her desk and wrote out a reply to her sister.

DEAR AMALIA STOP WONDERFUL NEWS STOP SO LOOKING FORWARD TO OUR DAY TOGETHER STOP MAKING PLANS FOR ENDLESS FUN STOP CANNOT WAIT TO SEE YOU STOP LOVE ELLIE

As for how they ought to spend their day . . . romps in the Luxembourg Gardens were out, not least because it was the middle of winter, but Amalia would probably wish to see Helena's studio and meet her friends from school. They would have dinner out, for Agnes was still in Antibes, and then they would go to a cabaret, or somewhere that played *le jazz hot,* and they would go dancing, too. She would invite the Murphys, and they would come into town for the evening, and it would be heavenly.

HELENA WAS AT the Gare du Nord to meet Amalia's train, having missed her watercolors class to collect her sister. She spotted her straightaway, so beautiful that she drew the attention of every man she passed, and so stylish that she might easily have passed for a Parisian born and bred.

Although she sincerely loved all three of her sisters, Helena was especially fond of Amalia, who had a rare sweetness to her nature, and an infectious sort of warmth that had a way of drawing others close. She was intelligent, too, and had been particularly good at mathematics; had she been born a decade later she might have aspired to a place at university.

Instead, she had married at eighteen and become the mother to three sons by the time she was twenty-five. With her husband, a baronet from deepest Derbyshire, she had a pleasant but distant relationship. Peter was about ten years older than Amalia, of middling height, very round about the middle, and had graying hair that was beating a slow retreat from his brow. He liked the sound of his own voice and at family dinners was much given to long-winded and ill-informed speeches about politics and world affairs. Though fundamentally a decent man he was also very dull, and she suspected that Amalia found him dull, too. Likely her sister knew as little of her husband's interior life as she did of her servants'. Not only did she and Peter have different interests, but they also lived different lives.

Amalia had always been the daring one among their sisters: she had been the first to bob her hair, wear rouge, and shorten her skirts. Yet it hadn't made a whit of difference to the way she lived, which was profoundly traditional. With little say in the upbringing of her sons, the youngest of whom had just been parceled off to boarding school at the age of eight, Amalia passed her days in shopping and visiting friends, overseeing the running of her homes, and engaging in some perfunctory charity work.

If Helena had married Edward, she would have had the same life.

The crowds on the platform parted, just for an instant, and she saw her sister, whose beautifully tailored coat and matching hat made her look like a fashion plate come to life.

"Amalia! Helloooo! Over here!" she called, waving her hand frantically. Amalia abandoned her sophisticated pose and ran pell-mell toward the platform barrier, brushing past it and the guard as if they were invisible, and when she reached Helena they hugged and even jumped up and down a little.

"Ellie, darling—you look wonderful. Simply *wonderful*. And your hair! It suits you so well at that length."

"Thank you. You're looking very well, too."

"Do you think so? This horrid winter has left me feeling quite wan. I'm absolutely desperate for some sun."

"Well, you'll get that soon enough. Where are the rest of your things?" Amalia had only a handbag with her, and as she'd never been one to travel light there had to be at least one steamer trunk nearby.

"The porter took them for me. He should be somewhere about—ah, there he is. Should we have them sent straight on to Aunt Agnes's?"

"Yes, that's best. Do you need anything from them? I was thinking we could go straight to Montparnasse now, so I might show you my studio and introduce you to my friends. They're very keen to meet you."

"And I them. I do so love reading about everyone in your letters."

"Vincent is in Antibes with Auntie A, so we don't have a car. I hope you don't mind taking a taxi."

Helena approached the porter and, after tipping him hand-somely, asked him to have Amalia's things sent on to her aunt's. She then steered her sister to the taxi rank outside the station. "We've a longish ride ahead of us, but it's interesting enough."

She asked the driver to take them to the avenue du Maine, nearly four miles distant, and in short order they were head-ing southwest along the rue La Fayette and, she realized, di-rectly past Sam's office.

It was the wrong time of day for him to be at work; at this hour he was likely still in his lodgings. It would be easy enough to send a *petit bleu* to the hotel. He would want to meet Amalia, she felt sure, and if he were to discover she had been visiting, and that he had been left out, it might hurt his feelings.

She composed the *petit bleu* in her head several times over before landing on just the right tone of friendly yet detached warmth. As soon as they got to the studio she would write it out.

> *Dear Sam—Short notice, I know, but Amalia is in Paris for the evening (en route to Biarritz) and we are going to Le Boeuf sur le Toit with the Murphys and Étienne. Arriving at nine-ish I think. You may well have to work but please join us if you are free. Regards, Helena.*

Looking out the taxi window, she realized they had crossed the Seine and were heading south on the boulevard Raspail. She leaned forward to direct the driver, and several minutes later the taxi had pulled up by the studio entrance on the rue du Maine.

She paid the fare and helped her sister out, and then led her beneath the wrought-iron archway and along the cobbled path to the building at the end. Up the stairs they went, and they had come at the best time of day, for the studio was flooded with sunshine and the paintings that crowded the walls were shining like stained glass windows, and it really did look like the sort of place where serious artists belonged.

Mathilde insisted they keep the studio in good order, so the space was clean and tidy and smelled only faintly of oil paints and turpentine. Each of them had a station set up by the bank of windows, with easels and small tables that Étienne had built from scraps of wood.

Running the length of the opposite wall was a narrow shelf with a lip at its edge, and on it rested more than a dozen of Helena's completed canvases, as well as her friends' work; hanging above, from wires strung from the crown molding, were bigger canvases, most of them belonging to Étienne.

"Here is some of my work," she said, suddenly nervous. "They're watercolors and pastels, in the main. I painted most of them in Antibes, although you can see—well, it's obvious, I suppose—that these ones are from Paris. I went to the markets one night, and these are . . ." She let her voice trail away. Better to allow her sister to look at the paintings in peace.

While Amalia looked over the paintings, Helena wrote out the *petit bleu* to Sam; fortunately she had a form tucked away in her handbag.

"I just need to post this," she told her sister. "I won't be a moment."

Helena ran out to the postbox on the corner, pushed her note to Sam through the special slot for pneumatic messages, and was back in the studio before Amalia had finished her inspection. When at last she turned to Helena, her eyes were bright with unshed tears.

"Oh, *Ellie*. I knew you had a talent for drawing, but I had no notion you were so accomplished."

"I've learned a great deal this year, of course."

"I can see that. These paintings, everything you've done here—they're wonderful. I'm so proud of you. And I rather wish I'd paid more attention when Miss Renfrew was trying to teach me drawing all those years ago!"

A clatter of boots on the stairs heralded the arrival of the studio's other tenants. Helena checked her watch and was surprised to see that it was past three o'clock already.

"Here come the troops," she joked, and then called down to her friends, "We're here!"

Étienne, Mathilde, and Daisy appeared at the door, with Louisette trailing behind as usual. Introductions were made, during which Étienne was at his most charming, and Amalia made a point of admiring the others' work with comments that were both intelligent and sincere—a rare combination, in Helena's experience.

"Daisy and I both need to go," said Mathilde after nearly an hour had passed. "I am needed at home, as is she. I am so very sorry that I cannot stay any longer."

"As am I," Daisy echoed. She and Mathilde shook hands with Amalia, said their farewells, and set off for their respective homes.

"Étienne, Amalia and I are going to Le Boeuf sur le Toit tonight. Would you like to come for dinner before?"

"Not tonight, alas. Shall I meet you there?"

"Yes—if we're late just look for the Murphys. They'll be there, too."

SARA, GERALD, AND Étienne had taken possession of a fine table at Le Boeuf sur le Toit when Helena and Amalia arrived, and had already finished their first round of cocktails. Of Sam there was no sign.

"So lovely to see you again," Sara said in greeting Amalia, for they, too, had become friends in the summer of 1914. "You haven't changed one bit."

It was impossible to look away from her sister, who was radiant in a bright red frock of beaded and draped silk chiffon, its short skirts only just grazing her kneecaps. It wasn't the sort of thing she usually wore at home, she'd confided to Helena, but with her husband and parents on the other side of the Channel she had decided to throw caution to the wind.

Helena was wearing her gold Vionnet frock, for it was too nice to leave languishing in her wardrobe, and in it she felt as pretty as she'd ever been. Not a patch on her sister's vivid beauty, of course, but well enough to sit next to her and not feel entirely out of place.

The others were drinking champagne cocktails, so she and Amalia ordered the same, and in no time at all she was staring at the bottom of her glass and wondering if it was too soon to order another. The cocktails were absolutely delicious, fizzy and light and not too sweet, and in short order she had gulped down a second one and was feeling quite enthusiastic about the evening and life in general.

"Who is the man playing the piano?" she asked Gerald, who always knew the answer to such things.

"It's Jean Wiéner. Can turn his hand to anything. Ragtime one minute and Bach the next."

"Is it just him onstage tonight?"

"No, but the cabaret acts won't come on until later. No one of note tonight, though they're usually quite—hey, look who's here!"

Gerald's attention was fixed on a point over her shoulder; she turned, and there was Sam.

"Hello, everyone. Sorry I'm late. I was out when Helena's *petit bleu* was delivered."

"I thought . . . I mean, I wasn't sure where to send it. I suppose I ought to have sent it to the paper."

"No matter. I'm here now."

"You are, and, ah . . . well, this is my sister, Lady Amalia Ossington. Amalia, this is my friend Sam Howard." When all else failed, her sense above all, she could at least fall back on good manners.

Introductions made, they shook hands and Sam took a seat on the opposite side of the table. When prompted by the waiter, he politely refused the offer of a champagne cocktail and instead asked for whiskey. "Any kind you have is fine."

He looked as if he had slept in his clothes, unfortunately, for his shirt was rumpled, his necktie was crooked, and his coat was pulled out of shape by the overflowing contents of its pockets. Helena could make a fair guess as to what they held: a notebook, pencils, a dog-eared *Plan de Paris,* his pocket knife, a handful of coins, and the remains of the sandwich he hadn't had time to finish at lunch. He needed to shave, for his chin was dusted with red-gold stubble, and there were dark circles under his eyes. Had she ever seen him so tired before? And yet he was so handsome that her heart fairly stopped at the sight of him.

It was impossible to keep up any kind of conversation, for the pianist had been replaced by a five-piece band playing American jazz. Feeling a little dizzy, Helena asked for a glass of soda water instead of another champagne cocktail, and when Sara went in search of the lavatory she and Amalia accompanied her as well.

It was cooler there, and far quieter, too, so they lingered awhile, powdering their noses and reminiscing about Sara's summer in Europe before the war. Presently Amalia tidied away her powder compact and rouge and fixed Helena with a long, assessing stare.

"I'd no idea that Mr. Howard would be so attractive," she said. "You never said a thing in your letters."

"I, ah . . . I didn't think . . ." Helena stammered.

"Who are his people? Apart from being Americans, that is."

"Didn't Helena say?" Sara answered. "His father is Andrew Clement Howard the Third. The steel baron. We may not have an aristocracy in the States, but if we did Sam's family would belong to it. I mean, they aren't *old* money—I think the fortune only goes back a century or so—but along the way they married into the old guard. Sam is as blue-blooded as an American can get."

It was a good thing Helena was sitting down; otherwise she'd have found herself on the floor. How had she not known something so important about him? And what did it mean that he had never told her the truth?

"Helena—what's wrong?" Sara asked. "Don't tell me you didn't know."

"I didn't. He never said a thing. Did you know?"

"Yes, but only because we know his parents. Perhaps he simply assumed that you knew."

"Of course I didn't. He never talked about his life in

America. And when he did, it was ordinary stories. The food you eat at Thanksgiving, how he misses going to baseball games—that sort of thing."

"Don't be too upset with him," Sara advised. "After all, nearly everyone here has some kind of story. Even you. Has anyone ever questioned your decision to live as Miss Parr and not as Lady Helena?"

"No, but it's just so surprising. If his family is that wealthy, why does he live like a church mouse?"

"Because he lives on his salary from the paper," Sara answered. "He hasn't accepted anything from his family for years."

Helena felt dizzy, as if she'd just imbibed an entire pitcher full of champagne cocktails, and her heart was pounding with something that felt very much like fear. Sam had seemed so different, so free of all the smothering constraints and expectations that had shaped so much of her life, and to discover that he, too, was part of that world was almost more than she could bear.

It would have been so easy for him to tell her the truth. The night they'd been caught in the rain, for instance, she had asked about his family, and he'd said he didn't wish to talk about his life in America. He had told her nothing—yet she, like a fool, had gone ahead and blithely emptied her heart and soul into his hands. She had told him *everything,* and he had responded with prevarication, half-truths, and silence.

A comforting hand touched her shoulder. "The men will be waiting for us," Amalia said. "Do you want to go home? Or are you fine to go back to the table?"

"We should go back to the table. I'll be fine," she fibbed, not wanting her sister to worry.

"Good for you," said Sara. "And remember that Sam hasn't changed. He's the same man he's always been."

"I know. It's simply a great deal to take in. That's all."

She stood, her legs a little shaky, and Amalia rushed over to embrace her. "Save your thinking for later. Now is the time for cocktails and jazz music and dancing."

Back at the table, Helena pushed aside her soda water and gulped down two champagne cocktails in quick succession. They proved very efficacious at redirecting her attention, and so when Sam got up to leave not a half hour later, explaining that he had to return to his office, she managed to say good night without drawing any undue attention to herself.

The rest of the evening passed in a blur. Étienne suggested they move on to a dance hall in Pigalle, which prompted Sara and Gerald to say a reluctant good night. "We've a long drive home to St.-Cloud tonight, and neither of us is an enthusiastic dancer," Sara explained. "It was so lovely to see you again, Amalia."

The dance hall was perfect: just seedy enough to feel exciting rather than dangerous, and so crowded that it didn't matter at all if one knew the steps to the dances being played at a blistering pace by its band. Étienne bought them a round of absinthe, which Helena was fairly certain had been illegal for some time, and she drank down her glassful as speedily as she dared. It tasted almost exactly like the licorice sweets she'd loved as a child, though less sweet, and if she hadn't been wary of its alleged hallucinogenic effects she'd have had another.

She and Étienne and Amalia danced without stopping for hours, and only when the band took a break at two o'clock in the morning did her sister plead exhaustion. "You and Étienne have class tomorrow, and I've a long train journey ahead of me."

Amalia was right, of course, though it had been heaven to listen to the music and dance and let every last one of her cares melt away. Étienne found them a taxi, threatened the driver with dire consequences if they didn't reach home safely, and kissed both of them, though chastely, before disappearing into the night.

They were home by three in the morning, and though Helena wanted nothing more than to flop into bed she took the time to change into a nightgown and hang up her Vionnet gown properly. She was rubbing cold cream into her face when her sister knocked at the door.

"Would you mind if I came in and slept here?" Amalia asked.

"I'd love it if you did."

And so they curled up alongside one another in Helena's big bed, and Amalia talked about her little boys, and Helena talked about her friends and her work, and presently they fell into an easy, gentle silence, both of them close to sleep.

"Are you happy?" Helena asked softly.

It was a while before Amalia answered. "I am. And yet . . . I'm not as happy as I might have been. I chose Peter because he was a good man. A safe, sensible choice for me. I am very fond of him, and of course I adore our boys. But I'm rather lonely at times.

"If I'd had a daughter," she went on, "it might be easier, I think. With boys, they leave so soon for school, and when they do come home, they aren't little anymore. They don't need me anymore. And the days are . . . they're rather hard to fill. I do envy you. So busy with your work, and your friends are so interesting. I did like them very much."

"Oh, Mellie," Helena sighed, using her sister's pet name. "I don't know what to say."

"Don't fret on my account. It's just the champagne talking." Amalia wiped her eyes with the cuff of her nightgown and smiled brightly at her sister. "Now, tell me more about Étienne. I knew who he was from your letters, but I had no idea he would be so handsome. Have you ever considered . . . ?"

"No, ah . . . no, I haven't." For a moment she considered trying to explain to her sister that Étienne was a homosexual, but she was too tired, and she wasn't entirely sure how she would react, besides.

"I see," Amalia said decisively. "It's Mr. Howard you're stuck on."

"Mellie! Whatever gave you that idea? He and I are friends, no more. And he isn't interested in me. Not in that way, at least."

"Allow me to disagree. He didn't take his eyes off you all night."

"Don't exaggerate. We really are only friends. And now that I know the truth about his family, and the way they live . . ."

"Yes?"

"I don't think I can go back to that sort of life. The life that Mama expects me to have—"

"The life I have," her sister whispered.

"Yes. Forgive me for saying so, but I don't think I can live in that world. I thought I did, once, but now . . . now I want more. I want something *else*. And if it means I never marry, then so be it."

"So be it," Amalia echoed sleepily.

"Good night, Mellie. I love you."

"Love you, too."

Amalia fell asleep in seconds, but Helena lay awake, her thoughts churning over the enigma that was Sam. How could she have been so wrong about him? It was clear, now, that she had imagined much of their closeness. She had been honest with him, as true friends must be, while he had remained apart and unknowable.

And those kisses they had shared? They had made a fool of her, for they had led her to conjure up a romance out of thin air. To imagine love where there was only a sort of tepid fondness.

She would miss him, of course, but those silly feelings would soon fade. Her heart was bruised, but it wasn't broken. And that was something, wasn't it? It was cold comfort to know such a thing, lying awake in the long and lonely hours before dawn, but it was all she had. It would have to be enough.

Chapter 23

With the vernissage for the Salon des Indépendants fast approaching, Helena threw herself into the creation of paintings for the exhibition. Maître Czerny would only choose one, but as he had so far disliked her every effort she had no real notion of what would please him best.

So far she had completed three works that she hoped would pass muster: a landscape in pastels of lavender growing over an old wall, which she had begun the day she first met Sam; a pen-and-ink drawing of a man who sold newspapers by the Pont Louis-Philippe; and the portrait in oils of the farmer's wife she'd seen at Les Halles.

She liked all three well enough; they were competently executed and perfectly decorative. But they lacked life, just as Maître Czerny had often complained of Daisy's work, and likely would say of hers if he ever bothered to take a closer look. They were inert, the sort of objects that were pretty and even rather interesting but not the slightest bit compelling.

One afternoon, a fortnight after her sister's visit, she arrived at the studio with Étienne and Mathilde; Daisy hadn't come to class that day, for her father had been ill and she was needed at home. Helena went to her easel, which was empty, and realized—why on earth hadn't it occurred to her before?—that she had nothing to do, for she had finished the last of her paintings the day before.

She opened her sketchbook, looking for some preliminary drawings to work up, and the only one that interested her was a spare, penciled vignette of the Train Bleu at the Gare de Lyon, at the moment when passengers were boarding for their journey south. So long ago that she had drawn it; so long, and yet it might have been yesterday.

"Mathilde? Étienne? Would you mind having a look at this?"

She flattened the sketchbook upon her table and stood back so her friends might see.

"I drew it last spring. It was my first day in France. I was on the Train Bleu and we'd stopped at the Gare de Lyon to take on more passengers. And I was thinking . . ."

"Yes?" Étienne prompted.

"I was thinking I might attempt a larger work, say a meter wide, with the train itself as the backdrop and the passengers in the foreground. Everyone would be moving, all rushing to board the train and say their farewells. At first glance it would look like one of those posters you see at train stations and on the Métro. The sort with an illustration of some exotic locale, and a slogan like 'Winter Is Pleasanter on the Côte d'Azur.' That sort of thing. But there would be more to it, for the longer you looked the more you would see."

"I like this idea of yours," said Mathilde. "I like it very much."

"But I paint so slowly. It would take me forever to finish. And we've only a month and a half until the Salon des Indépendants."

"Then paint faster," Étienne ordered. "You must begin now, before the muse abandons you. Don't bother with sketches—start with charcoal, on the canvas itself. Look at your drawing once more, and then shut it away. Your memories are all you need."

"I don't have anything large enough. My largest canvas is half that size."

"I have one that might do," he said, and he went to the corner of the studio where a half-dozen oversized canvases were leaning against the wall. Rummaging through them, he pulled the largest from the stack. "Here," he said. "Use this one."

"But you stretched those canvases yourself. You spent hours on them," Helena protested.

"And I am honored to know one will be used in a masterpiece by Helena Parr."

Adjusting her easel so the canvas was balanced securely, he picked up a stalk of vine charcoal and handed it to her. "Begin," he said, and then he and Mathilde silently returned to their easels.

Helena cleared her mind of everything but the memory of that moment in Paris, at the Gare de Lyon, still so clear in her mind's eye that it might have been yesterday. She drew and drew, and only when Étienne approached and gently touched her arm did she realize that night had fallen and hours had passed.

"That's all for today," he insisted. "We'll go to dinner now, and then I'll walk you home."

Standing back from the easel, she assessed the outlines she'd sketched on the canvas. Even at this early stage, she could tell that she was creating something original and new, something that was truly her own creation and not a pastiche of someone else's ideas and techniques. If she'd had the strength, she'd have continued to work through the night, but Étienne was right: food and rest now, and back to her easel as soon as the sun was up.

FOR EVERY MOMENT of soaring delight, however, there was a lowering counterpoint. It came the following week, near the end of her life painting class with Maître Czerny. The model had been a young woman, her skin rosy and clear, her face as wise and serene as an Old Master Madonna. Helena had been inspired to draw her face and hands alone, a pair of studies rather than a conventional portrait, and had done so using only charcoal and chalk.

The maître had spent the class prowling from easel to easel, but she had failed to attract his notice for most of the session. Only at the very end did he realize what she had done, and then his ire burst forth.

"Are you deaf, Mademoiselle Parr? Or are you a dullard? I asked for a compositional study. *Compositional.* You were meant to depict the model's entire form—but perhaps you thought you knew better than I. Is that it? Are you the master here?"

"I beg your pardon. I misheard you. I didn't intend to cause any offense."

"But you do offend me. Your tedious work offends me, as does your timid approach. You are tentative when you ought to be bold. You are—"

"Oh, do leave off!" she snapped, her anger overruling her sense. "I made a simple mistake, that is all. I misheard your instructions, and for that I apologize. But your behavior is indefensible, utterly so, and I am sick to death of it."

No one moved, no one breathed, and as she stood by her

easel, shocked beyond words by her outburst, the only sound she could discern was the thunderous beat of her pounding heart. She swallowed, felt a tide of sickness rise in her throat, but managed, somehow, to force it back.

Before Maître Czerny could respond, before he could begin to shout at her, she frantically began to gather her things, certain he would demand that she leave. What had she been thinking? It was nearly the end of the course; to fail now, to fall when the end was in—

"What are you doing? Did I tell you to leave?"

"No, but . . ."

"You aren't crawling away now, are you? Not after you have finally showed me you have a spine. Or would the Americans among you call it 'guts'?"

"So you aren't . . . ?"

"No. Put down your bag, Mademoiselle Parr, and try to pay attention from now on."

"Yes, Maître Czerny."

"Let this be a lesson to all of you," he announced to the class. "I roar, I growl, I hiss—but I do not bite. Learn how to stand your ground; otherwise the critics will make a meal of you. Understood? Yes? Then that is all for today."

Helena, Étienne, and Mathilde went straight to the studio after class, not even stopping to buy bread and cheese for lunch. Helena's hands were shaking so badly that she wasn't sure she'd be able to hold a brush, so Étienne unearthed a bottle of brandy he'd tucked away for emergency purposes and persuaded her to swallow several fiery mouthfuls. It did make her feel a little steadier, and she was thinking that she might be able to work on her Train Bleu canvas after all, when Daisy burst through the door.

"Where have you been?" Helena asked. "We haven't seen you for days."

It was evident from the expression on Daisy's face that something dreadful had happened. Mathilde led her to the settee and they gathered around her protectively. "What is the matter? Why are you so pale? Étienne—fetch her a brandy."

"Thank you," Daisy said, trying to smile. "I suppose I ought to explain." She took a deep breath, as if to settle her nerves. "My father died the day before yesterday." Before they could respond, she rushed on. "He'd been ill with a cold for weeks, but then it settled into his lungs, and he got pneumonia, and that was . . ."

Daisy's eyes welled up with tears, but she brushed them away impatiently with the back of her hands.

"I am so very, very sorry to hear it. We all are," Helena said.

"He was very agitated at the end. He kept asking me to forgive him, to please forgive him, but I thought he was talking about the way he'd kept such a close watch over me.

"He died at dawn, and it had been days since I'd slept, so I went to bed for a few hours. And then I woke, and I knew I had to make some decisions. Daddy hadn't ever talked about where he wanted to be buried, or what he wanted for his funeral, and I thought it might be recorded in his will, or somewhere else in his papers. So I went into his office, and I searched through his files, and I found . . ."

She paused and, accepting the brandy that Mathilde offered her, took a large sip, coughed delicately, and handed back the glass.

"Did you find what you needed?" Étienne prompted.

"I did. He wanted to be buried at home, in America, next to Mother, although he didn't say anything about a funeral, so I've no idea what to do about that."

"Perhaps one of his friends at the hospital?" Helena ventured.

Daisy shook her head. "It's not . . . there's more. I found something else. Something *awful*."

Étienne grasped her hand. "Go on, *ma belle*."

"One of the drawers in his desk was stuck, and I pulled at it, and it came flying out and tipped onto the floor. And inside it was . . . was . . ."

They waited for Daisy to find a way to describe what she had found, and as they did so Helena couldn't stop her imagination from running wild. Demands from creditors? Evidence of a mistress? Risqué photographs?

"Inside was a letter," Daisy said at last, her voice shaking. "It was from the man I loved, and for so long I'd thought him lost, but he wasn't, and all this time . . ."

She began to cry, wrenching, tormented sobs, and Étienne gathered her close, whispering soft, encouraging endearments into her ear until she was able to speak again.

"I met him in 1918, right at the end of the war. We didn't know one another for very long, but I loved him. I did. He was sent back to America, and we weren't able to say good-bye, and I tried to find him. I even asked Daddy for help, but he said it was no use. That it was better to forget. And I believed him. Why did I believe him?"

"Are you speaking of Daniel?" Helena asked, recalling their conversation about Daisy's time at the Studio for Portrait Masks.

"Yes. Daniel Mancuso."

"How did his letter come to be hidden in your father's desk?" Étienne asked gently.

"It wasn't for me. Daniel had heard I was sick with the flu, and came by the house to ask after me. Daddy told him I was dead, and Daniel sent a letter of condolence. That's what I found. I don't know . . . I mean, I don't understand why my father didn't simply destroy it."

Daisy reached for the brandy and took another fortifying sip. "I know I ought to be sad, and grieving for my father, but I'm so angry right now. How could he do such a thing? He didn't even know Daniel."

"What will you do now?" Mathilde asked.

"I have to take my father home. He wanted to be buried next to my mother. I guess I owe him that much. After that . . . I'm not sure."

"Do you know how to find him? Your Daniel?" Étienne ventured hesitantly.

"I know he was an engineer before the war, and that he grew up on the Lower East Side in New York. I suppose I'll start there." She wiped her eyes decisively and took a deep breath. "I'm leaving in two days. I'll worry about the house and everything in it later."

"Is there anything we can do to help?" Helena asked, her heart aching for her friend.

"Listening to me, just now. That was enough."

"Where is Louisette?" Étienne asked. They hadn't noticed before, but for the first time since they'd met Daisy, she was alone.

"Gone. Sacked. But I'm not heartless," she said. "I gave her a reference, and enough money to live on for a while."

"You were perfectly justified," Helena assured her.

"I couldn't bear the sight of her. I couldn't. She was always so unfeeling. So cold. I thought of asking her why, but in the end I didn't. It wouldn't have changed anything."

"What of your paintings?" Mathilde asked.

"Do you think you could take care of them? At least until I've a better idea of what will happen."

"Of course we will."

"I need to go. I'll write as soon as I arrive."

"You must write," Helena insisted. "We shall all be holding our breath until we hear from you."

Daisy hugged them, one by one, and stood back to take a last look at the studio.

"Au revoir, mes amis."

Chapter 24

28 March 1925

Dearest Mama,

Thank you for your letter, and for the recent photograph of you and Papa. I think it is the first one I've seen of him in which he's smiling. Usually he looks rather fierce, as if he is only just restraining himself from shouting at the photographer or complaining that the room is too hot and someone needs to open a window.

I do apologize for not writing as often as I did in the autumn. You mustn't fret—I assure you that I am happy, and healthy, and still enjoying my stay here in Paris. If I haven't written it's only because I am so terribly busy. I am still attending classes during the week, and then, in the evenings and on Saturdays, I spend every spare moment at the studio I share with my friends from school. We are all working frantically to finish off our paintings for the Salon des Indépendants—the exhibition at the end of April I mentioned in my last letter—although Mathilde and Étienne are rather farther along than I.

I really must get back to work on my painting—it's a large canvas *depicting the Blue Train to Antibes, with everything in it looking as it ought to do (I am sure Papa will find this reassuring), without even a hint of abstraction or any puzzling motifs. I am feeling tremendously pleased with it and have high hopes that it will be received well by visitors to the exhibition. Once it is finished I shall take a photograph so you can see what it looks like, and I'll describe all the colors, too, as they are such an important part of the piece.*

I do hope you and Papa are well, and enjoying the spring weather.

With much love from your devoted daughter,
Helena

Another chore accomplished, and done well in spite of everything. It was an assortment of half-truths and outright lies, for she was the farthest thing from happy. She hadn't seen or spoken to Sam in weeks; she was worried to death about Daisy; and she was anything but confident about her work.

It was Saturday evening, the end of another long day in the studio, and she had dashed off the letter to her mother while Étienne washed his brushes and swept the studio floor. Mathilde had gone home early, leaving just the two of them to continue on to dinner at Rosalie's.

"A good day?" Étienne asked as they strolled along the boulevard du Montparnasse.

"I suppose. Every time I stand in front of the canvas, though, I feel there's more I need to add. More I need to say, if that makes any sense."

"It does."

"Which of your paintings will you submit to Maître Czerny?" she asked, weary of fretting about her own work.

"I'm not certain, not yet."

She thought of the paintings he'd finished, hanging on the back wall of the salon, all of them superb; any one might become the talk of that year's Salon des Indépendants. "What about the—"

"It is tiresome of me to persist in asking," he interrupted, "but I cannot help myself. In my mind I can see it, see *you*, so clearly."

"See . . . ?"

"Your portrait."

Not again. He had asked her a half-dozen times at least, and she had always been very firm in her refusal. "Étienne, you know how I feel."

"I do, but I cannot help how *I* feel."

"Is there no one else you wish to paint? We could find you a model. The young woman from our life class the other week— she was lovely."

"She was, but she didn't inspire me as you do. Why do you refuse me, Hélène?"

"I told you already—I don't like being the center of attention. I never have."

At some point in the last few minutes they had stopped walking and stood facing one another as passersby brushed past them impatiently. The silence between them grew and grew, so tangible she could nearly taste it.

And then it came to her. This was her year to live, but yet again she was allowing fear to rule her. Did she truly care what strangers thought of her? No. Would it help a dear and cherished friend if she were to say yes? It would.

"I've changed my mind," she told him. "I'll sit for you."

They began late on Monday afternoon. The sun had already begun to set, so Étienne turned up the lanterns until they hissed and sparked, bathing the entire studio in warm, enveloping light.

Étienne had set the least battered of their chairs a few feet away from the little coal stove; the light was soft and kind, and she felt less exposed, there in the corner of the studio, than she'd have done in the middle of the room or next to the windows. Not certain of what pose he wished her to adopt, she sat up straight and folded her hands in her lap.

She was wearing her golden Vionnet gown, as Étienne had asked her to do; not only was it the loveliest of all her frocks, but it was also the most comfortable. Her feet were bare, also at his direction; she had done nothing to her hair, she wore no jewelry, and her face was entirely bare of cosmetics.

Helena perched on the uncomfortable chair, the tips of her toes just touching the floor, and without moving her head she allowed her gaze to drift over the studio, the paintings on the walls, the calm and studied movements of her friend, and she thought of all that she had done, and all that had happened to her, in the space of a year.

Last spring, she had promised her parents she would return to London, but so much had changed since then. *She* had changed. And she wasn't certain, now, that she could ever go back.

SHE SAT FOR Étienne three more times that week. He didn't show her his preliminary sketches, nor the painting as he worked on it, and she didn't ask. The composition was on a grand scale, larger than life-size, and while she was curious to see what he had created she was also a trifle apprehensive.

After Helena had finished posing for Étienne, he worked steadily on the portrait for another week, and only then was he ready to share it with her and Mathilde. He made a great ceremony of the moment, insisting that they close their eyes until he had arranged the canvas on an easel and unveiled it properly.

At last the command came. "Open your eyes," he called out.

Helena had thought she would know what to expect. She had assumed the painting would be of a woman, dressed in gold, seated on a chair. The painting did depict one woman; but it also, astonishingly, encompassed two portraits.

An invisible line ran vertically through the middle of the canvas, and while the left half of the woman was depicted in a neoclassical and entirely realist manner, her right half was an entirely abstract exercise in Cubist forms and shapes. It was at once a technical tour de force and an exposition of the strengths and limitations of two vastly different schools of expression.

"Well? What do you think?" Étienne looked so nervous, so uncertain. Did he truly not see the brilliance of his creation?

"With this painting, you will set this world on fire," she said, willing him to believe. "It will be the talk of the Salon."

"Mathilde?" he asked.

"I agree with Helena. This painting will change everything for you. It is *magnifique*."

He smiled shyly, then shrugged, affecting a nonchalance that Helena was sure he didn't feel. "Nothing is certain until Czerny agrees to submit it to the Salon. Until then, all we can do is hope. And drink champagne."

"But it's only three in the afternoon," Helena protested.

"You English and your rules. In Paris, dear girl, it's *never* too early for champagne."

Chapter 25

"You look awful, *ma belle*. Have you eaten anything this morning?" Etienne asked.

Helena shook her head. It was nine o'clock in the morning, she had been awake for at least five hours, and her insides were as hollow as a drum. But hungry was better than nauseous, and if she'd tried to eat even a scrap of breakfast she would have been sick to her stomach.

Any minute now, Maître Czerny would enter the academy's *grand salon*, and he would begin to select the paintings for submission to the Salon des Indépendants. All her work, everything she had done over the past year—it had all led to this moment. Before the hour was out, the maître would see *Le train bleu*, would pass judgment on it, and she would know, once and for all, if she was an artist.

Etienne had already set *La femme dorée* on his easel, and their fellow students had gathered around, shaking his hand and congratulating him, a few looking to Helena as they recognized her features from the painting. It was past time that she removed her own canvas from its fabric wrapping and set it on her easel, but she couldn't bring herself to reveal it to the rest of the class. It would look so amateurish next to Étienne's masterpiece. It would look wrong.

"Good morning," came the maître's booming voice from the doorway.

"What are you doing?" Étienne whispered frantically. "Put *Le train bleu* on your easel. He's about to begin."

She nodded. Swallowed back the tide of fear that threatened to choke her.

Crouching down, she drew out the canvas she sought, unwrapped it carefully, and then she set her portrait of the farmer's wife upon the easel.

"Hélène, *no*. What are you thinking? Change it while you—"

"*Eh bien*, Monsieur Moreau. I knew you would not disappoint me." The maître stood between her and Étienne, and he was smiling, something he did so rarely that it looked quite wrong on his face. "How have you titled this work?"

"*La femme dorée.*"

"It is exceptional. Painted in haste, I see, but that adds a certain charm. A boldness that I like very much."

"Thank you, Maître Czerny."

"On to Mademoiselle Parr. The subject of *La femme dorée*, I believe?"

"Yes, maître," she answered.

"He has immortalized you," he said, his eyes flickering over the painting on her easel. "What do you call this?"

"I, ah . . . *Femme de fermier*, maître."

"Very well. If that is all you can manage. A sentimental pasiche, but I suppose it will look well enough in some bourgeois sitting room. Ah—Monsieur Goodwin. What do you have for me?"

She stood there and waited for her pulse to slow and the

tightness in her chest to loosen, and when she could breathe again she turned and tried to smile at Étienne.

"Why?" her friend asked, and he sounded nearly as heart-broken as she felt.

"Not now," she whispered. Pleaded.

"I will go to him. I will explain there has been a mistake."

"No. No, it's fine. I wasn't ready, that's all."

He reached out and grasped her near hand. "*Courage*. One day you will show *Le train bleu* to the world, and the world will take notice. Of this I am certain."

ALTHOUGH HELENA WANTED nothing more than to hide away and lick her wounds in peace, there was no time, for she and Mathilde still hadn't finished their costumes for the ball everyone was attending that Saturday night. And there was no question of not going, for Auntie A and the Murphys and nearly everyone else in her circle of friends would expect to see her there. Everyone apart from Sam, of course. She had no idea if he was going, though it seemed unlikely. Sam wasn't the sort of man who would feel at home in an outlandish costume.

As she and Mathilde hadn't felt inclined to spend much on outfits they would only wear once, they'd gone in search of inexpensive frocks that might be easily transformed. The sale racks at Printemps had yielded a pair of sleeveless shifts in an inky blue artificial silk, and with only a little effort over the course of several days they had turned the plain garments into quite inventive costumes.

The theme of the ball was "Soleil et Lune," and with that in mind Mathilde decorated her frock with starbursts of sewn-on silver and gold sequins, since she planned to remove them and use the garment for Sunday best thereafter. Helena, who could afford to be a little more cavalier with her clothing, painted hers to resemble Van Gogh's *The Starry Night*. Though the cheap fabric of her frock had gone a little stiff and scratchy once the paint had dried, the overall effect was very striking.

It was a little lonely getting ready on her own, but Mathilde and Étienne had balked at the expense of a restaurant meal that cost more than two francs, the going rate for dinner at Rosalie's, and had said they would meet her at the ball around ten o'clock. Instead, she and Auntie A were dining with the Murphys, who never passed on the chance to attend a costume ball.

So Helena borrowed her aunt's gramophone and listened to Bessie Smith as she made up her face, put on her frock, buttoned up her new dancing shoes, and decorated her chin-length hair with diamanté hairpins. By the time she was ready to join her aunt downstairs, her mood was more buoyant than it had been for weeks.

Although it had been Agnes's idea to go to the ball, her aunt had refused to wear an actual costume. Instead she had unearthed a gunmetal-gray ball gown from before the war, which looked marvelous on her, and draped enough jewels about her person to make Cartier himself weak at the knees. In her hair was a towering diamond tiara in the Russian style, a wedding gift from Dimitri, and about her neck she'd hung ropes of baroque pearls, cabochon sapphires, and diamonds, some of the jewels as big as a gooseberry. Her wrists were covered with stacks of bracelets, too, and she'd pinned an enormous stomacher-style brooch to her bodice.

"You'll be the belle of the ball," Helena told her aunt, "but aren't you worried about thieves?"

"Not in the least. My real jewels are in the safe at my London bank—these are paste. Not inexpensive, mind you, but nothing like as valuable as the real thing. Shall we be on our way?"

The Murphys were staying the night at their pied-à-terre on the quai des Grands Augustins, only yards away from the restaurant where Helena had spent that dreadful evening with Jean-François d'Albret in January. Fortunately both Sara and Gerald had suggested another restaurant for dinner, one across the river on the avenue des Champs-Élysées, and Helena had been spared the ordeal of a second visit to Lapérouse.

The exterior of Fouquet's was that of a perfectly ordinary Right Bank café, its masses of tables and chairs crowding the pavement outside. It would be a pleasant place to pass an hour or so, not least because of its excellent view of the Arc de Triomphe only a quarter mile away.

Inside, the restaurant was true to its Belle Époque origins, with starched white tablecloths, polished brass fittings, chairs upholstered in oxblood-red leather, and waiters who looked to have been working there since the dawn of the Third Republic. The Murphys had already arrived and were seated at a large, round table in the center of the dining room.

Cheeks were kissed, they took their seats, and Helena belatedly realized that her friends were dressed in a perfectly conventional fashion. But Sara, always observant, reached across the table and patted her hand reassuringly.

"Gerald designed our costumes, and as you can imagine they're a little too outré to wear to dinner. We'll dash home and change after dinner."

"Are we expecting anyone else?" she asked, noticing there were two empty places at the table.

"We, ah . . . we ran into the Fitzgeralds earlier today," Sara explained. "And they asked if they might come to dinner."

"It's already half past eight," Gerald said. "Let's not wait for them. Waiter? We're ready to order."

Helena had a difficult time choosing from the menu, for reading through the list of first and second courses and *plats principaux* was enough to set her stomach growling. After dithering for several minutes she finally settled on terrine de campagne to start, with turbot in béarnaise sauce to follow and coq au vin for her main course.

As their various choices for a first course were being served, a commotion started on the street outside and quickly moved to the foyer of the restaurant.

"That must be Scott and Zelda," Gerald said, not even looking up from his foie gras.

"It is," Agnes said. "Making a grand entrance. As usual."

Mr. Fitzgerald was arguing loudly with the restaurant's maître d'hôte. It was hard to make out what they were saying, as his half of the discussion was conducted in very bad French, but it seemed to have something to do with his automobile, the unacceptable location in which it had been left, and his unwillingness to have it moved.

By the time Mr. Fitzgerald had come to some sort of agreement with the beleaguered host, Helena was quite prepared to discount him as an insufferable boor, the sort of person one crossed the street to avoid. Her poor first impression was only bolstered by the unease she saw in everyone else's expression, Sara's most of all.

"I had *so* hoped . . ." whispered her friend.

"I know, my darling. Don't fret. I'm sure they'll behave," Gerald reassured her.

As the Fitzgeralds approached, Helena couldn't help but stare, for there was something about them that simply invited such attention. They were a good deal younger than the Murphys and radiated a confident sort of glamour that put her in mind of film stars. It was as if they expected to be admired, to be watched, and rather than shrink away from the limelight as she would do, they actually relished every moment.

"I'm ever so sorry we're late," Mr. Fitzgerald announced once he and his wife had reached the table, kissed cheeks with Sara, said hello to Gerald, and been introduced to Helena and Agnes. "You know how it is."

"Scott wrote like a madman today," said Mrs. Fitzgerald. "He sat himself down at the dining room table and didn't get up for *hours*. I spent the whole day tiptoeing around like a little old mouse." Finding this amusing, she began to laugh, and it was such a merry, infectious sound that Helena, and everyone else, began to laugh as well.

Mrs. Fitzgerald was young, no more than twenty-three or twenty-four, and had a round, sweet face, dark and expressive eyes, and a small mouth that she'd painted into a fashionable cupid's bow. She wasn't beautiful, not really, but there was something indelible about her, as if once seen she could never be unseen, and she fizzed with an energy that felt nearly kinetic in its intensity.

She also had a most unusual accent, her words all smoothly honeyed vowels. But it was charming, just as Zelda Fitzgerald herself was charming, and Helena found that she quite liked the woman. Mr. Fitzgerald, however, was more of a puzzle. He was older than his wife, perhaps in his early thirties, and was slight and fair with beautiful gray-green eyes. Yet there was an indistinct air to his expression, as if the better part of his thoughts were focused elsewhere, and his gaze never seemed to truly focus on her or anyone else at the table.

Gerald had ordered several bottles of fine Burgundy for the table, but to his evident consternation Mr. Fitzgerald ignored the wine, instead demanding round after round of American-style cocktails. It was rather shocking to Helena, accustomed as she was to a single aperitif before dinner and then one glass of wine, two at most, with her dinner. It certainly didn't seem to make him happier or more content with the company he kept. Like a child presented with a bowl of boiled sweets, he seemed interested only in the here and now, the delight of consumption, and was unconcerned by—or perhaps accustomed to—the inevitable aftereffects.

Talk at the table was strained, though Agnes and the Murphys did their best to carry things along. Discussion turned first to Mr. Fitzgerald's work, for his third novel had just been published.

"Scott's first two books were grand successes," Sara explained to Helena and Agnes. "We're all quite certain *The Great Gatsby* will be, too."

At this Mrs. Fitzgerald giggled, or perhaps it was only a hiccup. "Everything Scott touches turns to gold. Doesn't it, honey?" She drained the last of her cocktail and set the empty glass on the table. Her pretty face was shiny with perspiration, and she had begun to handle her cutlery and the stem of her cocktail glass with exaggerated care.

Mr. Fitzgerald's face reddened, but Sara spoke before he could answer. "How is your Scottie liking Paris? You would love the child, Helena. Such a dear little thing. Not even four and she knows her entire alphabet forwards and backwards. She's even learning to speak French."

"I hate Nanny," Mrs. Fitzgerald said, her expression grim. "And she hates me, too—I know it. I hardly see Scottie anymore.

Whenever I pop into the nursery, that woman tells me they're busy with lessons, or playtime, or mealtime, or naptime."

"Now, come on, Zelda," Mr. Fitzgerald said. "You know we agreed that a settled routine is best for Scottie."

"Yes, and where does that leave me?"

"If you ever thought of anyone apart from yourself, for one single second of the day, you'd admit that Nanny is right. The world doesn't revolve around you—"

"So says the great man of letters. The saving grace of American literature."

"Now, Zelda," Sara interjected, "you haven't told us what you're wearing to the ball. Have you something fun planned?"

"We're not going," Mr. Fitzgerald answered, his voice sharpening to a sneer. "Zelda's too *tired*."

"It's too late to change our minds. We'd be the only ones there without costumes," Mrs. Fitzgerald said evenly, her eyes fixed on a point at the far side of the restaurant.

"Gerald and Sara don't have costumes," he countered.

"We're actually planning on changing. Just so you know," Sara said mildly.

"And we've been out every night this week already. Can't we just have a quiet evening at home?" Mrs. Fitzgerald asked, her voice beginning to quaver. "Just the two of us?"

Mr. Fitzgerald glared at his wife, the air between them fairly simmering, before he stood up so abruptly that his chair tipped over. "I'm going for a walk."

"I had better go," Mrs. Fitzgerald said, and she hurriedly kissed Sara goodnight before rushing after her husband. Together, nearly embracing, they gingerly negotiated the distance between the table and restaurant entrance, and as they vanished from sight Mrs. Fitzgerald began to cry.

"Well," Sara said presently. "I do apologize. Poor Zelda has been feeling a little lonely, what with Scott being so preoccupied with the new book, and Nanny being so zealous in her care of the child."

"They weren't at their best tonight," Gerald agreed.

"When are they *ever* at their best?" Agnes said abruptly. "This is the third time I've met them, and it's always the same. He ends up sodden with drink, she's miserable because of it, and the evening ends in tears. So undignified."

"Agnes is right," said Gerald. "I like them—how can you not like them?—but they do have a way of wearing you down."

"I know," said Sara, "but they're so young, and—"

"Remember how they woke us all up, even the children, in St.-Cloud last spring? That's what I mean."

Sara sighed, remembering. "We scarcely knew them—I think we'd met them once or twice before, but that was all. And then one night—"

"One *morning*," Gerald corrected.

"One morning, it must have been three o'clock at least, there they were, in our garden, tossing pebbles at the bedroom windows and shouting at us to come down, come let them in. Come get dressed and go out with them. And something about their being booked to sail on the *Lusitania*? So silly. Of course it woke the children, and all the servants, and then the dogs started barking . . ."

"I've known people like that before," Agnes said, her expression suddenly grave. "Always their own worst enemies."

"Who, Auntie A?"

"Dimitri's relations. And look what happened to them. First against the wall when the revolution came."

As DINNER CAME to an end, the Fitzgeralds still hadn't reappeared, and Gerald declared himself tired of waiting.

"We're off home to change. We'll see you there."

It was a short ride to the Théâtre de la Cigale in Pigalle, where the ball was being held. Neither of them spoke much on the fifteen-minute journey, and Helena could only suppose that her aunt was, like her, feeling a little exhausted by the Fitzgeralds' carryings-on at dinner. It had been a strange, somewhat fractured evening so far, and she could only hope it improved once they arrived at the theater.

Helena hadn't thought to ask Agnes who was hosting the ball—it wasn't the Comte de Beaumont, who was known for the extravagance of his parties, and it wasn't any of the other artistic or literary luminaries in her aunt's circle. She didn't recognize anyone in the crowd that was milling about the entrance, and compared to Agnes's usual set of friends it seemed rather a young crowd.

Very likely it was a student ball, then, for that would explain the incredibly risqué costumes on many of the guests. One young woman who passed by, shivering, was naked apart from a layer of gold paint and a few strategically placed feathers.

Without quite meaning to, Helena found herself separated from her aunt, but there weren't so many guests that she'd never be able to find her again. Instead she wandered around the theater, which had been cleared of seats for the occasion, and discovered Étienne and Mathilde in a matter of minutes. Étienne was dressed as the Sun King, Louis Quatorze, and looked terribly handsome in his golden suit and powdered wig.

"Where on earth did you get that costume?"

"I've a friend who's a dresser at the Opéra. Isn't it perfect?"

"It is. I especially like the—"

The compliment died on her lips, for just then, at the very periphery of her vision, she caught sight of a flash of auburn hair. She turned her head, and her heart stuttered in recognition.

It was Sam, wearing his ordinary clothes, without even a mask or funny hat to offer the appearance of fitting in. Sam, standing with strangers, one of them a young and fashionably dressed woman. She was laughing at something he'd said, her hand clutching at his jacket sleeve, and though her eyes were hidden by a silly little mask Helena could tell the girl was gazing up at him adoringly.

Of course it was no business of hers that he was here. There was no reason, even, for their paths to cross. He had his friends, and she had hers. She would not allow herself to be jealous of the woman who stood at his side and touched his arm in such a familiar, knowing way.

"Will you dance with me?" she asked Étienne, and he took her by the hand and led her to the front of the theater. Onstage, a band was playing American jazz music, and though the rhythm was infectious the dance itself was unfamiliar to her.

"It's the Charleston!" Étienne shouted in her ear. "I'll show you what to do!"

He took her left hand in his and set his left hand at her back, and then he showed her how to step back and forth, then kick from side to side, then pull away so their arms were outstretched and there was room enough for diagonal kicks between them. All this was accomplished lightly and speedily, with turns at each rotation, and in no time at all she had mastered the basic steps and was dancing as gaily as anyone else there.

They danced for ages, song after song after song, stopping only when the band announced they were taking a break. Mathilde had gone off with someone she knew from the École des Beaux-Arts, so Helena was alone, waiting for Étienne to return with some drinks, when Sam came over and sat next to her.

"Hello," she said, and offered a careful smile. "I hadn't realized you were coming. I wouldn't have thought you'd be interested."

"I'm not, to be honest. I got strong-armed into it by a friend at work. His wife's younger sister is visiting, so they asked me to keep her company."

"Ah," Helena said. "Are you having a good time?" Of course she didn't really care, but it was polite to ask.

"Not really. She's a nice enough girl but dull as . . . well, you know. Dull as a twenty-two-year-old from the Midwest, I guess you could say."

She thought, but was too well-bred to say, that such a girl was exactly what he deserved. A dull, dutiful, and obedient girl who would never ask him questions or push at him or expect anything more than dinner and a chaste kiss at the door.

"I miss you," he said. "I feel as if we never see one another anymore."

She wouldn't look up. Couldn't, else risk him seeing, and understanding, everything. So she inspected the flaking paint on her frock and then, once she could be certain her voice was steady, she answered. "I've been busy with school. Preparing my work for the Salon des Indépendants."

"When is it?"

"The vernissage is next Saturday," she said evenly.

She waited for him to say he would be there, or that he

should have liked to be there but was busy with work or some other obligation, but he remained silent.

Étienne reappeared just then, fortunately with a tall glass of seltzer for her, and he and Sam shook hands and greeted one another warmly. She gulped nearly all of it down, then, feeling much restored, resolved that she would dance some more.

"Étienne and I are off to dance again," she announced.

"And I had better get back to my friends." With this he bent his head, kissed her cheek quickly, and disappeared into the crowd.

She spent the rest of the evening dancing with Étienne's friends, with men she knew from the academy, and even with a few strangers. Every time she looked over their shoulders, her eyes searching the room, she found Sam, and his gaze was invariably fixed on her.

She danced and danced, and then, not long after midnight, the instep strap broke on her left shoe. Étienne and Mathilde were set on staying, so she wished them good night and went in search of her aunt. She found Agnes sitting with the Murphys, who were dressed as South American deities; Gerald told her the names, which contained an alarming number of consonants, and which she promptly forgot.

"Would you mind if we went home?" she asked Agnes. "The strap on my shoe is broken, and I'm feeling quite tired."

"Of course we can go. Did you say good night to Sam? I saw you talking with him earlier."

"No . . . he was busy with his friends."

As they departed, she couldn't help but look over her shoulder one last time. He was watching her, just as he'd done all evening, but rather than wave good-bye she turned her back and followed Agnes into the night.

Chapter 26

Later, when the ordeal of the opening reception was done and she could think clearly again, she'd feel badly about the lie she was about to tell her aunt. But not today.

"Étienne is feeling nervous about the vernissage," she announced as she and Agnes were finishing their lunch. "I told him I'd go over with him a little early. Do you mind?"

"Not at all. What time do you want me there?"

"The invitations say six o'clock, but no one is ever on time for these things. Any time after that is fine."

"You and Étienne will take a taxi? Promise?"

"I promise."

They would do nothing of the sort, for Étienne was God only knew where, and she was going to make the journey on the Métro, contrary to her aunt's wishes. If the Salon des Indépendants weren't being held at such a distance from the city center she'd have happily walked, or even taken a taxi. Most years it took place at the Grand Palais, but this spring it was being held at the Palais de Bois, a good three and a half miles distant.

On any other day, she'd have been happy to make the journey

with Agnes, but her aunt was so transparently delighted by Helena's inclusion in the Salon that she all but burst into applause every time their paths crossed. It didn't matter that the Salon was a nonjuried exhibition that anyone might enter; simply the fact that Helena's painting would be seen alongside the works of established artists was enough to delight Agnes's generous heart.

The afternoon crept by in glacial fashion, with little for Helena to do beyond fret and pace. At four o'clock she began to get ready, and by half past four she was ready to depart.

As she said good-bye to Agnes and walked north across the Pont Louis-Philippe, Helena found herself wishing that she had planned to meet up with Étienne or Mathilde, for they would understand and likely be just as nervous, too. It was too late for a change of plans, however, for she'd no idea where either friend was that afternoon. There was nothing for it but to get on the Métro and see for herself where her painting had ended up.

Helena had never been on the Paris underground trains, but as a frequent tram rider she had a good idea of what was expected. The station entrance was only a few minutes' walk away, its distinctive Art Nouveau canopy and sign quite impossible to miss. She sprung for a first-class ticket, which was ten centimes dearer than a second-class fare, and descended to the westbound platform.

The Metro didn't seem terribly different from the Underground back home, which she'd used often; her parents hadn't minded, just as long as she'd had a footman or maid with her. Nearly every wall was tiled in white, which helped to brighten the dimly lit halls and corridors, and scores of eye-catching advertising posters lined both sides of the platform.

She didn't have long to wait for a train, and though it was near the end of the workday and the second-class carriages were becoming crowded, there were plenty of empty seats in the first-class carriage she boarded. It was odd to sit by a window and see only darkness beyond, and if she were bothered by enclosed spaces it might have been disturbing; as it was, the relative quiet and solitude of her journey was exactly what she needed.

Porte Maillot was at the end of the line, at the border between Paris proper and Neuilly-sur-Seine, and the station was all but empty as she climbed the stairs to the exit. Blinking a little in the late afternoon sun, she looked around, trying to find her bearings, and then descended again to the ticket hall to ask for directions to the Palais de Bois.

Fortunately it wasn't far, just a short walk across the edge of the Bois de Boulogne, and as the afternoon was warm and sunny this final part of her journey helped to further steady her nerves.

She'd been furnished with one ticket by virtue of her membership in the Société des Artistes Indépendants, the only prerequisite for inclusion in the Salon, and this she handed to a waiting attendant in return for the exhibition catalog.

Pausing just inside the entrance, she searched through the catalog for her name, an easy enough task given that artists were listed alphabetically by surname. She found it on page 242.

Parr (Helena), née à Londres (Angleterre)—
  Anglaise—51, quai de Bourbon, 4e.
2602—Femme de fermier—600 fr.

It was far from her best work, and she knew it, but it was too late to change her mind. At least Maître Czerny had deemed one of her paintings good enough for inclusion in the Salon, and she could now say she'd had her work displayed at an exhibition in Paris. That was something, after all.

The one other time she'd seen her name in print had been the announcement of her engagement in the *Times* more than a decade before. It was strange and wonderful to read her name, her true artist's identity and not the triple-barreled dynastic surname she'd always thought rather pretentious, and below it to see the title of a painting that she had created—and even a price. Six hundred francs was a great deal of money for a work by a totally unknown artist, but perhaps someone, apart from Aunt Agnes, might like the portrait enough to buy it.

She edged a little farther into the exhibition hall, rather surprised at how modest it was compared to the luxuriously decorated Grand Palais, where the Salon had been held the year before. The building had the air of something temporary, and while she was uncertain of its history it felt rather like a remnant of a past exposition or world's fair.

Approaching an interior wall, she was surprised to discover that it consisted of nothing more than a wooden frame covered in burlap. The light was wonderful, however, with many clerestory windows and skylights, and the paintings had been arranged sensitively, with a reasonable amount of space between the canvases.

It came as no surprise when, upon entering the first large room of the exhibition, she found her own face staring back at her. Étienne's portrait of *La femme dorée* had been given a wall of its own, and as it was by far the largest canvas in the room, and arguably the most striking, it was attracting a great deal of attention.

She came a little closer, but rather than push to the front, to stand by her friend, she hovered at the edge of the crowd, a little nervous that someone would recognize her as Étienne's model. But no one made the connection, much to her relief, not even when Étienne beckoned her to his side.

He had never looked more handsome, or more happy, and she prayed that tonight would be the moment when her friend received the acclaim he was due. A glass of champagne in his hand, a half-wilted gardenia in his buttonhole, he embraced her dramatically and managed to spill most of his drink down the front of her frock.

"*Désolé, ma belle*—but it is champagne, and champagne never leaves a stain."

"I'm so proud of you. Just look at the admirers. People are standing ten deep to catch a glimpse of the extraordinary portrait by Étienne Moreau."

"I disagree—it is you they have come to see. The most beautiful woman at this exhibition. Have you found your painting yet?" he asked.

"No. This is as far as I've got."

"Me, too. Do you want me to come with you?"

"Of course not. You stay here and enjoy your success. I'll look for Mathilde's, too."

"Come back as soon as you've found it. Promise?"

"I promise. Though it might take a while." She flipped to the back of the catalog and held it open for his inspection. "There are more than thirty-five hundred paintings on display here. Wish me luck!"

She found Mathilde's a quarter hour later, and to her relief it had been hung at eye level on a wall that was well lighted; her friend would be pleased. The painting, of children playing in a garden, was attracting some favorable attention, though nothing like the same level of excitement as Étienne's.

Finally, after the longest twenty minutes of her life, Helena ran her painting to ground. It had been hung high on the wall in one of the final rooms of the Salon, in a dark corner with very little light, and in the time she spent hovering at the room's entrance not one person took a second look or even seemed to notice it.

It was silly to stay, not when there were so many other works to see and admire, so she forced herself to turn around and leave the farmer's wife behind. It came as a great relief when, only two rooms along, she found the Murphys, standing among a small crowd of admirers who had come to see Gerald's latest painting. It was the one of clockworks that he'd begun in Antibes the summer before, and was so enormous that it took up an entire wall.

"Helena! Look, Gerald—Helena is here."

"Wonderful! We were looking for your painting, but no luck yet. Have you come across it?"

"Yes. It's back that way, the second room on. It's rather hidden, though. Luck of the draw, I suppose."

"You should be very proud all the same," Sara said loyally.

"Thank you. And congratulations, Gerald—I should have said so right away. I love the painting."

"Thank you. We'll see you later, won't we? At the party?"

"Of course. I suppose I had better try to find my aunt. Until later, then."

Not in any particular rush, she wandered back through the exhibition hall, trying to absorb what she saw, although the sheer volume of work made it difficult to take everything in. Helena was standing in front of a small canvas, a still life that combined pointillist techniques with Cubist perspectives, when she heard the familiar accent of Maître Czerny.

She looked around, mentally preparing herself for a brief conversation with her teacher, but he was nowhere in sight. Perhaps she had been mistaken. But then he spoke again, and it really was his voice, only it was coming from the other side of the wall. A wall that was made of air and stretched burlap.

He was speaking in English, with a man who had a vaguely Australian accent, and they were commiserating with one another over the general laziness and ineptitude of art students. It was nothing she hadn't already heard a hundred times. And then—

"Of course this year's crop of students was the worst yet. Nearly all of them hopeless—apart from Étienne Moreau. Did you see his work when you came in? Striking, very striking."

"One out of how many?"

"Thirty to begin with, then a dozen or so by the end. I have to watch myself—can't scare off all of them."

"Understood, my dear Fabritius."

"The monied and hopeless are there to support the poor and talented—we know it, even if they don't."

"As it has always been. One in a thousand, if that, has the talent to make a life of it. And yet we persevere."

"If it hadn't been for Moreau I'd have gone mad, I tell you. Impossible to manage, like the best ones, but I think he'll go far."

"And his fellow students?"

"I've forgotten their names already."

They walked away, laughing gaily over Maître Czerny's last remark, and she simply stood and stared at the odd little still life before her until all she could see were meaningless, form-less dots, and still the words turned and turned in her head.

Monied and hopeless. One in a thousand. Forgotten their names already.

It was far too hot inside. She would faint if she stayed where she was. So she walked to the nearest exit, skirting the main rooms, praying to escape before anyone she knew found her.

She burst through the first door she came across, gulping in great breaths of cooling air, and when she felt a little steadier she walked to a nearby bench and sat down.

All along, she had been wrong. When she had believed she was progressing, improving, she had been wrong. When she had thought she might, possibly, have some small amount of talent, she had been wrong.

When her friends had told her that her work was good, they had been wrong. They had been lying to her, out of kindness no doubt, but still—it had all been a lie.

And the year she had begged for? The year in Paris she'd been so certain would transform her life? It had been a twelve-month of delusions, nothing more.

"There you are."

She didn't look up, couldn't look up. Not him.

Not Sam, not now.

"Why are you here?" she asked dully.

"Why am I here? How can you ask such a thing? I'm here because of you."

"Oh," she said. "Thank you."

"Something's the matter. Did something happen in there?"

"Nothing happened," she lied, and tried to remember what it felt like to smile. It was impossible, so she conjured up an approximation and pasted it to her face before turning to face him. "It was too warm inside."

"I saw your painting. I'm proud of you."

"Thank you."

"We've all been looking for you—it's nearly time to go to the Murphys'."

"What time is it?"

"It's just gone eight o'clock."

She had been sitting on the bench for an hour and a half. The sun had nearly set, and she hadn't noticed.

He led her inside, where she endured the embraces and compliments of her aunt and friends, and then they were in the car and on the way to the Murphys' flat, and Sam would not leave off watching her, his concern impossible to ignore.

She would not speak of it with him, or with anyone else. She had made a fool of herself, but it wasn't a killing blow. It wasn't the sort of thing a person could die from, not unless they were very silly and self-involved.

Tomorrow she would figure out what she was meant to do—but tonight she would set it all aside, all of the heartache and disappointment, and she would be happy for her friends. For a few hours she would be happy, and then, in the morning, she would begin again.

Chapter 27

The Murphys' pied-à-terre occupied the top two floors of an ancient building at the corner of the quai des Grands Augustins and rue Gît-le-Coeur. Although the staircase and corridors of the building were shabby in the extreme, Sara and Gerald's apartment was a marvel of modern décor. Its floors were painted a glossy black and its walls a bright white, and the only touch of color in the sitting room came from red brocade curtains that hung at the floor-to-ceiling windows and framed a marvelous view of the Seine and the Sainte Chapelle. Unusual flower arrangements further brightened the rooms—one was nothing more than stalks of celery, their leafy tops intact—and on top of the grand piano was an enormous metal sphere that most guests took to be a piece of sculpture but was, Sara confided, actually an industrial ball bearing. Altogether it wasn't Helena's idea of homey comfort, but it was the perfect venue for a cocktail party.

It had been hours since she'd eaten, but rather than help herself to any of the food in the dining room she went straight to Gerald and ordered up one of his near-lethal cocktails. Its effects were gratifyingly numbing, and after following it with three glasses of champagne Helena decided that she was quite happy with the world and her place in it after all.

For a while she hovered at Agnes's elbow, not trying to insert herself in any of the conversations that ebbed and flowed around her, and then, suddenly, her head was pounding and she'd had enough. One of the sitting room windows was open, so she stood before it and gulped in deep breaths of night air, clearing her lungs of the fug of cigarette smoke and too-strong perfume.

Someone came to stand behind her, and without turning she knew it was Sam.

"Ellie. Something's wrong. Don't say there isn't."

"It's nothing. I made the mistake of drinking one of Gerald's cocktails on an empty stomach. That's all."

"You aren't happy, not even close to it, but you should be. Just look at what you've achieved."

This angered her so much that she whirled around to face him, but her head started to spin and she had to clutch at his shirtfront to steady herself. "I learned today that I was wrong," she said when her vision finally cleared. "I was wrong to think I had a future as an artist."

"What happened?" he asked, his expression a curious mixture of anger and disbelief.

"I overheard Maître Czerny talking to someone, I don't know who. He didn't use my name but he was talking about me. He said I was monied and hopeless and I was there only to support the students who are poor and talented. He said he'd forgotten my name already."

"That *bastard*. I could kill him."

"But he was right. I've always had a feeling I wasn't good enough. That I was fooling myself to think I had any real talent. And now I know for certain . . . oh, *Sam*. What will I do now?"

Her eyes filled with tears, too many to blink away, and when she tried to hide her face he held her fast and wiped them dry with his thumbs.

"Sorry. I never seem to have a handkerchief. Right—this is what we're going to do. You're not having fun, and I don't think you should have anything more to drink. I'll walk you home and we'll talk, and everything will be all right. Sit here while I get your coat and tell Sara and Agnes where we're going."

Seconds later he was back at her side, guiding her downstairs and across the bridge and past the cathedral. He kept her close by, his arm supporting her, making sure she didn't stumble on the cobbles, and when Vincent opened the door Sam did all the talking.

"Good evening, Vincent. Lady Helena isn't feeling well, so I brought her home early. Could you have a pot of tea and some plain toast brought to her room, please? I'll take her up now."

"Mr. Howard, I hope you understand that—"

"On my honor, Vincent, I swear you have nothing to worry about. I would never do anything that might upset Lady Helena or her aunt."

Suitably mollified, Vincent went off to sort out Helena's tea and toast while Sam steered her in the direction of the stairs. When she stumbled at the first step he simply lifted her in his arms and, cradling her close, walked up the steep staircase with no apparent difficulty.

"Is your room here on the second floor?"

It was hard to talk, for she was so very tired, but she had to correct him. "This is the first floor. Silly American."

"Fine," he said, and kissed her hair. "If you say so. Which one of these doors is your room?"

"Far end . . . left side."

The door was ajar, so he shouldered it open and carried her across the room to her bed. He set her down and then, stooping a little, tucked a strand of hair behind her ear. His touch, whisper-soft, was the nicest thing she had ever felt.

"I had better go, otherwise Vincent is going to have a heart attack."

"Don't. Not yet."

She struggled to her knees, set her hands on his shoulders, and kissed him before he could stop her. At first he didn't respond, his mouth refusing to soften under hers, so she wrapped her arms around his neck, as she'd once seen Theda Bara do in a movie, and, opening her mouth just a little, let her tongue dart out to touch at his lips.

This had the effect of melting his reserve, and he pulled her close and kissed her so fiercely that she felt certain he had changed his mind and did desire her after all. But it only lasted a few seconds before he pulled away, gently but firmly, unwound her arms from around his neck, and took her hands in his.

"Ellie, no. You're in no fit state—"

She clutched at his arms, trying to draw him into an embrace, but Sam evaded her grasp and took another step back.

"I said no. You're not—"

"But I love it when you kiss me. I would seduce you if I knew how . . ."

"Are you trying to kill me? Listen—you're upset, you're three sheets to the wind, and Vincent has probably got his ear to the door right now. And we both know he wouldn't think twice about chopping me into little pieces if he thought it might please your aunt."

This struck Helena as one of the funniest things she had

ever heard, and it was some time before she was able to stop giggling and catch her breath. She started to talk, but her tongue suddenly felt swollen, and her mouth wouldn't behave, and on top of everything else she discovered she had a frightful case of the hiccups.

"Si—*hic*—silly man. Was Auntie A—*hic*—who gave me th' idea. She said we should be lo—*hic*—lovers. So she won' care."

Sam was shaking his head, but she knew she had to explain, had to make him understand. "Auntie A says I'm in love with you."

"Are you?"

"I don' know. Never fell in love be—*hic*—before. Would be silly to love you."

"Why, Ellie? Why would it be silly? Because I—"

"Because you're jus' like Edward. You're Edward in an Amer—*hic*—American suit. Thas' wha' you are, an' it makes me *sad*. So, so sad . . ."

She looked up at him, and of course he was so tall she had to tilt her head right back, and everything around her started to spin and shift. Her stomach turned over once, twice, and her throat seemed to close up—and then, before she could warn Sam or turn away, she vomited all over his front, and it went on forever, and in that instant she really, truly, wished she could die and never have to look him in the eye again.

He didn't turn away, which was very surprising, but instead stayed where he was and rubbed her back, even as she was throwing up all over his shoes. He said, "oh, honey," once or twice, and when it was over and she had stopped that awful empty retching, he fetched a towel from her washstand so she might wipe her face.

Even after the maid had arrived he only went as far as the

hall, and when she and her room were clean, and she had been dressed in a fresh nightgown and dosed with bicarbonate, he came in again to say good night. He had changed into a clean shirt and trousers, though neither fit him very well.

"Vincent lent me some of his clothes," Sam explained. "Do you feel any better?"

"A little," she whispered.

"I'll be back tomorrow, and we'll talk then. Try to get some sleep." He kissed her forehead, and then he was gone.

THE NEXT DAY found Helena feeling thoroughly wretched in both body and spirit. She woke at dawn, her head aching so badly that the slightest movement pained her, and immediately resolved that she would never, ever, *ever* let a sip of alcohol pass her lips again.

She staggered to her washstand, the distance between it and her bed stretching near to infinity, and met the sorry gaze of her reflection in the mirror above. She had never looked worse. Her face was smeared with rouge and mascara, her eyes were red and swollen, and her hair stood on end and smelled horribly of smoke.

Somehow she stayed upright long enough to wash her face and brush her teeth, which made her feel fractionally less disgusting. Back at her bedside, she swallowed two tablets of aspirin and, thoroughly exhausted, burrowed under her eiderdown and shut her eyes against the coming day.

If only she could shut her mind to the memories of her mortifying behavior. Sam had been so understanding, and she had rewarded his kindness by acting in the most shameless fashion—and then, when he had declined her pathetic overtures, she had vomited all over him.

That was all she could think about, her mind's eye replaying it again and again, and even once she fell asleep again the memory of those moments haunted her, chasing her through galleries of paintings by other artists, talented artists, and whenever she stopped to look for her own work Maître Czerny would spring up like a crazed Guignol puppet, shouting, "Useless! Hopeless!" and no matter where she searched, she couldn't find her Sam, for he had left her, too, and would never return . . .

"Helena? Helena, darling, it's Auntie A. May I come in? Helena?"

How long had her aunt been knocking? She sat up, untangled the sheets from around her legs, and rubbed the sleep from her still-swollen eyes. "Come in," she called.

"There you are. Oh, heavens—Sam wasn't exaggerating. Are you feeling better?"

"Not really. What time is it?"

"Nearly two in the afternoon. I thought it best to let you sleep. Sam is downstairs."

"He's what—he's *here*? Why is he here?"

"I expect to see how you're feeling. The poor man looks very tired, so you mustn't keep him waiting. Should I ask him to come up?"

"No, I'll come downstairs. I just need a few minutes to dress."

Once out of bed, she had to admit she felt a little steadier, and her head had ceased pounding quite so relentlessly. She dressed hurriedly, in an old frock that had seen better days, and, after brushing her teeth again and smoothing her hair, gingerly made her way downstairs.

Sam was in the *petit salon,* sitting on a ridiculous little fauteuil that was far too fragile for his large frame, and for some reason he was wearing his best shirt and coat, the ones he reserved for important interviews at the Élysée Palace. To her relief, his smile was wide and genuine, and when he greeted her it was with a heart-stopping kiss on her mouth, not her cheek.

"How are you?" he asked, guiding her to a nearby chair.

"Better. I felt like death warmed over this morning, but I went back to bed and that helped. Sam—I'm so sorry for last night. Please forgive me."

"There's nothing to forgive. You were right to be upset, given what you overheard at the Salon. And you'd had a long day, with hardly anything to eat. No wonder the drink went to your head."

She smiled ruefully. "I'm fairly certain I will never drink another drop of champagne or spirits again, not as long as I live."

"Are you still upset?" he asked.

"By what happened at the Salon? Yes. Of course I am."

"Surely you can see that Czerny was wrong," Sam reasoned. "He didn't say your name. He might well have been speaking of someone else."

"No," she insisted. "He was talking about me, and he was right. Just look at Étienne's work. That's the standard I need to judge myself against, and the truth is that I don't even come close."

"Oh, Ellie—"

"It really is the truth. I need to face it."

He looked unconvinced, but rather than press the issue he simply asked, "What are you going to do now?"

"I'm not sure. I think . . . I think I might like to travel. Go somewhere with Auntie A. Put all of this behind me."

"'All of this'?" he echoed. "What about your friends here? The life you've built for yourself?"

"I only ever planned on staying for a year. And I might return, one day. I haven't really thought about it yet. All I know is that I need to make a change."

"So that's it. You're just going to give up. One man criticizes you—the same man who has never given you the time of day, because he's an idiot—and you fall apart." Sam's voice was shaking, and when she steeled herself to meet his gaze she was taken aback to realize just how angry he was.

"But Czerny was right," she insisted. "I've known it all along, but I couldn't admit it. I was wrong to think I had enough talent to succeed as an artist."

"You aren't wrong. You *are* talented—anyone can see that. Your paintings are beautiful."

"So? Nearly anyone can produce a pretty picture. And that's all I'm capable of. Pretty, decorative pictures. A hundred years from now Étienne's work will be hanging on the walls of museums, but mine will be forgotten. I know that now."

"So that's your response? You falter once and decide you're done? I thought more of you. I thought you of all people would have the courage to persevere." His voice grew rougher, sharper. "But I guess all your talk of learning how to live was just that. *Talk*."

"Wait a moment—you're criticizing *me*? You say you dream of becoming a proper journalist, but you've been working the rewrite desk for years now, even though you're a better writer than all of your colleagues put together. Ten years from now, you'll still be sitting in that miserable office, deciphering cables and writing piffle about film stars, because you're scared to believe anything else might even be *possible*."

He took a deep breath, as if to steady himself after a blow. "You've no idea what I've been facing," he replied, his voice rising.

"If I've no idea, it's because you never told me. I've a pretty good idea, though, and it begins with Howard Steel."

He said nothing at first, the silence stretching thin and pale between them, and when he did speak his voice was eerily calm. "Who told you?"

"Sara. She assumed I knew. Apparently it's an open secret here in Paris. Can you imagine how foolish I felt?"

"I'm sorry, Ellie. If it's any consolation, that's why I came here today. I mean, I wanted to make sure you were feeling better, but I also knew it was time to tell you about my family. To let you know that I'm returning to America."

It wasn't possible—it couldn't be possible. She must have misunderstood.

"I beg your pardon . . . I don't think I—"

"I'm leaving Paris," he said. "I sail home to New York at the end of next week."

"Why? Why would you do such a thing?"

"My father isn't well, and he's asked me to come home. He needs me. My family needs me."

"And just like that you give everything up—leave everything behind?"

"It's something I've been thinking about for a while now," he muttered, his shoulders hunched like an old man's. "I've been wanting to tell you, but I . . ."

"Well, you didn't. Instead you let me waffle on about my family and Edward and the pressure I felt to live my life a certain way, but you were going through the same thing, too. Why didn't you just *say* something?"

"I wanted to. I did. But I was worried that it would come

to this, to my having to go home and leave you behind, and I couldn't even bear to think about it. It would have hurt to leave Paris, but to leave you . . ."

"Is that why you pushed me away? Said we could never be more than friends?"

"Yes. You'd spent years being treated like an afterthought by your fiancé and everyone else around you. I guess it seemed kinder to keep you at arm's length. Besides, we were only just getting to know one another. I didn't want to presume you cared for me."

"I did," she admitted, desolation gripping her like a vise. "I still do."

"Then why have you been so distant? For months you've been avoiding me, and when our paths do cross you barely give me the time of day."

"I didn't think you would notice. I didn't know you cared."

"Well, I did notice, and I do care. I care when you ignore me, and I care when you compare me to the man who nearly ruined your life. Is that what I am to you? Nothing more than Edward in an American suit?"

"No. No, of course not. I didn't mean that you were anything like him. Only that you both belong to the same world, with the same sort of impossible expectations and ironclad rules and people with their hearts and minds buried in the last century."

"So? I don't live in that world. I left it long ago."

"You did, but now you're going back. You're the heir to Howard Steel."

"It won't change me, Ellie. I won't let it."

"I'm sure you'll try, but how can you escape something that surrounds you? It's not as if you can leave work at the end of the day and go home to a shabby little garret. This life you have, here in Paris—it's *over*. Can't you see?"

"It's not forever. It's only until—"

"Until when? You inherit Howard Steel outright?"

"What else would you have me do? Stay here and let my father die at his desk?"

"Of course not. That's the thing, Sam—I agree with you. I honestly do."

He stared at her incredulously, disbelief etched across his features. "Then why are you so angry with me? I'm not going to change. I didn't before, and I won't now."

"I believe you."

"Then come with me. Come to America and make a new start."

It tempted her beyond reason, and it would have been the easiest thing in the world to say yes. If Sam were still the ordinary newspaperman she had fallen in love with, she'd have gone without a second thought. But he wasn't an ordinary man, and nothing could change that inescapable truth.

"No," she finally said. "I'm sorry—you'll never know how sorry I am—but my answer must be no."

Silence descended, dark and oppressive, broken only by the relentless ticking of a clock on the mantel.

"That's it?" he asked, despair shading his voice. "I leave and you stay?"

She nodded, not trusting herself to speak.

"Then I had better go." Crossing the space between them in two long strides, he bent low to kiss her quickly, fervently, his mouth hard upon hers. "Good-bye, Ellie."

Though she wanted very badly to run after him and take back everything she had said, she forced herself to remain where she was, dying by degrees, as he left the room and walked out the front door.

Pain bloomed in her chest, in the spot where her heart was meant to be, and it was so fierce and paralyzing that she could only breathe in short, shallow bursts. One day she would wake up, and the memories of this day would be gone, and she would think of her year in Paris, and Sam, without her heart stuttering almost to a stop.

One day she might think of him, and the look on his face just now, and she would not hate herself for it.

One day.

Chapter 28

The next day, Helena stayed in bed so long she gave herself a headache. It was nearly noon when Agnes came into her bedroom, yanked open all the draperies, and stood, looking quite fierce, at the end of the bed.

"It's high time you got out of bed and stopped feeling sorry for yourself," she announced. "I've asked the maids to run you a bath—do wash your hair, my dear, and give yourself a good scrub—and when you're done, come down to the *petit salon*."

"I don't feel at all well."

"Nonsense. There's nothing wrong with you that a hot bath, a good meal, and a long walk in the sunshine can't cure. Out of bed, now—and if you aren't downstairs by noon I shall come back and fetch you. Understood?"

Agnes rarely assumed the mantle of grand duchess, but when she did there was no defying her. Helena knew very well that her aunt would drag her downstairs by the ear if need be.

"Yes, Auntie A."

The bath did help her feel a little better, and then, when she went to find her aunt in the *petit salon*, she was given egg and cress sandwiches and a cup of hot tea, and only as she was finishing did her aunt begin the second part of her lecture.

"I never thought I would say this, but I'm disappointed in you."

Helena promptly spilled tea all down her front. "How can you say such a thing? You know what happened at the vernissage."

Agnes hadn't asked what had happened between her and Sam, but she must have suspected. Helena badly wanted to confide in her aunt, but to speak of their quarrel aloud meant that she'd have to think about the look on his face when he'd left. About how much she'd lost when he had walked away.

"I wonder if you recall the letter you wrote, last year, when you asked if you might come and stay with me. You told me that you had been at the point of death, and only then had you realized how much you wanted to live. Do you remember?"

"I do."

"Well, my dear, you've done a fine job of living this past year. I've kept my counsel and stayed out of your way, but I cannot stay silent now. You know how I can't abide self-pity, yet here you are, nearly drowning in it. That's why you are coming with me to London, to Rose's wedding—no, don't look at me like that. We leave on Wednesday morning, which gives you plenty of time to visit your friends and set their minds at rest. Poor Étienne was beside himself when he came by yesterday afternoon."

"Oh, *no*. I can't stand the thought of his worrying."

"Then go see him now. And sort things out with Sam, too. I was in the front hall yesterday when he left. Whatever you said, it cut him to the quick."

She shut her eyes against the memory of Sam's desolate expression when he had said good-bye, and focused on her aunt's advice. Agnes was right. Continuing to wallow in self-pity wouldn't help, and it wouldn't repair her friendship with Sam, or suddenly propel her to the heights of fame and fortune as an artist. She couldn't go back, she couldn't stay where she was, so she might as well move forward.

"I suppose I should pack."

"First you should visit your friends. As for packing, you only need enough for a week. Leave everything else here, and we'll sort it out after. You may wish to stay here with me, or go somewhere else. Either way I will only be happy if *you* are happy."

"Oh, Auntie A. What would have become of me without you?"

"You'd have managed perfectly well, and we both know it. Now, off you go to your friends. I'll have Vincent drive you—no, don't shake your head. I insist on it."

SHE ENTERED THE studio with a bright smile on her face and a bottle of champagne under her arm. She would apologize, assure her friends she was well, and together they would open the champagne and drink to future success. And then, if she could gather up enough courage, she would visit Sam and try to make things right between them before he left for America.

She paused at the door, suddenly apprehensive, but Étienne simply smiled and opened his arms to her. He held her tight as she cried and cried, and once she'd settled a bit Mathilde took her hand and led her to the ratty old settee, and she sat between her friends and told them everything, from the moment she had found her painting tucked away in a dark corner, to Czerny's bruising words, to her drunken departure from the party and its mortifying aftermath.

"We must have arrived at the Murphys' just after you left," Mathilde said. "Your aunt told us you hadn't been feeling well."

"An illness of my own making, I'm afraid. I'm so sorry I didn't come down to see you yesterday. I hope I didn't worry you too badly."

"Not at all, *ma chère*," Étienne assured her.

"Did you sell the portrait?"

"I did, and what is more—the Galérie Bellamy has asked to represent me, and they are holding a solo exhibition of my work in the autumn."

"Oh, Étienne! That is wonderful news!" She threw her arms around his neck and hugged him soundly.

"Enough, enough," he protested. "Mathilde—tell Hélène your news before she chokes me."

"Did your painting sell as well?"

"It did," Mathilde said, blushing faintly. "And the buyer has commissioned portraits of his wife and children."

"I *am* pleased. Both of you have done so well! We must open the champagne, but first I need your advice, and possibly your help. Now that the exhibition has begun, is there any way I can remove the painting that Czerny chose and hang *Le train bleu* instead? Am I allowed to replace one painting with another?"

"If it were a juried exhibition it wouldn't be allowed," Étienne reasoned, "but there are no prizes to be handed out, so you wouldn't be cheating, or depriving someone else of their space at the Salon. What do you think, Mathilde?"

"As long as we are discreet, and bring it in quietly, I doubt we'll have any trouble. If we do, we can say the frame needed to be reinforced, or something like that."

"Do we have enough time?" Helena wondered.

"More than enough," he answered. "The Salon is open late this evening, though we should try to get there soon, before the evening crowds arrive."

In the end, the only difficult part of the procedure was fitting the painting, well wrapped in a clean dropcloth, in the back of her aunt's car. Once at the Palais de Bois, they went straight to the room where Helena's other painting was hanging, and where there was, fortunately, just enough space to hang *Le train bleu* without interfering with other artworks.

Étienne vanished, having explained that he intended to speak to a few people about the painting, and before long a steady stream of people was entering the room and focusing their attention on Helena's painting. It was agony to stand nearby and listen to their comments, but to her great relief nearly everyone seemed to like it.

"What are people saying?" Étienne asked upon his return.

"Good things," Helena whispered. "Flattering things. I wonder if—"

Mathilde grabbed at her arm, her attention fixed on the entrance to the room. Helena followed her gaze to the man who stood at the threshold, and her heart nearly stopped beating.

Maître Czerny had arrived.

"Leave us," he barked at Étienne and Mathilde, and they stepped back obediently, though Étienne hovered within arm's reach. Helena's resolve wilted a little, for Czerny really did look very fierce, but then she remembered what he had said, and she straightened her spine and looked him in the eye.

He gestured at the painting. "This is your work?"

"Yes."

"Why is this the first I've seen of it?"

"I was afraid you would not like it."

"Yet you changed your mind. Why?"

"Because I no longer care if you like it," she answered readily. "I may be monied, but I am not hopeless."

Czerny winced, just a little, but he didn't apologize. Instead he approached the painting and examined it closely, taking his time, the seconds lengthening into minutes.

"As your teacher, may I offer an opinion?" he said at last.

"You may."

"This is good. I like it."

"Thank you," she said, in as gracious a tone as she could contrive.

"I will not deceive you with false praise, however. You are a good artist, but you will never be great. For that matter, neither will I. Few of us are touched by genius."

"Not everyone can be Shakespeare," she said, remembering her conversation with Sam.

"You English and your Shakespeare," he said, and wrinkled his nose disdainfully. "You may not be a great artist, Mademoiselle Parr, but you are capable of creating imaginative and highly decorative work. You might wish to consider turning to commercial art—posters and book jackets, for instance. You ought to consider it."

"Can one make a decent living with such work?" she asked, cringing at the vulgarity of her question. All the same, she had to know. Her future depended on it.

"Certainly you can. Would you like me to make some inquiries?"

She hated to ask him for anything, but it would be foolish to turn down his offer. "Yes, please. And thank you."

"It is nothing. Good luck, Mademoiselle Parr."

The instant he left the room, Étienne and Mathilde were at her side, their expressions an almost comical mixture of curiosity and fear.

"What did he say?"

"I hope he wasn't unkind . . ."

"He was fine. I am . . . I'll be fine. I think I know what to do next."

It wasn't what she had expected, or hoped for, but she wasn't going to turn up her nose at the maître's suggestion. He had shown her a way forward, a way to realize her dreams. A way to live independently, without recourse to her family's money.

But first, she knew, she had to see Sam.

"I must go," she told her friends. "There's someone I must see. Thank you for everything." She kissed them good-bye, and then ran from the Salon without a backward glance.

She had to tell him. She had to apologize and let Sam know that she had found her way—and so could he.

SHE HAD SENT Vincent home earlier, but rather than take the Métro now, she jumped in a waiting taxi and asked the driver to take her to the Hôtel de Lisbonne. There was a good chance that Sam would still be home at that time of day, and if he weren't she would simply take another taxi to his office.

No one challenged her as she walked through the hotel's modest lobby and started up the stairs, her heart hammering in her chest, her hands clammy with nerves. She knocked on Sam's door, lightly at first, and then harder when there was no reply.

"It's Ellie. Please open the door if you're there. I have to talk to you."

A door opened down the hall, and a man poked his head out just far enough to stare at her. She recognized him—he was one of the other deskmen at the newspaper, though she couldn't recall his name.

"Hello. I'm sorry for the noise," she said.

"You looking for Howard?"

"Yes. I had hoped—"

"He's gone. Moved out this morning."

Gone. Moved out.

"But he wasn't supposed to leave until next week," she said, her hand clutching at the door frame.

"Left this morning. Sorry about that."

She walked home in a daze, not even noticing when the sky grew dark and it began to rain. She was soaked through by the time she stumbled up the front steps of her aunt's house, and though she tried to be quiet as she crept along the front hall and toward the stairs it was no use, for her aunt burst out of the *petit salon* when Helena was only on the second step.

"Helena, my dear, where have you been? And why were you walking in the rain?"

She allowed Agnes to pull her into the *petit salon,* where she was wrapped in warm towels and given a cup of tea and allowed to collect herself. She had just swallowed the last of the tea when she noticed the newspaper clipping on the table beside her.

"It was in the paper today," Agnes said quietly. "I'm so sorry."

The *Tribune*'s Samuel Taylor Howard is departing these shores for the United States. Mr. Howard is leaving his chosen profession behind, much to the disappointment of his fellows here in Paris, with the intention of joining his father, Andrew Clement Howard III, in the management of their family's business concerns in America and abroad. He is sailing from Le Havre on the SS Paris and upon

arrival in New York City is expected to immediately take
up his position with the Howard Steel Company.

She let go of the clipping and watched it flutter to the floor. "I
knew. He told me. But he wasn't meant to leave until next week.
I thought . . . I thought I'd have a chance to say good-bye."

Tears rose in her eyes again, and with them came quiet, anguished sobs that left her drained and spent and nearly without hope. Agnes hugged her close and let her weep, and it was
a long while before she was able to speak again.

"I was so unkind to him. I said . . . oh, I said such *awful*
things, and now he's gone, and I think it might be my fault . . ."

"How so?" her aunt asked.

"He was upset with me, because he thought I was giving up
on my dream of becoming an artist, and of course he was right.
But I lashed out at him, and I said some very cruel things. I
told him . . . oh, Auntie A. I told him he should go back to
America. That he belonged there."

"What on earth possessed you to be so unkind?"

"I don't know. I was hurt, and so angry, and the words just
burst out of me. And the worst part is that I was wrong. He
had been trying to escape, just as I've been trying. All along,
he was trying to break free. And he was so close. If only I'd
been a better friend, he'd have seen it. He'd have seen it was
possible."

"Then be his friend now. Tell him what you just told me."

"I suppose I could write to him. Sara might know his address in New York."

"No," Agnes said decisively. "No, a letter won't do. You need
to go to him."

"What? Go to *America*? I can't. It's too . . . it's too far, for a start. And we've the wedding this Thursday."

"Then you can leave the next morning. You'll still arrive in America only a few days after he does."

"What if he refuses to see me? He left without telling me, or saying good-bye. Surely that means—"

"How can you know what *any* of this means if you don't go to him and find out? Now get started on packing your things, and I'll take care of everything else."

Chapter 29

One thing hadn't changed in the year since Helena had left London: the way she was treated by genteel society. Throughout the course of her niece's wedding day, she had been subjected to the same whispers, stares, cold shoulders, and knowing sideways glances that had blighted her life for so long.

She had expected it, steeled herself against it, and then, quite to her astonishment, had discovered that none of it hurt, not anymore. Once, such petty cruelties had defined her life. No more. Now, she realized, she truly didn't care.

It helped that she was dressed to the nines, or, as Mathilde would say, to the *trente et un*. Agnes had surprised her that morning with a new Vionnet frock and matching coat, which she'd had made from Helena's measurements after their visit in December. The outfit, made of silk chiffon and wool crepe the exact color of purple pansies, was exactly right for the occasion. With it she wore a matching cloche hat in finely pleated organdy, and a long rope of her aunt's biggest pearls, and she felt—she knew—she was the best-dressed woman there, with the possible exception of Agnes herself.

Of course Helena had expected it would be difficult to be thrown back into the same social circles that had once been so uncongenial to her, and of course she had known it would be hard to see Edward and his family for the first time in years. What she hadn't anticipated was how anxious she would feel over the fate of her niece, or how disenchanted she would be with the ceremony and attendant traditions, all of which felt like they belonged to an earlier age.

The expensive bridal gown from Paris had looked all wrong on Rose, its heavy satin far too overwhelming for her slight frame, while the family veil of Honiton lace, anchored by a diamond bandeau worn low over her forehead, had given her the appearance of a little girl playing dress-up.

That was the problem—she was a girl, only just eighteen, and the same age Helena had been when her engagement to Edward had been announced. If not for the timely intervention of the war, she would have shared her niece's fate of marriage to a near stranger and a lifetime of being bullied by a Gorgon of a mother-in-law.

The groom was Edward's brother, George, who had been a gangly adolescent the last time Helena had met him but was now a rather awkward and red-faced man in his mid-twenties. He was a barrister, which presumably meant he had some brains between his ears, and he did seem fond of Rose, which was a good sign. Helena feared her niece would bore her new husband silly, but perhaps, as neither knew to expect anything more, they might contrive to be happy. It was a lowering way to look at it, but truthful enough.

The ceremony and reception were exactly the same as every

other wedding she'd ever attended, featuring the same readings, the same music, and the same homily from the same chinless vicar who had been at St. Peter's Eaton Square for donkey's years. The breakfast afterward had gone on for far too long, with interminable and very dull speeches, and ostentatiously prepared food that had left her hungry for the unpretentious fare of Chez Rosalie.

If Amalia had been there, it would have been ever so much easier, but Peter was ill with a painful case of shingles and her sister had stayed behind at their country house to care for him. That was why, as soon as the wedding breakfast had finished, Helena had slipped out into the garden for some time to herself. But she'd been followed.

"May I join you?"

Looking up, she saw the man she hadn't been alone with since the day they had ended their engagement. Edward.

"Please do," she said, and she moved aside to make room for him on the wrought-iron bench. "How are you?"

"I'm well, thank you. Happy to be away from prying eyes. I hoped we might have a chance to speak, but I didn't want to set tongues wagging."

"Nor did I."

"I gather you were very ill last year. I'm relieved to see you looking so well."

"Am I?" she asked, and for a terrible moment she thought she might cry. They had been engaged for five years, but for all that he was nearly a stranger to her. "I'm sorry," she went on. "It's only that I'm rather tired. My aunt and I just arrived from Paris yesterday."

"Of course. You've been at art school."

"Yes."

"I'm glad to hear it. You were so talented. I ought to have tried to encourage you more, but I was a selfish idiot. Couldn't see past the nose on my face."

It was true, but he'd had other worries, too. It would be unfair of her to fault him on it now. "How is Lady Cumberland?" she asked instead.

"Do call her Charlotte. She detests the title. For obvious reasons. My mother, you know . . ."

"Of course. How is Charlotte, then?"

"Very well. Busy with her work, and the children, too."

"How old are they?"

"Laurence is four, and Eleanor is two and a half. We didn't bring them to the service, but you might have seen them running around before breakfast."

"I did. I thought they were very sweet." Laurence, she recalled, was a serious little boy, with dark hair and a quiet manner. His sister seemed his opposite, with fair hair and an engaging and rather precocious way about her.

"There was another child," she said, remembering. "A little girl with ginger hair. Is she Lilly's?"

"Yes. Her name is Charlotte, which never fails to delight me. She's just two now, and soon to have a sister or brother, as you may have noticed."

"Lilly seems very content."

"She is, yes. She and Robbie earned their happiness. But then, haven't we all?"

They were silent for a moment, and then they both started to talk at once, their words tangling together.

"No," she said. "You go first."

"I didn't know," he began, and he met her gaze unflinchingly. "The gossip, that is. The things people said after I broke our engagement. I was in . . . well, I was in a state, to be honest. I was pickled with drink and out of my mind with pain and self-pity, and I did a pretty good job of ignoring the world around me. I only realized what had happened months later, when Lilly told me."

"Oh," she said, not knowing how else to respond. She'd never expected him to do anything, of course, but it did help to know he was sorry for it.

"I wasn't sure what to do. I worried it would stir up bad memories if I wrote to you, or approached you in any way, and so I said nothing. For that I am truly sorry."

"It wasn't your fault. You did your best, and we both survived. You mustn't feel guilty. I don't blame you, or Charlotte, for any of it. Not one bit. Not least because you'd have made me very unhappy, and I you."

"I hope . . . I do hope you've been happy," he said. "In spite of things."

"I have been, especially this past year. I was very happy in Paris."

It was true. She had been happy there, really and truly content. She'd had work that sustained her, friends that understood her, and at the heart of it all had been Sam.

THE RECEPTION HAD ended, and Helena and her aunt were the sole passengers in an enormous automobile, driven by Vincent, that was conveying them back to her parents' house.

"Are you ready? Are your bags packed? We need to get you on your way."

"I'm ready, but I must speak to Mama and Papa before I go. I wanted to earlier, but there wasn't time."

Helena found her parents in the sitting room that connected their respective bedchambers. "May I come in?"

"Yes, do," her mother answered. "Come and sit next to me. I thought you looked very well today. Didn't she, John?"

"Yes, dear. Very well."

"Thank you. I have something to tell you," Helena began. "It's actually several things." Her parents exchanged apprehensive glances, but didn't interrupt.

"First of all, I'm not certain when I will return to London, or even if I will return at all. I love you dearly, and I will miss you, but I have been very happy in Paris and I wish to return there.

"Before that, however, I am going to America. I've, well, I've fallen in love with an American man, a friend of mine from Paris, but I made a mistake, and I let him leave without telling him, and—"

"Is this the American that Amalia met? The steel baron's heir?"

"It is, although that has nothing to do with—"

"Are you going alone? Without any sort of chaperone?"

"Yes, Mama."

Her mother swallowed, pressed her lips together, and then nodded. "If that is what you wish."

"Papa?"

"Is he a decent sort of man?"

"He is the very best sort of man, Papa. I promise."

"Then I suppose you must go."

"Thank you. Agnes knows Mr. Howard very well, and she can certainly put your minds at ease. I'll cable as soon as I arrive. Farewell for now."

Helena rushed upstairs and in the space of fifteen minutes changed out of her lovely frock and coat and packed away the last of her things. Agnes returned just as she was finishing, and with the help of Farrow the footman they carried her two suitcases downstairs, where Vincent was waiting with the same car that had brought them back from the reception.

"To Trafalgar Square," Agnes commanded as soon as they were settled in the car.

"Shouldn't we be going to Waterloo Station? That's where the trains for Southampton depart."

"Your ship isn't sailing from Southampton. It's at the docks here in London. We're going to the steamship line's offices first, to collect your ticket, and then to the ship."

When they arrived at the office Helena was appalled to learn that Agnes had already reserved and paid for the best available cabin, which cost the astonishing sum of £85 for a one-way fare. According to the ticketing clerk, it was a new ship, less than two years old, and offered only first-class cabins. "Your ladyship will be very comfortable on the voyage over," he promised.

"When does the ship arrive in New York?"

"First thing next Friday morning, ma'am."

She turned to Agnes, aghast. "Eight days? As long as that?"

"The express ships say they'll get you there in six," the clerk ventured, "but often as not they run into mechanical problems along the way. Our ships aren't as fast, but they're steady."

From Cockspur Street they set off at some speed for the docks in the east end, Vincent weaving through the late afternoon traffic at speeds that left her feeling rather ill. To Helena's great relief, her ship was still at the docks when they drew close, and looked to be nowhere near ready for departure.

"Good-bye, Auntie—"

"Not so fast, my dear. Here is some money for the voyage.

It's pounds, I'm afraid, but you can buy some dollars from the ship's purser."

"*Two hundred* pounds? I can't, Auntie A. It's too much."

"Nonsense. I should be very anxious if you left home with a penny less."

It suddenly occurred to her that she had no notion of how to find Sam once she got to New York. "I don't know Sam's address. What shall I do?"

But nothing could faze her aunt, it seemed. "I'll cable Sara and ask her to find out. The ship is sure to have a telegraph office on board—we'll get his direction to you, never fear. Now off you go, and bon voyage!"

Chapter 30

The SS *Minnewaska* slipped her berth and headed down the Thames and out to sea at five o'clock that evening, and though many of her passengers gathered on the promenade deck to wave farewell to England and any well-wishers remaining on-shore, Helena lingered in her cabin. She would venture out when the bell rang for supper, but until then she was content to be alone.

Her £85 worth of cabin was very pleasant, though far less luxurious than the first-class compartment she'd occupied on the Blue Train to Antibes the year before. It was about eight feet deep and about the same across, with good-sized windows on its exterior wall that ensured it would be bright as long as the weather held fine. It felt more like a sitting room than a ship's cabin, with parquet floors, chintz curtains, and a Sheraton-style desk and chair. There were two bunks, although only one had been made up, and a shallow wardrobe with hooks rather than a rail. Best of all, her cabin had its own bathroom, with a tub, sink, and WC.

No sooner had she unpacked her bags and settled in than the bell rang for the first seating at supper. She made her way to the dining room two decks below, a little hesitantly as she was still finding her sea legs, and was dismayed when one of the stewards led her to the captain's table. It would have been far nicer to dine with a smaller and less toplofty group, but her name and title had been noted, and her place would be at the captain's right hand for the remainder of the voyage.

Captain McKay and his senior officers were perfectly pleasant men, as were the other diners at her table, but the conversation was so staid and predictable that she all but fell asleep before the second course. There was no way around it, apart from claiming *mal de mer* and hiding in her cabin, and since she was a poor sailor to begin with there was every chance of her ending up confined to bed as soon as they hit rough water. She had better make the best of it while she still felt able to enjoy her food, if not the company at table.

When packing in London, she'd had the presence of mind to include paper, charcoal, and pastels, and for the first few days she busied herself with views of the ship and its fittings, mindful of Maître Czerny's advice. In order to win commissions as a commercial artist, she would have to build up a portfolio of work on related themes, and where better to begin than on a first-class voyage across the Atlantic?

So she walked up and down the decks and stretched out on a steamer chair and let the wind rush through her hair, and at night she stood by her window and stared at the dome of stars that silvered the endless velvet sky. When her attention wavered from the work at hand, she pulled out a smaller sketchbook, and she tried to recapture the moments of joy, fear, laughter, and despair that had led her away and across the sea. She drew Sam, many times, and she drew her friends and Agnes and dear old Hamish, filling page after page with portraits of those she loved.

Two days into the crossing, a telegram was delivered to her cabin.

SAM STAYING HOWARD FAMILY HOME NYC
TWO E SEVENTY-NINTH ST AT FIFTH AVE STOP
WORKPLACE FOURTEEN WALL ST FIFTH FLOOR
STOP HAVE CABLED DAISY STOP SHE WILL
MEET YOU AFTER CUSTOMS STOP ETIENNE AND
MATHILDE SEND THEIR BEST AS DO I STOP SARA

Late on Sunday night, the call went up—New York had been sighted in the distance, hours earlier than expected, and she rushed to the promenade deck above and shivered in her too-thin coat as a faint glow on the far horizon grew bigger and clearer, and someone nearby explained that they were seeing the lights off Long Island, and then a little later it was New Jersey in the distance, and then, at last, the ship began inching to starboard and they crossed through a narrow passage and emerged into an immense harbor.

Everyone rushed to the other side of the deck then, so they might see the great statue at close range, her torch lighting up the sky, but Helena stayed where she was. She was captivated by the sight of New York City ablaze with electric lights, and her artist's eye was fixed upon the strange modern skyline and its reaching towers, far higher than any buildings she'd seen in London or Paris.

The ship went straight to the piers on the Hudson River, on the west side of Manhattan, and by midnight they were neatly berthed—but no one could disembark until the following morning at eight o'clock, when the customs offices at the piers would be open and the SS *Minnewaska*'s passengers might be legally admitted to the United States of America.

It took an age for her to fall asleep, for she was terribly excited and a little nervous, too, but when she woke she felt rested and surprisingly calm. She was up and out of bed not long past dawn, and after a light breakfast of tea and toast with marmalade, which the steward delivered to her cabin, she dressed in her very best outfit: the pansy-purple Vionnet frock and coat she'd worn to Rose's wedding.

At eight o'clock she was one of only a handful of passengers making their way down the gangplank and across to the customs offices on the pier; the remainder, she assumed, were taking the chance to sleep in and have a proper breakfast in the dining room.

The customs officer was polite but officious, and was at first concerned that her visa for entrance to the United States had been issued in Paris, though she had set sail from London. Fortunately he accepted her explanation that she had originally intended to travel from Le Havre but had been persuaded by her aunt that a direct journey from London would be more agreeable. It wasn't an out-and-out lie, but it was certainly the first time she had ever been less than completely truthful with any sort of official.

When the officer had asked to see all the funds she had with her, she'd at first feared that he meant to extort some or all of the money, but it turned out he only wished to ensure that she had sufficient capital to support herself without resorting to public funds or charitable assistance. Last of all he extracted a payment of eight dollars, what he called a "head tax," which all foreigners had to pay upon entering the country.

By the time she emerged from the customs shed at the end of the pier, there was a sizable crowd milling around, and though she craned her neck and looked every which way, there was no sign of Daisy. She was just beginning to worry when she heard her name being called—no, shouted.

"Helena!!! Hellooooo! Helenaaaaa!"

And there Daisy was, pushing through the crowds, hugging her close and all but pulling the both of them off balance in her excitement.

"Come on—let's get out of this crush. We'll talk in the car. Give me one of those cases, won't you?"

As soon as they were seated and the driver had shut Helena's luggage in the boot of the car, Daisy turned to her friend and asked, "Where do you want to start?"

"It's not even nine o'clock . . . perhaps at his parents' house? Let me find the address again . . . here it is. Number two East Seventy-Ninth Street. Is that far?"

"It's a ways off, especially in rush-hour traffic. But it will give us a chance to talk. Tell me *everything*."

Helena shook her head. "You first. Why are you in New York?"

"It's complicated. I'm fine, honestly I am. There've been some sad days, but some good ones, too. I can't concentrate on any of that right now, though—I want to know why Sam is here and you're here. Sara's cable didn't say much."

"I suppose there wasn't time for a letter. Right—here's the potted version." And Helena told her friend the entire story, not sparing herself in her description of the morning after the vernissage, when she had been so wrongheaded and closed-minded in her rejection of Sam.

"Most of all I feel silly. Stupid, even. What was I thinking? I hurt him so badly, Daisy. I don't know . . . I can't be sure if he'll forgive me."

"I understand. Truly I do. I've . . . well, I'll tell you about it later. You're doing the right thing, though."

"I hope so."

Helena looked out the window, her attention belatedly caught by the utterly unfamiliar streetscape. Everything seemed so new, so modern, and the streets were so wide and straight, and the buildings so terribly tall. There were far more cars than at home, the streets clogged with traffic and crowds of pedestrians, and everyone she saw looked so busy and determined, and she wondered if any of them longed to sit down over a *café express* or pot of tea and simply watch the world go by.

The city felt so new, and not just new compared to London or Paris, but brand-new, so new its paint hadn't yet dried, and newest of all, to her mind, were the skyscrapers. With the exception of the Eiffel Tower or the spires of various cathedrals, she was fairly certain she'd never before seen a structure that rose beyond eight or nine stories—but already they'd driven past dozens of buildings that reached ten, twenty, even thirty stories high.

"All these skyscrapers . . . I had no idea. Which is the tallest?"

"I think it's still the Woolworth Building. It's sixty stories high."

"*Sixty* stories. Just imagine standing on the top floor. The view must be tremendous."

They'd been traveling north on a wide avenue, a huge park to their left, and she'd long since lost count of all the streets they'd crossed. The buildings they passed weren't as tall as they'd been farther to the south, but what they lacked in height they made up for in grandeur.

The driver turned right and pulled over to the side of the street. "Here we are, Miss Fields."

The exterior of the Howard mansion was a masterpiece

of French Gothic Revival architecture, with an intricately carved limestone façade that reminded her more than a little of Notre-Dame Cathedral. As they walked toward the main entrance, she half-expected to look up and see a gargoyle grinning down at her, and indeed there were any number of cheerful little creatures worked into the stone, among them a pair of putti supporting a copper lantern in the shape of Atlas and his globe.

The door swung open at their approach, and as they stepped inside they were greeted by a butler who had clearly been imported directly from England, complete with cut-glass accent and pristine white gloves.

"Good morning. May I help you?"

If ever there were a time to drag out her title, this was it. "Good morning. My name is Lady Helena Montagu-Douglas-Parr, and this is my friend, Miss Dorothy Fields. We are friends of Mr. Howard's, Mr. Samuel Howard, that is, and we were hoping to pay him a visit."

If the butler was surprised at the effrontery of two young ladies calling for the son of the house at nine in the morning, he was too well trained to betray it. "I am afraid that no one is at home, your ladyship. Mr. and Mrs. Howard are occupied with various engagements today, and Mr. Samuel Howard is at his offices on Wall Street. Would you care to leave a card?"

"I, ah . . . I . . ." she stammered. "If I could—"

"We would, thank you," said a voice over her shoulder. "Here you are. There's a note for Mr. Howard on the card. I would be most grateful if you could ensure he sees it."

"Of course, madame."

There was nothing for it but to return to the car. "If only we'd known," Daisy sighed, nearly as frustrated as Helena.

"Wall Street isn't all that far from the piers. Oh well—it won't be long now."

Daisy instructed the driver to head south again, and eventually the car turned left, then right, and they were on a street called Broadway, still heading south.

"We just passed City Hall," Daisy said presently. "We're nearly there."

The car turned onto Wall Street a few minutes later, and again the driver promised to wait. Number fourteen was a grand building, so tall Helena couldn't quite see the top, and its foyer was nearly as striking, with marble on the floors and walls, and a bank of elevators with brass so highly polished she could see her reflection in their doors.

The reception area of Howard Steel was exactly as Helena had expected: plushly carpeted, baronially paneled, and as quiet as a pharaoh's tomb. Its overseer, an immaculately dressed woman in her forties, was seated at a modest desk and at first did not appear to have noticed their arrival.

"Good morning," Helena ventured.

The woman looked up from the papers she was organizing and offered a crisp "good morning" but no more.

"My name is Lady Helena Montagu-Douglas-Parr, and I'm a friend of Mr. Howard's from Paris. I called on him at home earlier, but was told he was at the office today. I, ah . . ."

"Do you have an appointment?"

"No, I'm afraid not. I only just arrived—"

"Mr. Howard is in meetings all day. I can't possibly interrupt him."

"But I've come so far . . ." Helena offered, knowing it sounded pathetic but bereft of anything better to say.

"Yes. I imagine you have."

"Oh, for heaven's sake," Daisy interjected. "Here's my card. Lady Helena and I are at the Plaza. I'm sure you can contrive to put this in his hands the next time you see him. Come on, Helena."

They scurried back to the elevators, and by the time they were on solid ground again Helena's confidence of that morning had evaporated entirely.

"I had no idea it would be so difficult to see him," she said as they got into Daisy's car yet again.

"Everything is different now. He's the heir to Howard Steel. Imagine what sort of people that brings out of the woodwork."

"What should we do next?"

"Let's go to my hotel. The Plaza isn't much more than a mile away from the Howard mansion. We'll have a late breakfast, since I have a feeling you haven't eaten a thing so far today, and we'll make plans. He may be at the office all day, but he's got to go home at some point. If worst comes to worst, we'll sit in the car outside his house and wait for him."

The latter part of Daisy's plan seemed rather desperate, but what else could she do? And she was feeling quite hungry. Once she'd eaten, and had a chance to think, she would probably feel better. If only she could be sure of getting a decent cup of tea.

The Plaza hotel was terribly grand, the sort of place that she was certain Agnes would adore, and Daisy's suite of rooms was positively baroque in its splendor.

"Make yourself at home—there's a second bedroom I haven't even looked at, so you must stay. Do you want to eat in the restaurant, or would you rather have our breakfast sent up?"

"If you don't mind, I'd prefer to eat here. That way I can kick off my shoes and relax."

With breakfast ordered, they both collapsed onto the sitting room sofa, and after a moment's silence, Daisy began to laugh and Helena, unable to resist her friend's infectious giggles, joined in.

"Who would have thought chasing down my one true love would be so difficult? I mean, the woman at his office was awful. She looked at your card as if it were made out of *loo* paper!"

"Let's just hope she didn't flush it down the nearest lavatory. I wouldn't put it past—"

A loud knock sounded at the door, startling them out of their laughter.

"My goodness," said Helena. "The kitchen here is efficient."

"It can't be our food. I just put down the telephone. They're good, but not that good."

The knock sounded again.

"Hello?" Daisy called out. "Who is it?"

"It's Sam Howard, Miss Fields. I'm looking for Ellie."

Chapter 31

It was Sam. Somehow he had learned she was here and he had come for her. If he were done with her, he wouldn't have come, would he? It would have been so much easier just to—

"Helena! What do you want me to do?" Daisy hissed.

Helena stood, smoothed an imaginary wrinkle from her frock, and nodded. Daisy opened the door.

It was Sam, wearing a ridiculously formal pinstriped suit, which she didn't care for at all, and his hair was cut short and smoothed down and he wasn't the man she remembered but was still, all the same, the man she loved.

"If you'll excuse me," Daisy whispered, "I'll be in the Palm Court downstairs."

The door closed behind her. They were alone.

He took one step forward, then another. He was still so far away, but she hadn't the courage to cross the room and finish her journey.

"I can't believe it," he said.

"How did you . . . ?"

"Miss Thorpe, at my office—was she rude to you?"

"Not precisely. I suspect I'm not the first young woman to try to talk her way in to see you."

"Yes, unfortunately. You must have made an impression on her, though, because she gave me this." He held out Daisy's card, and Helena stepped forward, just to the length their outstretched arms could reach, and took it.

She's here, her friend had written.

"Will you sit down? Have something to drink?"

"Not just yet. I need to explain."

"So do I."

"I wasn't honest with you. Not completely. I didn't lie, but I left a lot out."

"Go on," she said, suddenly apprehensive.

"I made my parents a promise when I left, just as you had done with your family. I promised that I would return in five years. In fact, I all but swore an oath on the family Bible. Father wanted to retire long ago, but he gave me those years, and I didn't feel I could refuse him. There was no one else, after all."

He began to pace back and forth, fretful as a zoo-bound tiger, pausing only to loosen his tie and unbutton his high, starched collar. "I knew the day was coming. I only had six months left. And then I had a letter from Mother. She said Father's health was failing. That he needed to retire for the sake of his health. When I came to your aunt's the morning after your vernissage it was to tell you everything. I was going to explain why I had to return home. But then we quarreled, and I was so angry I more or less packed my bags and left."

"You were that upset with me?"

"Only at first. I was about halfway across the Atlantic when

I came to my senses. I actually sent you a cable from the ship, but you must have left Paris by then."

"I thought you had left without saying good-bye," she said, her throat clogging with sudden tears.

"The thing is, Ellie, you were right about *everything*. I had been living in fear, and it was time I faced up to it. I had no right to criticize you, none at all, because you are the most courageous person I know."

"So you've come back to take over Howard Steel?"

"No," he said flatly.

She went to the sofa and sat down. It was that or crumple slowly to the floor. "I don't understand. I thought you came home to take over from your father."

"When I left Paris, that's what I planned to do. But that lasted for less than a week. By the time I arrived, I knew I couldn't do it. Not even for my parents could I do it. That's the first thing I told them."

"How did they react?"

"They were disappointed, of course, but then I explained everything. I think they understand now."

The effort to make sense of Sam's revelations was very nearly making her dizzy. "If you aren't taking over, who is?"

"No one. A buyer approached my father a while back, and we've agreed to sell the company to him. Nearly all the proceeds will go to a charitable trust that my parents will manage. Eventually I'll take over, but only to disburse the funds to charity.

"You need to know that I'm walking away from the money. There will be some set aside for my children, but nothing like my father's millions. That's one of the things I've been struggling with all this time. What to do about all that money."

"It must be a relief," she said. "If only because rich men rarely make great writers. Or great artists, for that matter."

He swayed on his feet, and only then did she see how pale he was, and how dark the shadows were under his eyes. "I haven't been sleeping all that well," he admitted. "Perhaps I should—"

She reached out and grasped his hand, and then she pulled him closer until he was seated next to her on the sofa.

"Now it's my turn," she began, her heart so full she could scarcely speak. "I came to America to tell you that I was wrong. You *are* brave and I *am* proud of you. And you need to know that I love you. I lied to you in January, when I said I was content with being your friend. I want that, yes, but I want more, too."

"Thank God for that. Because I love you, too, and I do want more from you. I'm not prepared to settle for less. Not anymore." He tucked a strand of hair behind her ear, his touch infinitely gentle and reassuring. "I've a very important question to ask you now. What's your middle name?"

"I've several," she said, a little puzzled by his request. "I'm Helena Mary Angela et cetera et cetera."

"Right, then." He pulled a small, square box from his coat pocket, and, dropping to his knees before her, opened the lid and held it out. Inside was an old-fashioned diamond ring, the oval central stone surrounded by sapphire petals set in gold.

"Helena Mary Angela et cetera et cetera, will you do me the very great honor of becoming my wife?"

"I will," she said, her heart suddenly so full that it hurt to breathe.

She held out her left hand, so he might fit the ring on her finger, and with her right hand she pinched her leg, hard, just to make sure her imagination wasn't playing tricks on her.

"It's my grandmother's ring. I confessed everything to my

parents at dinner yesterday. This morning, Mother came to see me at work. She said she couldn't stand to see me so unhappy, and she all but ordered me to return to Paris and sort things out with you. And she gave me the ring."

"It's lovely."

"Do you want to have the wedding back in England with your family?"

"Not especially," she said, thinking back to Rose's uninspiring nuptials. "Perhaps we could have something quiet, here in New York, and then have a party in Paris with all our friends?"

He answered her with a kiss. It began as a delicate and respectful gesture, one that was perfectly suited to the emotion and solemnity of the moment, but Helena was done with chaste and tender kisses from the man she loved. She contrived to open her mouth a fraction, just enough that she might touch her tongue to his lips, and that was enough to push him over the edge. An instant later he was sitting on the sofa, she was astride his lap, and he was kissing her so passionately that she thought she might actually swoon, although she hadn't worn a corset in years and had always been a levelheaded sort of person.

Sam pulled away first, gasping for breath as he set his chin on top of her head and pulled her tight against his chest. "God, Ellie. You're going to kill me. Let's see about getting a marriage license first."

"Slave to convention. That's what you are."

"I'm afraid of your aunt Agnes, that's what I am."

"She lived in sin with Dimitri for years, so I doubt—"

"Don't tempt me. That reminds me. We need to visit my parents, or my mother will have my head."

"Will they be upset with me? For taking you away from Howard Steel, and back to Europe?"

"No. They know it was my decision alone. Besides, there's no reason they can't travel now that my father is retiring. Mother's always wanted to do the Grand Tour."

It occurred to her that, with the Howard millions dispersed, Sam would need to work for a living. "Do you think the *Tribune* will give you your old job back?"

"I don't need it. I've had an offer from John Ellis, the editor of the *Liverpool Herald*. He's asked me to be the paper's European correspondent. The pay is better than at the *Tribune*, and we can live in Paris or London—whichever you prefer."

"Definitely Paris."

"I'll have to travel a lot, but I thought you could come with me, at least some of the time."

"That ties in perfectly with my new profession."

"Your new . . . ?" he asked, mystified.

"Not entirely new. I spoke with Maître Czerny the day after the vernissage—no, don't make that face. Étienne and Mathilde and I smuggled in my other painting—*Le train bleu,* the one I'd been nervous about—and he saw it, and liked it. He told me I should consider becoming a commercial artist, designing travel posters or book jackets or things like that."

She wriggled off his lap and reached for her bag, which she'd left propped on the floor at the end of the sofa. In it was the portfolio of drawings she'd created on the voyage to America. He leafed through them slowly, his face a picture of delight and admiration.

"These are wonderful—although, to be honest, I love all your work."

"Thank you. I'm still . . . I mean, I lost my nerve, and I haven't quite got it back yet. But I've got to try, no matter what."

"That's the spirit. I wouldn't have been offered the job at the

Herald if it weren't for you. You were the one who encouraged me to focus on my writing, and it was the series I wrote on the Anglo-French accord—remember how long I worked on those articles?—that got me the job. I sent them to Mr. Ellis, just to show him the sort of work I was doing, and he liked them so much he offered me a job with his paper."

"Have I said before that I am terribly proud of you?"

"Not in so many words, but I'm glad to hear it. Now, are we ready to go? Do you have everything you need?"

"I think so—oh, no! I forgot about Daisy!"

"Why don't we join her downstairs?" he asked. "They can't serve us champagne, but we could have some tea."

"And toast the end of my year in Paris?"

"That, and the beginning of many more."

Epilogue

October, 1925
Paris, France

It was the night of Étienne's vernissage at the Galérie Bellamy, and if Sam didn't return home very soon they would be late. He'd been out all afternoon, busy with various errands, and Helena was beginning to worry that he'd lost track of time.

They had been married in America at the beginning of June, in the drawing room of his parents' cottage in Connecticut, though she still found it odd to call a house with forty rooms a cottage. Daisy had been her maid of honor, while Sam had asked his father to be his witness. They'd returned to Europe via London, where they'd celebrated quietly with her parents and sisters, and had been settled in Paris by the middle of July.

They'd found a small flat on the rue Vavin, just off the boulevard Raspail, and after digging through Agnes's attics and scouring every *brocante* market in the central arrondissements they had managed to furnish it; for decoration they'd hung its walls with paintings by Helena and her friends.

Of course Agnes had insisted on throwing a grand party for them, stuffing her home full of friends, acquaintances, and random fixtures of Parisian salon life. Of the guests, the only ones she could truly count as friends were Sara and Gerald Murphy. It had been great fun, but Helena had far preferred the much smaller gathering that Mathilde and Étienne had hosted a week later.

The weeks and months since then had flown by, for Sam had been busy settling into his position at the *Herald* and already he had traveled twice to Germany in connection with various stories he was pursuing.

Helena had been much occupied with her first commissions as a commercial artist, for Maître Czerny had kept his word and recommended her work to several art directors he knew. Already she had completed a poster for the Compagnie Internationale des Wagons-Lits, was working on a brochure for Thomas Cook, and was waiting to hear if she'd won the commission for a series of book jackets for the Clarendon Press in Oxford.

Just then she heard the scrape of a key in the lock, the sound of bags being deposited on the table, and before she could blink her husband was at the door of their bedroom.

"Hello there," he said, and his grin had something of the Cheshire cat about it.

"Hello," she replied, and hurried over to kiss him. "If you hurry, you've just enough time for a bath before we leave."

"Are you ready?" he asked.

"I am," she said, stepping back so he might admire her frock. She knew he would approve, for she was wearing the golden gown he loved so much.

"Put on your coat. There's something I need to show you."

"Now? You have to show me now? What about Étienne's vernissage?"

"We won't be late. I promise. Come on, now."

He led her downstairs and outside, but rather than flag down a taxi he directed them to the Métro stop around the corner.

"But this train will take us in the wrong direction," she protested.

"Humor me, won't you?"

He paid their fares and led them down another set of stairs, to the westbound platform, and there, right at the bottom of the steps, he stopped.

"Close your eyes. No, don't ask me why—just do it. I've got your hand. It isn't far, I promise. We're almost there . . . almost there. Now stop, and open your eyes. What do you see?"

"It's my poster!"

It was the commission she'd completed last month, a simplified version of *Le train bleu*. It really had turned out so well, the colors crisp and bright, the design dynamic and wonderfully modern. She'd worked on it for weeks and weeks, and the fee she'd received had amounted to very little, but none of that mattered now. Her work, her *art*, was hanging where it would be seen by tens of thousands of people.

"I noticed it right away. It was all I could do not to rush up to the other people on the platform and tell them, 'See that poster? My wife is the artist!' "

Sam picked her up and swung her around in a circle, and before he set her down he kissed her soundly. "Tomorrow we'll come back, and we'll bring my camera, and I'll take your picture in front of it. We'll send copies to your parents and sisters, and to my parents, too—"

"Yes, yes," she laughed, "but first we have Étienne's vernissage, and Auntie A is bringing an entire crate of champagne, and—"

"I thought you'd sworn off champagne for good after the, ahem, *incident*," he teased.

She slapped at his arm, affecting a look of deep affront. "What happened to your promise to never mention that evening again? And I only plan on having a sip."

She would go to the party and admire her friend's paintings and dance with her husband, and she would be as happy, in that moment, as she had ever been. And then, when the evening was done and they were walking home, she would raise her face to the silver glow of the moon. She would bathe in the moonlight falling so beautifully over Paris, and she would think of the girl who had so badly wanted to live, the girl who had simply wanted more, and she would thank her, then, for promises made and promises kept.

Acknowledgments

First and foremost, I would like to thank everyone who has embraced my books so enthusiastically. I am so fortunate to have such devoted readers, and I am deeply grateful to each and every one of you.

In the course of researching this book, I relied upon the collections of a number of libraries and archives. I would specifically like to acknowledge the Archives of American Art (Anna Coleman Ladd papers), the Beineke Rare Book and Manuscript Library (Gerald and Sara Murphy papers), the Bibliothèque Nationale de France, the National Archives in the U.K., the New York Public Library, and the Toronto Public Library.

I would also like to offer my thanks to those who were kind enough to help me with my research, either by answering my questions or by examining sections of my work-in-progress for errors. Susan Logan and John Barkley offered their observations on artistic techniques and the artist's path; Jennifer Yates cast her professional translator's eye over my French usage; Lori Barrett advised me on all things musical; and Erika Robuck provided invaluable suggestions regarding my characterization of several figures from the Lost Generation. Any inaccuracies or mistakes that remain are entirely my responsibility.

To my literary agent, Kevan Lyon, and her colleagues at the Marsal Lyon Literary Agency, in particular Patricia Nelson, I once again extend my heartfelt thanks.

Also deserving of my praise and gratitude is my editor, Amanda Bergeron, whose patience and understanding kept me writing even when I was convinced I had lost my way. I am also very grateful to Elle Keck in editorial, as well as my publicists Emily Homonoff, Lauren Jackson, and Miranda Snyder, together with Kim Therriault, for their ongoing support.

I would like to thank everyone who supports me and my books at William Morrow, in particular Tom Pitoniak, Emin Mancheril, Mary Ann Petyak, Serena Wang, Molly Birckhead, Jennifer Hart, Samantha Hagerbaumer, and Carla Parker. The producers at HarperAudio have once again created a beautiful audiobook and I am most grateful for their hard work. I am also indebted to everyone at HarperCollins Canada, among them Leo MacDonald, Sandra Leef, Colleen Simpson, Cory Beatty, Shannon Parsons, and Kaitlyn Vincent. Last but very much *not* least, I want to thank all of the sales staff in the U.S., Canada and the international division for their efforts on my behalf.

Closer to home, I'd like to thank the circle of friends whose love and support keeps me afloat: Ana, Clara, Denise, Erin, Irene, Jane D, Jane E, Jen, Kate H, Kelly F, Kelly W, Liz, Marissa, Mary, Michela, and Rena.

My heartfelt thanks go out as well to my family in Canada and the U.K., most especially my father, Stuart Robson; my sister, Kate Robson; and my beautiful children, Matthew and Daniela.

Most of all I want to thank my husband for his support, understanding, and love. And just so you know, Claudio—you are the hero of *my* story.

About the author

About the book

Insights,
Interviews
& More . . .

Read on

Meet Jennifer Robson

JENNIFER ROBSON is the *USA Today* and #1 *Globe & Mail* bestselling author of *Somewhere in France* and *After the War Is Over*. She first learned about the Great War from her father, acclaimed historian Stuart Robson. In her late teens, she worked as an official guide at the Canadian National War Memorial at Vimy Ridge in France and had the honor of meeting a number of First World War veterans. After graduating from King's College at the University of Western Ontario, she attended Saint Antony's College, University of Oxford, where she earned a doctorate in British economic and social history. She was a Commonwealth Scholar and an SSHRC Doctoral Fellow while at Oxford. Jennifer lives in Toronto, Canada, with her husband and young children, and shares her home office with Sam the cat and Ellie the sheepdog. ∽

Paris and the Lost Generation

THE TERM "LOST GENERATION," which has come to be attached to the group of writers and artists who came of age during or just after the First World War, was coined by Gertrude Stein, who overheard a garage owner bemoaning the laziness and lax work ethic of a young mechanic in his employ. The garage owner called the mechanic and his contemporaries "une génération perdue," and Stein, who knew the value of a bon mot as well as anyone, told Ernest Hemingway about the conversation. He used it as an epigraph in *The Sun Also Rises*, and many years later wrote about the phrase in his memoir, *A Moveable Feast*. It's worth noting that he then added, "I thought that all generations were lost by something and always had been and always would be."

In the years following the end of the Great War, thousands of expatriate writers and artists were drawn to Paris, lured in part by the buying power of the American dollar: by the summer of 1925, for instance, one dollar equaled twenty French francs. A decent meal might be had for two francs, a room in a hotel might be let for 200 francs a month, and nearly everything else was correspondingly cheap if your pay or savings originated in dollars. For example, William L. Shirer, who later became known for his work with Edward R. Murrow, earned $60 a month for his work as a deskman at the European edition of the *Chicago Tribune* (he arrived in late 1925, so his tenure didn't coincide with Sam's fictional sojourn there).

Shirer had just graduated from college, and had spent all his life up to that point in the American Midwest. Although he had planned on returning to the United States ▶

after a short stay in Europe, he instead decided to remain indefinitely. The allure of Paris was simply impossible to resist. "In this golden time one could be wonderfully carefree in the beautiful, civilized city, released from all the puritan, bourgeois restraints that had stifled a young American at home," he later wrote in his memoirs.

It was possible not only to live well in Paris, but also to live relatively free of intolerance, small-minded attitudes, and old-fashioned conventions, and to do so surrounded by like-minded people. It was also the case that Paris, perhaps more so than at any other time, simply felt like the center of everything. The most interesting fiction, poetry, theater, music, dance, and art was being created in Paris, and if that wasn't strictly true it at least *felt* true.

You may have noticed that a number of notable literary and artistic figures who lived in Paris in this period make no appearance in this book, or are only mentioned in passing. Among them are Ezra Pound, John dos Passos, Ford Madox Ford, Cole Porter, T.S. Eliot, James Joyce, Pablo Picasso, George Gershwin, Igor Stravinsky, and Jean Cocteau, and they are absent either because they weren't living in Paris in the period *Moonlight Over Paris* takes place, or because I couldn't establish a plausible connection between them and my characters.

The question of plausibility preoccupied me for many weeks when I first began to research this book. In the beginning, I wasn't at all sure if I would include any real-life members of the Lost Generation as characters. How likely was it, I asked myself, that Helena would have encountered any of these people? I soon realized that her background and interests made it not only likely, but also very nearly inevitable.

Ninety years on, it's difficult to reliably establish the number of Americans living in Paris in the 1920s, for official estimates vary considerably. The French census of 1926 counted just under 18,000 Americans living in France, with roughly half of them based in Paris and its suburbs; but that figure didn't include the thousands of undocumented visitors who had, for instance, overstayed their visas or had entered the country illegally. In 1923, an article in the European edition of the *Chicago Tribune* (yes, Sam's paper) cited a figure of 32,000 Americans living in Paris. The real number, which likely hovered somewhere in between these two estimates, fluctuated according to the exchange rate and other economic factors, and it also included all Americans in Paris, many of whom were businessmen with no connection to the arts. Historian Warren Susman has speculated that only one-tenth of American expatriates were writers or artists, which leaves us with a very rough estimate of two or three thousand men and women, to which must be added several hundred expatriates from other countries, most notably Britain, Russia, and Spain.

It may seem implausible that a newcomer to Paris in 1925 might have been able to attend a party and there meet a dozen or more famous writers and artists, but making some provision for exaggeration and hindsight, the people who belonged to the expatriate artistic community did socialize with one another, did spend great amounts of time in one another's company, and did tend to frequent the same cafés, restaurants, and bars. Paris, in that sense, was a small town— and like most small towns it was the sort of place where everyone seemed to know everyone.

Two of the most central figures of the Lost Generation were Sara and Gerald Murphy, although they would almost certainly have resisted being attached to any sort of label. Immortalized in Calvin Tomkins's long-form essay of 1962, "The Best Revenge is Living Well," and recently the subject of several biographies and novels, it is impossible to read or write about France in the 1920s without encountering the Murphys. My characterization is a sympathetic one, for they were simply the sort of people you wanted to be around—funny, charming, warm, witty, and interesting. They instantly made any gathering a success, and they retained their characteristic warmth of spirit and generosity even in the face of the two overwhelming tragedies that brought an end to their life in France. These were the death of their son Baoth in 1935, age 16, of meningitis, followed by the death of their other son Patrick in 1937, also at the age of 16, after a long battle with tuberculosis. After Patrick's diagnosis in 1929 they moved to Switzerland, where he might receive the most modern treatments available, and then back to the U.S. in 1934. After they left France Gerald never painted again.

During their years in France, the Murphys gathered around them a group of friends that included Archibald MacLeish, a famed poet and later the Librarian of Congress; Ernest and Hadley Hemingway; Pablo Picasso; and, perhaps most famously, Scott and Zelda Fitzgerald. The Murphys were partly the inspiration for Fitzgerald's characters Dick and Nicole Diver in *Tender is the Night*, although the literary notoriety that came with this connection always upset Sara. "I didn't like the book when I read it, and I liked it even less on rereading," she told Tomkins in 1962. "I reject categorically any resemblance to us or to anyone we knew at any time."

By establishing a friendship between Helena and Sara Murphy, I was able to create a pathway into the world of the Lost Generation, a world that leads her not only to Sam Howard but also to Gertrude Stein and ▶

Paris and the Lost Generation *(continued)*

Alice B. Toklas, the Hemingways, the Fitzgeralds, Sylvia Beach, and even such lesser-known figures as Rosalie Tobia, the proprietor of Chez Rosalie. Signora Tobia was a real person, mentioned by name in a turn-of-the-century directory of artists' models, and was known for her kindness toward many struggling artists, most notably Amedeo Modigliani.

Through the fictitious character of Aunt Agnes, whom I like to imagine as a cross between Margot Asquith and Madame de Staël, I was able to gain entrée for Helena into the salon of Natalie Barney, and introduce her to a group of women who were intellectually curious and socially daring. They included Peggy Guggenheim, Winnaretta Singer (the Princesse Edmond de Polignac), Djuna Barnes, Colette, Elisabeth Gramont (the Duchesse de Clermont-Tonnerre), Thelma Wood, Mina Loy, Nancy Cunard, and Romaine Brooks.

Consuelo Balsan, whose fictitious nephew by marriage proves so irksome to Helena, was a real-life figure, too. Born a Vanderbilt, raised in the very top drawer of New York high society, she became a duchess at the age of eighteen when she married the Duke of Marlborough. The marriage was an unhappy one, and resulted in separation eleven years later, followed by divorce in 1921. Later that year, however, Consuelo remarried, this time to Lt.-Col. Jacques Balsan, a pioneering French aviator.

No discussion of Paris in the 1920s can be considered complete without Sylvia Beach and her iconic bookshop Shakespeare and Company, which she opened in 1919. Beach is best known today for her championing of James Joyce, and her decision to become the publisher of his magnum opus *Ulysses* after it was deemed too inflammatory in its subject matter and language to be published in the United States or Britain. In addition to being a center of English-language cultural life in Paris, Shakespeare and Company also operated as a paid lending library, and nearly every acclaimed writer who spent time in Paris in the 1920s and 1930s had a subscription there. Beach closed her shop after the German occupation of France in 1940 and it never re-opened; the Shakespeare and Company of today's Paris bears its name as an homage to the original shop.

To learn more about the Lost Generation and Paris in the 1920s, please turn to my list of Further Reading in this section. ∽

Glossary of Terms and Places in *Moonlight Over Paris*

NEARLY ALL OF THE PLACES I mention in *Moonlight Over Paris* still exist, in one form or another; in a few cases the original building has been destroyed and replaced with a modern structure, though the street address remains (Chez Rosalie is an example). If you're interested in seeing what the buildings look like today, or would like to get a sense of where they are in relation to one another, I've created a *Moonlight Over Paris* map via Google Maps. Feel free to visit (and use the Street View option to take a closer look). The url is goo.gl/t18Q75 and a link is also available via my website at www.jennifer-robson.com

à demain: so long; literally "until tomorrow"

à la Véronique: a savory dish prepared with grapes

absinthe: an aniseed-flavored liqueur that was infamous for its allegedly hallucinogenic and toxic qualities, it was banned in France and much of the world from 1915 onward, with restrictions on its sale removed only in the early years of this century

Aéronautique Militaire: original name of the French Air Force from its inception in 1910 to its renaming as the *Armée de l'Air* in 1933

allô: hello; less formal than "bonjour"

American Field Service: established in 1915, the AFS provided ambulances driven by American volunteers to the French army until the entry of the United States into the war in 1917

ancien combattant: veteran; literally "old soldier" ▶

Glossary of Terms and Places in *Moonlight Over Paris* (continued)

Antibes: a small town on the Mediterranean coast that was popular among the wealthy for winter holidays; in the 1920s it also became a sought-after destination in the summer months

aquarelles: watercolors

arrondissement: Paris is divided into a series of twenty administrative districts, with boundaries that rotate clockwise from the center rather like the segments of a snail's shell. Each arrondissement is numbered, and often people will refer to the number as a destination in and of itself: for example, "the Eiffel Tower is in the seventh."

Belle Époque: literally "beautiful era," it describes the period from the end of the Franco-Prussian War in 1871 to the outbreak of the First World War in 1914, and is roughly analogous to the Gilded Age in the United States

Blue Train: nickname for the Calais-Méditerranée Express, the Blue Train (*le train bleu*) was a luxury rail passenger service that ran from Calais via Paris and Lyon to the resort towns of the Mediterranean

Le Boeuf sur le Toit: the famed restaurant and cabaret, established in 1921, which was known for its jazz music; its audience was a who's-who of the Parisian cultural elite

boulangerie: bakery

boulevard du Montparnasse: the central boulevard in the neighborhood of Montparnasse, along which many of its iconic cafés and restaurants were located

boulevard St.-Michel: the boulevard St.-Michel ran north-south through Montparnasse, roughly parallel to the eastern border of the Luxembourg Gardens, and was known colloquially as the "boul' Mich' "

boulots: compressed egg-shaped lumps of coal dust that were often used in place of firewood or coal

les bouquinistes: booksellers of used and sometimes antiquarian stock whose stalls can be found along the banks of the Seine

brocante: type of market that sold used or antique furniture and household goods

bunkum: useless talk or nonsense

cablese: series of codes, almost a language unto themselves, used by telegraphists and newspaper editors to shorten telegrams, or cables, to save on the costs of transmission; since cables were priced by the word, great efforts were made to combine words, create memorable acronyms or mangle accepted rules of grammar to reduce costs

café allongé: literally a "stretched coffee," an allongé is prepared espresso-style but with extra water. Other specialty coffees mentioned in *Moonlight Over Paris* are a *café au lait*, in which coffee is mixed with an equal amount of hot milk; a *café crème*, which is espresso combined with hot milk; a *café express*, equivalent to a shot of espresso; and a *café noisette*, in which a small amount of milk, sufficient only to turn the drink the color of a hazelnut, is added to a shot of espresso.

cami-knickers: essentially a camisole and knickers combined into one garment, these had superseded combinations as the undergarment of choice for young women in the 1920s, and typically were worn along with a soft-cup brassière

carte d'étudiant: student card

chambre particulier: private room

Chez Graff: a bohemian restaurant and bar in Pigalle known for its gay clientele

Chez Rosalie: a modest restaurant in Montparnasse that was popular among artists and students looking for a cheap and filling meal

Côte d'Azur: the stretch of Mediterranean coast from St.-Tropez to the Italian border; then, as now, a popular destination for the rich, famous, and glamorous

Cubism: an avant-garde movement, at its height in the first quarter of the twentieth century, which sought to break up and reassemble objects as abstract forms, and thereby encourage multiple points of view and a greater understanding of the artwork as a whole. Its most famed adherents were Picasso, Georges Braque, and Juan Gris.

dépêche-toi: hurry up; literally, "hurry yourself"

deskmen: term for the copywriters and/or editors at a newspaper; in the context of the Paris edition of the *Chicago Tribune*, Sam's employer, it was the staffers who spun short and often unintelligible cables into longer stories for use in the newspaper

désolé: sorry; literally, "desolated"

dessin: drawing or sketching

dessin à modèle vivant: live model drawing

devoré: a type of fabric, often velvet, in which parts of the nap are burned away, leaving only the fabric backing; this produces a patterned effect on the fabric

Le Dôme: properly Le Café du Dôme, this Montparnasse landmark was a favorite gathering spot for writers, Ernest Hemingway among them

Dona nobis pacem: translated from the Latin, "give us peace." Here it refers to the final movement of Bach's *Mass in B Minor* ▶

Glossary of Terms and Places in *Moonlight Over Paris* (continued)

École des Beaux-Arts: France's pre-eminent school of fine arts, based in Paris, and located in the Palais des Beaux-Arts in St.-Germain-des-Prés

Eighteenth Amendment: enacted in 1919, the Eighteenth Amendment to the United States Constitution banned the production, transport, and sale of alcohol, though not its consumption, and marked the beginning of Prohibition in the U.S. It was repealed in 1933.

Élysée Palace: analogous to the White House, it is the official residence of the President of France and is also the center for much official state business

en tout cas: in any event; at any rate

entrez: come in

European Edition: the official title of the *Chicago Tribune*'s eight-page Paris-produced newspaper; colloquially known as the Paris edition

fais des beaux rêves: sweet dreams; literally, "make beautiful dreams"

Fauchon: luxury grocer, first established in 1886, and still in business today

La femme de fermier: farmer's wife; name of the painting Helena originally submits to the Salon des Indépendants

La femme dorée: the golden woman; name of the painting Étienne submits to the Salon des Indépendants

fine à l'eau: brandy diluted with water; one of Hemingway's preferred drinks when he lived in Paris

Fokker C.IV: two-seat biplane introduced in 1924

"For He's a Jolly Good Fellow": immensely popular song at birthdays and most celebrations; the song "Happy Birthday to You" was not widely known in this period and would not have been sung at a birthday celebration in the mid-1920s

Fouquet's: first established in 1899, this traditional Parisian restaurant (its name does include an apostrophe) was for many years the venue for the annual French film awards, the Césars

Gare du Nord: one of the main rail stations in Paris in the 1920s, it served northern France and points beyond. Other stations in central Paris at that time included the Gare de Lyon (southerly destinations), the Gare d'Austerlitz (central and southwestern France), the Gare de l'Est (serving eastern France and Germany), the Gare Montparnasse (western and southwestern France), the Gare d'Orsay (since closed; now the Musée d'Orsay), and the Gare St.-Lazare (western France, including Normandy).

La Garoupe: name of the beach in Antibes where the Murphy family and their guests would often gather in fine weather

Gillotte's: officially called Le Rendezvous du Petit Journal, but known to all as Gillotte's, this small bistro was the favorite watering hole of the deskmen at the Paris edition

Grand Bassin: a large octagonal pond in the Luxembourg Gardens; much favored, then and now, as a place for children to sail model boats.

Le Grand Duc: a cabaret in Montmartre renowned for its American jazz music

Grand Palais: an immense exhibition hall located just off the Champs-Élysées in central Paris

grand salon: in a private home this might be the largest of several drawing rooms; in a public space, such as a school, it would be the largest classroom or lecture hall. A *petit salon* was simply a smaller or less grand version of the same.

Guignol and Madelon: puppet characters who are roughly equivalent to Punch and Judy in England

Les Halles: for centuries the central market for Paris, the glass-and-ironwork buildings at Les Halles (literally "the halls") were constructed in the mid-nineteenth century and demolished just over a century later. Today the area is a transit hub and shopping mall and in the middle of a large-scale redevelopment.

horaire: timetable

Hôtel de Lisbonne: the small and exceedingly modest hotel where many deskmen for the Paris edition lived; rent for a single room in the mid-1920s was the equivalent of ten dollars a month

Île de la Cité: one of two remaining islands in the Seine in central Paris, much of it is taken up by Notre-Dame Cathedral, the Sainte-Chapelle, and the Conciergerie

Île St.-Louis: the second island in the Seine in central Paris, it is mostly taken up by residential buildings, many of which date to the seventeenth century and are among the most valuable and coveted real estate in Paris

impasto: a painting technique whereby paint is laid on very thickly; can also refer to the paint itself when so applied

Jardin Luxembourg: see Luxembourg Gardens, below

le jazz hot: French term for American jazz music, particularly that originating from New Orleans

Lapérouse: one of the oldest restaurants in Paris, Lapérouse has been open since 1766 and is known for its luxurious private dining rooms and classic French cuisine ▶

Glossary of Terms and Places in *Moonlight Over Paris* (continued)

Latin Quarter: a Left Bank neighborhood in Paris, centered around the Sorbonne, that has long been a focus of student life and avant garde culture in the city

Luxembourg Gardens: created in the early seventeenth century, the public gardens ("Jardin Luxembourg" in French) are known for their manicured paths and flowerbeds, children's amusements (puppet show, carousel, and pond) and displays of statuary. The Musée du Luxembourg is located at the northern end of the Gardens.

Magasin Sennelier: an artists' supply shop, open since 1887

Maison Vionnet: the fashion house of Madeleine Vionnet, the designer famed for her pioneering use of the bias cut. She closed the house upon her retirement at the beginning of the Second World War, though her name is currently used under license by a Paris designer.

maître: literally "master," it is used as an honorific for teachers

Métro: the Paris Métropolitain is the system of underground trains, first opened in 1900; the iconic Art Nouveau entrances and décor of its first stations remain as highly visible landmarks throughout much of central Paris

Montparnasse: this neighborhood, center of much of the artistic and literary life of 1920s Paris, takes its name from the cemetery at its southern border

Musée du Luxembourg: Paris's first museum of contemporary art, it was later superseded by other museums, among them the Musée d'Orsay and the Musée Nationale d'Art Moderne. Today it functions as a display space for traveling exhibitions.

mutilé de guerre: a person left wounded or scarred by war; literally, "mutilated by war"

Orteig Prize: a $25,000 award for the first aviator who successfully flew non-stop between New York and Paris, it was first offered in 1919 but not won until 1927, when Charles Lindbergh crossed the Atlantic in his Spirit of St. Louis

pagaille: a terrible mess

Palais de Bois: an exposition space near Porte Maillot on the western fringes of central Paris; it has since been replaced by the Palais de Congrès

Paris Edition: the colloquial name for the European Edition of the *Chicago Tribune*

pédé: a derogatory and highly offensive term for a gay man

la peinture à l'huile: oil painting

petit bleu: a pneumatic message, so named for the blue color of the original message cards; literally, "little blue"

Le Petit Journal: large daily French-language paper that occupied most of the building in which the offices of the Paris Edition were located

Pigalle: a district in central Paris known for its nightlife and cabarets, among them the Moulin Rouge

pissoir: a public urinal

pointillism: an artistic technique in which tiny, distinct dots of color are used to create an image. The most famous practitioner of pointillism was Georges Seurat, who is best known for "La Grande Jatte."

Printemps: one of the great Parisian department stores, its competitors in this period included Le Bon Marché, La Samaritaine, and Galeries Lafayette

ravissante: gorgeous or beautiful; literally "ravishing"

rewrite desk: the area of a newspaper where editors (deskmen) reworked truncated cables into full-length pieces

Rive Gauche: the "left bank" of the Seine in Paris

Sainte Chapelle: thirteenth-century chapel located on the Île-de-la-Cité in Paris

Salon des Indépendants: the annual art exhibition of the members of the Société des Artists Indépendants. It was first held in 1884 and had the guiding motto of "no jury, no recompense."

saucisson: dried pork sausage

Shakespeare and Company: Sylvia Beach's renowned English-language bookshop, it opened in 1919 and closed in 1940. The current shop by that name first opened at a different location and under different management in the 1950s.

sou: coin of little value; term was unconnected to any specific unit of currency in France at that time

SS *Minnewaska*: a luxury ocean liner with the Atlantic Transport Line, she sailed the London–New York route between 1924 and 1931

St.-Cloud: a well-to-do commune, or suburb, located on the western fringes of Paris. Sara and Gerald Murphy lived here for part of each year in the early 1920s.

St.-Germain-des-Prés: neighborhood on the Left Bank of Paris that was the center of French intellectual life for much of the twentieth century

St. Peter's Eaton Square: church in the Belgravia district of London

Studio for Portrait Masks: the American Red Cross Studio for Portrait Masks, which was active from late 1917 to early 1919, was established and run by Anna Coleman Ladd, an American sculptor. The studio provided customized face masks for French and American soldiers and officers with facial deformities as a result of war wounds. ▶

Glossary of Terms and Places in *Moonlight Over Paris* (continued)

tartine: slice of baguette, typically day-old, that is toasted and spread
   with preserves or butter
The Falstaff: a café in Montparnasse, still in existence, that was
   decorated to resemble a traditional English public house
Théâtre de la Cigale: a theater in the Pigalle district of Paris with a
   long-standing connection to avant-garde culture
Third Republic: government of France from the collapse of the Second
   Empire in 1870 to the Occupation of France in 1940
toi aussi: you, too
Le Train Bleu: see Blue Train, above
vendeuse: saleswoman
vernissage: opening of an art exhibition; literally, "the varnishing"

An explanatory note on currency:

In the years following the First World War, the value of the French
franc all but collapsed, though its currency did not experience the
same dramatic devaluation as the Reichsmark of the Weimar Republic,
for instance. In 1925 one American dollar could buy 20 French francs,
while a pound sterling could buy 50 French francs. This meant that
expatriate Americans were particularly well-off in a city where a
decent meal could be had for one franc, a room in a hotel could be
let for 200 francs a month, and a journalist like Sam Howard was
paid $60 a month, which equaled roughly 1,200 francs. This happy
state of affairs only lasted until October 1929, when the beginning
of the Depression prompted many American expatriates to return
home. ∾

Reading Group Questions

1. Other cities in Europe—for instance Rome, Venice, Barcelona, Vienna, or London—are arguably just as beautiful and historic as Paris. Why, then, are we so drawn to the City of Lights? And what is it about Paris in the 1920s that we find so particularly fascinating?

2. Did you enjoy encountering real-life figures in the pages of *Moonlight Over Paris*? Is it possible to portray such iconic figures as F. Scott Fitzgerald and Ernest Hemingway with any degree of accuracy? Or has their fame obscured the real men behind the legends?

3. This novel is set six years after the end of World War I, but even still the characters and Paris itself are affected by those years. How do we see this with our characters? What do we see of this in the city itself?

4. Would a year in Paris, with all the freedom that Helena enjoys, have been possible for most women in that era? Or was it the case that her family's wealth and status made it more easily achievable for her?

5. If you were able to read the story of one of the other fictional characters in the book, whose would it be? Étienne's? Aunt Agnes's? Another of the secondary figures?

6. Music, visual art, and the written word play a big role in this story. Why do you think that Paris became such an epicenter for artistic expression during this time? Do you think the aftermath of the war played any part in this? ▶

Reading Group Questions *(continued)*

7. How does the character of Helena change and evolve over the course of the novel?

8. In what ways is Sam a typical man of his time? Are there ways in which he transcends the conventions and expectations of his era?

9. Do you think Helena ends up fulfilling the promise she makes to herself at the beginning of the book? ⌒

Further Reading

THE FOLLOWING TITLES represent only a fraction of the sources I consulted when researching *Moonlight Over Paris*, but if you are interested in learning more about the era, the people who lived through it, and the places that appear in my book, these books and articles are a good place to start. Most should be easily available through your local library or bookseller, though some are now out of print.

To begin, there is no better place to start than with John Baxter's guides and histories to Paris. Few people know the City of Lights better than he, and if you can't travel to Paris you can at least see the city through his eyes in *The Most Beautiful Walk in the World: A Pedestrian in Paris* and *The Golden Moments of Paris: A Guide to the Paris of the 1920s*. For a more general understanding of French life and culture in the interwar period, I recommend *Paris 1919-1939: Art, Life, and Culture* by Gérard Durozoi. For a history of art and artists in these years, *Cubism and Twentieth-Century Art* by Robert Rosenblum is an excellent resource.

The memoirs of the Lost Generation, though often unreliable in regard to details of their relationships and work, nonetheless contain a wealth of illuminating information on their day-to-day lives. Best known, of course, is *A Moveable Feast* by Ernest Hemingway, but I also recommend *The Autobiography of Alice B. Toklas* (which was actually written by Gertrude Stein), *Shakespeare and Company* by Sylvia Beach, *Paris Was Yesterday* by Janet Flanner, *That Summer in Paris* by Morley Callaghan, and *Memoirs of Montparnasse* by John Glassco.

For biographies of key Lost Generation figures, I recommend *Hemingway: The Paris Years* by Michael Reynolds, *Paris Without* ▶

Further Reading *(continued)*

End: The True Story of Hemingway's First Wife by Gioia Diliberto, *F. Scott Fitzgerald: The Paris Years* by Paul Brody, *Zelda: An Illustrated Life* by Eleanor Lanahan, *Gertrude and Alice* by Diana Souhami, and *Sylvia Beach and the Lost Generation: A History of Literary Paris in the Twenties and Thirties* by Noel Riley Fitch.

To learn more about the salons of Gertrude Stein and Natalie Barney, search out "The Stein Salon was the First Museum of Modern Art" by James R. Mellow (*New York Times*, 1 December 1968) and *Wild Heart: Natalie Clifford Barney and the Decadence of Literary Paris* by Suzanna Rodriguez.

For more information on Sara and Gerald Murphy, I recommend *Everybody Was So Young: Gerald and Sara Murphy— A Lost Generation Love Story* by Amanda Vaill, "Living Well is the Best Revenge" by Calvin Tomkins (*New Yorker*, 28 July 1962), and *Sara and Gerald: Villa America and After* by Honoria Murphy Donnelly and Richard N. Billings.

The memoirs of the men who worked at the Paris edition of the *Chicago Tribune* make for especially entertaining reading. The best of these are *The Start* by William L. Shirer, *The Last Time I Saw Paris* by Elliott Paul, and *The Paris Edition: The Autobiography of Waverley Root, 1927-1934*. *News of Paris: American Journalists in the City of Light Between the Wars* by Ronald Weber is an excellent resource as well.

Last of all, if you would like to read more fiction set in this period, I recommend *Villa America* by Liza Klaussmann, *The Beautiful American* by Jeanne Mackin, *The Paris Wife* by Paula McLain, *Call Me Zelda* by Erika Robuck, and *The Other Daughter* by Lauren Willig. ༄

Daisy's story continues in

"All for the Love of You"

an all-new short story in the anthology,

FALL OF POPPIES

Stories of Love and the Great War

Coming March 2016